KARMA RISING

RITA GRAHAM

AuthorHouse™
1663 Liberty Drive
Bloomington, IN 47403
www.authorhouse.com
Phone: 1-800-839-8640

© 2011 Rita Graham. All rights reserved.

No part of this book may be reproduced, stored in a retrieval system, or transmitted by any means without the written permission of the author.

First published by AuthorHouse 12/19/2011

ISBN: 978-1-4567-6259-9 (sc)
ISBN: 978-1-4567-6260-5 (hc)
ISBN: 978-1-4567-6261-2 (ebk)

Library of Congress Control Number: 2011905370

Printed in the United States of America

Any people depicted in stock imagery provided by Thinkstock are models, and such images are being used for illustrative purposes only.
Certain stock imagery © Thinkstock.

Because of the dynamic nature of the Internet, any web addresses or links contained in this book may have changed since publication and may no longer be valid. The views expressed in this work are solely those of the author and do not necessarily reflect the views of the publisher, and the publisher hereby disclaims any responsibility for them.

DEDICATION

To my delightful Family, my Children, my Sisters and my Brothers and my Dear Friends—to my Beloved and my Loved Ones who have gone before—and to every stranger who was kind, you have blessed my life with your love.

Because your shadows fall on every page of this book, I know that God gave it to me to give to you.

FOREWORD

Rita Graham has established her singular, richly textured voice in the canon of music. Now she has channeled it into a novel that resonates as affectingly as her soaring vocal riffs.

Karma Rising is soulful in every sense of the word, earthily wise but also informed, in every narrative twist, by the transcendent. It introduces us to Ceeoni Jones, a resourceful, independent-spirited woman, who assumes the leadership of a storied, old theater on the hallowed turf of the Underground Railroad, only to discover a corpse during her first day on the job.

Tales of murder and suspense usually do not shimmer with spiritual reflection, but Graham uses her research and personal insights into past-life regression to explore larger questions and themes beyond the usual whodunit. Can a woman achieve an unshakeable sense of self even while the past—in this case, the events of another century, which provide a velvety and sinister backdrop—haunts the bounty of her present?

As her prismatic story shifts and shuffles time and point of view, Graham evokes a bygone era with the scrupulous detail of a daguerreotype. However, she celebrates the flesh along with the spirit, this world as much as the next (or the last), and mysteries as much as certainties. This promising new author has minted her own distinct genre, I think, of Reincarnation Gothic.

Graham first enchanted me, along with every other spirit within hearing range, with her singing at another old, storied theater rumored to be haunted, the Holly Theater in Dahlonega, Georgia. As I grew to know her better, I quickly realized that she is a passionate reader, an original thinker and storyteller of coruscating honesty and clarity.

Still, her meditative thriller startles with its breadth, depth, and sweep.

The novel's dialogue, too, swings with a certain musicality, syncopated occasionally by a wry and knowing aside. Even when she was performing in the spotlight, Graham evidently was paying rapt attention to the mannerisms and machinations of those around her; she conveys the speech of music-makers, visionaries, artistic strivers, spiritual seekers, and other nonconformists with pitch-perfect naturalism.

Graham also feels such discernible compassion for the characters in the aptly named city of "Starcross, Georgia" that these pages practically warm to the touch; they vibrate with the same melismatic energy that animates her interpretations as a songstress. *Karma Rising* is a masterwork of rhythm and blues in the sense of its steady, irresistible pacing and old sorrows tempered with the revelations of catharsis.

Candice Dyer, Writer-at-Large, Atlanta Magazine; Author, "Street Singers, Soul Shakers and Rebels With A Cause—The Music of Macon"

PREFACE/INTRODUCTION

Karma Rising weaves a suspenseful tale around a subject that isn't widely known or understood. Under light hypnotic suggestion, and sometimes spontaneously, it is a common occurrence for ordinary people to speak of past lives they believe they have lived. Some demonstrate competence in previously unknown skills or describe accurate details of other times and other places, while many lapse into foreign accents and/or languages.

Through the simple process of past life regression, most people can 'return to another time' where they easily resolve present compulsive behavior as well as painful and/or unfinished issues they perceive originated from a past life. And there are those bizarre episodes of deja vu, when we have all experienced the certainty we've been places we've never been, all of which causes many to believe that the human soul survives death. Although there are various theories attempting to explain this very common phenomenon, no one knows why.

The basic premise of the fascinating subject of Past Life Regression has been accurately presented in the Karma Rising story. Also incorporated are elements of actual past life regression testimonies taken from verified reports.

The Starcross Manor and Theatre were inspired by two elegantly restored structures: the Rattle N' Snap Plantation, built in 1842 in Columbia, Tennessee; and, the 599-seat Morton theatre, built in Athens, Georgia in 1910 by African American, Pinky Morton.

Starcross, Georgia does not exist. All historical incidents and anecdotes are factual, to the best of the author's knowledge.

ACKNOWLEDGEMENTS

Karen O. Kaplan, who patiently typed the first draft from my handwritten text.

Doreen Flummerfelt and Joi Williams who gave their time and expertise.

Dr. Rosie Milligan whose clear thinking illuminated the path.

Attorney Sheri Long Cotton who offered advice, encouragement and awesome "tekkie" skills, as well as the considerable ingenuity of her gifted son, artist Lonnie Long Jr., who designed and illustrated the cover.

PROLOGUE

Kar-ma, noun
[noncount]1 often Karma: the force created by a person's actions that is believed in Hinduism and Buddhism to determine what that person's next life will be like 2 informal: the force created by a person's action that some people believe causes good or bad things to happen to that person

The evening she arrives in Atlanta to manage a restored theatre, Ceeoni Jones spontaneously recalls a long-forgotten conversation she'd had with her friend Di, about Karma. Ceeoni is surprised when Di's words echo verbatim in her memory. She could almost hear her friend's voice saying,

"*Relationships are the hardest lessons in the world. There are Universal Laws all humanity has to learn. Not just in romantic relationships, but in all relationships—brother to brother, stranger to stranger, parents to children, neighbor to neighbor, nation to nation. The Laws of Karma are the rules that govern our Souls' decisions to repay the Spiritual Debts we owe one another. The debts are made according to the ways we behave toward each other.*

"*Although the belief in Karma comes from Eastern Religions, the Christian Bible states, 'Not one whit, not one tittle of The Law shall go unfulfilled', which means that we will reap what we sow.*

"*The metaphysical interpretation of that is whatever a Soul does to another, every bit of that Spiritual Debt must be paid. If it's good, good returns. If we fail to learn the lesson, then we are destined to repeat it, in some way, until the lesson is learned. The Soul chooses how it will learn, and the people in our lives are teaching us, and learning from us, constantly. We can't escape it, for learning these lessons is our major purpose for taking on this earthly form.*

Actually, our relationships are as intricately wired and intertwined as are all living molecular structures . . . throughout many lifetimes."

In spite of Di's fascinating explanation, Ceeoni has her doubts about Karma, especially the idea that each Soul learns lessons throughout many lifetimes.

All alone during her first night's exploration of the Civil War Era Starcross Theatre, Ceeoni is drawn into a terrifying spiral of 19thCentury realities. Her view of life itself is shattered as danger from the dark past lurks in the shadows of Starcross.

xxx

"Steeped in Southern American culture, murder and mayhem, KARMA RISING navigates plot twists and turns to solve a myriad of mysteries, completing a jigsaw that is ultimately satisfying and inspiring."—Wild Times Magazine

"Spellbinding, enchanting and bewitching! As Graham masterfully weaves the plot together, I couldn't turn the pages fast enough. KARMA RISING surprises and delights the reader with the power of rich, absorbing and action-packed story-telling!"

—Judy Joy Jones, The Judy Joy Jones Internet Radio Show
Author, "Mother Theresa, When A Saint Calls, Surrender"

E-Mail: RitaGrahamsKarmaRising@yahoo.com

CHAPTER ONE

She glanced at the calendar as the telephone rang. Friday, November 3, 1997. It rang several times, but her assistant wasn't picking up. Oh well. She rolled her chair away from the computer and answered, "Ceeoni Jones." The voice on the other end boomed with a silky, lilting Southern drawl she associated with Dr. Martin Luther King, Jr., and courage. The loud voice assaulted her ears,

"Miss Ceeoni Jones? My name is Homer Dinsmore of Dinsmore & Associates. The resume of your work history was brought to my attention by a private research firm. After careful consideration, I'm offering you a contract to manage the 600-seat, state-of-the-art Starcross Theatre for the Performing Arts in Starcross, Georgia, just outside Metro Atlanta.

"The timing is perfect, Ms. Jones. We are aware that your contract with the Wilshire Ebell is up for review in a few days, at which time you can choose not to renew it." His voice underlined the word, 'not'.

"Your contract with us includes your townhouse and car, over and above your $75,000 annual salary, plus an attractive bonus package, and stock options in Dinsmore & Associates, Developers, Inc.

"You have one week to complete your affairs in Los Angeles and get settled in Atlanta. We open next Friday with a two-day celebration featuring jazz pianist, Joe Sample as the star attraction. We took into account the fact that you'll need time to become acclimated, therefore, we've already booked the first eight weeks. Our goal is to establish a rich tradition of variety arts programming, and we think you'll approve of how far we've come.

"Should you decide to accept this offer, your one-way ticket to Atlanta is awaiting pickup at Delta Airlines. Please let me know your decision right away. You were chosen because we're certain you're the guiding force the Starcross Theatre needs." Silence.

Ceeoni made a concerted effort to say something, but she succeeded in only moving her lips. She tried a small sound as if clearing her throat, "Ah—uh—Mr.—uh—Dinsmore?"

"Please call me Homer. Ms. Jones, we're on a really tight schedule, and we do need your answer today."

Today?? A silent scream reverberated in her head. Today?? He didn't stop to apologize. He kept talking in that commanding voice, like a man accustomed to getting results, today. "Please call me back at (404)555-0238. My office will find me, and you and I can discuss what we're trying to do down here. By the way, in case you're interested, yours was the last resume we reviewed out of a total of over fifty prospects," he chuckled, "you were most definitely not an easy person to find."

Stunned, she held the phone for a few seconds until she realized he was gone. She stared at the tiny yellow anthers peeking at her from the centers of the African violet blooms on her desk. *Is this a prank from an unknown enemy? If it's a real job offer, I'll have to move to Georgia now. NOW? Jesus! And out of fifty prospects, why me? Why did he choose me?*

Her assistant, the ever efficient Nell Porter, rushed into the room excitedly waving a sheaf of papers.

"Ceeoni, I can hardly believe this myself, but you just got a killer job offer from Atlanta starting yesterday, at a brand new-correction, I should say, at an old theatre that's probably better than new!"

The heavy-set impeccably attired figure hovered over Ceeoni's cherrywood desk, smiling, anxiously awaiting a reaction.

"Well, I don't know—Nell, I just spoke to some audacious character named Dinsmore, in, ah—Starcross, Georgia. Hey, you're from around Atlanta somewhere, aren't you?"

Nell adjusted the power bow of her red silk blouse, sat the papers down and perched on the desk corner, "Yeah, I'm from Decatur, GA, but wait, you actually spoke to Homer Dinsmore?"

"Un huh."

"Homer Dinsmore called you, personally?" Nell asked, gesturing toward the papers,

"Ceeoni, I bet the stock options alone are worth a fortune. Oh wow! Forgive me, but I couldn't help but read while I retrieved this from the machine." She smoothed her stylishly relaxed long black hair, and settled into a quiet confidential tone,

"Ms. Jones, you've hit the jackpot! Homer Dinsmore is one of the leaders of Atlanta's sharp, black grown-up entrepreneurs. God only knows what you'll decide, but here's what any Atlantan would tell you."

Nell's comments about Homer Dinsmore went on for a full twenty minutes, and she added some of the buzz about the Starcross Complex. As Nell got up to leave, she half-whispered,

"I won't breathe a word of this to anyone, and I'm going to let you have some privacy to mull it over," she giggled, "You don't have much time, Ceeoni Jones, you've gotta' mull quick!"

Ceeoni hit the speed dial and left a message for her dear friend, Diana Underhill,

"Di, call me! I just got a dream job offer from Atlanta by way of Out Of The Blue, and if I take it, I'll have to leave right away! Help! Ciao!" She quickly poured a cup of coffee with shaking hands, knowing in her heart that her tidy life had suddenly taken a sharp, dramatic and surely risky, turn.

Dream job, she was under the impression she already had her 'Dream Job.' Her life had consisted of very hard work. She'd spent long hours, sometimes around the clock, starting from the experimental works-in—development format at the 99-seat Equity Waiver Theatre of the Inner-City Cultural Center of Los Angeles. After years of assisting the assistant, building scenery, scrambling around for props, staying up all night to gather and build costumes, trying to fit whole productions into teeny-weeny budgets, soothing nerves and delicate egos, and solving problems of every variety, she'd fallen out of love with traditional theatre and found her professional niche in variety arts programming.

The hard-won prestigious position of managing the 1,270-seat Wilshire Ebell Theatre was her reward for years of solid effort. At the age of 34, she considered herself at the apex of her career. She didn't think anything could be better than this. Now this one call had completely rearranged her thoughts into a mishmash of excited anxiety.

Homer's offer had caused her to face up to the fact that her Dad, Diana and her job were the only factors binding her to California. Nell Porter knew the Dinsmore Company to be a highly successful development firm that built communities all over Georgia. It dawned on Ceeoni that she was at what Diana would label a "Destiny Point", and deep inside she knew she'd never rest if she didn't toss out her usual trepidations and take this chance. You go girl—go ahead and step out on space.

Diana returned her call with the Reverend O.C. Smith, Minister of the City of Angels Church of Religious Science, on a three-way hookup. Di's voice, filled with curiosity and enthusiasm said,

"Ceeoni! I got your message—somethin' about a job offer in Atlanta, startin' yesterday? I figure this one requires some serious prayer, so 'The Rev' is on the line."

Di's perception was on target, as usual. The Reverend O.C. never failed to soothe Ceeoni's soul in his gentle uplifting ministry, just as his classic recordings had never failed to soothe her teenaged angst. She had worn out her copies of his "Little Green Apples", and Gordon Parks' haunting ballad, "Don't Misunderstand," from the old "Shaft" movie.

Ceeoni told them every detail of Homer Dinsmore's call. She described Nell's glowing remarks concerning Dinsmore & Associates, and she related the details of the signed contract that had popped out of her fax machine minutes after Homer hung up. Ceeoni finished talking and Rev. O.C.'s question went straight to the core of the matter,

"Ceeoni, you've got to ask yourself how you feel about leaving Los Angeles and every single thing you know, to take a chance on the complete unknown. In other words, can you do that? You don't have to answer now. We can meditate over it, and you can get back to me."

She answered without hesitation, "I'm thrilled beyond belief! I guess I've mentally started packing already." She heard Diana's barely audible gasp, but 'The Rev's' "Aha!" was reassuring.

"See there?" he said, "All you have to remember is that there's a reason for everything, and sometimes we're blessed enough for the important reasons to be revealed. Your heart knows the way—go and have faith that you'll find your reasons."

"Diana—I—" But Di had already decided that no excuse was necessary.

"Well, Cee," she said, "you know how much I'll miss you, but this may very well be the best move you've ever made. I'll be over to help you get organized." Their conversation closed after O.C. sang, "The Lord's Prayer", at Di's request. His beautiful baritone created a moment that Ceeoni would forever hold in her Treasure Trove of Precious Memories.

Ceeoni immediately dialed Homer Dinsmore's Atlanta office, to prevent second thoughts from changing her mind. She waited while his secretary connected her call.

"Mr. Dinsmore? Ceeoni Jones. Ah, I-I've decided to accept your offer." He sounded relieved, "Whew! For a moment there, I thought you were gonna' fool around and miss all this good stuff we've got waiting for you." Ceeoni laughed, knowing she was going to like this Homer Dinsmore.

x x x

Friday night, she put the finishing touches on the E-Mail, her letter of resignation, which would come as Manna From Heaven to second-in-line Nell Porter. The click of the 'send' button clanged like the closing of a gigantic door. Refusing to look back, she propped herself up with a pile of bed pillows and turned her attention to the heavy information packet that had arrived that evening at her Hancock Park apartment, by special messenger. It contained a substantial bank draft, a contract, a glossy real estate sales brochure that touted the new Starcross Lakes Estate Community, and a history of the Starcross Theatre. The Starcross Theatre website was still under construction.

She read that the theatre had been built in 1868 by a Letty Starcross Bramwell, on the site of an old church that had been part of the Starcross Manor. Ceeoni smiled to herself. That Letty Bramwell must've been some super-cool lady! For many years up until the

Civil War, she'd worked with the Underground Railroad, helping a number of slaves escape to freedom, one by one, right under the noses of their owners, one of whom was her only son. Toward the end of her life, she ignored the existing segregation laws, and bequeathed every inch of the Starcross property to a former slave, even though her son still lived on the premises. Ceeoni would've loved to have been a fly on the wall when that news circulated around 1874 Georgia. Letty Bramwell's estate executors had discovered a legal loophole that allowed Starcross to remain in the family of the former slave who inherited it.

The brochure didn't say what transpired until Dinsmore acquired it from the descendant of a former slave named Baldwin, in 1975. Around 1900, the property was struck by lightning. Although it didn't burn the theatre down, the remains of a partially burned human corpse was found out in front and was buried on the premises. The grounds were crumbling by the time Dinsmore began restoration of the Starcross Theatre and Manor, in conjunction with the development of an upscale, gated community of 100 exclusive estates, just across the road. This modern estate community featured a restaurant, clubhouse, private school, man-made lakes, riding stables, natural rock swimming pools, waterfalls, an 18-hole golf course and tennis courts covering an area that had once contained slave cabins and cotton fields. The brochure also boasted that the 1997 Heavyweight Boxing Champion of the World, Evander Holyfield, owned a spectacular estate a few miles from Starcross.

Dinsmore had fully restored the theatre far beyond its former glory. The latest sound, lighting and technical wizardry made the 600-seat theatre competitive with the best of Atlanta's theatrical venues, including the Variety Arts Theatre, Spivey Hall and the 14th Street Playhouse.

Now, Ceeoni faced the multi-faceted task of managing a performing arts center opening in a few days in a new environment, without her familiar support staff and trusted purveyors, but somehow she knew she could handle what was required, with style.

Everything that could possibly go wrong in a venue, anything that could prevent success had already happened to her, including a major California earthquake during a performance of August Wilson's,

"Piano Lesson." She had the feeling that Murphy's Law had been discovered lurking in the shadows of a moldy old theatre, waiting for some unsuspecting soul to open the curtains and unleash it on the world. North American Van Lines Relocation Services called her the next morning to say they had been engaged for her move to Atlanta, Georgia. Eddie Jones, who always supported his daughter's every decision with enthusiasm, pitched in to store things Ceeoni couldn't part with, while she and Diana scurried to mark things that were to go. The wrenching packing decisions were finished, and finally, early on Thursday morning, November 9th, teary-eyed and numb, Ceeoni hugged her Dad and Di, and left Los Angeles, promising to call as soon as she got situated.

She spent most of the flight to Atlanta in a state of semi-shock. The sudden and drastic move had necessitated a whirlwind of activity filled with instantaneous decisions that afforded her little time to internalize the downside possibilities of her new job.

Homer had made it very clear in their many telephone conversations that some people thought his luxurious Southside Starcross Community would fail. He said that some who lived anywhere but on the Southside, believed that folk 'Down There' suffered from terminally malignant poverty of spirit and services, and they would not, and could not support his grand vision. He'd laughed, a loud infectious chuckle,

"Ms. Jones, in spite of the skeptics, all but a few of the estates are sold. We've begun Phase II to build larger and more expensive homes to meet the demand. To top it off, the Starcross Restaurant is another facet of my dream come true." In a more serious tone he added, "Now that we've got the place up and running, the Starcross Theatre is up to you."

A feather touch of apprehension tickled her spine, but no comment to his remark had been necessary. They both knew the theatre's viability depended on a multitude of variables that would only be revealed after she was thoroughly committed.

She had everything to gain, and everything to lose, but as crazy as it was, she felt confident. She couldn't help but agree with Homer's ideas because her experience had taught her the ingredients for success, and Homer seemed to intuitively know what they were.

Homer's savvy and generosity were refreshing. He'd ended one of their conversations with the statement, "By the way, Ceeoni, if you have a good idea that takes you over budget, remember, you have carte blanche to make it happen. I trust your judgment."

CHAPTER TWO

At 5:20pm, one week to the day after Homer's first call, the 747 rolled to a gentle stop at Atlanta's Hartsfield Airport. Ceeoni was one of the first to embark. Had she been able to relax, Homer's first class perk would have been more enjoyable.

She smiled at the gorgeous woman holding a sign with STARCROSS printed in bold black letters. The woman barely touched Ceeoni's outstretched hand, and she didn't return her smile. Her shiny plum lips hardly moved as she spoke.

"Ms. Jones," she said, "I'm Minette Coulter. I don't mean to rush you, but I do have another appointment within the hour. Oh, and before I forget, these are your keys." She handed Ceeoni a key ring, each key marked with a letter. "You'll need this key code to know which key goes to what, and these are the keys to your rental car." She gave Ceeoni a grey leather packet, and walked away without saying another word.

Ceeoni figured she was supposed to follow wherever the very unusual Ms. Coulter was leading. Ceeoni had the capacity to enjoy life's little wonders, and the cute hi-tech train that took them from the gate to baggage claim was one of them. Minette didn't speak to Ceeoni as the driver loaded her luggage into the limo, but Ceeoni had been in the presence of so many odd modes of behavior in her life, she figured this Coulter person either had a private axe to grind, or she was just plain peculiar. Whatever it was, it wasn't Ceeoni's problem.

Minette sat on her side of the car, while Ceeoni turned her attention to the scenery along the freeway, affording slivers of city views. What looked like the tops of downtown buildings was straight ahead for a few minutes and, eventually, the car turned onto an unmarked lane lined with aristocratic single red brick homes, sitting a half-block off the street. She almost forgot Minette's presence until she heard the lighter click, followed by the sharp odor of cigarette smoke.

Thinking she'd possibly been too super-charged to accurately read the lady's attitude, Ceeoni tested the water, "I understand the weather is turning cool in Atlanta this time of year."

Without looking in Ceeoni's direction, Minette tossed her hair, and blew a large smoke ring,

"Yes, it is November."

Ceeoni waited but since no further response was forthcoming, she went back to her window, as the car pulled through the iron gates of a townhouse complex built in the Stratford-on-Avon style. Negotiating the winding brick walkway on high yellow pumps, Minette waved her cigarette to punctuate her clipped, rapid fire explanation of the convenient location; close to the airport, downtown and the Starcross Theatre. Ceeoni kept up with the sensational, probably size fourteen Chanel suit and wondered again if Minette was as cool to everyone, or was it a personal thing?

"Ms. Coulter," she said, "I'm really curious about the theatre. I'd like to go there if it's OK?"

"Of course—ah, use the silver 'A' key. Don't forget you have a code when you're trying to gain entry."

Ceeoni opened the door and went inside, but Minette stood in the doorway and blew smoke in Ceeoni's direction.

"Sorry, I won't be able to accompany you," she said, without looking at Ceeoni, "Homer thought you might like to go to the theatre. I hope you don't mind going alone."

"Oh, that's quite alright, I have an excellent sense of direction."

Minette hesitated, "Ms. Jones—"

"Ceeoni, please."

"You may call me Minette." For a moment, Ceeoni thought she might be warming a bit, but the haughty demeanor didn't change. "I have a unit just like this in the next lane, with different decor, of course. Would you like the driver to take your luggage upstairs?"

"Yes, thank you." Ceeoni tried again, "Minette, would you like to come in for a while? I'd like to know—"

"No," Minette interrupted, "I have to go. I think the directions and the theatre map are fairly clear. Homer had another pressing appointment, he sends his apologies for not being able to meet you. He'll call you when he can. Oh, and your rental is the red Buick outside. They had it sent over earlier; nobody was free to bring one of Homer's vehicles." Keeping her hand on the doorknob, Minette remarked, "Cee-o-nee, is it? Interesting name."

"It comes from Yemen. My Father named me."

"How nice," she mumbled. "So, I must be off. Do you need me to go over those directions with you?"

"No thanks, Minette, I can find my way."

With a flick of her ashes and an impatient toss of her heavy auburn hair, Minette was out the door, nodding curtly at Ceeoni's assurance she would be just fine. Actually, Ceeoni was better than fine—she breathed a sigh of relief, and spent a few minutes taking note of the condo's art deco charm. Shades of grey and pale blue, with accents of deep blues and pumpkin, defined the three stories of compact, cozy space.

She liked what she saw, but she would unpack and leisurely explore her new residence later. At the moment, she was eager to be on her way to Starcross. She quickly freshened up and changed from her comfortable calf-length boots and chocolate shirt-dress, into a beige jumpsuit, chosen because she'd never worn it, and because it reflected her sense of bright, new beginnings. She looked forward to going to the theatre alone, to poke around without time constraints and to be free from having to make appropriate conversation. Anyway, Minette didn't seem like the sort of company with whom Ceeoni would want to share a moment as special as seeing her theatre for the first time.

xxx

She located Starcross easily. The directions led her down Cascade Road, through a residential area of expensive looking communities and small businesses. She turned onto a road that appeared to be cut through a splashy, multi-colored forest, and after several miles, she came upon an elegant illuminated white sign with gold letters:

STARCROSS LAKES ESTATES
STARCROSS RESTAURANT
STARCROSS THEATRE OF THE PERFORMING ARTS

While reading the sign, an unusual feeling came over her. She slowed the car, trying to identify the new feeling, rolling it around in her mind until some glimmer of truth revealed itself. Oh! It was a strong sense of familiarity, familiarity in this place she'd never been. How strange! Soon, it would be too dark to see. She was glad she hadn't wasted any time, and hadn't gotten lost.

She gripped the steering wheel in nervous anticipation, and slowly maneuvered the Buick around a long hairpin turn that wound through a leafy glade. It opened out into a wide lane with a tall boxwood hedge on the right, and a steep, curving hill on the left. At the top of the hill sat the Starcross Theatre.

Well, Ceeoni, you did it—all the way from the Los Angeles Basin to Georgia. Hopefully, it will be worth the price tag hanging on the big bridge you burned.

She parked off the road in a seemingly planned viewing site, a slightly elevated concrete apron on the right, with room for several cars. She cut the engine and felt her heartbeat accelerate as she gazed at the breathtaking panorama before her. The brochure had contained a rather flat photo of the theatre. How did the photographer manage to miss this naturally wonderful angle? She made a mental note to have the photo changed on the brochure and website.

She read the words that stretched out above the portal of the Greek Revival building on the hill:

STARCROSS THEATRE OF THE PERFORMING ARTS

No wonder Dinsmore & Associates had taken on the task of meticulous restoration. Such shining beauty had to be preserved. The theatre stood like a sparkling architectural jewel in a scene from a Civil War movie. Ten large supporting columns were accented dramatically with dancing, reflected multi-colored shadows that bounced across the circular driveway from an ornate fountain. The theatre and the fountain spewing shifting patterns of pastel water into the air, reminded her of every graceful antebellum mansion she'd ever seen or imagined. She had arrived just before sunset, and she decided that it was the exact moment when the theatre's facade was most beautiful. The fading sun's red-orange rays painted highlights of gold swatches around the majestic setting. She would come to realize that no matter what hour she saw it, the theatre, surrounded by an honor guard of huge magnolia and pine trees, moved something in her spirit. Ceeoni immediately dismissed the nagging feeling of familiarity, telling herself that emotional exhaustion coupled with a life-long love of plays and movies had blurred the lines separating imagination from reality. Yeah. This first sight of the old theatre mingled and overlapped with cherished memories of great characters and dialogue that lived in her head.

She re-started the engine, turned up the steep driveway to the well-lit empty parking area behind the building, and slid into a space. Gathering her new Gucci attaché case and bag, gifts from her former staff at the Ebell, she took a moment to glance into the rearview mirror. Wide dark eyes against her golden tan complexion showed no sign of fatigue. Not bad for staring at the ceiling most of the night, night after night, for the past week. She felt eager to meet the challenges ahead, and she couldn't wait to see inside the theatre.

Following the written directions, she found the correct key and the light switch. She disarmed the security system and noted that each door off the hall led to well-appointed rooms that lacked nothing. Dressing rooms, a large wardrobe/laundry area and bathrooms, with showers, were obviously up-to-date-additions, with lighted mirrors everywhere. She smiled, remembering the single mirror in the Inner-City Cultural Center's main theatre and the amazing confusion that ensued when a cast was dressing. There were no shortages here. With every imaginable amenity, the backstage of the Starcross rivaled or exceeded that of the finest houses she'd ever seen. Her thoughts were invaded by a noise. The gentle closing of a door? The sudden movement of a foot? Every hair on the back of her neck stood up.

"Hello?" She waited. Silence. "Is anyone there?" She sensed that she wasn't alone. Her heart thudded, violently.

"Hello?" She couldn't guess where the noise had come from, but she instinctively began to tiptoe as she moved faster down the hallway. Making no sound, she reached the stage entrance and opened the door to total blackness. She propped the door open with her attaché case until her eyes adjusted. The stage lights control panel was in the most obvious place on her left, and with shaking hands, she rushed to turn up every light in the house. Stepping out on stage, Ceeoni breathed a sigh of wonder—the descriptive conversations with Homer and the photos hadn't prepared her for the mixed emotions that rushed to her head. Somewhere in her consciousness, this exact auditorium existed. She knew the arrangement of the dusky rose seats included outside aisle chairs raised much higher than usual, offering a clear view of the stage from every seat. She looked up, and for a brief instant, a full house, a complete audience of men and women dressed in elegant 19th Century evening attire, waited in flickering gaslight for the curtain to rise. Astonished, she blinked and the vision was gone.

Goodness, Girl, you really are in need of a full night's rest, something you haven't had since you heard the word, 'Starcross'. She crossed the stage and carefully sat down on the piano bench. She'd never thought she'd seen something that wasn't there before, but then, she'd never been so completely unsettled, either. The past few days had been unreal, she just needed to collect herself.

Her tremors slowed as she raised the cover of the brand new 9' Steinway Concert Grand Piano, and ran a glissando over the keys. The natural acoustics in the auditorium reminded her that the newer buildings never seemed to duplicate that special full resonance. She'd scheduled the piano tuned before each performance, but when she picked out a few chords of "Piano In The Dark", she knew the tuner guy wouldn't have much to do. Telling herself that the noise she'd heard could've been caused by an item that wasn't securely fastened, she thought no more about it. Also, she rationalized that the apparition she thought she'd seen was probably jet-lag induced.

The atmosphere did have that stillness she'd experienced many times in the past; a kind of quirky energy that settles in the air prior to opening night that has been known to adversely affect dress rehearsals, as well as cause the breakdown of equipment and nerves, usually all at the same time. Coincidental luck had already solved one major crisis when the Star Attraction, pianist, Joe Sample, cancelled on Tuesday, three days before the opening celebration. Homer had called her right away to discuss last minute alternatives.

Karma Rising

"Cee," he said, "Everybody else we've booked is locked into surrounding commitments, what do you think?"

She suggested jazz guitarist Earl Klugh or the brilliant pianist, Chick Corea. She also mentioned jazz vocalist, Diane Shurr, and one of her favorite pianists, Adam Delayno. Homer sounded pleasantly surprised when she mentioned Adam Delayno's name.

"Ceeoni, we're currently in negotiations with Adam's people over a property deal. Come to think of it, I told Adam about the theatre, and he expressed interest in eventually performing for us. I guess I didn't think of asking him because time is so short, he's not in the country and he usually appears in larger venues." He added, "If we're patient, maybe we can book him on an off-day, since he's moving here."

Ceeoni became very still when she heard this tidbit of news. A small but clear voice echoed through the recesses of her mind. Adam Delayno? Adam—Adam, here—where—where—you—? Mentally, she scolded herself for descending to a new level of insanity. To Homer, she very calmly responded, "Well, it wouldn't hurt to ask. I've never met Mr. Delayno, but some artists may consider it a privilege to be the first to perform in a theatre in over 100 years, especially a theatre once owned by a former slave."

"Ceeoni Jones!" Homer shouted, "After all, the worst he can say is, 'I'm already committed, or 'It's short notice' or plain old 'Hell no!'" She heard Homer call to his secretary, "Get me Adam Delayno on the line!"

He called her back at 6am the next morning, which meant that it was 9am in Atlanta, but it was OK, because she wasn't sleeping anyway.

"Good morning, Cee—Adam Delayno agreed to open for us this Friday! We're changing our advertisement blitz from Joe Sample to Adam Delayno. We should do well since he's never appeared in concert in Atlanta."

Ceeoni sat straight up, wide awake, "Oh, great, Homer, that's wonderful! An artist of Adam's stature is sure to draw capacity crowds once the word is out."

She knew that the handsome, enigmatic Adam Delayno, internationally famous pianist/composer, had a large following. The

Rita Graham

Starcross Theatre was too small for him, which would assure overflow crowds. In spite of being one of his devoted fans, Ceeoni had never seen him in concert. Curiosity stoked her imagination whenever she thought about him or heard his music. For years, Adam's records had exerted an indescribable effect on her psyche. Now that the time when she would actually meet him was drawing near, the sharp stab of pleasure she felt surprised her in it's intensity.

CHAPTER THREE

Ceeoni pushed her musing aside, quickly closed the piano and checked her map for the route to her upstairs office. The map led her up a metal stairway to a door marked with her name in brass. The lights came on automatically as she entered the room. It was a near replica of her office at the Ebell! They had done their research thoroughly. Her treasures were placed almost where she would have put them herself. It was all there, her signed Tiffany lamp, her green oriental rugs, her NAACP Image Award, posters from past shows and presentations she had been a part of, and Violette, her African violet, was flowering beautifully on her desk. Her favorite framed snapshots sat on the carved mantle of a beautiful black marble fireplace. Graduating shades of emerald green, with light green and sky blue touches enhanced the subdued atmosphere.

Entering the large bathroom, she couldn't stop smiling. The color scheme was the same, and the room had a fireplace. She noticed that the fireplace was double-sided; identical to the one on the same wall in her office. A fireplace in the bathroom! Homer had said that some rooms had been converted from their original purposes.

She pulled the handle of the frosted, engraved shower door and indirect lights inside popped on, illuminating the careening bloody body that lurched forward and nearly knocked her over with its weight; the man's eyes and mouth frozen wide open in a silent howl of stark terror. Shocked, she screamed. Stumbling backward, she fell against the sink behind her, and caught herself, breathing hard, heart pounding, sobbing, stomach churning, heaving, she ran for the stairs. Clutching her briefcase, dark curls flying, shoulder bag bumping against her hip, her boots slipping on the metal stairs, she ran unsteadily, her wet palm sliding down the railing, while a pulse boomed like tympani drums in her throat. She ran down the hallway, nearly fell out the back door and ran to the car. Her head snapped around in all directions, as she fumbled for the keys. Suppose the killer is still here! That must've been the noise she'd heard—the murderer, nearby, watching, waiting? Shaking, she opened the car door, jumped in, started the engine and double-checked that the doors were locked.

She dialed 911 and shouted, "Help! Please! I found a dead man at the Starcross Theatre, right in the shower! There's been a murder!" She caught her breath and tried not to sob. Thank God for the cellular phone. Still trembling uncontrollably, she wiped her eyes and told 911 she would wait for the police. She checked the front of her suit and was relieved that her beige jacket was free of bloodstains. She must've backed away from the falling corpse quicker than she thought. She made an effort to slow her breathing as she watched all sides with the motor running. Oh! She'd forgotten about Homer Dinsmore. He answered on the first ring, "Hey Ceeoni! Welcome to Starcross. Sorry I couldn't—"

"Homer," she sniffled, her voice raspy from screaming, "I—I'm so scared! I found a murdered man in my shower stall, right there, in the theatre—in the—in my office!"

"What!!?" Homer's voice thundered in her ear. Ceeoni tried not to babble, but her words tumbled out on top of each other,

"A body, a man, covered with blood, So much blood—Oh God! I've called the police, but they're not here yet, and—" He cut through her trailing sentence, "Don't move. I'm nearby. I'll be there in a minute."

She began to feel a little better knowing that Homer was on his way. Her violent trembling subsided, but her eyes shifted from the rearview to the side mirrors. The thoughts running through her mind were meeting dead ends. Who was the murdered man? She had the impression he was a middle-aged, middle-sized man, with a medium brown complexion. Wearing what had been a very expensive charcoal suit, he looked prosperous, even in death. But why my office? Was the corpse killed or placed in my office deliberately? And the door was locked. Did the killer have keys?

Police sirens tore through the cool November night air. What a comforting sound! She took a deep breath, and noticed that the Starcross Theatre was beautiful even from the rear. She looked up and saw stars. Stars! She couldn't wait to tell Di about all of this. In just a few minutes she had more to discuss with her friend than she'd had in years; the horror of discovering a dead body, a murdered person—in her office, her new office. She knew Di would be intrigued by the account of her first few hours in Georgia. Ceeoni leaned back and forced herself to calm down by focusing on the celestial array gleaming through the moonroof.

Before her older sister had married and moved to Europe, she took Ceeoni for a day trip to the Grand Canyon. Ceeoni's 10-year old heart had been filled with the wonder of stars hanging over one of the world's most spectacular sights. Thinking about that now helped take her mind off of the bloody nightmare in the office upstairs.

From that high point in the Starcross parking lot, she could make out rooftops and colored floodlights showing through the trees, beyond the boxwood hedge, which must have been the homes of the new Starcross Lakes Estates development.

Sirens screeched louder as headlights came speeding up the driveway, blue lights spinning. Ceeoni gratefully ran to meet the two plainclothes detectives who got out of one of the cars. She told her grisly story in gasps as she attempted to open the theatre door, with trembling hands. Detective David Saxon, who was in charge of the investigation, gently took the keys and opened the door for her. He introduced himself, and within minutes he had learned why she was at the Starcross Theatre that evening, and her cel phone number.

They stood at the foot of the metal stairs dodging the crew of investigators carrying equipment. Out of the crowd that suddenly filled the area, Ceeoni heard someone call her name. She had no idea what Homer Dinsmore looked like, but she could never mistake his loud voice,

"Ceeoni, I'm—"

"Homer?" She intended to hold back her tears, but when he put his arms around her, all her pent-up emotions poured out in a torrent of sobs. He held her patiently, with her face buried in his broad chest until her weeping turned into little sniffles.

Detective David Saxon's statement was addressed to no one in particular, "I've been informed that we need a key to Ms. Jones' office." Homer handed his keys to Detective Saxon's red-haired partner standing at his side, then leaned down to whisper into Ceeoni's ear, "You think you can go back upstairs now? I don't want to leave you by yourself."

Homer Dinsmore, six feet, two hundred pounds of rock-solid energy, wore his shoulder-length silver and dark brown hair pulled back in a ponytail that was as wavy and unruly as hers. Bristly brows almost hid his beautiful eyes of the most unusual shade of dark gray. She thought he was very handsome with all that silver against his olive brown skin. With his reptile boots and gray western-style suede jacket, he reminded Ceeoni of a tan hero from a classic western movie. He could have been any age over 35, and he exuded an easy, relaxed aura that warmed the air around him.

Upstairs, Homer didn't ask her to go into her office. She watched the police and technicians from the doorway, and got out of the way of the stretcher removing the full body bag. Someone handed her a steaming hot cup of rich coffee that opened her sinus cavities, and helped slow her inner tremors.

Homer came out and walked her down the hall,

"Ceeoni, I know Detective Saxon wants to question you further, but he prefers to wait until after the initial investigation of the crime scene." He paused, "Apologies aren't worth a damn at this point, but I hope you know we didn't bring you all the way to Starcross just to scare you half to death. I realize how overwhelming this must be for you—something so horrible actually falling on you before you can even un-pack. It has occurred to me that it won't be easy for you to be alone in a new environment. What I'm saying is you're welcome to stay at my house until you're ready to look into a shower stall again. Someone is always there and we have plenty of room. With your consent, I'll take your keys and have your luggage brought over from the townhouse. There's much to attend to tomorrow, and we're depending on your expertise to oversee those critical last minute touches. Anyway, nothing more can be done here." Ceeoni agreed to stay at Homer's and wondered what his lucky wife was like.

xxx

Climbing into the front seat of Homer's shiny, restored 1959 Rolls Royce Silver Cloud, Ceeoni felt fatigue start to creep into her bones. Her watch read 8:30. Only a little over an hour had elapsed since she entered the Starcross Theatre for the first time, but it seemed like a week. She felt disoriented and frazzled, and she knew Homer was right, she didn't want to be too far away from other people, and she would really have to fix her mind in order to go back into that office bathroom. She was thinking of possibly asking Homer if she could change offices, when he seemed to read her thoughts.

"You know Ceeoni," he said, "we can move you from that office, if you'd like."

"Well, I don't know. Maybe I just have to get over the initial shock before I can feel at ease in there. Do you know what it was originally used for?"

"It was the owner's office when the theatre was built in 1868. Did you have a chance to read about Miss Letty in the brochure?"

"Oh, yes," Ceeoni laughed, "who could forget her? I'll bet she was the most stubborn woman in these parts."

"One who'd rather die before taking 'No' for an answer," Homer said. "I heard the family was considered stand-offish in the community. Well, everybody except the son. He was a real playboy type, lots of drinking and gambling. Nobody knew much about Miss Letty, but long after her death, her part in the Underground Railroad was revealed by people she'd worked with in other locations. All I've heard is bits and pieces of gossip. I would imagine that since she was a freedom fighter, she probably didn't have much in common with her slave-owning neighbors."

"I'd love to know more details of her life. It's a shame how facts get lost in history."

"Yeah, for example, nobody knows anything about the charred bones that were found in the wreckage in front of the theatre. Oddly enough, your office in the rear of the theatre wasn't badly damaged. Most of the damage was up in the front. In your office, most of the wood was intact. The roof hadn't leaked in that end, either. It was as if it had been vacuum-sealed. We had to break an old lock to get into that room, after we removed the debris blocking the door. That part of the restoration was easy, but other areas required much more work. We think that your bathroom was originally Miss Letty's sitting room/bedroom. Before that, we believe the area had been a meeting room in the old family church."

"So that's why the double-sided fireplace."

Homer chuckled, "Nice, huh? Actually we had already added a bath just under it, so it was easy to extend copper pipes. We left the fireplace untouched because the construction was solid, it's so pretty, and you never know, you might want to light it up sometime. It does get cold in Georgia. Still, Ceeoni," he said, "keeping that space is entirely up to you. Even though I feel like it should be your office, my crew can do the same decor in another room."

She knew Homer had gone to a lot of trouble to put that office together for her. She thought it would be childish to ask him to go to more trouble to change offices, simply because a dead body was discovered there. In truth, courage is one of the main attributes that divides the women from the girls.

"Homer," she said, "I've made up my mind that no murder or murderer is going to intimidate me. Since that office belonged to a brave, stubborn woman, I'll try to carry on the tradition and keep my lovely office, thank you."

Homer laughed and pulled out of the space. Ceeoni was about to ask Homer about the murder victim when he seemed to be thinking out loud, saying, "I wonder how he got into the theatre, and the office? I guess Basil had plenty of enemies, being a wealthy man himself, and having access to Adam's millions. But what would someone gain by murdering him? I mean, kidnapping for a ransom would be more reasonable—why murder?"

"You knew the murdered man?"

"Yeah, I've known Basil for years. You know, in spite of the ugly publicity we're bound to receive, the bottom line is that Detective David Saxon has a sharp analytical mind, and a fine record. I've known David since he was a snot-nosed kid. Before he went to college and earned his Golden Boy reputation at the APD, he used to work on the Kid Krews that assisted my construction gangs. He's very thorough, and I know it's just a matter of time before he uncovers something. Crooks always slip up, no matter how smart they think they are. I believe the same emotional torment that inspires someone to murder is the main factor that obscures his or her ability to understand that nobody can anticipate and/or control unforeseeable circumstances."

He paused as he slowly negotiated a turn.

"Homer, you mentioned Adam—Adam who?"

"Delayno, Adam Delayno."

"Was this Basil connected to him?"

"Oh, you couldn't have known. That's what makes this murder all the more peculiar. The dead man is Basil Cassidy, Adam Delayno's business manager."

Ceeoni thought the phrase 'odd coincidence' was beginning to sound like a gross understatement. Homer went on to explain,

"See, Basil handled the business end of Adam's career for years, and he made Adam and himself, very rich. I guess Adam's lawyers will complete the deal Basil and I were about to conclude. I was supposed to meet Basil and Adam tonight at the Starcross Manor to go over some final details of the sale. Instead, I had to call Adam to inform him that Basil had been murdered. Someone must've really wanted him dead to have stabbed him over forty times. Ceeoni, when you called to tell me what happened, I was waiting for Basil to let me know he'd arrived at the Manor.

"Adam and his personal manager are staying at the Manor, but the rest of the band is downtown at the Marriot Marquis. I agreed with Detective Saxon that there was no need for Adam to rush over here tonight, because he will speak with everyone concerned tomorrow."

Ceeoni thought all of this was getting deeper by the minute. "Adam Delayno is staying at the Manor?"

"Uhhuh, the Starcross Manor is the property Adam Delayno is buying from my company."

Her heart began to beat faster—Adam Delayno, right here—not just in Atlanta, but here—right here in Starcross—my, my, my—Out loud, Ceeoni said, "Oh?"

"Yeah. Adam appreciates the Manor's history, which is much older than the theatre. Miss Letty's Father built the house in the year of Miss Letty's birth, 1782. Seems that her Daddy, Charles Starcross, was an artist of some fame as well as fortune. He painted a few dignitaries and early presidents, including George Washington. The story goes that for some reason the Civil War didn't decimate their fortune, and Miss Letty was still rich after the fighting was over. Everybody tried to hide their valuables as the war moved closer to Georgia, but few people got away with it. Most hidden valuables were found and confiscated. Somehow, Miss Letty was able to rebuild the Manor bigger and better, and lived to see her theatre become a thriving venture."

"When did she die?"

"In 1874, she was 92."

"I read where she dedicated the theatre to her husband who was also an artist."

"Yeah, Miss Letty met her husband in Europe, where her only son was born. One thing I'd like to know is why Starcross became a cotton plantation, with slaves, when Miss Letty was a committed abolitionist. Nobody knows why they did that because they already possessed tremendous wealth. That's part of the mystery of the past."

"Well, how did you discover the information you have?" she asked.

"I spent as much time as I could with the Baldwin Sisters, who lived over in the West End. They sat on their porch, weather permitting, and told the Starcross history to anybody who would listen."

Ceeoni was definitely fascinated, but the murder at the theatre was uppermost in her mind. A murder so closely connected to the major artist featured in their kick-off presentation was more than a mess.

"This is the worst time for a gory crime to happen here, Homer." He didn't reply, and she wished she hadn't said what was on her mind.

In the same spot where Ceeoni had parked earlier, he stopped the car and turned toward her.

"I'm way ahead of you, Cee. I've spent the last few years pumping the concept that a venue on this side of town is a great idea. I've been planting the message at every opportunity in order to stimulate interest in the Starcross Lakes Estates sales, so I'm acutely aware of the devastating publicity hanging over us right now. Our current business with the murder victim is bound to complicate the situation, and will, most certainly add all kinds of speculation to the gossip. By publicizing the meaningful history of Starcross, we've gradually been building interest. The last thing I want to see is some God-awful, cheap sensationalism blared all over the damn news. The sooner the police can wrap this up, the better!"

Ceeoni wondered if the Starcross Theatre opening should be postponed, but she knew it was Homer's decision, to be made without any prompting. She watched the rainbow lights play on the fountain, as Homer re-started the car. Her focus blurred for a moment, while the fact that Adam Delayno was buying the Starcross Manor buzzed around in her head, setting little exploding charges.

x x x

Her thoughts eventually drifted back to their conversation, "The brochure said that you restored the Starcross Manor, as well."

Homer immediately warmed to the subject, "Yes, we did. It was filled with incredible challenges, because there were no guidelines to follow. We were flying blind all the way. We worked around a solid existing framework in some places, and there were irregularities everywhere, but it turned out to be a wonderful house."

"How many rooms?"

"Twenty-six in all. We didn't have time to print a brochure on it, because Adam bought it just days after I decided to sell. Most plantation homes weren't as large as Starcross, and of course, they had no bathrooms, only water closets. In those days they built the kitchens in separate buildings because it was too hot to cook indoors, in summer. It wasn't until around the middle of the 19th century that they started building the kitchens indoors."

Ceeoni was thinking how much fun a big house like that would be—26 rooms!

The car turned through the iron gates of the Starcross Lakes Estates, past a manicured park-like entrance and soon, lavishly elegant estates began to flow by, each architectural design uniquely different from the other, just like the brochure photos.

"When did you start building the estates?"

"In 1990, nearly ten years after we started the restoration. I know that sounds like a long time, but I kept the whole complex on a back burner. Some thought the restoration was my hobby, but it was really more of an obsession. I had to fit it in while I built other things. At first, I envisioned the Starcross community as a small group of exclusive estates, maybe fifteen or twenty, but the demand increased, and we had the acreage, so it grew. Now there are 68, and it seems like we can't build them fast enough."

"Homer, you're a whirling dervish," she said, feeling like she'd known him all her life.

He waved at one of the white-gloved parking attendants as they passed the Starcross Restaurant.

"I can't wait to try the restaurant, what's their speciality?"

"Oh, I don't know—we do keep grits and biscuits on the menu. Minette changes the menus regularly to include cuisine from around the world. We'll go over there soon, you're in for a treat."

"Minette?"

"The restaurant is her baby, she's the manager over there." Ceeoni decided not to comment on the subject, except to say, "Oh."

"Well, whatever your tastes, I think you'll like it. And speaking of likes, it's chilly tonight. I took the liberty of asking Weber to build a fire in your suite."

"Oh, I like that idea—I do—but tell me, how did you know I'd want to stay?"

"Because I know if I'd only had a few days to adjust to a new job in a strange city, and some dead dude, dripping blood, fell into my lap right after I'd arrived, I'd be over-joyed to stay in the bus station all night, just to have some company. Here we are."

Homer unlocked one of the carved mahogany double doors that opened onto an elaborate foyer that stretched up three stories to the very top of the house, where stars twinkled through a large four pointed star-shaped opening in the ceiling. He pressed a button on the wall and the opening closed.

"It's nicer in the summer. The rain falls inside through a fine screen and keeps the plants watered. Too cold for that on a November night."

"What a great idea!" Ceeoni could imagine rain and sunlight streaming in on the garden of lush plants arranged around the dark blue reflecting pond in the center of the entryway. African artifacts, masks, fertility dolls and paintings hung from the stair wall. A massive chandelier made of all sizes of dimly lit glass bulbs appeared to be suspended in mid-air over the wrought-iron spiral staircase. Homer's house was just like him, big, warm and flamboyant.

"I love the decor, especially that lamp," she said.

He answered her unspoken question as they climbed the stairs to the second level. "I redecorated after my divorce, I think I just needed to change the energy around here, sort of setting the mood for newness in my life."

Ceeoni couldn't help but wonder about the dynamics of that divorce, but Homer didn't offer anything else. He opened the door to her suite, and stepped back to allow her to enter, "If you need anything, simply pick up that phone and someone will answer. The meeting is at 9am, and one of us will send you a wake-up call, if you like."

"Yes, thank you. 7am will be fine. Homer, I'm grateful for your hospitality. My nerves of steel turned to jelly tonight."

"Try to get some rest." He kissed her cheek and left.

The combination living room/bedroom suite contained a sitting area and two queen-sized beds. There was a fully stocked bar hidden discretely behind mahogany cabinet doors. Chocolate carpet and overstuffed twin sofas matched the tan raw silk drapes. A cheery fire threw prancing images on the walls, changing the expressions and moods of the hanging red and black Masai masks. The masks were a bit much—she felt as though their eyes were following her around the room. She stood on a chair and took the six masks down, "OK fellas, you can rest on the closet shelf until which time I build up some artistic appreciation for your fearsome countenance."

She opened the silk drapes a little and peeked through the creme sheers covering the French doors leading out to the small balcony. The balcony looked down on a dark blue natural rock swimming pool, surrounded by large tropical plants, with a tall cascading waterfall at the far end. She hastily drew the drapes to answer a knock at the door.

"Yes?"

"It's Weber, Ma'am. I have your luggage." Weber, a slender, friendly-faced man, wearing a silk version of the traditional white Korean Karate Gi uniform, brought in a tray carrying fragrant noodle soup, corn muffins, hot lemon zinger tea, and her set of keys before bringing in her luggage, "I hope you enjoy your stay, Ms. Jones. Homer told me about today's tragic event. If you need anything, I'm only as far away as the phone."

"Weber, may I ask how many people live here?"

"Oh, just the two of us, Ma'am, which is probably why we're happy to have an honored guest." He bowed slightly and took his leave.

Once she got a whiff of the soup, she decided her tummy wasn't so queasy after all. She ate the wonderful concoction, hung up her clothes and soaked in rose scented water in a garden tub big enough for six. Wrapped up in a fluffy beige towel, she called Di, in Los Angeles. Getting no answer, she left a message,

"Girl, you won't believe all the drama! All hell broke loose up in here tonight! And let me repeat, Hell!—I mean I just got here and already, well, I'll tell all the vivid and gory details when we talk, but here's a preview. Since I left you and Dad a few hours ago at LAX, I discovered a murdered corpse. Yes—Pause—Gasp! A stone, cold deader-than-a—door-nail brother in my office bathroom. Remember I told you yesterday that Adam Delayno is replacing Joe Sample for our opening tomorrow night? Girl, get this, the corpse was Adam Delayno's business manager! Yeah, the stuff is sloshing, making deep waves. This isn't a joke and I do hope I haven't lost my mind, but Di, everything else is Positively Yummy! P.S., Fantastic isn't an adequate word for the single, as in unmarried, hunk of rompin' stompin' male refinement who owns the Starcross Complex. And, this man seems to have the uncanny ability to answer questions I was thinking, without my having asked them. Oh yeah, Starcross is stretching my sanity! What sanity? Hit me back! Ciao!"

Ceeoni fell asleep with all the lights on, still wrapped in her towel. The soft sofa molded itself around her shapely form, as the hot bath, the snack and the crackling fire combined to sedate her emotional rollercoaster. She never saw the shadow that moved slowly and silently outside her second-story balcony doors.

CHAPTER FOUR

Ceeoni awakened to the sound of Weber's soothing voice on the intercom, "Good morning, Miss Jones. I'm reminding you of your 9am meeting. Breakfast is ready. Would you like a tray in your suite, or would you prefer to come to the dining room?"

She took a minute to remember where she was.

"Yes, oh, good morning. I'll find my way to the dining room."

"I'll take you to the theatre, or you can drive, its close, your choice," he said. "Thanks Weber, I'd appreciate a ride." She rolled off of the sofa to prepare for the busy day to come. Horrifying flashbacks of the night before assailed her as she showered and found her 'work clothes'; black sweater, pants and boots. She kept seeing Basil Cassidy's open dead eyes, staring at her, watching—

Ceeoni Jones, what have you gotten yourself into?

She sat on the bed, and scolded herself, Now, you gotta' pick one! Which will it be? A Banner Day or Regrets R Us?

She shook off her fears, mentally bound and gagged her very loud, persistent critical factor, which she thought of as 'The Voice of Reason' aka 'The Sane Ceeoni,' and closed her inner ears to negative noises. It was time to get moving and get to work. Homer was counting on her.

Jake Clark, the Starcross Assistant Manager, had a resume that stated he knew nothing in life but theatre, and as a dancer, he had, among other things, understudied Gregory Hines. The major shows this consummate pro had been apart of read like a list of Broadway's Greatest Hits, Cats, A Chorus Line, Dream Girls, Jelley's Last Jam, and on and on. Homer told her that Jake had sustained a back injury that ended his career in dance, but he'd made a transition into theatre management. He didn't look like he'd ever had a bad cold. Jake's credits in production and management were nearly as extensive as the performing end of his career.

When they met, Jake made an elaborate bow as he took Ceeoni's hand, "Ms. Jones, you have no idea how happy I am that you decided to join us here at Starcross." He even bore a slight resemblance to Gregory Hines, and he exuded the same kind of dancer's fluid movement and energy.

"Ceeoni, please, Jake," she answered, "I'm impressed with your remarkable background."

"Why, thank you, Ceeoni. When Homer told us you were his number one choice, I thought he'd been reading my mind, or consulting a psychic."

"How about that mind-reading number?" she laughed.

"Yeah, he does that a lot." Jake winked at her and added, "You'll find there's plenty of unseen stuff in the air around here. Anyway, your reputation has preceded you. I personally believe that if you do half of what you did at the Ebell, we'll be fine. Actually, I remember hearing about you when you were at Inner-City, as well."

"Oh, if you're familiar with that theatre you must've been aware of our intense limitations there." She took the chair he offered her, before he replied,

"But isn't that what all of show business is about—finding many ways to take an audience beyond all awareness of any limitations, except that which is feeding the senses?" His Gregory Hines eyes held hers until she nodded, "You're so right, Jake." Ceeoni thought of the years at Inner-City as her Dark Ages, because of the tremendous effort required to stay afloat professionally, financially and emotionally. At that time in her life, she'd had been too numb to examine her senses.

The rest of the staff joined them, right on time. She'd been supplied with everyone's resume while she was still in California, and they were well chosen. More hiring was necessary, but she approved of Jake's starting line-up. He'd added little descriptive notes to each work record to help her sort out strengths. For example, on Becky Jewel's resume he'd noted, 'enthusiastic, cooperative and flexible.' She was the tiny, fresh-faced Assistant Stage Manager who looked like she should be in junior high school.

After introductions and an opening statement of team confidence, Ceeoni spoke;

"Ladies and Gentlemen, I'm certain you're aware of the crime that was discovered here at the theatre last night, and I can assure you, the police are doing everything they can to get to the bottom of it. Does anyone have any questions?" She paused, and no one said a word. "OK, I promise you I believe in short meetings, and this one is adjourned."

The group gladly dispersed to get about his or her tasks. She was very pleased with the staff's level of professionalism. They already exhibited that familiar mix of quiet efficiency sprinkled with outrageous banter that was common to an effective unit. The morning continued with round after round of checking and double-checking the weekend's arrangements. Everything was falling into place when Homer's call interrupted the flow.

"Ceeoni, Detective David Saxon needs to have a few words with you, and he insisted that we get together for lunch." Lunch! She didn't have time for lunch! She'd been too busy to even think about the murder. She knew that soon after 12noon on any performance day, curtain time would be in her face in what seemed like minutes. Lunch was something she wished she could forego, but she guessed Homer wouldn't have called if there was a way around it. She sighed in resignation as Jake crossed her path,

"Jake, I've gotta go to lunch, and I can't get out of it. I wanted to be here for the Tech rehearsal."

"Go ahead, we can hold it down until you get back."

"Can I bring you anything?" she asked.

"No thanks, Moveable Feast will be along with their baskets of sandwiches and fruit in—," He glanced at his watch, "a half-hour."

"Sounds like what I should be doing, but I'll be back by 1pm Sound Check. A missed light cue can go unnoticed, but the sound has got to be perfect. I want to hear it with my own ears."

Homer picked her up for the short drive to the Starcross Restaurant. Ceeoni was extremely grateful they'd chosen somewhere close. Detective Saxon was waiting out in front when they arrived. The restaurant's Greek Revival design was in keeping with the Starcross architecture—ten tall columns, with a facade nearly identical to the theatre's.

She was curious to see what Homer had done with the interior.

Ceeoni followed Homer to a rear table, where they sat opposite Detective Saxon.

"Well, I've got a bit of good news," David began, "We've asked the media not to release the murder story until tonight."

"Thanks, David, I didn't think that could be done."

"Homer, I wish I could keep it out of the public eye a little longer, but I held the info as long as I could."

Ceeoni patted Homer's hand, "Hey, that's good, very good. On the positive side, that'll give us a day of theatre-goers' walking word-of-mouth publicity. I've heard Adam Delayno puts on a great show, which should give them plenty to talk about."

"Hopefully, the good stuff will outweigh the news of the murder," Homer said.

The waiter appeared at their table, "Good day, everyone. Good day, Mr.Dinsmore. My name is Steven, and I'll be your server today. May I bring you something from the bar?" They asked for coffee, and the slender young waiter quickly returned with a decorative black China coffee pot before he took their orders.

"Nobody asked me," Homer said as he passed the sugar, "but we have some gulf shrimp that tastes like they swam in here and jumped into the salad this morning."

David said he only wanted coffee, but Ceeoni and Homer ordered shrimp salads. The salad turned out to be the stuff shrimp salad dreams are made of—fresh, sweet and ice cold, with a light herbal dressing.

"Homer, my compliments to you and the chef," she said, "everything was especially delicious."

"Well, I'll have Minette pass that on. She's the one who implements my wishes."

David Saxon turned to Ceeoni, "Please tell me exactly what happened last night."

She reiterated the details of her chilling exploration, remembering to include the strange noise she'd heard.

"So Homer, you were at home?" David asked.

"I played a round of Chess with Taurus Weber."

"Oh, yeah, Weber."

"I was waiting for Basil Cassidy to call me to let me know he was on his way to meet Adam and me at the Manor," Homer said.

As David spoke, his eyes took on a flat, police look, typical of law enforcement officers, "Yes. If needed, you will make the details of your business with Basil Cassidy available to us?"

"Of course. Just let me know what you want, and when. I take pride in keeping complete, accurate records. My attorney can supply anything my office doesn't have."

"Damn, I still haven't had the opportunity to speak to Delayno today."

"David," Homer said, "Your best bet would probably be to wait until after the concert tonight, or possibly tomorrow. Basil had no family that anyone knows of. Adam is taking care of his final arrangements. Basil wished to be cremated with no ceremony of any kind. Adam is also trying to get halfway settled, and he probably has to make some preparation for tonight's concert. I left one of my cars for him to run errands with one of the band guys from Atlanta. There's no telling where they are."

It was obvious that Detective Saxon considered Adam a suspect, and Ceeoni couldn't blame him. She knew of many artists who didn't get along with their business people. She'd been privy to infamous tales of horrific artist/agent conflict, scary shouting matches, threats, revenge and bitter, expensive litigation.

Ceeoni glanced at her watch. Time was growing short. She had to get back to the theatre.

A smiling man walked up to the table, wearing an elegant burgundy African robe, blonde hair escaping from the sides of his matching kufi. The man held out his hand to Homer,

"My friend!"

Homer beamed as he got up and hugged the robed figure,

"R.C.! So good to see you again!" He gestured toward Ceeoni, "This is Ceeoni Jones, our General Manager at the theatre, and this is Detective David Saxon, who is in charge of the murder investigation, meet. R.C. Ponder, Adam's personal manager. Please join us."

R.C. carried a snappy monogrammed brown leather attache case, obviously custom crafted.

"Happy to meet you, Ms. Jones, Detective Saxon." R.C. sat down and pulled some papers from the attache case, which he handed to Ceeoni.

"Ms. Jones, I guess these go to you." She took the hard copy contracts, and wondered at the wave of sadness that welled up with unshed tears as she saw the flourish that was Adam Delayno's signature at the bottom.

With a sincerely concerned expression, R.C. spoke to Detective Saxon,

"Detective, we don't know what to make of the tragedy that occurred here. I know I can speak for Adam when I say we're completely at your disposal in regard to your investigation."

David's response snapped back in the clipped, official mode,

"Your flight arrived at Hartsfield from Kennedy at 2:08pm, Thursday. If you, or another member of Delayno's entourage wanted to kill Basil Cassidy, you would've had plenty of leeway. Mr. Cassidy's murder was placed at approximately 4:30pm."

R.C. appeared to be comfortable with David's cold demeanor as if subtle attack rolled easily off of his sensibilities. He looked directly at David,

"Yes, that would've been quite enough time, wouldn't it? We'll make our where-abouts known to you, along with witnesses to corroborate our testimony."

"David," Homer interjected, "It's more than puzzling, but I have faith that you and your excellent staff will solve it."

"I appreciate your vote of confidence. Oh, and one more thing, do you know what time the last person left the theatre before Ms. Jones arrived there?"

"Yeah," Homer answered, "I went straight home. Jake had to take some papers to Ticketron before they closed at 5:30." David nodded and sat back in his chair. Homer signaled for the waiter. R.C. ignored David as if he had suddenly disappeared.

"Ms. Jones," R.C. said, "we're really looking forward to the concerts this weekend. I've rarely seen Adam so hyped." She noticed R.C.'s slight northern European accent, the long sandy braid he

Karma Rising

pushed back over his shoulder, and the happy sea green eyes with their crinkly laugh lines. This guy would make you smile even if you hadn't planned on it.

"We're looking forward to them, also. Have you spent much time in Atlanta?"

"Ms. Jones, this is my first trip here, and oh, oh, oh what a town! We've been reading everything we can find about Georgia since Adam is bound and determined to move here. Now, I think I'm glad he chose this area. We've noted the fact that many artists and recording companies are based here, with more moving in all the time. And I understand there's quite a bit of emphasis on cultural activities. From what I've learned so far, I think my family will love it."

Ceeoni wasn't sure if she would love it or not. She took a moment to survey the restaurant's decor and color scheme. The black velvet chairs and booths, the waiters' sharp, all black attire, huge ferns hanging from translucent ceiling panes that reflected shadows on the peach-streaked black carpet, blended into a tranquil scene. A narrow beam of track ceiling light illuminated a single coral rose in the center of each table.

"I like the ambiance here, Homer," she said, "Did you decorate?"

"Nah, my ex-wife. She liked the restaurant better than she liked me."

Ceeoni tore her eyes away from the delicate fountain under the graceful archway dividing the dining area from the bar. She could've watched the hidden pale gold lights turn tiny water droplets into liquid sunshine, for hours. The thought forced her to realize the time.

"Oops, please forgive me. Everything was great, but I work across the street, and I must get back." The detective stood,

"Ms. Jones, I can give you a lift, if you like."

"OK, Detective."

Homer blew her a kiss, and R.C. waved,

"I'll be there in a few minutes," R.C. said, "I'm doing the sound check."

Leaving the restaurant, Detective Saxon took her arm,

"Hey You, let's drop the 'Detective' stuff. Please call me Dave, and I'll call you Sweetness." When she didn't respond, he added, "Seriously, I've checked your background and your flight from LA, and I've eliminated you as a suspect. Everyone in Delayno's band took the shuttle to the Marriott downtown after they arrived. R.C. Ponder and Delayno left in a limo, supposedly on their way to Starcross Manor to meet Basil Cassidy. I've surmised that Homer didn't meet your plane because of that appointment."

She replied that she was thoroughly accustomed to the typical mad rush that was ever present in her business, and had thought nothing of Homer's absence, or Minette's haste. She couldn't help but notice the warm, reassuring grip he maintained on her arm. And, she couldn't help but wonder who is Detective Saxon's prime suspect? R.C? Adam? or Homer? And what about Minette? Why had she been in such a hurry? Ceeoni made no comment, and David, mistaking her silence to be interest, whispered in her ear,

"Now that I know you're not the killer, and if you don't have a date tonight, will you join me for a drink after the show?" When he leaned over to open the door for her, she noticed his long, thick lashes over what is known as classic 'bedroom eyes.' Nevertheless, she politely declined his offer, "Well, Detective, ah, I mean, Dave, I have no idea what time we'll be finished, and even under normal circumstances, after days of preparation, a performance and a reception, I'm always too bedraggled to socialize."

He persisted, "Coffee? Tea? A Smoothie? How about coming over to my place to read some of my police reports?"

"Ouch!" she laughed, "Police reports?"

"Yeah, I had a lady once ask me if she could read some of my most bizarre police reports. I had a hard time getting it across to her that they don't let us bring them home."

His smile was appealing, and the short ride up to the theatre was pleasant, but she didn't want to go out with anyone just yet. "Thanks, but I need some time to adapt to my new environs."

He flashed her another one of those dimpled wonders, "I'm a patient man, Ceeoni Jones, I can wait."

She was certain that the detective's smile had the ladies rolling in the aisles all over town. As she climbed the stairs to her office, she reflected on relationships. Over the years, it was her work that had cushioned her disappointments and heartaches. One marriage, a couple of affairs and a few minor flirtations had all, for one reason or another, failed to last. She was more careful as more maturity set in. Broken romances took a terrific toll on her emotions, and she didn't bounce back easily. Each wrecked romantic excursion seemed to require longer periods of recuperation Ceeoni Jones was a happy person, who was hoping to find another happy person. She dreamed of meeting the one man with the perfect combination of integrity, mischief, kindness, loyalty, sexy madness and soul, with tolerable imperfections, who was searching for the same things, and would find them in her. That's a Tall Order—does such a man exist? And most of all, would she ever find him? She often wondered if relationships were as difficult for others. In her love life, it seemed there was always something missing, something that should have been there, but wasn't.

x x x

She looked around the office for her attache case, and noticed one of her framed posters was hanging at a lopsided angle. The poster was from "The Meeting," a powerful play about a hypothetical meeting between Dr. Martin Luther King, Jr. and Malcolm X, in which the philosophies of non-violent social change and its opposite, collide. Thinking about "The Meeting" always reminded her of her ex-husband, Bobby Moraku. It was the second production they had worked on together.

Bobby Moraku, full of fire, had brilliantly maneuvered through the maze of Hollywood politics and blatant racism to become an important filmmaker/director. After making an easy move from directing a few highly acclaimed off-Broadway productions, Bobby's successful film career surprised everyone, him included.

He was ten years older than she when they met. She had just begun her stint at the Inner-City Cultural Center Theatre. Bobby's work was already well known. She'd heard about the achievements that Bobby Moraku was making, and she was thrilled to be a Production Assistant on a play that he'd written. She had no idea who was going to direct. All she could think of was how wonderful it would be to have such a bright addition to her sparse resume, and she expected she'd learn some bigtime tricks of the trade.

Unfortunately, the day of the first production meeting was one of the rare occasions when she was late, and very late, at that. Her little white Mustang convertible had reached the point where all the systems were beginning to fail. When the starter refused to kick over that morning, she'd scrambled to catch public transportation. From the slow-as-Christmas Crenshaw bus, the fast Pico Blue Line dropped her near the Inner City Theatre, where she'd tip-toed quietly into the meeting that was already in full swing.

Her entrance caused a slight pause in the somewhat pompous speech a man she'd never seen before was making. She smiled what she hoped was a winsome, apologetic smile, but the man ignored her. She wondered who he was. They always brought in a guest director for an important work, especially when the play had as much New York Juice as a Moraku show. She figured this good-looking stranger must be someone important.

The producer pointed to a saved chair. Ceeoni lowered herself into it as gingerly as she could, but the wooden chair emitted a long, loud creak, anyway. There were eight people around the table, and seven of them knew her well, and knew she was seldom as klutzy as she appeared that day. The stranger making the boring speech didn't know her, and his look of glaring disgust in her direction told her he didn't care to. She wanted to say something, apologize maybe, but it was apparent that a great deal of finesse, skill and nerve was required for some brave soul to attempt to get a word in edgewise, as long as his gigantic ego had the floor. The meeting wore on, while the man led them point by insignificant point through the script. Finally, she'd had her fill of this guy's inability to perceive the subtle interplay that would enrich a pivotal scene between the two lovers. Or at least, the way he said he was planning to direct the big love scene, the audience would never see what the scene could portray. She waited for the man to take a breath in his monologue, a breath that never came. He droned on and on, until she couldn't take it. When she raised her hand, he ignored it. Finally, she broke in.

"Ah, excuse me, but shouldn't they be closer during Mark's speech? Right now he's across the room from her, but since he's

Karma Rising

saying such tender words, it seems he should be straining toward her, reaching out, so to speak, sort of on the edge of his chair?"

The man, whom she assumed was the director, stood up. He didn't speak for several seconds.

"And just who are you?" he asked, in a sharp tone.

"Ceeoni Jones," she replied in a small voice.

His brown eyes narrowed in his chiseled face, and she saw further evidence of his anger in the sudden flare of his nostrils,

"You were tardy, Ms. Jones! What, may I ask is your position regarding this project?"

She bit her lip. Too late! She realized she had already committed a Grand Faux Pas. This was a person not to be opposed, under any conditions. But she couldn't back down now. She had to play it out. She was able to smile about it later, but while it was happening, she'd felt like a small antelope that had put her head into the lion's mouth.

The shocking impact of the stranger's sudden intense furor had momentarily diminished her ability to think on her feet. She was about to try to answer him, but his demeanor had become so threatening, she decided to hold her peace to see what this egomaniac was going to do. His tall, slim frame was tense with rage as he slowly picked up his folding chair, never taking his flinty eyes from hers. She didn't know why he was so angry, and she didn't know what to do to save herself from whatever he had planned. The thought that he intended to hit her with his damned chair ran through her mind. He stood at the head of the long table, staring at her, breathing hard, with the chair in his hand.

"Maybe I'm not making myself clear, Ms. Jones, what is your position? Answer me!"

She ignored his demand and his stupid chair. She concentrated on staring back at him, to keep from running out of the room in a trembling mass of frustrated, humiliated tears.

Suddenly, he threw the chair, hard. It sailed over the heads of the theatre's artistic director and the technical director, who appeared to be frozen in disbelief. The chair smacked against the wall with a loud bang, followed by pieces hitting the floor like wooden wind chimes. No one moved. This was all so ridiculous, she would've laughed if she hadn't been so angry. Her emotions took her past caring what this jerk or anybody else thought. She began to snatch up her papers and notes, as she glared at him. Her voice shook, and she could feel tears forming in her eyes, as always, when she was upset.

"W-Well," she sputtered, "please accept my humble apology for whatever mortal sin I've committed in your sacred sight, but Moraku wrote a love scene here that is crying for the steady hand of a sensitive director who possesses empathetic vision and insight—"

The man's expression changed, like the sun showing up in the midst of a blustry storm. Smiling, he spoke softly,

"Ms. Jones! Ms. Jones! Ms. Jones, my name is Bobby Moraku, and I do like to think my work reflects all of those attributes."

Her engines were full throttle, ready to do battle. But everybody around her was smiling! Bobby Moraku! Oh God No! She blinked to collect herself, as Jack Jackson, ICCC's Managing Director, got up and put his arms around her,

"Ceeoni, remind me to tell you about the first time I saw him do that chair thing. He put a whole cast and crew in terror, which turned out to be an expedient method of securing everyone's lasting and respectful attention. I told our staff about it before Mr. Moraku arrived; sorry you weren't present to be forewarned."

Bobby Moraku came over and held out his very warm hand to her,

"I'm so glad you like my play, Ms. Jones. Can we get to work now?" She wasn't ready to feel happy just yet. It took a while for her back to un-stiffen and for her breathing to slow to normal. Before the close of that fateful meeting, he passed some script pages around the table. She glanced at the top of her page. He had written, 'Will you have dinner with me—now?' And the script changes included her recommendations for the love scene.

They were inseparable from that day on. When they married in a hasty champagne haze at Las Vegas' Caesar's Palace six months later, she was far too besotted with his hazel eyes, his great mind, his dependence on her and the heat of their passion to give any credence to the danger signs. She believed they had loved each other, but Bobby's world was like the song, 'What's Love Got To Do With It?' She learned love had nothing the hell whatsoever to do with it.

Karma Rising

After they'd been married for three years, it was clear that Bobby's genius required endless all-night accolades from a large, varied female audience. Ceeoni moved into the extra bedroom, disgusted with him, and more disgusted with herself for hoping he'd 'change'. Her friend Di said she was just plain disgusted,

"Ceeoni, sluts like your husband don't change, they just get older than their years. Once he's broken down and sick, you get to be the brave woman who had the stomach to stick it out in pain, while he spent years at the Ball." It wasn't funny, but Ceeoni had joined in.

"You know I know, Di, or he ends up with some poor trusting soul who thinks she's won something, only to find that Mr. TreasuredPrize has had such a good time at the Ball, he's burnt out and too tired and/or mad at the world to spell the word, fun, let alone have any!"

Ceeoni had tried to stick it out. She helped him fine tune his writing and directing skills, and helped him soften his sharp edges to more readily display the warmer side of his persona, so that his Jekyll and Hyde flip-flops became nearly invisible. She typed his plays, screened his offers, acted as a sounding board for his ideas and fears, and offered constructive suggestions in all areas of his career. Bobby Moraku became an even more adept mover and shaker than he was when they met.

Ceeoni realized he was irresistible in his profession, in business, and to women, lots of women. At first, she felt extremely neglected. There are all kinds of abuse, and her marriage taught her that neglect is as devastating as all the rest. He had wide mood swings, and she never knew when he was coming home sober and silent, angry and abusive, or with some weird new combination that always ended in angry and abusive. She reached a point when she dreaded the sound of his key in the door.

Bobby was going on location to Vancouver, Canada, to shoot his first feature film, at the same time their marriage was picking at the final shredded thread of the last straw. She'd packed his bags for the trip, and they had only two hours to plow through traffic from their Beverly Hills condo near Wilshire Boulevard and Comstock, to LAX. Mr. FilmProducer/Director was already a little drunk from meetings and celebrations. She pulled their midnight blue Mercedes

Benz up from the subterranean garage and parked it in front of the building in order to load the last of his luggage.

She found him standing in the kitchen, whispering into the telephone. Weaving and swaying, barely standing was a more adequate description. He attempted to pour Johnny Walker Black Label Scotch into a tumbler, although more of it splashed over his hand onto the floor, while he held the phone stuffed between his shoulder and his ear. He looked up, saw her, then he mumbled something into the phone and quickly broke the connection, which made her skin crawl.

"Bobby," she said in a flat tone, "You don't need another drink." He ricocheted off of the kitchen counter, bounced off the doorjamb, then swirled around to face her with bloodshot, unfocused eyes and shouted,

"Stop trying to tell me what to do! You're supposed to be my wife, dammit, not my mammy-jammin' mama! Why in the hell can't you acquiesce like a woman should? You're always tryin' to exert some stupid ass power over me!"

"Power? Power?! Oh, Bobby, I'm just saddened because you don't seem to have power over yourself!" Swaying, he belched, and reached out for the wall to steady himself. The gesture made her feel pity for him, and a glimmer of hope that something might be salvaged. Maybe, just maybe, if he stopped drinking so much, they could—

"Bobby, look," she began, "Today is a marvelous day for us. Today begins a new phase in our long-nurtured 'Harvest of Dreams'. We can put all this behind us and turn over a new leaf—we've worked too hard for this day just to throw it all away now—"

His harsh laughter stabbed at her pride and her heart. When his laughter turned into a coughing spasm, he was forced to stop and take a deep breath,

"We? What 'we'? Hot Damn! Now that's a joke! Have you forgotten that I was freakin' successful before I ever laid eyes on your sorry ass? All these years, all you managed to do was get the hell all up in my Goddamn way!"

She stood there, unable to think of anything to say, even if she could muster the energy to say it. He staggered into bathroom while she, numb and trembling, sat down in the dark living room.

That night, it finally became clear in her mind that her marriage was totally impossible. She was still sitting on the sofa, holding her car keys in her hand, when a car horn signal was followed by the slam of the front door. From the balcony, she watched her husband load his luggage into a tan Jaguar, with the affectionate assistance of the driver, an exotic young woman in a backless leopard catsuit, the seams of which threatened to break apart by the jiggling furor of her bouncing curves. Ceeoni could hold back neither the uncontrollable laughter or the unchecked tears that flowed simultaneously down her face.

The divorce came with a very generous cash settlement, a quick-claim deed to the Beverly Hills condo, and the pink slip to the Mercedes. She banked the money, and sold the rest. Diana stayed with her for a few months afterward.

"Well, Ceeoni," she said, "You can't say he done you wrong in the financial department."

Ceeoni played Donny Hathaway's 'Gone Away,' a poignant ballad of lost love from Roberta Flack's first album, until it wouldn't play anymore—The song burned in her heart—'You were mine, for only a minute and if I hurt you, I didn't intend it—you are gone away, I keep telling my mind—you're not gone to stay—yet I believe sometime that I've lost you baby—I've lost you baby, and you are gone~'

Years passed before she could think of that night, or hear that song, without feeling the bleak emptiness all over again. After it was all over, she'd constantly asked herself if she had done her best. Her heart knew they had never been right for each other, still, she wished him well.

He'd recently completed his sixth major film, and although not of Oscar caliber, they were good pictures, and they made money. Mutual friends told her tales of Bobby's multiple personal relationships that remained inevitably soaked in Bobby's typical brand of alcoholic infidelities and deceptions, like 'All My Children In Another World As The Stomach Churns.'

Work kept her from mentally re-living and re-writing scenarios in which things came out differently. She didn't know what made relationships stay vibrant and romantic. She knew if she had to do it over again, she wouldn't settle until she was sure that honor was apart of the equation.

The very attractive Detective David Saxon was showing signs of what Ceeoni thought of as 'The Curse of High Visibility.' This common malady is brought on by physical attractiveness, status in the community, in one way or another, and is exacerbated by having money, or the appearance of being successful, in one way or another. This condition can really be toxic in one who possesses a combination of popular desirable qualities. One of the patient's common symptoms is a glaringly shallow perception of affairs of the heart. Someone suffering from 'The Curse' may never realize the depths of caring and understanding that two people can reach, because he or she doesn't have to. Like her ex-husband, one can flit from partner to partner, pretending to be in love with someone, without bothering to get to know anyone.

CHAPTER FIVE

Thinking of her failed marriage reminded Ceeoni of the many hours she and her friend Di had spent discussing one of their favorite subjects, relationships. From their earliest years, they'd discussed how to get along in school and in every situation.

One particular conversation came to Ceeoni's mind. On a beautiful sunshiny afternoon, another perfect day in L.A., she sat in the kitchen of Diana's California ranch stucco home in Baldwin Hills, keeping Di company while she prepared her famous baked zucchini casserole. Ceeoni recalled that they vegged out on that do-nothing day, while a sparkling clear view of miles and miles of Los Angeles glistened through sliding glass doors.

"Relationships are the hardest lessons in the world," Di said, as she added fresh basil to the dish. "There are Universal Laws all humanity has to learn. Not just in romantic relationships, but in all relationships—brother to brother, stranger to stranger, parents to children, neighbor to neighbor, nation to nation. The Laws of Karma are the rules that govern our Souls' decisions to repay the Spiritual Debts we owe one another. The debts are made according to the ways we behave toward each other." She waved a spoon to emphasize her point.

"According to the Bible, 'Not one whit, not one tittle of The Law shall go unfulfilled." Di continued, "The metaphysical interpretation of that is whatever a Soul does to another, every bit of that Spiritual Debt must be paid. If it's good, good returns. If we fail to learn the lesson, then we are destined to repeat it, in some way, until the lesson is learned. The Soul chooses how it will learn, and the people in our lives are teaching us, and learning from us, constantly. We can't escape it, for learning these lessons is our major purpose for taking on this earthly form. Actually, our relationships are as intricately wired as the molecular structures of life itself."

Ceeoni privately smiled at Di's ability to speak in capitalized superlatives. Nevertheless, she'd captured Ceeoni's undivided attention.

"So Di, is that what they're teaching you in those new-fangled courses you're studying?"

"Yeah, but what makes the Theory of Karma so compelling is the whole new fearless way you learn to look at life and the world, and I believe it, too. According to the Laws of Karma, we live many lifetimes, learning, interacting with all types of Souls, strictly for the purpose of learning how to treat each other."

"Oh yeah. OK. Of course. Many lifetimes, huh?"

"Ceeoni, don't throw it out. Millions of people believe in reincarnation, and have irrefutable evidence of past lives." Di sipped her wine, "And, laugh if you want, but this reincarnation stuff is very hip. The people in our lives are drawn to us, even the ones who hurt us, and we are drawn to them, for the express purpose of working out Karma, or balancing Karma. We recognize one another from past lives. We all spend a second or a lifetime with someone just for the purpose of spiritual development."

"Well, Di, I never heard of anyone who believes in Karma."

"Now you do, but look around! You know those odd couples, the ones people are always trying to figure? Like, I wonder how those two got together? Or why is this difficult person my supervisor? Or, out of all the people in the world, why is he my neighbor? Etcetera. Ceeoni, I believe that pairs, or groups all have soul-to-soul-connections. These connections aren't Soul Mates. A true Soul-Mate is the one person with whom each Soul can attain the highest states of love, passion, and spiritual evolvement, although we all have different types of Karmic connections with others."

Not knowing what to say, Ceeoni mentally sifted what her friend had said.

Di dug into the casserole, and handed Ceeoni her plate,

"Anyway, Cee, I'm beginning to think my Soul Mate isn't alive in this life."

"Whoa! Di, what happened to 'It Ain't Over Til' Its Over'?"

"Maybe I'm working out other Karmic Debts this time."

"Aw, cut it out—it's not like you to be negative. It's your job to keep us positive, remember? I'm the careful one who worries and is hard to convince of anything!"

Diana waited until Ceeoni took a bite out of the Italian dish, "So, how is it?"

"Girl, please—this is one of the world's greatest recipes! But Di, I most definitely did hear you say we're getting out of this alive after all, but tell me, does anyone know how to get it right? What I mean is, can we do anything about the human predicament and make good Karma?"

"It ain't easy. It takes practice. All the regular stuff applies. The Ten Commandments aren't suggestions. Keeping it going is the hardest thing, you know, doing unto others, and all that, everyday, in every way. I think the first step is to realize that being aware of this fact is the key, that is, being spiritually aware, caring for all relationships as if we have to pay for everything we do. I'm learning that the only way to attain real happiness comes out of total spiritual awareness. That's because when you're spiritually aware, in every instance, you treat yourself and others with loving care, which makes good Karma."

"You know that doesn't come easy to a lot of us peons down here on the ground. A lot of us think whoever gets the most stuff, wins."

"Yeah, right, but there's no luggage rack on a hearse, and no U-Hauls hooked up to the back, either. The stuff people would lie, cheat, steal and kill for, can't be taken with them."

"O.K., but—Di, you know how impossible some folk can be. How do you get around the feelings that just rise up when someone is simply awful? What's the secret?"

"No secret. Simply put, its unconditional love; loving unconditionally, that is, treating everyone and everything with love."

"Love unconditionally? I think only holy people like Mother Theresa can do that."

"Ceeoni, we all have to try. There's a hidden truth in loving unconditionally. Loving people doesn't mean loving the mistakes we all make. You know, fear, and flaws in human belief systems can cause us to be unlovable, and that includes the menace to society types. It is said that the lack of harmony between the loving, real inner self and the illusionary belief system, is what manifests physical disease. If we learn to see the inner light and separate it from the sometimes flawed belief system that people have been taught, and/or that we've taught ourselves, the light in everyone is very bright."

"Yeah, well," Ceeoni said sarcastically, "Some folk have gone to great lengths to cover up their inner light."

x x x

Each time she thought back on that conversation, she was aware of how much easier unconditional love was to say, than to do, especially in marriage.

Looking around her Starcross office, she did a mental checklist, and was heading for the door when she remembered her lucky pen. She went back to her desk, but the gold-trimmed Montblanc wasn't there, and it wasn't in her case. Now where did it go? She cherished that pen, it had been a gift from Di to commemorate the production of her first show back in '85.

"Planet earth calling!" Jake tapped on the door, and handed her a stack of messages. She forgot about her missing pen.

"Oh, Jake, thank you. I know I must be a little late. How's it going?"

"Actually, you're right on time. They had a devil of a feedback whine in one of the speakers that has, prayerfully, been corrected. Be thankful you weren't in the house. We've tested and retested the system. It should sound better than Carnegie Hall. You know Homer insisted on nothing less than top of the line equipment." They approached the stage door, and Ceeoni walked ahead, saying,

"I've seen great systems neutralized by an engineer who didn't know how to get the best out of it." Glancing over her shoulder, she read the confidence in his eyes.

"I think you'll like what you're about to hear."

A series of rich piano chords flowed from the Steinway, as she sat down in the front row of the auditorium. R.C. Ponder, standing in for Adam, played slowly, checking how the piano mike picked up every tone. After the sharp, pure sound that filled the room dissipated, R.C. jumped off the stage and sat beside her.

"Beautiful Ceeoni, you're just starting here?" he asked.

"Yes, and I love this part already." They watched Jake make recommendations to the technical director, who was up on a ladder, adjusting lights. Several band members tuned up, while guitar runs, the hollow pops of conga heads, and the saxaphone's chromatic scales intermingled into a warm, familiar dissonance.

"I don't know why," R.C. said, "but this whole place has something indescribable about it. I can't quite put it into words. It's like there's a heavy vibe here. Adam is crazy about the Manor. We talked about this same thing very briefly and he said he feels something special, as well. Today, he explored the whole house, just like a kid. He had a strange reaction to this beautiful antique piano in the solarium that literally stopped him dead in his tracks. When he tried it, it was even in tune. He played that piano until his schedule tore him away. He said it's the oldest piano he's seen outside of a museum, and he's wondering if Homer knows how valuable it is."

"Do you suppose Homer left it there accidentally?"

"I've known Homer for many years, and he's usually on top of things like that. I would guess he left it there deliberately, but Adam would never second guess. We plan to discuss the piano soon, possibly this evening. In any case, Adam has to have it. If it isn't included in the sale, he wants to buy it."

"How long have you been with Adam?"

"Hmmmm—almost eighteen years now."

"Eighteen years? That means you were there at the very beginning of his career."

"Time zooms by, doesn't it? It seems like just a few months ago. I wandered into one of Adam's recording sessions, by mistake, and ran straight into him. I said, 'Excuse me,' and he put a water glass of Jack Daniels in my hand. They were standing around listening to playbacks of what they'd just recorded. The music blew me away. I said something like, 'Who is this?' Adam asked, 'Do you like it?' When I told him it was fantastic, he said, 'Thank you, it's my stuff.'

"Playbacks are some of my favorite things," he said, "especially Adam's playbacks. I guess I'll never get tired of studio-sitting. Every time I hear his recordings, I hear something new; the colors and textures are intertwined and layered, and the notes he chooses are unique. I can hear the same song by another artist, and that arresting quality just isn't there."

"I've thought the same thing about his work," she agreed.

"Also, you know how you can meet someone, and you feel like you've known that person all your life?" Ceeoni knew that feeling well. "That's how we were. Aside from the music, I knew Adam was my friend, even if I never saw him again. We talked about his music, and my career as a promo representative at CBS International in London. He asked if I was looking for another job, and I told him 'I'm always looking for another job until I find the right one.' He asked if I'd ever toured and I replied that I'd never even been on tour, actually. 'Great,' Adam said, 'I've never toured before, either. We can learn together.' He was nineteen, and I was twenty-two. I've never regretted it for a moment."

"He made up his mind fast," Ceeoni laughed.

"Yeah, it took a while to get used to that. He does it all the time, usually when I least expect it. But every now and then, he'll go on for months and months, until something happens to force him to make a decision." She was enjoying the conversation filled with little clues to Adam's personality, all of which she found stimulating,

"Sounds like you really know him."

"He's not an easy person to know. I think he waits to see if a person touches his spirit in some way. He's happy to have a small circle of friends." R.C. looked around at the decor, and changed gears. "This is one hell of a venue. I certainly hope the murder doesn't affect the crowds. People need to partake of this."

Ceeoni changed the subject, "Oh, speaking of the murder, you worked closely with Basil Cassidy. What kind of person was he?"

"Oh, he was very distant. I don't think anyone was close to him. He bragged about having no family or children. We worked together for over fifteen years, but all we ever talked about was money—how to invest it to make some, and how to re-invest it to make more,"

R.C. sighed," Basil was a good man. Every artist needs someone who can handle money as well as Basil did. He'll be missed."

"You said he'd been Adam's Business Manager for fifteen years? How does one find a good Business Manager?"

"Once an artist's career starts to take off, all sorts of people turn up offering their services, and other artists volunteer recommendations. In this case, Basil was a staff accountant at CBS in New York and Adam was on his list of accounts. Basil had talked Adam into separating his two strongest singles onto two separate album projects instead of on one album, like the company wanted. In those days, a new artist had no right to defy the company's decisions, but Adam got away with it. It helped that the A&R guy didn't seem to have a clue as to which of the potential singles was stronger than the others. Adam held his ground, and the two albums created twice the expected revenue.

"Adam knew it was Basil's quiet suggestion that had brought the potential for two back-to-back hits to his attention. We decided to stop by Basil's Manhattan office to express our thanks. Basil, as usual, was wearing one of his impeccable suits, which was probably the only suit in the building. Mind you, this was the early eighties, and everybody else was in costume. Basil's secretary was wearing orange satin shorts! But I had the feeling that his well-organized style was an indication of how he approached his work, and I was right. Adam said, 'Basil, you've helped to make me a ton of money and I'm wondering what I can do for you in return?' Basil poured out three glasses of French champagne and answered, 'I appreciate your gratitude, and I was hoping you'd ask me that question, or give me the opportunity to ask you for something.'

"I could tell Adam was surprised. He was making more money than he ever dreamed, and he was in the process of paying people for everything. I think he was waiting for Basil to give him a monetary figure, and that would be that. Instead, Basil said, 'I want to work for you. I want to handle your money because I think you'll be making a lot of it for a long time.'

"I knew Adam had given financial management some thought, but he hadn't made a move. Basil continued, 'The one condition I would impose is that I could be based in Atlanta, without having to travel. I'm really tired of the New York Shuffle. Can we make a deal on a year's trial? If you like my work after a year, I stay.' It sounded fair. They shook hands and it turned out Basil had a Midas Touch that brought profit from every endeavor.

"It's no secret that the only place where they had any disagreement was Adam's free spending habits. Basil wanted him to save for a rainy day, and Adam doesn't believe in rainy days."

Ceeoni realized that time was getting away from her.

"What a story!" she said, handing him one of the embossed cards Homer had left on her desk, "Duty calls. Please page me should you or Adam need anything."

She left the auditorium smiling, thinking that she and Adam Delayno had at least one thing in common. She didn't believe in rainy days, either.

x x x

As the day wore on, she knew everything was ready. At 5pm she could see the stage manager's flu was giving him and everybody else a case of the blues, so she sent him home. She was certain the assistant stage manager, Becky, could handle everything Adam's concert required. The catering company had been setting up all afternoon, unloading the buffet supper for more than six hundred guests. Her watch read 5:30; time for a bite and a quick change of clothing. After having worked out every detail she could, she was on automatic pilot. From this point on, the night would take care of itself.

The caterer, Windsor Jordan, of Mary Jordan Caterers, set the buffet in the Grand Ballroom, adjacent to the lobby, to give the crowd access to both areas. Homer had said that Windsor is the brother of Vernon Jordan, a high-powered Washington, D.C., attorney, and a close confidant of President Clinton's. The late Mary Jordan, their Mother, had run her catering company in Atlanta for nearly fifty years, until the mid-eighties. What an amazing feat for any woman at any time. And what bravery it must've required for a black woman to have her own thriving business in the South before, after, and during the Civil Rights Movement.

Ceeoni and Homer had worked out the buffet menu with Windsor by phone: Pate, four different types of bite-sized biscuits; broccoli, cheese, turkey sausage, shrimp; lox; beluga and lumpfish caviar; pastas; steamed and raw veggies; cheese; fruit; sliced turkey; sherbets; tarts; four Champagne Fountains, and five portable bars. She gratefully accepted Windsor's sample tidbits, and acknowledged his expertise with a big smile and a plateful of delectables.

Slipping out through the stage door exit, she found the rental car right where she'd left it the night before. She got in and cranked the engine. She noticed the brakes felt a little mushy when she backed out, but it was only a short distance to Homer's; down the steep driveway, across the road, through the gates, to the end, turn right, and on to Homer's house at the end of the lane. She started down the long slope of the driveway. Halfway down, she applied the brakes to slow her descent and nothing happened! She kept pumping the brake pedal, but there were no brakes. She couldn't believe this. The brakes had seemed fine the night before. Fortunately, no cars were coming as she approached the main lane. She frantically pumped the brake pedal and yanked the emergency brake, but the car kept moving, going faster. Picking up speed, the red Buick hurtled across the road. She was too afraid to move. Jumping was out of the question. Fear told her to scream, and she could hear her heart in her ears, but common sense told her to hold on and steer for the boxwood hedge. Tears clouded her vision, but she gripped the steering wheel with both hands and held on as momentum caused the car to leap the curb and plow into the shrubbery that lined the concrete wall bordering Starcross Lakes Estates.

The airbags hadn't inflated. And though the impact jolted her a little, she was unhurt. She felt dizzy as she sat there, listening to the hissing sound coming from under the hood. She opened the windows and breathed deeply, trying to get her bearings. One of the caterer's white vans was going up to the theatre, and the young male driver called out,

"Hey, Miss, you need some help?"

"Oh, yes, please, can you drop me down the lane a little way?" She knew she appeared rattled by the look of alarm on Weber's face when he met her at the door. "Ceeoni! Are you all right? What happened?"

"I'm fine, really—just a little shaky. But I'm OK. The brakes on my rental car failed, but I was able to steer into the greenery at the entrance." He walked with her to her suite.

"Do you have time for a rest? I can make a cup of something that will soothe those nerves." His genuine concern helped her to relax.

"Hey, Weber, that sounds great."

"Ms. Jones, you're about to receive another one of Weber's Super Quick Remedies for Traumatic Experiences. You've gotta' be in good shape tonight." He started to leave, then turned back and added, "I'll call the rental company about that car."

She fell across the bed and closed her eyes. A half hour was all she needed.

Weber returned with a mug of Green Tea that made her want to sing. She took a shower that finished the job of revitalization.

Brakes fail everyday, but she wondered if these had failed on their own. All the rental companies check those systems thoroughly before the cars are rented, don't they? At the thought of the murder and the brakes going all the way out, she felt butterflies start to flap their little wings in her stomach, but she made up her mind not to let them get started. She said one of her affirmations over and over, 'I have faith that all is in Divine Order' until those pesky butterflies flew away.

Within a few minutes, she was ready for anything. She pulled her shoulder-length curly hair on top of her head and secured it with old fashioned invisible combs. She had decided on a suit by Geoffrey Reed of New York, one of her favorite young black designers. The emerald green tuxedo jacket hugged her small waist and flaring hips, and the long velvet skirt, split up to mid-thigh, made her feel that the four-figure price tag was worth the glamorous feeling it gave her. She had worn the suit only once, for a preview of Bill Duke's film, "The Cemetery Gang."

It happened to be the first time she'd seen her ex-husband since he staggered out of her life, and she was so glad it was a dressy occasion. She always felt extra confident in formal clothes. Di said it was the under-developed side of their Emotional Quotient, because she felt the same way. Surprisingly, the meeting between her and Bobby Moraku was something they both needed. Because it was early, he was still sober, and because a small part of her would always love him, she didn't snub him when he flirted shamelessly with her. She had waved to him from across the lobby, and he winked at her while suggestively licking his lips. Instead of turning away, she smiled slightly to declare peace. She happily noted that her cheeks weren't burning and her heart wasn't thumping, but it was useless to pretend she wasn't glad to see him. She could never hold a grudge, not even a big one.

During the film intermission, he waited for her outside the Ladies Lounge, leaning against the wall wearing a formal Versace white-on-white leather ensemble, complete with silk shirt and scarf. He put his cigarette out in the tray by his side when he saw her,

'Ceeoni' he called, 'Come here.'

He was still scoring high marks on the crude-o-meter.

She didn't want to come there. She kept walking in the opposite direction. Bobby followed. 'Girl, I just want to have a friendly conversation, you know, see how you're doing and all, you know—'

She stopped and faced him. His appreciative glance told her the green velvet was doing it's thing. She remembered how easy it was to get lost in his hazel eyes, but that was from another time.

'I appreciate your concern, but I—' He interrupted her with probably one of the most sincere apologies of which he was capable. 'Baby, you're lookin' so good to me. I don't see nothin' wrong with two people who used to be married, talkin' for a little while.' She looked into his eyes, and realized the agony of the past had become only a distant shadow in her heart. He touched her cheek. 'Ceeoni, I'm doin' alright these days, but as good as it is, Baby, you were the best part of my life.' Any reservations she might have had, melted instantly.

Right away, he changed the subject, as if what he'd said had slipped out. Although she had to fend off his attempt to caress her shoulder and pull her closer to him, he ended up telling her about his latest projects, and inquiring about hers. All in all, it was a healing interlude, a healing that had been a long time coming and an affirmation that all the Bobby—trauma had been laid to rest forever.

CHAPTER SIX

Her watch read 6:45. Curtain time was 8:30. She called Weber to ask him if he'd take her to the theatre, but the knock on her door announced Homer Dinsmore, looking wonderful in a black Armani tuxedo that must've been what Armani had in mind when he designed it.

"Ceeoni, Weber told me what happened. How are you feeling?"

"Weber's tea was like a shot of B12."

"Good, we can't have your elbows dragging. You've gotta' show this town how it's done. Naturally, the car will be checked out. Rental companies are extra careful about the brakes."

"Yes, I thought so too."

"Anyway, that was just something for you to drive until you decide which one of these cars around here you want."

"Homer, I can send for my VVV."

"VVV?"

"That stands for 'Vivacious Vintage Volvo,' it's at my friend Di's."

"Well," he chuckled, "You can sell it if you want. Remember, a car is included in your contract. By the way, you look lovely." Homer reached into his pocket, and handed her a small antique silver box.

"I took the liberty of bringing you something I hope you'll accept. I found these at the theatre, in an old sea trunk. I don't know who they belonged to. I had them appraised, just to be sure they weren't some elaborately designed costume jewelry. It turned out they're most definitely the real thing. The stones are perfect. My Ex refused to wear them because she said the opals are bad luck if the owner is not a Libran. Coincidentally, you were the only Libran out of the resumes we considered."

"Is that why I was chosen?"

He closed her hand around the little box with both of his. "Of course not. I didn't choose you Ceeoni, I knew you were the one. Now that you're here, and I've had the opportunity to get to know you a little better, it seems fitting they should belong to you."

Happily surprised, she opened the box. A pair of exquisite earrings nestled in black velvet; large black opals, surrounded by a ring of brilliant, blue-white diamonds, dropped from a large diamond stud. The opals flashed fire with the slightest movement. As she held the earrings up to the light, streaks of dazzling color glittered in the stones' blackness; blood red; deep purple; electric, cobalt blue, and rich, vibrant emerald green. Holding the earrings, she felt a rush of teariness well up in her throat. She swallowed, and quickly removed her modest emerald studs. When she slipped the opals into her ears, Homer's warm smile gave her a feeling of peace,

"They're not only perfect, they're perfect for you, Ceeoni."

She was astonished at the deep-seated rush of emotion she experienced with the earrings on. A new small voice from the edge of her usual awareness said, 'Oh, I will wear them with my new black taffeta gown!', to which the Sane Ceeoni spoke silently from the back of her head, 'What's going on? I don't own a taffeta gown!'

Ignoring her inner mind, she kissed Homer's cheek,

"Oh, thank you! Homer, you've done so much for me. I want you to know I'm grateful, and I'll do everything I can to make the Starcross Theatre the best it can be."

He offered her his arm,

"I believe you will do exactly what the Great Spirit brought you here to do. Hey, I'm very glad you weren't hurt in that rental car fiasco. If you find you don't feel well later, please let me know, OK?"

In the car, she caught a trace of one of her favorite fragrances,

"Homer, do you have one of those perfumed car hangers with a lavender scent?"

"So, you noticed it too? The scent's in that silver box the earrings came in, or maybe it's just in the earrings. That's the box they were in when I found them. Possibly the scent has had over 100 years to sink in. You'd think if anything, it would have a moldy aroma, rather than one of fresh lavender."

"Do you suppose the earrings are 100 years old?"

"It's hard to say, because I know nothing about them. The appraiser said they're in a rare antique setting, probably dating back to the early 19th century. He said it's hard to find opals like that nowadays."

"I'm curious. Just where in the theatre were they found and how in the world were they left undiscovered after umpteen years?"

"You know, 'peculiar' is our middle name around here. Up in the office, which is your office now, a heavy beam had fallen over the locked entrance to your bathroom. Only upon close examination did we realize the beam was obscuring a door. We didn't even know a room was there until we removed the debris from the hallway. We had to go through some real changes to get up there in the first place, because the old wooden staircase was rotten. Since we have no idea what happened here for many years, the Baldwin Sisters thought lightning struck the building, maybe around 1900, about the same time a high fence was constructed around the Theatre and Manor.

"None of the surrounding area was developed when I became aware of the property. They had signs up everywhere, warning people that it was 'Private Do Not Enter.' People said it was haunted. Vandals had stolen what seemed valuable over the years, but it must've taken guts like iron for anyone to have stayed around here at night. The buildings were overgrown with thick kudzu, and they said that strange noises were heard, and lights were seen at odd hours. Back in 1975, we found evidence of brave squatters who'd added to the general mess."

"Fascinating. Oh, and what is kudzu?"

"Kudzu, kudzu. It's everywhere in Georgia. Kudzu is an ivy-like vine that covers even large trees, making them resemble silent shrouded phantoms, gathered beside the roadways holding secret conferences in the summer. Then in winter it drops its green leaves and looks like old brownish-gray ropes. You'll be seeing plenty of it, and sometimes it's almost pretty. Anyway, looking at your office from the outside of the building, after the kudzu was removed, we had no idea what kind of room it was, and wait until you hear this. When we found that wooden beam lodged in front of the door, it was stuck so tightly, we finally had to cut it up to remove it. We broke the lock on the door, and behind it, was what is now your bathroom. As I said, that's when we decided it must've been a sitting room/bedroom."

"So, the earrings were in that room?"

"Yes, we found just a few things there; a desk, an antique piano and a rosewood bed, which I had moved to the Manor. There was a beautiful rug covering a large stain of blood on the floor, and there was the sea trunk. The trunk sat on the rug, as if placed there on purpose. Although the rug was a hand-woven Persian, I had it burned. It looked like it had been used to cover the bloodstains. Look, I hope this isn't too gory for you."

"N-n-no." Ceeoni felt her heart flutter. "I want to know."

"Well, there were several people standing around the day we broke through into that room; my wife had stopped by; a distant cousin of mine who teaches art at Spelman College was there; Weber, who had been with me all day that day and David Saxon. He was just a kid then, also there was David's childhood friend, the redhead guy who is now his partner at the APD, along with three or four guys on the clean-up crew. They watched us get the room open. It was pretty exciting. We all agreed that it appeared no one had been in that part of the theatre since before the turn of the century.

"When the trunk was opened, all I found was some gauzy bluish fabric, maybe material for curtains. I got on my knees to reach into the trunk to pull out the fabric and my finger struck a loose brad among the brads along the bottom of the steamer. Seems the loose brad was really a lever that released a false bottom. Suddenly, the false bottom flew up and underneath it I found that little box. Strange, huh?"

Ceeoni felt a fast tremor begin in her stomach, then it passed as quickly as it came.

"There's a tale to sizzle one's innards, the whole thing sounds like a 'Twilight Zone' kind of moment to me. So mysterious—"

"Yeah, while everybody oohed and ahhed over the room, I just put the box in my pocket to surprise my wife with the earrings later.

The memory is still vivid in my mind. Ceeoni, I swear something as cold as the grave came over me when I pulled the rug back and saw the blood stains. The one explanation that crossed my mind was connected to the fact that this property survived Sherman's fiery march across Georgia. Maybe the blood was from that time, but God only knows why the opals were stashed in the trunk."

"I guess we'll never know."

"I can tell you that even with the daily ups and downs, weird secrets, and years of an amazing outgo of sweat, tears and money, Starcross has brought nothing but Magic into my life. I know this sounds corny, but there's something wonderful here; I believe it'll spread to everyone who touches it, even in small ways. That's one of the reasons why I've been anxious to open the theatre to the public I see it as a way to share the Magic."

He got out of the car to come around to her door. Knowing the small probability of hiding anything from Homer's observant glance, she nevertheless dabbed her cheeks with a quickly found tissue, to keep him from seeing that her eyes had inexplicably overflowed with tears.

x x x

Ceeoni suggested sitting in the balcony and Homer agreed. She preferred the balcony in order to read the crowd's reaction to everything happening onstage. Since she'd received no page from R.C. Ponder or Adam Delayno, she surmised all was going well backstage. They could call if they needed her. She had a policy never to disturb the energy flow before or during a performance unless it was absolutely necessary. Tonight, more than ever, she needed to sit still and compose herself. Every Opening Night was always preceded by unexpected nerve wracking events, but Starcross was stacking up to head her list of nerve wracking Openings of All Time. Always, what made it worthwhile and one of the main reasons she had stayed high on her profession for so long, was Opening Night. Everyone can feel excitement hanging in the air. Her many splendored euphoria at Starcross came from the fact that she was managing a brand new performing arts center, where anything was possible. And privately, after years of listening to Adam Delayno's recordings, she waited for the curtain to rise on this concert artist whose music had penetrated her soul.

Di always said that Life Changing Events, or "Destiny Points", are clear and obvious. The thought that she'd been led to this place, that Starcross was where she was supposed to be, was both thrilling and frightening.

She looked down at the full house. The audience represented many walks of life; the obvious creme de la creme: Adam's loyal fans, carrying CDs and promotional posters purchased in the lobby; and the curious who wanted to see what the Starcross Theatre was all about. Jake said both nights had sold out the remaining tickets within hours after the radio announced Adam Delayno as the featured artist.

Homer smiled and waved while Ceeoni hovered somewhere above Mt. Olympus. Amid the hum of conversation and coughs, the excitement in the auditorium escalated. The tension in her nerves felt taut, like strung piano wire, waiting for the Maestro's hands to fill her with his music. She could feel vibrations of anticipation rippling through the crowd, blending with her tripping and racing pulse. Needing something to do, she opened the program in her lap, and Adam Delayno's photo smiled at her from the second page.

My goodness, he's handsome. Although she had approved the program last week via computer, she read his bio again. Adam Delayno and his brother, Samson, grew up in a foster home in Detroit, Michigan, abandoned by their mother. Ceeoni guessed their mother was another member of the inner-city legions whose insurmountable problems gave her little resources to care for her small sons. She was believed to be deceased by the time Adam was three years old. They never knew their father.

A quote from his teacher, a Miss Cora Lee, said, 'At the age of five, Adam climbed up on the piano bench in kindergarten, and began to play little songs. He played scraps of nursery rhymes, commercials, and bits of themes from television scores. That moment was one of the greatest experiences of my life; seeing this tiny, under-nourished waif demonstrating mature, sophisticated understanding of melody and harmony sent chills all through me. I could play in church, but I'd never taught music.

Karma Rising

'That day, I bought a first year music book, which was a waste of money because he played the whole book the next morning! Adam and I embarked on an adventure that lasted until he was eleven, when I realized he knew more about music than most teachers would ever learn. Even then, his mastery of classical piano was of concert quality, but he just loved that blues and jazz music.'

Adam's London office had sent several photos, two of which she'd approved because of their charm; a skinny, grinning fourteen-year-old Adam, after he'd won a national piano competition, hugging his foster mother and Miss Cora Lee, the teacher who believed in him. The second photo was twenty years later, in almost the same pose, the same two ladies hugging a grown-up Adam after a sold-out concert at Osaka, Japan's Festival Hall.

His first album captured a vast audience and he gained international recognition by the time he was twenty years of age. The rest of the bio mentioned his 23 top selling albums and CDs, his productions for and with other artists, and his upcoming production with Quincy Jones. She was glad she didn't meet him before the concert, and she knew part of the reason she was reluctant to meet him in the first place. It was about keeping her illusions for as long as she could. Meeting him, and finding him to be a Royal, Boring Pompous Asspect would take away one of her most cherished flights of fancy. She had dreamed about him once; a vague cloud of music, Adam and love. The heat of that wild dream had lingered and played havoc with her imagination for a long time afterward.

Over the years, she had sometimes been extremely disappointed when meeting some of her favorite celebrities. Their private personalities were a complete surprise, sometimes very warm, sometimes cold and petty, and the public persona was a poor thermometer. She had wondered, over and over, what kind of person is Adam Delayno? What kind of spirit is the conduit and custodian of such magnificent music? Music comes from the Universe, through the musician, just as all art comes through the artist; however, many talented people have been known to think it was all their idea. Could Adam Delayno's wonderful musical ability be his only saving grace? After identifying with his music for half her life, she was now wondering if he had anything to do with the savage murder of his Business Manager.

Minette Coulter slid into the seat next to Homer, infusing the air with the scent of White Diamonds. She was a vision in a yellow knit halter gown, clustered with yellow rhinestones on the bodice, thin yellow rhinestone straps, with a dangerously low neckline. Her shiny auburn curtain of hair that hung over one eye was pushed back with long, gold—tipped fingers, then she would toss her head, which caused the hair to fall back over her eye again, and again. Oh, well, we the people all have our special eccentricities. Minette's tanned, polished skin glowed, enhanced by swinging, shimmering yellow rhinestone earrings. Ceeoni acknowledged Minette's quick little obligatory wave with a smiling nod as the term 'Femme Fatale' came to mind. While the house lights slowly dimmed, Minette and Homer shared a brief exchange that was beyond Ceeoni's hearing.

A hush swept over the auditorium.

Behind the curtain, the band began to vamp one of Adam's biggest hits in a walking, funk/jazz feel, where the bass and percussion set the groove to ride right on Ceeoni's heartbeat. The curtain opened slowly and a pale pink spotlight pierced the dark stage, picking up Adam Delayno strolling out of the wings. Wearing a soft, white African robe with silver trim around the v-neck and down the front, he rewarded the loud burst of applause with a shy smile. She'd had no idea he was so tall and beautifully proportioned. Masculine grace and confidence emanated from his slightest gesture.

Everything was timed to perfection. At the exact moment he reached the pianos center stage, the band came to a clean break. Standing at the electric stack in the silence, Adam raised his right hand high into the air and came down hard on a chord just at the downbeat—pale lights suddenly switched to fuchsia, the groove kicked back in without missing a stroke, and the crowd went crazy.

Wearing identical white robes, the band was arranged on separate black risers of varying heights around the Steinway and Adam's stack. Ceeoni forgot everything as she watched him. His lighting patterns were a work of genius, they dramatized and punctuated each movement of every song; underlining, emphasizing and flowing with the textured, painted sound, they provided visual pump to the grooves. His emotions lay bare in the subtle turns of his head, in each movement of his body; in his frowns of concentration, the count-offs of the tempos, and the trace of a smile that passed across his face when he closed his eyes to listen. His excitement was catching. Everybody felt it, and clapped with him—the crowd became one with Adam and the music.

At the end of one of his high-energy hits, the stage went to blackout for a moment before a gold baby spot came up on Adam's face as he sat at the Steinway. Touching the keys in a pattern of lush chords, his deep voice slowly embraced the words,

"The great Isaac Hayes co-wrote the next song. On this wondrous night, I want to share it's beauty with you."

Suddenly he looked up; his eyes searched the audience and then stopped, as if he was looking straight at her. Ceeoni knew he couldn't possibly see her, but it appeared that he could. His small puzzled frown passed in an instant. What could he be thinking? He looked away, focused his attention on the keys and played a sensuous, yet tender version of 'Deja Vu'.

The mystical lyrics fit the bewildering sensations she was feeling about this time and this place.

'Deja Vu', could you be the someone I once knew, is it you?—I keep remembering me, I keep remembering you, Deja' Vu.'

She could almost believe he was playing the haunting song just for her and her alone. Her rational, sane Ceeoni couldn't help but marvel at her own vivid imaginative excesses.

Adam segued from the ballad to a fast Latin percussion vamp that turned into Duke Ellington's 'Caravan.' The blasts of hot horns in rich harmonies sent her, and an enraptured audience, flying on sound waves out through the roof to frolic among the stars. Standing, he drove one of his hits after another. The blend of exciting new songs; delicious old standards; and re-workings of music from a variety of composers, brought the crowd to its feet.

Too soon, during the closing vamp of the last tune before intermission, Adam walked off the stage, dripping with perspiration. He looked strong and exhilarated. With each step, the robe opened all they way down the front and swirled in his wake, revealing his long sculptured thighs in clinging white pants and his muscular chest, naked except for a shimmering medallion on a silver chain.

She hung onto the final chord's reverberation, tingling all over, fully aware that she was breathing hard, as if he'd just made love to her. The house lights came up and she felt herself falling to ground zero.

"You never really know the extent of an artist's greatness until you see him live. He was electrifying!" Homer whispered.

She could only nod. She hadn't fully returned from a world of shadows, colors, music and visions ruled over by a merciless Black King who held her captive in a prison made of dreams.

Ceeoni noticed Minette hurrying to collect her evening bag and her yellow wrap. Smiling to herself, she waved two fingers in their direction and almost ran up the aisle. Ceeoni had a hunch that Minette was rushing to try to get backstage. If true, it would take an amazing lack of savvy and empathy for anyone to even think of stepping into a performing artist's space in the middle of a concert.

Homer got up to speak to someone passing by. Halfway through the 20-minute intermission, Ceeoni saw Jake beckoning in her direction from the first floor in an effort to get her attention. She waved back, realizing that the serious expression in his eyes said something was wrong. She quickly ran downstairs to find the backstage area in a tizzy. A dozen or so people milled around one of the dressing room doors. She noticed that Adam's dressing room door was closed. Two theatre security guards attempted to disperse the small knot of onlookers that included some stage crew and several band members, already changed into royal blue robes. A very attractive woman bent over the figure on the sofa, whom she realized was Minette. Minette? Minette had been away from her seat for only a few minutes. What was she doing back here anyway? Ceeoni spoke to the woman attending Minette,

"Did she fall? What happened? I'm Ceeoni Jones, general manager of the theatre."

The woman straightened up, "Oh, hi—they didn't tell me you were so beautiful. I'm Claudette Dinsmore-Walker, Dr. Walker." She smiled and held out her hand, "It's a good thing I was near the stage door. It appears someone hit Minette over the head, then attempted to strangle her with her own scarf. See?"

She pointed to the yellow wrap draped around Minette's neck.

"I was right outside when Jake tried to open the stage door from the auditorium and we saw her knocked out cold in the hall. Her body was partially blocking the doorway. I had Jake raise her head carefully, and I immediately loosened the scarf. It may have saved her life."

Minette coughed and tried to sit up. Dr. Walker adjusted the pillow behind her head,

"I don't think she knows what hit her—as far as I can tell, she was hit on the right temple from outside of her range of vision. Please be still, Minette."

R.C. waved to Ceeoni from the doorway and pointed to his wristwatch. Remembering the full house she said,

"Oh, R.C. go ahead and start. Jake, please keep the press out of the loop. If they get any ideas, tell them Ms. Coulter had a fall."

"I think the worst injury is to her pride," Dr. Walker said, "but she may have a mild concussion. Hold this cold towel on her forehead. I wrapped up some ice from the water pitcher. The paramedics are on the way."

"Dr. Walker, we appreciate your kind concern. Is there anything else we can do to make her more comfortable?"

"Not a thing. Just keep her quiet until the wagon gets here." Minette looked woozy, but she still tried to get up while pushing the towel aside.

"I've gotta'—"

"Minette, you must relax," the doctor said, "We want to be sure your vital signs are normal. Ms. Jones, I'm going to get back to my seat to enjoy the rest of this fabulous evening. It was a pleasure meeting you, and I know the Starcross Theatre will be a smashing success."

As she heard the band start up, Ceeoni thought how she would have loved to have been out there. She watched Dr. Walker's creme chiffon cocktail dress float gracefully as she turned away. Her hair, skin and eyes were in the same honey blonde color range. Was this lovely woman Homer's sister, cousin, or ex-wife?

Ceeoni reluctantly sat in the dressing room with Minette until the paramedics arrived. Minette had finally quieted and Ceeoni guessed that she was as caught up in the music as everyone else.

For the second half of the concert, the crowd response was even greater. Closing her eyes to visualize Adam's face, Ceeoni enjoyed Adam's exploration of different types of music. He ignored the superficial lines that divided one kind of music from another, and simply composed and performed great songs. She listened as he talked to the audience, teasing and cajoling, he took them to peaks and valleys with the deft skill of a sensual sorcerer.

Detective David Saxon came in with the paramedics. "Minette," he said, "I'll get your statement as soon as they've checked you out. How do you feel?" Minette's answer was swallowed up in the paramedics' bustling emergency attentions.

After Minette was taken to Crawford Long Hospital for observation, Ceeoni was able to watch the last moments of the concert from the wings. Adam and the guitarist played an intensely passionate version of Carlos Santana's, 'Europa Suite.' The song and the way they played it, combined with the candle-like reflections on Adam's face, caused tears to well up in her eyes again, while the Sane Ceeoni's awed whisper echoed in her head,

'Girl, I hardly know you.'

Adam played two more curtain calls, but the audience still wasn't ready for him to leave the stage. Standing ovation followed standing ovation until finally, making the peace sign, he took another bow.

"That's the signal," R.C. said to Becky, who immediately closed the curtains. Adam exited stage left. Ceeoni stood on stage right, deliberately.

CHAPTER SEVEN

She rushed over to the Reception Ballroom, thinking of Adam Delayno. Marvelous scents of the buffet supper permeated the entire building. The buffet lines lengthened as people talked excitedly and champagne flowed. Homer, accompanied by a bevy of smiling attractive women, hailed her,

"Ms. Jones," he said, "Meet the President and some members of the Metropolitan Atlanta Chapter of 100 Black Women, who need to talk to you about block tickets for their organization."

It was music to Ceeoni's ears.

She met the handsome Mayor of Atlanta and his wife, several Atlanta City Councilmen, CNN and Turner Broadcasting executives, the Fulton County Commissioner and the gracious Lady Atlanta Police Chief.

After an hour elapsed, Ceeoni figured Adam Delayno was probably not going to show for the reception. R.C. Ponder, in a formal navy embroidered robe and Kufi, caught her eye and raised his glass in greeting. She returned the gesture and made her way to his side to click her glass to his.

"Here's to a great concert, R.C., Adam is a stunning performer. I know tomorrow will be even better, and I'm looking forward to seeing all of it this time."

R.C., the soul of perpetual good humor, possessed an easy personality sure to smooth over any pothole in the road. His green eyes crinkled into a happy grin.

"He'll be glad you enjoyed it. I haven't had a chance to speak with him, but I'll make it a point to let him know management is pleased. Hey, whoever attacked Ms. Minette must have been either crazy or really stupid, with over 600 people and a few police around, eh?"

"I was thinking the same thing. I've been wondering if it's sabotage to make sure the theatre fails, or if someone resents Homer's hiring an 'outsider,' so to speak."

"Ceeoni, are you thinking your being here could be the reason?"

"Oh, I don't know. The corpse was in my office. I'm wondering if that was deliberate."

"Well, I see what you mean. But I think theatre sabotage in general is as good a guess as any. A man like Homer might have inspired quite a bit of hateful envy."

"Oh, R.C., none of it makes a bit of sense! There's a killer among us! Who knows how anyone can feel resentment to the point where they'd commit murder?"

"The killer knows, Ceeoni, the killer knows, but Dear Lady," he offered his arm, "enough of these dark shadows. My glass is empty and, if you'll please be so kind as to accompany me to the champagne fountain, I'll tell you all about my beautiful wife and my eight beautiful children."

"Eight?"

"Eight. And I'd have more if my Juno would agree. Unfortunately, she says that she's done her part; she's had some, now it's my turn to have some. I keep telling her George Foreman's wife didn't say that." At that moment, Homer joined them, wearing a relieved expression,

"I just called the hospital, and Minette is fine. Weber's going to pick her up. I offered her a place at my house until she feels better, but she wanted to go home. She said home is the only place she can really relax. The restaurant was closed tonight, anyway." Homer refilled his glass from the fountain, "If nothing else, at least she'll get a badly needed rest."

"You know, something's gotta' turn up to help us get the person or persons who's behind all of this, or we're gonna' feel it at the box office, at the restaurant and the estates. I sure as hell don't want to be sitting out here all by myself. R.C., we may have to close for a few weeks just to air out the bad gossip. Where's Adam?"

"Oh man, in all the years I've known him, he's always hated receptions. If the buyer doesn't put reception attendance into the contract, Adam won't attend. He may still be in the dressing room—let's check it out. C'mon, Ceeoni!" But something inside her froze. True to her uncharacteristic behavior of the past few days, a wave of anxiety swept over her and she felt like her feet were glued to the floor.

Homer reached for her hand, "Don't you want to meet him?"

"Oh, yes, ah, yes, I do, but I have something to pick up from the box office. It'll have to wait 'til tomorrow."

The quizzical expression on Homer's face told her he recognized a flimsy excuse when he heard one.

She left the ballroom and wandered out to the lobby, seeking a quiet place where the party noises would fade into the background of her thoughts. The souvenir vendors were closing down. She found a chair facing the glass doors. Surprise! She thought she'd outgrown high school crush stuff years ago, but here she was, acting like she'd never met an attractive man before.

A thick gray mist hung over the night, suspending the fountain in a surrealistic cloud of pirouetting diamond beads, spinning in contours of polychromatic hues—life imitates art. The fountain reminded her of an extravagant computer generated fantasy. She guessed the people remaining would hang around until the fog let up before driving home. There was plenty of food and booze; the original plan was to keep the party slammin' until the last person left. Homer wanted the Starcross opening to stay on people's minds for weeks to come.

Movement from the corner shadows turned out to be Detective David Saxon, slumped down in one of the plush chairs. He sat up, flashing his dimples.

"Hey Pretty Lady, I was just waiting to see how long you were going to pretend you didn't see me."

"Hi, David. I'm trying to unwind from the terrors of opening night and our very own assailant's latest caper."

"Mind if I join you?" He sat in the chair opposite hers, "It's OK, ignore me anytime. I was enjoying watching you watch the night. You look like a sexy green goddess in that outfit." He sipped from the drink in his hand, "Yes, this is Courvoisier, yes, I'm off duty, and hell no, I'm not driving."

When she laughed, he used the opportunity to say, "Baby, if you hang out with me, I'll have you laughing like that all the time. A woman as gorgeous as you is supposed to stay happy." She thought his dimples were amazing, but she didn't respond.

"OK, Ceeoni, be that way. One day you may feel differently and I'll be there." He paused, but she didn't address his prediction. He sighed and changed the subject.

"Well, on the serious side, the Starcross Slasher, as he's been dubbed by the precinct, is leading us on a merry chase. So far, he's left no clues, or the clues are so obscure, we haven't found them yet."

"David, like Homer said, you haven't had much time. Everybody's certain new clues will emerge."

"Thanks for the confidence. I know we'll bust the right move, to quote my Junior K-A-Psi frat brothers. I was really hoping to talk to Delayno tonight, especially since I discovered he and Basil disagreed over Delayno's purchase of the Manor." He took a deep draught from his glass, steeping the cognac on his tongue before saying,

"Basil considered the purchase frivolous and way over-priced, probably because he owned a luxury condo in Buckhead that cost only a fraction of what Delayno is laying out for the old Starcross place. From what I can gather, their disagreements over the years were always for the same reasons; Basil was the financial conservative, trying to curb Delayno's high rollin' excesses. Delayno got away tonight before I could reach his dressing room."

She heard the edge of snide contempt in his tone and asked,

"Would that be enough of a motive for Mr. Delayno to kill his business manager? And if so, why would he attack Minette?"

"I'm grasping at straws here, Ceeoni. Even I have enough sense to know Delayno had no way into the theatre or your office." His eyes narrowed, "Or did he?"

David answered his own question, then, described a scenario,

"That would depend on who had access to the keys! Now suppose you were coming into a strange city to take possession of a piece of property of which your business agent disapproved. You meet this person at the property, you have an argument, kill him in a fit of rage—ahh! But you stumble upon a set of theatre keys, left accidentally on the property, or on your ring. You stash the body in the theatre. The keys in your hand are labeled for easy identification, and no one is around. Imagine—over the years, you've accumulated plenty of reasons to be angry. Ceeoni, it definitely fits. Since the theatre and your office were locked, I must base any theory on the existence of another set of keys."

She followed his supposition by repeating her question,

"But why would he attempt to choke Minette?"

"Look at it this way. Whoever attacked Minette may not have been laying for her. Maybe he just didn't wanna' be seen."

"Why would Adam not want to be seen backstage? He had nowhere else to be."

"Suppose she caught him doing something he shouldn't have been doing?"

At that point, she thought the conversation had taken a confusing turn, "Well, I can't imagine what, but you're the expert. I realize you have to consider all the angles. Oh, by the way, the brakes on my rental car failed this afternoon. It was all I could do to bring my runaway vehicle to a safe stop."

"Yeah, I got the word. They're checking it over for prints and evidence. Look, all I'm saying is that we must consider the fact that Delayno is the main person who had possible motive and opportunity to have murdered Basil Cassidy."

She got up and took a few steps toward the ballroom, "It's been an incredibly long day—I'll see you later." A loud protest flashed through her mind, firmly declaring,

'No, no, no! Adam Delayno is incapable of murder!'

David stood and showed her how deep his dimples were,

"Don't forget what I said about you and me, sweet Ceeoni."

She felt his eyes following her as she went back to the Ballroom. Detective David Saxon was grasping at straws in more ways than one.

The party was still going on full blast. A tape R.C. had supplied was programmed with Adam's recordings, interspersed with contemporary and traditional jazz cuts; Miles Davis' 'It Never Entered My Mind' was playing. Throughout the evening George Duke, Kenny Burrell, Nina Simone, Eddie 'Lockjaw' Davis, Kevin Mahogany and others, pulled her attention away from conversations.

Somebody had read her mind when the music was chosen. R.C. answered her question.

"Oh, Adam always programs the tapes. He enjoys that task more than anybody else. Actually, I think it's because he doesn't trust us to tap into that stream the way he can."

People were disappointed Adam hadn't attended the reception, but Homer said he purposefully didn't include it in their contract, saying, 'Let him maintain an aura of mystery and let the public clamor for more. I knew he would hardly have had time to recover from the flight from London and a New York concert the night before flying here. He had the right to choose whether or not he wanted to attend an after-party.'

In the luxurious atmosphere, the music and the mood would hold until the sun came up. Ceeoni sat at one of the tables, and watched the clothes go by. Some folks were people-watchers, but she was a clothes-watcher. She had been warned that people didn't dress up in Atlanta, but Atlanta had pulled out all the stops for this affair. Exciting outfits; dresses, tuxedos, cocktail suits and Afro-centric ensembles, worn with flair, paraded by. Homer, across the room, was spinning what she was beginning to think of as Prince Charming's Web. It was obvious he was loved and respected by people who had known him for years, and he managed to instantly charm those he was meeting for the first time. Right away, he drew them in with his habit of listening carefully, letting them know he was sincerely interested in what they had to say. Two Atlanta Journal-Constitution reporters happily accompanied him to her table.

"Ceeoni, are you ready for an interview?" Homer asked. The reporters took photos while she and Homer spoke of her career, and their vision for the Starcross Theatre's future, leaving out any mention of the murder.

As the evening finally came to a close, the crowd dispersed, and the caterers were packing up when Homer said,

"Anytime you're ready, we can leave, and if you're not too tired, I've something to show you."

"Oh, I'll get my bag."

She hurried from the ballroom, to the backstage entrance off the lobby, and up the stairs. In her locked office, her attache case with the schedule in it wasn't where she knew she'd left it. Now who in the hell's been in here moving my stuff around? There was nothing in the case except the list of theatre employees, their resumes, Adam Delayno's two-day contracts, and a few blank contract forms. She found the case on the floor, instead of on her desk. Nothing was missing. The only conclusion she could draw was that Homer or Jake had been in there, or Detective Saxon was right about the existence of another set of keys.

Her mellow mood was short lived. She looked around carefully as she opened the door to the deserted hallway. Running nervously down the stairs, she was grateful for the deep slit in her skirt. Outside, the maintenance people moved in and out of the building, taking out large containers of trash, and joking with each other. It was 1:30am, and the still heavy fog hung heavy over the parking lot. Homer's car idled near the back door. She mentioned the misplaced attache to him while getting settled in the front seat.

"My dear, Jake and I were both in the theatre all evening. We had no reason to go to your office. I don't know what to make of your misplaced case, but the investigation is in full force and all we can do is wait until more facts come to light. I wish I knew what was going on, and most of all, why?" His gray eyes held hers, and she believed he was sincere. She touched his hand.

"It's so scary. Whoever it is, is still busy, still hanging in there, turning up where least expected. But what about another set of keys. Is it possible?"

"I suppose anyone could have a set of keys made, but Ceeoni, please bear with us. I know in my heart we're going to be all right. Whoever is causing all these horrors is bound to slip up; it's inevitable. Everything good in life has its detractors and saboteurs. I know you can't help thinking that maybe you made a bad decision to come here, but I hope you'll see us through this. I've believed you were destined to be here from the moment I read your resume, and I've always been able to trust my intuition. As a matter of fact, my intuition was a major source of dissension in my marriage and it continues to raise eyebrows in my business. I can't explain how I know things, I—I think I've always known, without a doubt, that we're all where we're supposed to be."

Rita Graham

She felt his infinite kindness so completely, she could almost touch it.

"Homer, I've been here for only two days, but I feel an identification with the theatre, and you." She leaned over and kissed his cheek.

At the end of the driveway he turned left, just past the theatre he turned left again down a hard gravel road, lined on both sides with tall, graceful trees. Headlights revealed the trees' dark burgundy leaves.

"Wow! What are these trees? They're magnificent!"

"You ain't seen nothin' yet. These scarlet leaves are their winter wear. Wait'll you see the unforgettable show they put on in the spring. They're called dogwood trees and they cover this lane with downy, delicate blossoms for a few weeks every year, making this driveway look like Fairyland."

"Did you plant them when you restored the property?"

"I think the dogwoods have always been here. I took out dead trees and put in new ones. Dogwoods are all over the place in Georgia. You know, no matter where I am in the world, I always have it in my mind to get back to Atlanta in time to see the dogwoods bloom in late March or April." He drove very slowly down a winding lane that she later learned was about two and a half blocks long.

"We even have a Spring festival in Piedmont Park dedicated to the blooming of the dogwoods."

"Let me guess—the Dogwood Festival?!"

"You're learnin' fast, girl!"

"Well, they're so pretty now, I can imagine what they'll be like in the spring. What's down here?"

"Adam went to a recording session at LaFace Records, and after I told him you might like to see the Manor, he cordially invited us to check out the restoration."

The car inched along as Homer talked. The closer they got, the more excitement she felt.

"I can't wait to see it! The restoration of a 26-room mansion must have really been something."

"It was a 16-room house at first, but we added six baths and four sitting rooms, and that was without knocking out walls. We put the baths in what used to be called water closets in some areas, and added walls in three huge bedrooms. And was it full of problems! Originally constructed with hand-hewn pine beams connected with wooden pegs and grooves, we were able to keep most of the original beams because they were solid, as were some of the window frames, which came as a complete surprise. I expected termites and wood rot everywhere, but even the foundation was strong. We improvised an acrylic paste to fill the columns that were being eaten up by some weird fungus, but now they should last another 200 years. It looked like they added the kitchen around 1825. We put in all modern wiring, and amenities, and considering its history from 1782 and the storms it's weathered, it turned out really well. There was a graveyard in the back, with all the markers missing. We brought in earth, covered it, and planted a flower garden. Across the way, we built a waterfall that flows into a pool we made from an existing reflecting pond, and then enlarged it with natural rocks found on the property. To me, it turned out to be one of the loveliest spots in Atlanta."

"So this is the house Adam bought."

"Yes, and let me tell you one of the reasons Basil Cassidy objected to Adam's purchase of the property. Adam bought it sight unseen, over the telephone, after I'd only told him about it. I sent him photos of Starcross Manor after we'd made the deal." Ceeoni said exactly what was on her mind. "I never heard of anything like that."

"Me neither. It was a real first for me. I had met R.C. and Adam in Tokyo at the very beginning of Adam's career, and it was R.C. who started the whole thing when he called to ask for some brochures of available Atlanta real estate. Adam rejected everything I sent. I even told him of other developments in the area, but he wasn't interested in anything until I mentioned the Manor restoration. He seemed quite taken with the Starcross history, especially Miss Letty's Underground Railroad activities. He asked a few questions about the distance from Starcross to the airport and downtown Atlanta. I started rattling off the Manor's special features, but he interrupted with, 'It's wonderful, I'll take it. You and Basil work out the details, I'll move in as soon as I get back to the States'. Now, I've lived my life depending on my intuition, but it shocked me to hear somebody else make a big instantaneous decision like that. I was taking a few moments to recover, when he added, 'By the way, how much is it?'

"Basil Cassidy and I had met in the 80s when he bought a unit in a condo village I developed. When I got in touch with him concerning Adam's purchase of the Manor, he asked me not to sell it to him. He said Adam didn't know what he was getting into, buying a big money pit like that. I couldn't stop the negotiations on his word, Adam Delayno's name was on the bottom of the check. We ended up working it out in spite of Basil's objections."

"Oh wow, Homer, be sure and include that one in your autobiography."

The fog was heavier here and there. "Homer, please, I think I'd like to walk the rest of the way—I love to walk on foggy nights."

"Oh? OK, if you wanna' stroll on gravel in those little shoes, it's just a short distance from here."

They walked slowly. The cool foggy night surrounded and covered her like a gossamer blanket snuggling her body in a dewy embrace. Homer held her hand.

"Everything about my acquisition of Starcross was unusual. By the time I found the property, all of these old mansions had been taken over by one historical society or another. I was elated to learn that the Baldwins had managed to keep the Starcross property, which I discovered was because it was part of a trust with Lloyd's of London."

"A trust?"

"Yeah, the Baldwin Sisters told me about the Lloyd's Trust, and the real estate maintenance account, and that was how I found the rightful heir. Well, the heir had no interest in even visiting Georgia, and he couldn't explain large sums missing from the account. He was a very alone and broke old man when I found him, and he was very happy to sell it."

"So, he was a Baldwin?"

"Yes, it went like this, Miss Letty left it to Elijah Baldwin Starcross, a freed slave, who in turn left it to Phineas Baldwin, also a freed slave. I bought it from Phineas' great-grandson. At first, I thought Elijah and Phineas were the same person, until I received the records from Lloyds. I don't know if they were related; the Aunts didn't know, either. The trust was set up by Elijah Starcross in 1877, for maintenance and upkeep of the property. I had to promise Mr. Baldwin I wouldn't report the missing funds to the authorities before he'd even discuss selling it. The missing money was probably the main reason he didn't put it up for sale. I can only guess he cashed checks trumped up to look like reasonable maintenance expenses. He must've lived like a king all his life."

"I wonder why none of the Baldwins ever came back here."

"Well, you have to remember the times. Before the 70s, the racial climate in the South made it very difficult for Blacks to want to give up lives they had made in the North. Anyway, ever since I found it in 1974, I think Ol' Elijah was saving Starcross for me."

"Homer, that's downright eerie!"

"Well, it all fell into place, dovetailing, so to speak. Dr. King led the push to move Civil Rights forward and Georgia became almost as livable for Blacks as anywhere else. As usual, we still see the vicious face of hatred, but now the law is on our side, whether they like it or not. I bought Starcross planning to live in it."

"Why didn't you?"

"My Ex hated it. She said it was spooky, and she vowed she'd never stay one night in that 'rat hole'. Oh, Jake said she just happened to be there tonight when they opened the door and found Minette. Did you meet her?"

"Dr. Walker? She appears to be a very nice lady."

"She is," he sighed. "We finally faced the truth that had been living with us for a long time. She didn't want kids, I love kids. She had a demanding career, and I like my lady up under me most of the time. She said I was selfish in that area."

"I think we all need someone with similar interests and a similar concept of how to spend time."

"They should teach that in school. Anyway, we'll always love and respect one another, but we knew we weren't in love."

"Oh, I do know what you mean. My now extinct marriage had more problems than love. I've often wondered if we were ever in love. Who knows? I'm beginning to agree with my best friend that having a Soul Mate isn't for everyone."

"Hey, that's the term Claudette used, Soul Mate. She said this guy she's married to now is her Soul Mate, and now they have a wonderful little boy. That let me know one can certainly rearrange one's priorities when given the correct set of inspirational circumstances."

She smiled, remembering Diana's definition of a Soul Mate. 'One with whom a Soul can reach the highest states of love, passion, and—and spiritual evolvement'. The question of how one finds the elusive Soul Mate was uppermost in her mind when they rounded a bend in the road, and Starcross Manor stood among the trees in a drifting veil of mist.

Slivers of moonlight streamed in rays through the surrounding dogwood, pine and oak, casting dappled silver specters that seemed to float in a gentle breeze against the front of the mansion. She couldn't move or talk, and she couldn't believe her eyes or her feelings. It was as if a gigantic chord in her heart had been struck. Deep and resonating, it sang tenderly inside her, and brought tears to her eyes. Her emotions had been tossed and turned about in the past few days, but now, the noise of confusion was still, and a blissful happiness folded its wings around her. She was overwhelmed by a sense of giddy gladness—to be back.

"People think the Manor is an architectural twin to the Starcross Theatre, when actually, it's the other way around," Homer said, "The theatre was built 86 years after the Manor. We think the Manor's Grecian colonnade was added before the Civil War, which was all the rage then, and Miss Letty built the theatre in the same style in 1868."

She was only half listening and didn't respond to his statement. Her eyes followed every inch of the ten massive columns, the carved double doors, and the oak tree in front, now much larger than she remembered. She'd seen many houses like Starcross in photos and movies, but this was the most unique house she'd ever seen. This 215-year-old mansion was her home, or it had been her home, and she knew that better than she'd ever known anything. No wonder the theatre was so familiar. She had a quick mental flash of the interior; a fleeting vison of what it had looked like when—when?

Homer regarded her with questions and concern in his eyes,

"Hey there, Ceeoni? Is everything alright?"

She couldn't answer. Language was too far away. Unsure of what to do, he waited until she was ready to respond. Finally, she turned to him with a glowing smile,

"Homer, there are some things for which there are no words. C'mon, let's go inside!"

CHAPTER EIGHT

Anticipatory flutterings of her own heartbeat drummed in her ears as Homer opened the front doors. The green marble foyer was almost exactly as she remembered. She ran from room to room, amazed that the colors of each room were so like the way they were in the unknown recesses of her mind; the green living room, the royal blue parlor, the huge library and the Rose Room. Her jumbled thoughts echoed, what miracle had created this miracle? Homer, breathing hard, hurried to keep up with her, his eyes wide; filled with astonishment.

"Wow!" he exclaimed. "I can't say I've ever seen this kind of reaction to the place! You sure you haven't been here before?"

"Of course I've been here before! Or, I think I've been here. Homer, I just know, I know this house!" She couldn't hold back the tears. "I know—"

"Ceeoni?"

"These aren't tears of sadness. Look! This is the dining room, right?"

Speechless, Homer could only nod.

"See how big the fireplace is? In those days, there were hearths for warmth and light cooking in every house. The metal door on the right is a warming oven." She opened the door, revealing neatly stacked racks inside.

"Oh yes! I remember this little compartment," she half-whispered.

He gestured to the dining room chair beside him, but she couldn't sit. "No, no thanks."

"Cee, I wish I knew something about what you're experiencing."

"Oh, I can't wait to tell my friend, Diana. She's full of theories about Deja Vu. I know she'll have plenty to say about this!"

She stood about two feet from a doorway, "Test me, OK? Now watch, this is the solarium, right?" He nodded. She covered her eyes with one hand, "Windows go all the way around the corner, this way." She pointed to the left. "The French doors to the garden are on the left also. Through these doors to the right, there's a hall with another set of French doors leading to the kitchen and dining room, right? There are shelves on either side of the doors. OK, I want to go in to check it out."

Still covering her eyes, she extended her other hand for Homer to lead her into the room.

"Open Ceeoni!" Homer shouted as he stared at her. She uncovered her eyes, squealed and clapped her hands. She wasn't surprised that everything was as she'd described it. "Damn!" he laughed, shaking his head in disbelief.

She stopped laughing at the sight of the gleaming antique piano in the solarium corner.

"That piano! Oh no! It doesn't belong here." She wondered why that seemed so meaningful.

"No, that's the one I found in the room next to your office; you know, your bathroom, which was Miss Letty's sitting room."

"R.C. mentioned this piano today. He said Adam fell in love with it."

"It's his now, maybe he'll play it for us someday."

She felt a pain go through her heart, and hot, fresh tears threatened to spill from her eyes. Her inner voice of sanity chastised, 'Ceeoni! What's the matter with you?'

Homer patted the piano, "I really love this piece. It was in great shape, considering it was built around 1835 and had been sitting up since God only knows when. I was reluctant to sell it, though. They told me it was priceless. It didn't fit my old house in the Cascade, or my new house in the Estates. When Adam decided to buy the Manor, I included it in the sale. I figured he, of all people, would appreciate it."

"Well, according to R.C., you were right." She lifted the keyboard cover. Despair, thick and heavy, seemed to ooze out of it. She closed her eyes, and gently let the cover back down. When she stumbled slightly, he grabbed her arm.

"Cee? Maybe you ought to sit for a while."

"I'm OK, really, whatever it was has passed." He held her arm to steady her as they climbed the winding stairs.

"You know these are all the wrong paintings, don't you?" She gestured toward the art hanging on the stairwell wall. "These are all new."

"They certainly are. I didn't find much around here that could be salvaged. The fact that Miss Letty's theatre sitting room was closed to any intruders is what saved the sea trunk, the rosewood bed and the piano, otherwise, they would've been destroyed or stolen long ago."

"I remember a painting that used to hang right—" Ceeoni ran up three steps and said, "here! I remember the face of the Confederate Colonel. I can recall—his eyes, his cold eyes." Her face wore a puzzled frown, and Homer politely didn't pursue the rest of her recollection.

Upstairs, her knowledge of the house was as uncanny as it was downstairs. R.C.'s and Adam's clothes and personal effects were in masculine disarray. She was happy to note there were no feminine articles anywhere in Adam's room. She knew immediately which one was his room. Sheet music, electric pianos, and CD's were everywhere. She saw Homer glance at his watch.

"Oh, Homer, I'm so sorry! We need to go, but I don't think I can sleep."

"Don't let my droopy red eyes fool you, I don't think I can sleep, either."

Outside, she nodded toward the oak in the front yard.

"There used to be a swing hanging from that branch, although I remembered the branch being closer to the ground." He hesitated before he took her arm.

"Ceeoni, I got up in that tree myself and cut the shreds of rope outta' there, right after the sale papers were signed. It was one of the first things I did."

After they left the Manor that morning, their lives and their perceptions of life itself were forever changed.

x x x

At her suite, Homer opened the door,

"We should try to get some sleep, we're going to need it tomorrow."

"Homer, I can't think of anything to say."

"Good, don't try. Allow me to thank you for showing an old magician a side of magic I didn't know existed." He kissed her forehead, and left.

She sat staring into the boudoir mirror for a long time. The diamond and opal earrings caressed her cheeks and sparkled in her eyes. Nothing in her face had changed, the changes were inside. She made a cup of fragrant rose hip and chamomile tea, added a double shot of brandy from the bar, and sipped it during her bath. When she called Di in Los Angeles it was after 3am in Georgia, but just after midnight in L.A.

Diana Underhill was the only 'family' she had in the United States. Ceeoni's blood sister, Sarah, seven years older, had married a professional soldier and lived in European luxury with him and her three beautiful children. Their mother had died after Ceeoni was born, which could have been a real tragedy if her Dad, Eddie Jones, hadn't been the person he was. Long before it was fashionable for men to take full charge of their children, Eddie Jones was a single parent who did everything for his little girls, except comb their hair. Ceeoni always joked that early photos of them looked like they were wearing big fuzzy hats. By the time Ceeoni and Diana became 'Best Friends' in third grade, Diana had demonstrated a natural ability to twist Ceeoni's tight curls up into ponytails, Afro—puffs, and other popular elementary school styles—a blessing that saved Ceeoni from the wretched embarrassment of being laughably different throughout those tender years of awkward, exaggerated and misinformed self-assessment.

Eddie Jones provided for his daughters, and anybody else who was around, very well on a postal worker's salary. Di fit into their family as if she'd been born to it, becoming the sister to Ceeoni that Sarah could never have been. As she got older, Ceeoni realized Sarah's spirit just wasn't wired into the big sister mode. Quiet, independent and incredibly beautiful, Sarah focused on and planned for a life straight out of Architectural Digest, Glamour and Ebony magazines. She achieved her lifelong goal of attaining her version of a storybook lifestyle, when she married a good-looking West Point graduate, and moved into a castle in Germany. Ceeoni thought if the castle came with the dull, military-type husband, Sarah could have it.

Diana was the person Ceeoni talked to when everything went wrong, as it always did going through school. They shared the details of their challenges, triumphs, and crushing defeats. Diana got on her knees and prayed with her when Ceeoni's soft spoken party animal Dad nearly left this life from a heart attack, right after they graduated from Fairfax High. Everyone agreed that Diana and Ceeoni had prayed him back to health.

That same year, Ceeoni confided in Di when she broke up with her first boyfriend, an even-tempered jock who had the horrendous habit of sleeping through movies, plays and concerts, where he occasionally emitted an open-mouthed, head-snapping snore.

Ceeoni and Diana helped each other as much as they could, and when help wasn't possible, each was there to listen to whatever arrows outrageous fortune had slung into the other's life. Tonight, she needed to talk to Diana, not her Dad, who was busy enjoying his second marriage after dating his bride for ten years; not her sister, whose reality consisted of what she could see, hear, touch and spend. Diana would not only understand, but would have plenty of input.

The phone rang twice, and Di's 'Hello', was a letter from home

"You know," Ceeoni said, "we always vowed never to allow fear of the unknown to stand in the way of success, money or love. But Girl, these last two days have tested my resolve many times over. I know strong people who would be on their way to the airport tonight."

"I got your strange message. Whassuupp? Please begin at the beginning, and don't leave out a single detail."

"Let me tell you Di, I should probably be more afraid than I am, and I'm scared, but I'm determined to see this through. First of all, God only knows why this murderer killed his victim in my office.

What I've been thinking is, did he know it was my office, as in let's scare the hell outta' the new girl? You know what I mean?"

She told Di everything that had happened from the time she'd arrived on Thursday afternoon, up to her stunning, elaborate Deja Vu experience at the Starcross Manor. She left out only one thing—how a sharp new inner voice weaving around her conflicting thoughts of Adam Delayno had been messing with her mind.

It is said that you recognize your friends, you don't choose them. Diana and Ceeoni had grown up in a lovely time in L.A., before drugs, guns, poverty and overcrowding had spilled a hoard of fearful possibilities out into the streets. Di had always wanted to be a writer, and Ceeoni had always wanted to work in some area of entertainment, preferably the theatre or music. They were never at a loss for something to talk about, especially after Di enrolled in the School of Parapsychology at UCLA. Ceeoni was working at the Inner-City Cultural Center by then, and Diana had already sold a few TV scripts. Di's metaphysical studies inspired never-ending conversations and speculations. That night Diana was enthralled with Ceeoni's account of the Starcross episode. She stopped and asked questions from time to time, and when Ceeoni was finished, she was quiet for a while.

"Cee," she said, "this is really something! I need time to assimilate what you just told me. But, Ms. Jones, may I take a moment to digress and inquire, what in the world is that great big, fine, sleek Adam Delayno like?"

Ceeoni laughed nervously, and wished she didn't have to tell the truth.

"Ah, Di, you're going to be ready to hang me up by my thumbs, but, well, I haven't met him yet." This time the silence dripped with acid.

"Di? Are you there?" The reply was slow and quiet, with emphasis on 'you'.

"Do you mean you were in the same building with Adam Delayno, all evening, and in his house, in his house (!) for the rest of the evening, and you didn't meet him?"

"No, but the way everything went down, there was—"

"Oops," Di growled, "then, I'm going to have to ask you to submit your resignation from the Vixen Club, by taking your card and your privileges, for conduct unbecoming any self-respecting Fox! You know you're slicker than that!" Ceeoni couldn't suppress her giggles,

"No, I plan to keep my card. All I need is a fair opportunity to bring this meeting about with smmoove class and su-wah-vey cool!" The laughter did Ceeoni good; she was beginning to feel like herself again. Di suddenly screamed,

"Cee, Ceeoni! I just remembered! One of my favorite instructors is in Atlanta right now, as we speak, doing some research at Emory University. She's going to be there for a while. Her area of specialization is past life regression. She's a past life therapist! Oh, this is deep! What a coincidence for Nasrene to be right there while you're going through some kind of Spiritual Revelation. Strike that! There are no coincidences or accidents! Now look, I'm going to give you her number. I've told her about you and, if you recall, I told you about her. She's absolutely vibrant, knowledgeable, down to earth and yet, spiritual."

"Di, I don't know—"

"C'mon Ceeoni! This is important. After what you've been through the past few days, and especially after Spirit pulled out all the stops at the Manor, you need to talk to Nasrene. This isn't the Psycho Friend's Network. In regression, past life visions are re-run, so to speak, by your own subconscious mind, like forgotten memories. You lived at Starcross in another time! Who were you? A past life regression, or a series of them, may help you understand why you had that vivid Deja Vu. The way Nasrene does it, the process couldn't be easier. Ceeoni, I want you to go and get regressed. Do you promise?"

Ceeoni reluctantly agreed,

"OK, OK—I'm willing to try anything that will help me understand. My belief meter shot straight up tonight. I guess my reservations are based on what can be called, 'stomp down confusion.'

"Oh, Ceeoni, I know, I know it must've shocked your system. But look, if nothing else, regression will give you a clear picture of the fact that your Soul is on an Eternal Journey. Many people are convinced that whatever the reason, the information that comes from previous lives, or the information they think comes from previous lives, helps them solve problems in their current lives. Real or imagined, the facts cannot be ignored. Past life regression works. I know Nasrene Asher fairly well, and I'll bet when she hears about your adventures in Georgia, she'll be standing at your door with her tape recorder loaded."

"Well, I'll tell you, last night wasn't one of those measly little psychic impressions that zip across your mind, like knowing who's calling before the telephone rings. This was full and complete, and I knew things I didn't tell Homer, like the fragrance of Gardenias and Roses floating in bowls all over the house, and the pattern on the large green Ming Vase that once stood on that green marble table in the foyer."

"Wow!' Di breathed," Could you see yourself?"

"I was trying hard to see myself, but I think I was a nebulous form, among several nebulous forms. The earrings Homer gave me, and the antique piano in the solarium seem to be connected, somehow."

"See there? That's why you've gotta' get in touch with Nasrene. Wait a minute, here's her number, OK, ready? (310) 555-3218, got it?"

"Yeah, I wrote it in my book. I'll call and invite her to the theatre for the Saturday night concert. Hey Di, I've probably frozen your ears, so I'll let you go. Hopefully, this toddy will drift me off to dreamland."

"Now, remember you promised to call Nasrene right away. And, get back to me with a blow-by-blow account the minute you finish knocking Adam Delayno's eyes out."

"Di, why do you want to go there? You know I've always loved his music, but he might be a real jerk, plus, you know his world is draped with actresses and supermodels."

"Girlfriend, just be your same old remarkable self. Tell me the truth—aren't you at all curious about him?"

Ceeoni's answer came in the form of a question,

"Di, have you heard anything about Adam Delayno's personal life?"

"No, never. I think of Adam Delayno as the Dark Duke of Mystery. I've never heard a word of scandal about him. I read where he'd been married, but that's all. His private life is very private."

"Not a good sign, Di," Ceeoni chuckled, "All that enigma could be hiding something sinister or shallow or silly. And don't forget the regular git-low, down and dirty types who surprise no one when they finally get busted and go to jail." After a hard laugh, Di signed off,

"Please try to behave yourself. And call Nasrene! Love you, Ciao."

Ceeoni curled up and tried to sleep, but her thoughts kept her awake through the wee small hours of the morning. The enormity of the knowledge that some part of herself retained memories of another time, in another place, flashed in her mind's eye like a big day-glo sign. She finally fell asleep, recalling visions of Starcross and a group of faceless shadowy figures. One figure stood apart in shadows, isolated and angry. The other dream people she encountered were warm and loving, but she couldn't identify anyone. The only thing she knew about the caring people was that she loved them all—very much.

CHAPTER NINE

Ceeoni Jones had been in Atlanta since Thursday afternoon, and on this third day morning, she had a whole new awareness as well as a whole new life. She knew she should be tired, but instead, she was at the highest level of excitement she had ever experienced. The ringing telephone announced Homer's big voice.

"Hey, Cee! I've gotta' run out, can I bring you anything that doesn't have to be tried on?"

"No thanks, but I was wondering if you would take me to see Starcross Manor again?"

"Oh, I'm sorry, Adam signed the final papers this morning. I'm on my way to take our attorneys back to Buckhead."

The disappointment slipped out in the tone of her voice,

"Oh, I see." It was almost a gasp.

"Now don't give up. We can always clear it with the new owner. This deal has been in the works for several months, and now that it's finalized, I can turn my attention to the theatre, the Estates, or anything else I damn well please. Adam's personal effects are due to arrive any day. It's not my house any more, and frankly, I'm glad it's over. I worked like a Georgia mule to get the entire property in the shape its in now, while juggling the building of various planned communities, along with a few other things."

"Let's see, you bought it in 1975, then you started the restoration in 1981. All tolled, that's a span of twenty-two years!"

"Yeah. If I'd known it would take so long and cost so much, I might not have been so gung ho," he laughed, "but don't start me lying, Ceeoni, I would've done it no matter what it took."

"Were you married?"

"Was I married! I bought it when Claudette and I were broke newlyweds. She was still in medical school. I had it for over five years before I could afford to do more than go over there and dibble and dabble by myself. Starcross was, well Ceeoni, it was something I had to do. I spent so much money and energy on it, Claudette started calling it the Dinsmore Albatross. She got so she hated hearing the name 'Starcross.' The restoration seemed to go on and on because I had to fit it in and around my life, and I couldn't bear to half-do a single task over there, all of which was real hard on our marriage. There I was, all excited about the inch-by-inch restoration of two marvelous buildings, and Claudette couldn't figure why anybody would want to do a thing like that. What thrilled me was a colossal drag to her, but that was then and this is now. For the first time in many years, I have a sense of freedom."

"Well, I don't know how you could let it go, but after last night, I guess I'm biased. I know you did a real job on it, because it parallels my memories so accurately—I guess they were my memories. Oh, and speaking of my memories, please don't tell anyone about my experience, OK? I think people would decide I'm ready for the 'Home.'"

"You know I'll respect your wishes. But truthfully, I don't have anyone to tell. Most people wouldn't believe it. Then, there are those whose faith in the devil and demons is so unshakable, they'd be certain you're possessed."

"Yeah," she added, "like the European inquisitors and the Salem witch hunters, whose motto was, 'if we don't know what it is, it must be evil, let's kill it!'"

"You got it, Cee! I know if I could somehow take my wallet calculator, the 'one-dollar wonder' I give to customers, back 100 years in a time machine, I bet they'd burn my behind at the stake, or boil me in oil."

"Or get down on their knees to worship your magic." Ceeoni lowered her voice, "And you know, in the wrong neighborhood, you'd better be real sure your time machine was able to whisk you and your 'tool of the devil' out of there before they caught up with you, you warlock, you!"

"Cee, how do you feel after being yanked through a window in time?"

"Spanking brand new, but I'm still trying to sort it out. In spite of what anybody may think, what happened to me felt natural, you know? There was nothing weird about it, except I can't imagine how it could be possible. I guess what I'm trying to say is I'm not anxious to know what anybody else may think."

"Well spoken, and well taken, I'll see you at the theatre."

After she dressed in black sweater and pants, Weber knocked at the door and handed her a set of keys, "Homer said if you don't like the silver BMW sedan, we've got some others out there. This is the one he hoped you'd drive. Oh, breakfast is ready."

She had toast and tea with Weber in the kitchen, and left for the theatre singing a Mickey Stevenson song, *Somebody Told Me 'Bout Jesus*, from a show called *The Gospel Truth*.

It was a miracle there were no serious injuries resulting from the latest attacks. She and Minette were both OK. At least in those instances, fate was working against the killer's plans, but where would he turn up next? Homer didn't seem upset as a lover might have been at the news Minette had been injured, which reinforced Ceeoni's decision that they were not a couple. At first, she thought they might be, until she noticed more traces of Minette's chilly self-absorption, completely opposite Homer's thoughtful ways. We are one of only two types of personalities, those who feel connected to others, and those who don't. Minette seemed to fall into the group who 'don't.' Ceeoni couldn't imagine Homer in a close personal relationship with one so disconnected, no matter how physically attractive. She'd be willing to bet Minette would change that if she could.

x x x

R.C. Ponder waved at her from the stage.

"Miss Ceeoni, you look absolutely, positively gorgeous this morning!"

She grinned at him. Today, his ever-present African robes were dark brown with a darker trim,

"I just found out that my wife and three of my children will be here soon!" he announced, as he jumped off the stage to join her.

"Hey, that's wonderful, R.C.! Do you get to see them often?"

"Not as often as I would like, but we set Adam's schedule so it isn't as brutal as it could be."

"Does he take long tours?" she asked.

"Oh, it depends. Most years, we're usually moving fast from April to early November. A few years, we cut the tours short because of overdue recording deadlines, but those were exceptions to the rule. Thanksgiving and Christmas are always at home, except in the event we're presented with some irresistible situation, or a favor that must be honored. We usually record from January to April, and some 'Live' recordings during the tour, but those are rare. My wife comes to visit often, sometimes bringing kids. Our kids have visited museums and sights around the world that most kids only read about."

"Do you take them along?"

"Sometimes, they've been on safari, they've seen the Pyramids, walked the Great Wall of China, eaten mangoes off the trees in the Philippines, romped with wallabies in the Australian Outback and explored many other places."

"Oh, wow! I never thought of it like that. I always thought touring is generally uncomfortable."

"Well, once we realized what made touring uncomfortable, we avoided those things."

"Like what?"

"We take time to arrive, situate and repair, physically and psychologically. Everybody doesn't do that. We've seen bands tour for 90-180 days, and more, without a break. It can be very inhumane. Some managers believe a day off is a dollar lost. We don't schedule trips back to back without two or three days' rest on either side, with no rehearsal and no travel, and we've never lost money by doing it that way. We avoid Hit-And-Runs like the plague."

"Hit-And—And-Runs?"

"Yeah, that's a scheduled concert in a city where no hotel is provided; in other words, the show comes in, performs the concert, and gets back on the bus or plane that night after the performance. They're never fun, but at times, we've been forced into it. Now and then, a city's hotels are filled, but we make sure that real rest is possible on the next stop."

"Yuk!"

"Ceeoni, I promise, if I ever get to take you anywhere, I'll never include one of those horrid things. Rest is like true love, there's no substitute for it. Adam believes in the best hotels, transportation and pay because if he's going to pay the IRS or the crew, he'd rather pay the crew. It's really sad that some organizations would rather pay the IRS well, and shortchange the little folks who are helping them make all the money."

"Adam seems like a considerate person."

R.C. turned to face her, "He is." Oops! It was time to change the subject. She didn't want to sound personally interested in someone she'd never met, and she saw the sharp curiosity in R.C.'s eyes.

"Will your family be staying at the Manor?" she asked.

"Only for as long as it takes Juno to decide where she wants to live. I like the look of the Estates across the way, and she usually likes what I like. We have a house in London and an apartment in New York whenever we need that much city."

Enjoying R.C.'s contagious warmth and enthusiasm, she also noticed how he put the stagehands and crew at ease with his joking.

She touched his arm, "Hey, I don't know my way around yet, but I'll be glad to offer your family any assistance I can. I'll bet moving from one country to another can be a jarring experience, especially with children."

"Now you've said the word! My wife loves to shop. If you two could find some of the malls, it'll enhance my existence, because she'll bug me until I can take her."

"Consider it done, I love to shop, too."

In search of the sound engineer, Ceeoni ran into Jake.

"Oh, the sound guy will be back in less than a half hour. One of the speakers blew a fuse, which was good to know sooner, rather than later. He won't be long."

"Jake, I've got to close my eyes for a moment. Please call me upstairs when he returns."

The view outside her office window had darkened as thunder rumbled in the distance. In L.A., rain was a tremendous blow to audience attendance, but with all these trees, she knew audiences had to be accustomed to torrential rainstorms, as in *Rainy Night In Georgia*. Refusing to think about the murder, she closed the drapes, curled up on the couch, and pulled her old afghan over her head. Within seconds, she was asleep.

In the dim light, a shadow quietly moved toward the sofa where Ceeoni slept. She stirred a little, and the shadow stopped, frozen. Just then, the telephone rang, and in the time it took her to roll over, find her way out of the afghan tent and answer the phone, the shadow was gone. Sitting on the sofa, she shook her head and rubbed her eyes. She sensed that something in the room had changed.

"Ceeoni, I'm so sorry to disturb you," Jake apologized, "but you're needed down here."

She threw some water on her face, hurried from the dreaded bathroom, freshened her makeup in the office and ran down the stairs. The bathroom had been cleaned meticulously, but it was just too soon to feel right there. The atmosphere still had a funny vibe. She met Homer as he came in the back door.

"Good afternoon, ma'am!" His handsome face beamed with exuberance.

"Hey, Homer, today's the day!"

"Every day's the day, but after last night the grapevine's 'a hummin'! My phones have been jumpin' off the hook."

In the theatre, on the stage covered with equipment and cable, R.C. watched the piano tuner working on the Steinway, while the stagehands set speakers and adjusted monitors. Several people stood around. Everything appeared to be in a state of normal chaos. She didn't see Jake. Now where did he go?

She saw the fashionable brown felt hat first, a wide-brimmed affair that swooped down on one side. The glamorous brown leather swing coat, leather pants and boots—it looked like, like—the woman's face turned toward Ceeoni and recognition clicked in her head.

Oh! "Diana?!! Is that—Oh, Di! This is too much! Am I glad to see you!" She hugged her Dear Friend. "I was in dire need of a pleasant surprise. When did you get here?!"

"Lessee," Di counted on her fingers, "One hour and thirty-eight minutes ago. I couldn't bear the thought of leaving you all by yourself with a murder, an attempted murder, a killer stalking a restored 129-

year-old theatre, a mysterious historical mansion, along with Adam Delayno—I repeat, Adam Delayno, live, and in concert." They hugged again. Ceeoni saw Jake over Di's shoulder.

"Jake—there you are. Di, you've got to meet everybody! Jake here is my assistant, and this is Homer Dinsmore, who owns Starcross, and R.C. Ponder, Adam Delayno's personal manager—Everybody, this is my friend, Diana Underhill."

Ceeoni's observant glance didn't miss the not-so-subtle electrical current that passed between Di and Homer. His eyes fixed on Diana's loveliness. It was as if Homer had developed a new voice she had never heard him use when he quietly said,

"So glad to meet you Ms. Underhill."

Diana smiled in a way that Ceeoni had never seen before, in all the years they had been friends. "My pleasure, Mr. Dinsmore," she murmured.

For a split second, Ceeoni had the sensation of peering into someone's window, because Di and Homer were gazing at each other, excluding everyone else, as if they were alone. She guessed if a tissue were held up between them and released, it would stand suspended on the charged air.

R.C. ambled back to the piano, but Jake broke the spell when he noisily picked up two folding chairs.

"Where would you ladies prefer to sit?"

Homer inspected his own shoes. Ceeoni figured they waited for her answer. "Oh, thank you, Jake, just inside the wings."

Homer, silently advertising his newly energized aura with glances in Di's direction, stood outside of Ceeoni's and Di's earshot, as they watched the stage preparations. Di leaned toward her, saying,

"Girl, that Homer is gorgeous, gorgeous! Talk about a Silver Fox!" Her uncanny James Brown always sounded like it didn't come from her soft voice, "Good God!" She frowned and touched Cee's shoulder, "But Cee, you aren't, well, are you? You know, are you and—"

"No, I'm not, he isn't, and we aren't, but I bet Minette Coulter, you know the lady who runs the Starcross Restaurant?"

"You mean the one who got hit in the head?"

"Yeah, I believe she would, if she could. I don't know what the story is, but there's a story somewhere. Homer doesn't appear to be any way but all business."

"Really?" Diana purred.

"Yeah, he seems to have a rare combination of honesty and worldly sophistication, you know, the rare kind who wouldn't allow himself to be chosen."

"I wouldn't have anyone who was any other way," Di laughed. "The other kind already wore me out."

Homer, who appeared to be not at all sophisticated at the moment, still lingered, keeping an eye in their direction, well, in Diana's direction.

Ceeoni, I swear, I heard bells and whistles when I looked at him."

"It's OK, Di, he looked like he was hit with bells and whistles when he saw you."

Di half-turned toward Homer with a little smile, crossed her legs, then turned away, pretending like she didn't see him.

"So what time did you leave L.A.?"

"After I talked to you last night, I packed a bag and caught the first thing smokin', around 8:30 this morning. I couldn't sleep anyway. Thuffering thuccotath, Theeoni, therth a thittling thituathon thimmering here! I plan to stay as long as I can. Just lead me to an ATM and a Mall in a few days."

"I'm so glad you hopped that plane. Your being here will help keep me grounded, if that's possible at Starcross. This ain't your average, everyday run-of the-mill ordinary restored theatre and mansion."

"You know me well enough to know I had to see it for myself. All these seductive mysteries are titillating to my metaphysically oriented mind."

"My schedule should allow us to see some of Atlanta next week."

"Who cares about sightseeing? I only want to visit Spelman and the University Center, the King Center, and Starcross Manor."

Di's elbow nudged Ceeoni's side as Homer Dinsmore headed in their direction. An elegant figure wearing a navy blue cashmere overcoat, sweater and slacks, he moved like a man who had made up his mind, and was ready to take action.

"Would you ladies like to use the next hour to get settled in the town house, or my house?" His 'my house' dropped to the husky tone that Ceeoni had noticed earlier. She knew Diana wouldn't want to stay alone.

"If you don't mind," she said, "I think we'd both enjoy your lovely home until the murderer is caught. There's so much room in my suite with those large beds; it's big enough for several people, even if they don't like each other."

Di hesitated, "Well—"

Homer appeared crestfallen. Di glanced slowly from Ceeoni to Homer and finally answered,

"That sounds OK to me."

Homer instantly brightened up. He grinned like a teenager as he swung Di's garment bag over his shoulder, and grabbed up her huge second piece. Di's 'few things' usually consisted of several outfits for any and all occasions. Homer carried those bags like they were empty.

"Miss Di, you're in good hands. I've still got things to do here, and since I can't get away, I'm just going to have to trust you'll get settled in."

Homer tried to raise his right hand,

"Scout's Honor! C'mon Di, let's blow this joint!"

As they walked away laughing, she could've sworn she saw stars in Diana's eyes.

Ceeoni was satisfied with Saturday night's state of readiness when she left the theatre. Back at Homer's, Di told her she and Homer had grabbed a sandwich in the kitchen with Weber and the rest of the time they'd talked and talked. She said the same thing about Homer that Ceeoni had felt, like she'd known Homer Dinsmore all her life.

CHAPTER TEN

Getting dressed for that evening at the theatre was a fiasco. Ceeoni and Di critiqued each other as they tried on several Saturday Night Specials. Di was beautiful no matter what she wore. Her short, medium brown stylish haircut, set off her wide smile and dramatic, almost round eyes. She had a knack for finding the perfect garment to minimize what she called her 'soulful' hips. Tonight, she finally decided on a drop-dead red satin, strapless knee-length dress, a wide satin belt, and red satin stiletto sandals. The addition of a red faux fur cape, the same length, created a fabulous effect.

Di had already chosen Ceeoni's outfit, after rummaging through the closet several times.

"Here," she insisted, pushing the garment into Ceeoni's arms, "No argument! This is Da Bomb, guaranteed to stop clocks, eyeballs and hearts!"

"Diana," Ceeoni laughed," I don't want to stop hearts!" She slipped on the gown named Old Faithful, because wearing it never failed, never failed to make her feel like royalty. The straight, barely there, backless silk crepe, was worn with a matching floating chiffon shrug. A quick survey in the mirror showed that the gown was still keeping up its end of the bargain, emphasizing all of her best features. She opened the silver box and added the ultimate accessory.

Diana looked closely as Ceeoni affixed one of the opal earrings,

"Oh, wow, Ceeoni! So those are the opals! Girl, they must've cost a couple of years of our combined incomes. I remember seeing a black opal ring in one of those incredible Las Vegas jewelry stores; the stones were smaller than yours and it cost over $100K. They say opals are bad luck if you're not a Libran. Is Homer into astrology?"

"I don't know. He said it just seemed like the earrings should be mine."

"Ceeoni, that's another reason why we should get in touch with Nasrene Asher. What's happened to you here feels like some past life phenomena to me."

"Yeah, well, it feels like plain old weird to me." The diamonds twinkled as she secured the other earring,

"OK, Di, tell me the truth, tell me you won't think I'm crazy! Go on, tell me."

"Alright, Bud, I don't think you're crazy, but wait! What kind of a question is that? I'm the one carrying around pyramids, crystals, magnets, et al, and you never thought I was crazy, or did you?"

Ceeoni turned to meet the amused curiosity in her friend's eyes,

"Di, this is serious, and I can't hold it any longer." She took a deep breath and said, "I heard a voice clearly echo in my mind at the exact moment Homer gave me the opals."

Di's eyes widened, "You did? What did it say?"

"It said, 'I will wear them with my new black taffeta gown', and you know I don't own a taffeta gown!"

After a moment of silence, Di asked, "What did the voice sound like?"

"This voice is quite distinct. At first, it didn't sound like anybody, but after I thought about it, maybe it's my own voice, but as it would be if it were amplified, off in the distance, oh, it's hard to describe."

"Well, you can stop trippin'! I fully understand what you mean. I started hearing a voice several years ago, but I didn't mention it to anyone except Nasrene. She said it goes with the territory of expanded consciousness."

"Expanded consciousness? Did you think you were cracking up when you first heard it?"

"I was deliberately trying to develop an inner voice," Di answered, "Rather, I was meditating to clear my conscious mind, to bring the ever-present inner voice of the deeper mind to my awareness."

"Ever-present—?"

"Yeah, Cee, the voice you heard is natural. It's always there, whether you can hear it or not." She winked, adding, "I must say, now that you're evolving spiritually to a state of higher consciousness, it certainly looks good on you. You look like Fresh Long Green, Queen!"

Ceeoni spun the boudoir chair so that she faced the mirror. She couldn't compare what she saw with Di's slang description for 'money', but there was something more-vibrant. The deep purple gown brought out the rich purple flashes in the opals, and the diamonds lit up her eyes.

She picked up the BMW keys, "You riding with me, Ms. Underhill?"

"Oh, no, no no! Homer asked me to go with him. But I'll walk you out. Cee, do you believe in love at first sight?"

"Is there such an animal? It seems to me it could be a sure way to complicate one's existence unnecessarily; sort of like bungee-jumping without taking time to check the harness, and even then, the harness could be faulty. Why?" Ceeoni already knew why.

"Well, since friendships can be instantaneous, like our friendship, as a point of fact, why not love relationships, you know, Souls recognizing each other's hearts?"

Ceeoni's rational mind answered, "Well, I guess it happens, but the odds against it are, uh, you know what I mean."

"I can't factor the odds," Di answered, "You and I grew up together. Nothing in our lives ever fit the norm, the typical, the average, or the 'evens'! I don't know about you, but I believe I have to let the Universe take care of the stupid odds!"

x x x

The parking lot was nearly full, and inside, the theatre hummed with tempting buffet scents wafting through the air. Windsor and his Mary Jordan Caterers were at it again. Fashionably dressed people gathered in congenial groups in the noisy, jovial atmosphere. She spoke to R.C. and met the Time Magazine reporters who were to cover a story on the Starcross Theatre featuring Adam Delayno. Ceeoni recalled hearing a radio interview with Adam back when she'd first become deeply affected by his recordings. The interview didn't reveal much about him personally, but she never forgot his description of music. He'd said, 'Music is love in search of a word.' Over the years, she'd heard no sweeter definition of something that could never be defined.

She ran into Jake, whose worried eyes announced his alarm before he whispered, "Adam isn't here yet!"

"It's only a little after 7:30, he might've been delayed. He's got time." In spite of her calm response, a cold chill ran slowly down her spine. In the past, she'd discovered that getting excited in the face of an impending crisis didn't help. If the main attraction or a key cast member hadn't shown by the half-hour call, that's when she flew into remedial alternatives. Her mind began to frantically sift through worst-case scenarios.

Minette slithered around Ceeoni and Jake in the backstage hallway. Although beautifully attired in a pale gold lace evening suit, her face wore a distracted, glassy-eyed stare that set her features in hard lines. Ceeoni called after her,

"Minette, how are you?"

Minette kept walking, but turned her head slightly, mumbling, "Fine."

Ceeoni didn't see a bruise on her forehead, possibly because her thick hair had been combed to fall over nearly half of her face. Now what could be happening with her? Or was it a darker side of her usual dark side?

"And," Jake asked in a half whisper, "Adam's car phone and pager didn't answer, and neither did the house. What do we do now?"

Diana and Homer came through the stage door, smiling as if they shared a big secret.

"C'mon," Homer urged, "Let's get to our seats before folk start assuming they're cancellations. I don't want to be shufflin' around when the concert begins. Hey, you two look very un-festive. What's up?"

"Adam's not here yet," Jake said, "And his phones don't answer. R.C. is up front with Time Magazine. Maybe he has some idea why Adam's been delayed."

Homer immediately headed for the Lobby with Di at his heels. They looked great together. No wonder Minette had appeared irritated. She'd probably seen them on the parking lot, and those smiles alone were enough to put a jealous-hearted onlooker into a real blue funk.

Ceeoni realized she had to move fast, "Jake, it's nearly curtain time, please talk to the audience. You know what to say, tell them the old 'there's been a slight delay' stuff. Give me a good 45 minutes to see if I can locate him. I'm going over there!"

She prayed that Adam wasn't stuck behind an immovable accident on the freeway, or off somewhere totally inebriated, as she'd once found a famous comedian, a few minutes before curtain time. He'd passed out in the limousine, on the way to the theatre, and it took her and two others to get him out of the car, at which time he'd vomited all over her aqua North Beach Leather suit. She couldn't watch his act again, not even on television.

Ceeoni's phone rang as she pulled into the Manor circular driveway,

"Talk to me," Homer shouted, "Have you heard from Adam yet?"

"I'm at the Manor now. Maybe he's suffering from jetlag, and overslept." She didn't believe a word of that.

"We'll be right there. You know Di won't let me leave her at the theatre."

From the background, Di's voice rang out over the wire, "Di isn't going to let you leave her anywhere!"

In front of the mansion, a flood of impressions flowed through Ceeoni's mind. She felt herself sitting on the second floor sunporch, drinking cool lemonade from a slender crystal glass. When—? It was amazing how pictures clicked in her inner eye, like brightly colored slides. But she couldn't see herself. She wondered if she would ever become accustomed to the idea that she had been her exact same self, in another time, with another body, another identity. But what identity?

The locked dark money-green Cadillac parked in the drive wore the license plate, HD6, identifying it as another one of Homer's loaners. Shivering a little in the cool air, she rang the doorbell many times. Although the drapes were drawn over all the windows, she was able to see through the drapery crack in the room she remembered as the parlor. The bluish cast of a TV set playing in front of a half-eaten sandwich and a bottle of beer, attested to a simple unfinished activity. She rang the bell again. Again, delicate chimes echoed throughout the house. Behind her, Homer's Rolls screeched to a halt. He and Di ran up the half dozen stairs, holding hands. Homer held up a key,

"This is R.C.'s, I'm hoping someone Adam knows picked him up, and they're just running late getting back to the theatre. I spoke with him around 6:30. He said he was going to grab a sandwich and get right over, but he does know a lot of people in Atlanta. You know how an old friend can turn up at the last minute and—" His sentence trailed off, as if he realized his scenario was wishful thinking.

Their search of all twenty-six rooms; library; six bedrooms; six new marble baths; four sitting rooms; ballroom; English Pub Room; nursery suite; living room; dining room; parlor; Rose Room and the solarium yielded no clues. Ceeoni was again struck by Homer's attention to minute details in crafting and re-creating the restoration. While they looked under beds and in closets, Di kept remarking in amazement at Ceeoni's familiarity with the floor plan. They found the Cadillac keys with another house key and a cellular phone on the dresser in Adam's bedroom. Ceeoni stared wistfully at the two electric pianos that had been placed in a v-shape by the window. She tried not to think Adam may be hurt, or something worse. They looked at each other as Homer spoke the obvious truth,

"If Adam left the house under his own steam, why didn't he take his phone and his keys? This is like another odd piece in a crazy patchwork quilt! He was here, and now he's gone, and I've got a theatre filled with people anxiously awaiting one of the biggest stars in the history of jazz, and he's freakin' disappeared!" He slammed the keys down on the desk, "Damn—Damn! We've gotta' notify the police!"

Jake answered on Ceeoni's first ring, "I knew it had to be you. He's not there, is he?"

"Oh, Jake, Jake?" When his silence said more than words could say, Ceeoni's frustration poured out,

"We're living the ultimate professional nightmare. Tonight, the nameless fears that crept around inside my head during those tense nights before every opening have materialized, although not even my vivid imagination could've come up with all of this. We've got the disappearance of a major celebrity along with the murder of the celebrity's business manager, all within the theatre's first hours."

"So now," he groaned, "We do the usual?"

"Yeah, tell them they have a choice of a refund or a rain check. The media will probably splash the whole thing everywhere, but we can't stop them."

"Tell him to feed those people," Homer shouted, "Keep the music playing, turn it into a party. We've gotta' pay for all that stuff, anyway."

"I heard him. Cee, tell him it's done. That should ease some of the pain."

"Thanks, Jake. Call if anything develops, oh, and if you're a praying person—"

"That's the first thing I did. Don't worry about the theatre, I'll hold everything down here."

x x x

Detective Saxon met them a few minutes later in Homer's exotic living room, and visibly brightened up when he saw Diana. Ceeoni, sitting at the bar with a coke, could've sworn the detective licked his chops when she introduced him to Di.

"Ms. Underhill," Detective Saxon purred, "Is this your first visit to Hotlanta?"

"Yes, it is," she answered, as David, looking into her eyes, sat down on the sofa next to her. He leaned in a little closer,

"So, what do you think of our city, so far?"

"Well, I like the airport and Starcross a lot," she answered with a smile, but her eyes shifted away from his penetrating gaze.

"You mean they've kept you in since you've been here?"

Watching the scene, Ceeoni thought, 'There he goes.' Homer, obviously tired of the little drama, interrupted, "David, Ms. Underhill arrived early today. I plan to see to it that she enjoys all that Atlanta has to offer."

"Of course, Homer." Nobody missed the 'back off' edge in Homer's voice. The detective cleared his throat and switched gears over to his professional police mode, "Now everyone, if you don't mind, please tell me where you were this evening, and what you saw. Please include everything, you never know what might prove to be important."

After the brief questioning, Weber left with Detective Saxon to join the police search.

Diana, deep in concentration, punched up numbers on her phone saying,

"Ceeoni, I'm glad I couldn't reach Nasrene when I called her earlier. I was trying to invite her to the concert, but the line was busy. It sounded downright peculiar to get an old-fashioned busy signal in this era of advanced technology, but I kept getting one."

"Di, Baby," Homer said, "Now that the concert is off, if you catch up with your friend, ask her if she's free to join us for dinner tonight."

In the pulse-pounding avalanche of events, Ceeoni had forgotten about. Di's friend from UCLA, Nasrene, Nasrene somebody. Pacing the floor, Homer talked out loud to himself,

"There were people at the theatre tonight that I know and respect; people from CocaCola, City Hall, Atlanta Life Insurance, the governor's office and members of the King Family. Dammit, I'm not going back in there to face their condolences along with the pity in their eyes, 'Everythings' gonna' be alright! Hang in there, Buddy, etc. Hell, I know everything is gonna' be alright! I just don't know when!" He stopped pacing, and pulled his keys from his pocket, "C'mon, let's get out of Dodge. Ceeoni, you and Di have been cooped up here, and Atlanta is an exciting, romantic city. All we can do here is sit around and speculate on the worst possibilities. Jake's got the theatre, David's got the investigation, let's catch the wind!"

While Diana persisted in trying to reach her friend's number, Ceeoni gathered the used glasses to wash in the wet bar sink. She knew that nothing could ease her tossed emotions except realistic breakthroughs. She wished again that all the drama was over, that the killer was caught, and Adam Delayno was back, alive and well, to which the Sane Ceeoni asked sarcastically, 'So what's Adam Delayno to you, anyway?'

"Oh, I see! I had the wrong area code!" Di said, "Nasrene's number isn't 310, it's 323! Oh, hello, Nasrene? Hey, this is Diana Underhill. I'm in Atlanta! Following you around! Ha! Yeah, uh-huh. Hey, I've got a fascinating story for you, but you need to hear all the details of this one because I've got a feeling the answers are all up in your arena.

"I remember you said all so-called coincidence is spiritual intent. I have a friend here, and she's in the middle of the strangest vibe! Nasrene, this is beyond textbook cases of deja vu. And I can tell you one thing, it had me so fired up, I would've hitch-hiked to get here if I had to. We wanna' tell you about it, can we take you to dinner? Now, you can? Great! Oh? A really good restaurant? Here, tell Homer. He's an Atlanta native. Homer, this is my friend, Nasrene Asher." He took the phone.

"Hi, yes, I do, and it's one of my favorites, we'll be glad to pick you up. Oh? Well, OK, if that's what you prefer. We'll take you back to Emory after dinner. It's 9pm now, we'll meet you there around at 9:30."

"Her roommate will drop her off," Homer said, already on his way to the door. "They've been going there so much, they know how to get there. You may like this place, ladies. It's truly unique."

x x x

The Showcase Eatery on Old National Highway, College Park, featured brick and wood decor with high exposed beams from which unusual items hung, entertaining one's vision. Ceeoni enjoyed the odd assortment of musical instruments lining the walls, along with vintage photos of jazz musicians mixed in with a hodge-podge of collectibles.

The chubby young waitress seated them after hugging Homer. "Girl, he said, "You know I have to get in here to see you and have my herb tea! Is my Big Gulp back there somewhere?" She responded to his two-fingered signal with giggles and a tray of two pitchers of iced tea.

"One pitcher is never enough," he explained.

The tea proved to be light, sweet and spicy.

"They should sell this by the barrel," Di said, "Ooowee, Ceeoni. I can't wait to see what Nasrene is going to say about your episode of deja vu. Homer, considering your strong attraction to Starcross and your determination to restore it, you probably had a past life there, also!"

Homer's answer, "I wouldn't be at all surprised," was interrupted as a lovely woman, whom Ceeoni assumed to be Nasrene Asher, waved at Di while silently sliding into the booth across from him. When he hesitated, she gestured for him to continue. Homer nodded, and kept talking,

"Well, where was I? Oh, when I was a kid, I worked with the SCLC in the Civil Rights Movement, and Dr. Martin Luther King, Jr. Dr. King inspired me to do something meaningful in my life."

Ceeoni gasped, thinking, 'My God, this man actually knew Dr. King!' She had to pause and re-focus on what Homer was saying.

"Dr. King helped me get my first job with a construction company while I was in high school, and he helped me qualify for college. When I graduated from Morehouse with a degree in business, I got married, thinking I would work at the construction company for a while, and maybe teach sometime in the future. Soon, I got the opportunity to work as an apprentice with a developer on a planned community, and I studied hard. Pretty soon, I got the idea to build my own community one day, but it certainly never occurred to me to restore anything.

"Anyway, back in '74, I was out searching for a small parcel of land at a bargain rate. My plan was to buy enough space for a few houses, just to get started. I drove around for weeks before I found it.

"The road to Starcross was overgrown. I parked the car and walked, without having a clue there was anything in those woods, until I saw the 'Private Property—Keep Out' signs. I learned early in life that I can trust my intuition, and something told me there was a path near there. The path led me to Starcross, and the greatest adventure of my life.

"The whole place was in ruins, but for some reason, I could imagine it as I wanted it to be, and I knew I could do it. I embarked on a search for the owners, but I kept ending up in blind alleys. I found the Baldwin Sisters by accident when I mentioned in passing to young David Saxon, who delivered my newspaper, that I'd discovered a fenced-in theatre and mansion, covered with kudzu, abandoned in South Fulton. He replied, 'That sounds like the old Starcross property the Baldwin Sisters talk about all the time.' David showed me where the sisters lived, and the info they gave me got the ball rolling. I can't tell you how elated I felt about that property!

"Starcross turned out to be much larger than I thought, 500 acres in all, but fortunately, it was a lot cheaper than it should've been because of low real estate values in the area. It took months to research the owner and I spent every dime I could borrow, plus, I was forced to endure endless objections from family and friends. Ah, but I was overjoyed when it was mine at last! My wife knew it dominated my thoughts from the moment I saw it, and she was totally convinced that I'd lost my mind."

Nasrene had taken Homer's hand while he told the story, and she had paid close attention to every word until he finished.

"You know," she said, "when we find ourselves fascinated with a place, as you were, there's usually a reason, even though we may never know exactly what it is."

Di, Ceeoni and Homer proceeded to tell Nasrene details of everything that had happened from Thursday afternoon, up until Adam's disappearance, which alarmed her.

"Look, this is scary," she said quickly, "Adam Delayno is either in terrible danger or he's already been killed. Whatever this Soul is seeking, it is clearly malevolent enough to go to any lengths to get it, and clever enough not to leave any obvious clues. Homer, do you have any enemies?"

"I guess everybody unknowingly steps on somebody's toes throughout life, but I have no enemies I know of. Besides, why would this person murder Basil Cassidy? And if Adam Delayno is in danger, how would he fit into the picture?"

"I'm thinking about the theatre," Nasrene said, "I mean, the murder and any other crimes could be the method the killer is using to cause the Starcross Theatre or the Starcross Development to fail. I'm new to Georgia. Look, is there a competitive theatre or developer in the area?"

Homer laughed and shook his head,

"Oh no, they're so busy scrambling to put all the good stuff in other parts of the city, especially north of downtown. They haven't discovered South Fulton, yet."

"Well," Nasrene said, "Adam Delayno is a big star. If something happens to him here, the publicity would close you down before you could blink. According to everything you've told me, I don't believe he would just not show. It seems that Ceeoni's deja vu may have something to do with what's happening here, but considering the circumstances and your intense dedication to the property, Homer, with your consent, I'd like to work with you first." Diana gave Ceeoni the 'See-there-I-told—you-so' nod.

Homer replied slowly, "I don't understand what's going to happen, but I would love to know why Starcross meant so much to me. What's surprises me is that once the restoration was over and the Manor was sold, it's like leaving an old relationship. I have a sense of completion, a sort of a been-there-done-that-wore-out-a-case-of-tee-shirts feeling."

Nasrene's spontaneous delighted laughter made everybody laugh with her.

"I know exactly what you mean; that's the feeling we have when karma with a person, place or thing, is balanced, paid or fulfilled. But remember, no one knows what will happen with past life regression. You may want to go back to a place in time that relates to Starcross, but then again, you may not. What we'll be doing is trying to see if anything comes up that is buried in your deeper mind, relating to Starcross. I believe that there is always spiritual guidance in past life regression; that the visions are deliberate. I think we all see what we need to see in those fleeting impressions. I've witnessed tremendous healing on many levels because of it, so let's get started. We can't waste any more time. Homer, is there somewhere we can go to be quiet for a while?"

"Sure," he replied, "I'll get them to fix us up something to take out." Nasrene and Homer recommended the Champagne Shrimp with brown rice, which was ready in a few minutes.

Nasrene, sitting in the front seat with Homer, answered their questions concerning past life regression and therapy. She swung around in order to talk to Di and Ceeoni at the same time. Her ebony satin skin, sable eyes, and coppery, wavy hair reminded Ceeoni of the dramatic beauty seen in Brazil and the Caribbean Islands.

She spoke of all the unusual things ordinary people have been known to do during past life regression; speaking foreign, sometimes ancient or 'dead' languages, playing musical instruments, and having verified knowledge of all sorts of things to which they'd never been exposed.

"There are hundreds of books on the subject of past lives; Edgar Cayce, Dr. Ian Stevenson, and Dick Sutphen are only a few authors who have written about the phenomena," Nasrene added, "however, there are many more, and there are past life therapists in every major city, and organizations of healers who use PLT whose memberships include psychiatrists, psychologists and medical doctors. No one knows the reason, but whatever the reason, many people believe they've lived before, many lifetimes, in many cases. I've regressed dozens of men and women from all walks of life, and I've read thousands of case histories, and in all my exposure to it, past life regression never ceases to amaze me."

Homer, keenly interested, asked, "How does one discover past lives?"

"I prefer a light state of relaxation, but there are other ways. I know people who are convinced their dreams show them past lives, and there are those who have spontaneous episodes of deja vu, like yours, Ceeoni. Actually, experiences like yours aren't at all uncommon, but most people just shrug them off. The process I use is very simple, and I can bring you out of that life if it becomes too painful. Homer, we may discover why you were drawn to Starcross, and Ceeoni, apparently, you were here, as well. I would like to regress you next, to see if anything fits."

Ceeoni thought about the isolated, angry energy form she'd encountered in her vision, and wondered why she hadn't mentioned it. Was it herself she'd seen? She closed her eyes as the car slipped through the imposing iron gates of Starcross Lakes Estates.

"Is this the way to the Manor?" Nasrene asked, "This looks so new."

"No, I thought we'd go to my house."

"If it's possible, Homer, I think the old Starcross Manor may be more conducive."

On the way to the Manor, Ceeoni reached Jake on her phone. "We're blessed," he said, "It wasn't as much of a madhouse as I'd anticipated. Most people chose a rain check, and there are only a couple of dozen refunded tickets. So it's cool, and the party is kickin'. I supervised the rental company load-out, and I let R.C. leave Adam's equipment here until they can pick it up. Has anyone heard anything about Adam yet?"

"No."

"Oh God," he sighed, "I've never seen anything like this, and, oh, tell Homer the caterer will give us a break on tonight's invoice. We've all talked to the police. R.C. was frantic, and I think joining in the search with Detective Saxon and the police gives him something to do to keep his sanity. I'll be closing down as soon as folk clear out. Do you want me to call you then?"

"No thanks Jake, only if something comes up. Ciao."

By the time they arrived at the Manor, the police had left. Nasrene asked Homer to choose where he would be most comfortable for his past life regression, and he picked the room between the solarium and the hallway to the kitchen, the Rose Room.

Decorated in shades of pink and rose, the room's cozy elegance, down to the smallest decorative knick-knacks, were very much as Ceeoni remembered. How could this be?

Nasrene was the first to finish the wonderfully seasoned still-hot repast. She anxiously waited with her tape recorder and notebook until everyone settled down and Homer said he was ready.

He stretched out on the dusky rose velvet sofa. Nasrene switched on the recorder and began the relaxation techniques in a quiet voice, as Di and Ceeoni watched intently from the opposite sofa. Soft light from the rose lamp emphasized Homer's gentle, handsome features, and accented the caring expression in Diana's eyes.

While settling into the room's familiar comfort, Ceeoni said a prayer in her heart for Adam Delayno and all the people connected to this frightening and wonderful place called Starcross.

CHAPTER ELEVEN

"Homer," Nasrene said evenly, "You are now going back to a time that relates to events occurring in your life now. You will remember everything. It will be like watching a movie. Can you tell me where you are? There was a long silence. Then they were shocked to hear the low tones of an old woman's voice emanating from Homer's mouth, in a shaky whisper.

'I'm at Starcross Manor.'

Di and Ceeoni watched, frozen in mute, wide-eyed amazement.

"What year is it?" Nasrene asked.

'1874'

"How old are you?"

'92'

"What is your name?"

'Leticia, Leticia Starcross Bramwell!' Ceeoni gripped Dianna's hand as the wispy voice added cheerfully, 'But folks call me Miss Letty!'

Miss Letty said that Starcross was built in 1782, the year she was born, and she'd enjoyed a happy childhood as the only offspring of a wealthy landowner and his beautiful wife. Her Father, a respected artist, hired a governess who recognized and nurtured Letty's natural aptitude for music, therefore, Harpsichord lessons had been added to writing, embroidery and French studies. Leticia took pleasure in thrilling parlor guests with her considerable musical talent. By the time she was eighteen, she responded to the urging of one of her Father's associates, and became a professional concert pianist, which was a very bold undertaking for a young woman.

She toured Europe many times, playing for audiences of aristocrats and royalty, accompanied by her childhood governess, who fulfilled the dual role of chaperone and coach. When the dear lady expired from consumption during the tour of 1807, the grieving twenty-five year old Letty elected to honor her obligation; she finished the tour alone, in spite of wars and rumors of wars in her path. She recalled being afraid, but it was during that tour that she met her lifelong friend, Avajay, and because of Avajay, she met her beloved husband, Thurman Bramwell, with whom she shared complete happiness. Many years would pass before she would face the sickening, helpless dread of encroaching war again.

After Miss Letty and Thurman were married, Avajay accompanied Letty and her artist husband as they traveled the world. Letty performed concerts and her husband painted, multiplying their fame and fortune. In 1817, after the birth of their son, Talbert Starcross Bramwell, she learned that a scarlet fever epidemic had swept over Starcross, taking her vibrant parents to early graves. Reeling from shock and loss, she and Thurman moved back to Georgia, taking their newborn son and the East Indian Avajay with them.

Avajay, companion, friend and teacher, taught them the existence and care of the Eternal Soul and the Spiritual Path, thereby instilling ancient knowledge of the Past, Present and Future Continuum. They followed the dictates of their destiny and disregarded the barbaric laws of the land by enthusiastically joining a secret group of abolitionists, led by a firebrand Episcopalian friend of Thurman's.

Propelled by their faith, Avajay's visions and Thurman's ingenuity, they became a part of a system by which slaves, who had the courage, could escape from the South. When Thurman died suddenly in 1827, Miss Letty and the clairvoyant Avajay knew they had to carry on, in spite of the danger of discovery. With only a small staff of indentured servants who ran the house and gardens, they continued their work, careful not to arouse suspicion.

After Thurman's death, the sale of a few of his paintings quadrupled her wealth. Miss Letty asked her young cousin, Wayne Starcross, newly graduated from Harvard Law School, to assist her in the management of the Starcross Estate. She knew this arrangement galled her only son, the hedonistic Talbert Bramwell, who saw it as a crushing blow to his ego, representing his failure to bully his Mother into relinquishing the family finances to his reckless control.

Slave trading had been declared illegal in the United States in 1808, yet tens of thousands of Africans were sold into slavery by other Africans for profit and who, in some cases, had to choose between trinkets, or the serious end of the slavers' firesticks.

More slaves were smuggled into the country as the fast and efficient cotton gin increased the demand for slave labor to plant cotton. The Southern mindset assumed that all sane folk aspired to own slaves. She even knew of black slave owners. Miss Letty said she'd heard rumors that it was her fear and/or lunacy that prevented Starcross from being the great slave plantation it should have been, and that her son's incessant parties were a brave front of pretense; mere shadows of his family's long gone prosperous years. Anyone knowledgeable in the international world of fine art knew better, but in their remote area south of Marthasville, nobody would have believed that the sale of a single Bramwell portrait would fetch the equivalent of three years' profits from a large cotton plantation.

It broke Miss Letty's heart to see her son become the victim of his own brooding meanness. After he'd been asked to leave two universities due to drunken and disorderly conduct, he returned to his family home, more sullen than ever. With a generous allowance and idle time on his hands, he longed to indulge the passion of his life, to turn Starcross into a cotton-growing plantation, with slaves.

Talbert's reasons, of course, were selfish. As a money generating business, Starcross would give him exclusive control over finances that would allow him greater excesses. Also, it would elevate his status among his slave-owning peers, sons of families who had always owned and bred slaves. Talbert, caught up in the enthusiasm of his dreams, regularly practiced the art of wielding the whip; its zinging snaps could be heard from the barn, unsettling the sweet Starcross evenings, causing Miss Letty to cover her ears against the sinister sounds. Determined, he continued to badger his Mother for years in every way he could, but she held her ground, telling him that her Father, Charles Starcross did not build his family home to become a plantation.

She never stopped missing her late husband's quiet strength and she prayed that she would be able to prevail when Talbert's frustration reached the inevitable boiling point. Her husband, like her, had believed life's greatest purpose was to be a friend to man. Avajay's visions had revealed to them that Miss Letty's destiny in this incarnation was to work for the cause of freedom, and to guide a Great Soul who would need her protection.

When Talbert was a beautiful, perfect baby, she thought he was the Soul of Avajay's prophecy, but early in his life she realized her son's Soul had much to learn. Always a self-centered child, Talbert's antagonistic behavior increased at the age of ten, after he found his Father's lifeless body on the solarium floor. Soon, he became a stranger she knew she could never trust.

Their furious disagreements came to a curiously abrupt end in the fall of 1848, when opportunity smiled on Talbert Starcross Bramwell. He stumbled upon a way to quickly change his fortune. Miss Letty learned the whole truth much later. Her cousin, Wayne confessed that he regretted the day he told Talbert about Sybil Baldwin, a maiden lady, 32 years of age, who had returned to Georgia after living abroad most of her life. The only child of a wealthy shipbuilder who also owned a huge South Georgia plantation, Sybil was well educated, high spirited and, although she wasn't as beautiful as some who threw themselves at Talbert everywhere he went, Sybil was almost pretty, and filthy rich. Her Mother's death soon after Sybil was born, had left her to a loving Father who raised her with all the privilege his dotage could buy. Talbert had seen her once when they were children. He'd told his Mother how a skinny, plain girl never took her eyes off of him at Wayne's eighth birthday party.

Fuel was added to Talbert's fire when he learned that Sybil believed that owning slaves was the only proper way of life. She could keep an entire staff scurrying around the clock to satisfy her insistent demands. She was a girl after Talbert's own heart.

x x x

Talbert's plan went into effect when, fearing his anger, Talbert's cousin Wayne Starcross gave in and allowed Talbert to accompany him to Sybil Baldwin's New Year's Eve Charity Ball. Wayne told

Karma Rising

Miss Letty that Talbert never spoke a word during the more than two days' ride from Starcross to the Baldwin Plantation.

Talbert was very tall and extremely handsome, and, as the son of a distinguished family, he knew he would be a most welcome uninvited guest. At Baldwin, none of the fluttering debutantes and matrons had heard telling rumors that this fine figure of a man's Mother didn't own slaves and was some sort of weird recluse, who held the family purse strings with an iron hand.

On that crisp December night, the ballroom was in full sway, glowing with sparkling decorations, food, drink and fashionable guests from miles around. All movement in the Baldwin ballroom came to a standstill when the princely stranger appeared, seemingly from out of nowhere. His cousin had described Sybil to him; Talbert knew exactly what the prey he intended to capture looked like. That evening, Sybil was radiant with her curvaceous figure draped in the finest white Spanish lace. Her long, thick brown curls were pulled away from her face, minimizing her irregular features and enlarging her rather small eyes. She exuded the youthful, regal self-confidence that only education, travel and advantage could bestow.

Attired in a flawlessly tailored black silk evening outfit, accented with a creamy ruffled cravat, Talbert stood poised in the doorway. People in the room realized that something had just happened. All heads turned. Talbert's eyes searched the faces until he found her. His gaze rested on Sybil. He saw no one else. He caught and commanded her full attention. She turned away from a thin, attentive suitor to face Talbert with an inquisitive half-smile. Holding her eyes with his, he handed his cane, white gloves, top hat, cape and scarf to the waiting slave at his side, then walked slowly toward Sybil and bowed deeply. He kissed her extended hand and caressed it while he spoke softly to her. Even his cousin, Wayne, was impressed with Talbert's courtly approach, so much so that when he was forced to tell Miss Letty about it, Wayne could relate each moment of that first encounter in minute detail.

Sybil was swept off her feet. She was his before he asked her to join him in the dance. At the stroke of midnight, heralding the year 1849, she breathlessly consented to his rather matter-of-fact request for her hand in marriage.

Her Father, Jasper Baldwin, could deny his daughter nothing, but naturally, he had reservations about Sybil's two-hour courtship. His consolations were Talbert's good looks and his wealth. It was common knowledge that Talbert's family had far too much of everything, for an only son to have to stoop to gold-digging.

During the nuptial arrangements, Jasper was impressed with Talbert's modest request that slaves be added to Sybils's dowry; he respected Talbert's true explanation that he wanted to expand the Starcross business by planting cotton. Generous to a fault, Jasper committed Baldwin slaves, but he made it clear that they had been bred by his Father's hand, and were not to be abused or over-worked. Talbert agreed to what he regarded as a most peculiar stance. But then, Talbert would have agreed to anything.

Jasper was eager to get the wedding behind him in order to return to his shipyard. He selected the strongest, best trained slaves to plant and harvest cotton and to attend to Sybil's every demand. He added equipment to build and furnish cabins in the style that any modern plantation would require.

Talbert told his future Father-in-law that his poor sweet Mother was gravely ill and probably wouldn't be permitted by her physicians to attend the wedding. Since Talbert was well over the legal age of consent, it was fitting and proper for his cousin to handle the legalities of the union, representing the Bramwell family. Wayne carefully concealed the fact that Talbert had only a monthly allowance under his personal control, as per Talbert's instructions. Wayne did as he was told. He was very young and had not yet outgrown a childhood respect for Talbert's penchant toward a seething, unpredictable volatility.

Wayne smoothed over all the rough spots of the negotiations and even produced a warm congratulatory message, supposedly from Miss Letty. Miss Letty said she was amazed to eventually discover how adeptly Wayne had discouraged Jasper's overtures to visit Starcross before the wedding, citing unpredictable January weather and Miss Letty's delicate condition. It was the only time in his life that Wayne Starcross betrayed Miss Letty's trust. Only an act of God could have stopped the inevitable chain of events.

When the wedding arrangements were nearly completed, Jasper expressed his deepest concern regarding his daughter's betrothal. He explained to the couple that because of madness in the family, they must not have children. Being so close to the materialization of their separate dreams, Sybil and Talbert agreed. Children were not apart of Talbert's plan, anyway, and Sybil was too much in love to care.

Sybil and Talbert were married in a quiet winter ceremony in the Baldwin Chapel in February, 1849, with Wayne Starcross representing the Starcross-Bramwell family. Back at Starcross, Miss Letty had been curious as to what could have kept Talbert away from home for so many weeks, and she hoped he hadn't gotten himself killed. When the details of his whereabouts were revealed, Miss Letty finally realized that Talbert's long cherished dream had come true.

Homer stopped speaking. Transfixed, Ceeoni and Di were motionless.

Nasrene's whisper broke the silence,

"Well, well, well—I wonder if the illustrious. Miss Letty has more to say." She waited a few minutes. Homer remained in the relaxed state.

"Miss Letty," Nasrene asked, "Would you like to continue?"

In the still of the Rose Room there was no sound for several seconds, until Miss Letty's voice returned. This time she sounded weaker and emotionally drained.

x x x

'I recall that March day was dark, threatening rain. Avajay and I, tending a cauldron of corn and lima beans, heard the startling noises of horses and creaking wagons. Avajay opened the dining room window, then closed it quickly; her eyes shadowed by an unreadable expression, 'Letty,' she said, 'I believe its Talbert.' I heard the perplexed question in her tone. Talbert? Outside? I had enjoyed the peace of his absence, but after all, Starcross was his home. I braced myself, certain I was about to be confronted with an unpleasant surprise over one thing or another, but horses and wagons? I hurried to the front door and was met by an unfamiliar, resplendent black coach being vigorously wiped down by several slaves I'd never seen before, while others unhitched the team. The shining coach was heading up a line of wagons, wagons filled with slaves, men, women and children, back down the lane as far as my eyes could see. Good Lord! Enough slaves to work a plantation!

'The caravan had come to a halt, and a very much alive and well Talbert, wearing a seldom seen smile, assisted a tall young woman in dark blue velvet down from the coach. He nodded to me and said, 'Mother, I'm so glad you're feeling better. May I present your daughter-in-law, Sybil Baldwin Bramwell' Talbert turned to the man with kind eyes beside him, adding, 'And my Father-in-Law, Jasper Baldwin.'

'Avajay's somber expression transmitted a silent message that I could not ignore. As Sybil greeted me, I struggled to stifle any outward signs of my bitter chagrin at being elaborately outfoxed.

'When Sybil inquired politely after my fragile state of health I knew by her condescending manner that I was being regarded as a feeble-minded old fool and, whether I liked it or not, Talbert had won. After the brief introductions, my son refused to look at me. I stood in the cool air, with no choice except to welcome them with open arms, and back up whatever fandangled lies Talbert had told to have his way, to have his plantation.

'It wasn't until the slaves were busy constructing temporary common shelters, under the supervision of Talbert's newly acquired overseers, and the wedding party had retired to their chambers, that Avajay had the opportunity to talk to me.

'You did that very well,' she said. 'had you shown the slightest opposition, it would only create greater unhappiness for the new Mrs. Bramwell and accomplish nothing. Her Father is departing in the morning, and we must be ready to help the poor girl when she meets the real Talbert Bramwell.' She lowered her voice, 'Besides, it's too late. I've already seen the pregnancy that is to be, and the sinister cloud of tragedy in her light brown eyes.'

'Well, it wasn't long before it became obvious that building cabins and planting cotton required more work than Talbert had ever encountered. His wife's immediate, feared and unwanted pregnancy added to his frustration, all to which he responded with a glowering, resentful bearing. Although the slaves gave him no trouble, he expected trouble at every turn. His days were filled with a multitude of tasks that prohibited his usual dalliance, leaving him little time for drinking and whoring with his old friends of the landed gentry. Talbert got what he wanted but he lost what he had, and he knew it.

'Sybil had come to Starcross accompanied by a shirt-tail cousin she was grooming to become her personal maid, a large blond girl of twelve years. This girl was the strangest child I'd ever seen. Avajay said that the girl, Roxanne Baldwin, was a tortured Soul whose scorching and searing evil flared like a white-hot fire in her heart. Her physical development was far beyond that of a typical twelve-year-old, and her behavior was the kind that caused men to ignore their women. Handy with needle and thread, Roxanne assisted the slaves who kept Sybil's wardrobe, and, after her chores were done, Roxanne would tailor her own clothes, making bodices a little tighter causing her full breasts to bulge out over the tops of the garments.

'Sybil wasn't around when Avajay and I noticed how the girl flirted shamelessly with Talbert, every time she could. At the end of the day, Roxanne would take her sewing into the parlor and wait patiently for the jingles and clip-clops of the horse's bridle and hooves that announced Talbert's arrival. If Sybil came downstairs, a demure Roxanne would lower her head over her sewing. Otherwise, Roxanne would greet him, flushed and animated, dominating the conversation and trying to narrow the distance between Talbert and herself. I could see that he hated the girl, but he would never tell his wife of her bold ways. Talbert was thoroughly accustomed to brazen women and Roxanne helped to divert Sybil's attention, which gave him more time to sneak away to the Coach Stop Inn or to the taverns of Marthasville, I mean, Atlanta, they had renamed it in 1847.

'As it was, within a few months, Talbert began to spend most of his time away from home. Home to him had soon become nearly impossible. He could barely tolerate his wife's pregnancy, a state that caused her to become bigger, clumsier and increasingly more demanding. Oblivious to my consternation, and ignoring his wife's complaining tears, he would get up in the middle of the night and ride out for parts unknown, sometimes staying away until the next afternoon.

'One morning, as I was about to leave my bedroom, I saw Roxanne tiptoe past my partially open door. I widened the crack a little to see where she was going, but I guess I should have known. Talbert, dressed in black riding boots, black shirt and breeches, was headed for the stairs. Roxanne moved fast, considering that the far too large gold satin dressing gown, obviously pilfered from Sybil's armoire, hung off of her, and dragged on the floor. Talbert's sneer expressed his feelings, he looked at her as if the gown showed more skin than he cared to see on a twelve-year old. Roxanne laughingly grabbed his arm as he attempted to pass. When he pulled away, she hung on fast. A strap fell off one shoulder, but she succeeded in wrapping an arm around his neck, moaning and whispering in her oddly thin, hollow voice, while trying to snake one leg around his. He reached up to extricate her grip,

'Keep quiet, dammit! Don't wake Sybil up!'

'But most of her weight was swinging from his neck, while the fingers of her left hand clawed at his belt buckle, and he couldn't pry her loose. During their tussle, one full breast escaped and bounced against his chest. Giggling, she tugged at his arm, attempting to pull his hand toward it, but Talbert had reached the limit of his patience. He jerked his arms free. The sudden movement caused her to release her hold, and she slid, gasping and coughing, down the length of his body, to lay sobbing at his feet. His deep baritone spoke so slowly and quietly through clenched teeth, I could barely hear what he was saying,

'Never, ever do that again, or by God, I'll have you horse-tromped like a slave and sent the hell away from here!'

'She stared at him, her furor matching his, her twisted, tear-stained features had reddened and swollen into a grimace of pure hatred. She turned her head, gagged and vomited viscous brown liquid that splashed onto his polished boot. I thought he was bending to hit her, but instead he wiped his boot with a handful of the gown, while she, unmoving, watched him.

'Talbert,' she hissed, 'I'm warning you!'

He straightened up, frowning,

'Roxanne, you're too damn daft to warn anybody of anything. Cover yourself and clean up this Goddamn mess!'

'After he strode away, Roxanne shakily smoothed the gown, wiped her mouth with the back of her hand, and then began to sing in a tuneless soprano singsong. It was the first time I had seen evidence of her lunacy with my own eyes. She got to her feet, and her face turned toward me allowed a full view of her blank expression. She lifted the hem of the stained gown with both hands, and taking slow, teetering baby steps, I heard her repeat the phrase, over and over as she tip-toed down the hall,

'I'll pay you back, Talbert, someday, I will, I will, I will. I'll pay you back, Mister-son-of-a-bitch, bitch, bitch, LaLaLaLa—'

'Shocked by what I'd witnessed, I went first to fetch someone to clean the hall, then I hurried to find Avajay to tell her what had transpired.'

Homer stopped talking, but he continued to wring his hands in a gesture typical of an old woman's anguish. Nasrene awakened him after suggesting again that he would no longer feel any pain from that lifetime, and he would remember everything.

CHAPTER TWELVE

Homer opened his eyes, smiling. The smile grew wider when he saw Di and Ceeoni sitting there.

Nasrene felt his forehead,

"That was very impressive. How do you feel?"

"It was—it—was—amazing!" He spoke with his full natural, masculine voice, "The visions were so vivid. I was a woman! Over a hundred years ago. I was in a woman's body! I—I was Miss Letty! Damn! No wonder!" He sat up, "Now I know why I had to have Starcross. Nasrene, now I understand! When can we do this again?"

"I'm not sure, but I'd wait at least a little while. That must've been extremely stressful."

"Are you OK? It's always been an incredible experience for me. I'm glad I know what it feels like."

"I'm good, except I still feel dregs of Miss Letty's anxiety concerning Roxanne's infatuation with Talbert."

"Yeah, Homer," Diana said, "I picked that up, and it sounds like she had every reason to be anxious. Roxanne was something else, even at the tender age of 12. I bet her Soul is involved in what's happening here and now."

"I think you may be right, Di, but who knows for sure?"

"Well, you asked that I go back to events in my Soul memory that are affecting my life today," Homer said, "I don't know how it connects to the murder, but I can feel that there's some tie."

"Whatever it is, there's much more here than anyone could've imagined," Nasrene said as she packed up her notes. "Reincarnation is a rebirth of the Human Soul into all kinds of bodies, into all kinds of life situations, human bodies, that is. The great psychic

Edgar Cayce said that once a Soul has evolved to the human state, it doesn't revert to an animal's body. Homer, your Soul appears to be highly evolved. I'm struck by the seemingly intentional outpouring of information. I think the Soul develops spiritually, in a never-ending upward spiral, learning lessons of love. When completely evolved, the Soul will eventually become 'perfect in God,' to quote a phrase from the Bible.

'Metaphysicans say that the Soul, no longer needing a body to learn, becomes a Being of Light. Souls turn up in each other's lives in unusual roles, to learn. For example, your brother last time may be your daughter this time. The mailman this time may have been your aunt in a past life. The Bible states that we are to be separated one from the other, you know, father from son, brother from brother, etcetera. I believe it's because we are in fact one in spirit, and our earthly bodies and relationships are learning tools that teach us lessons of total love. I think the Bible is saying that we are to be separated from our concept of earthly relationships."

"Whoa! Thanks for that bit of insight," Homer said, "If I hadn't seen myself in that life, I never would've believed it. After that, I'll believe anything!"

"Well, wait'll you hear this. I learned of a housewife of Irish extraction who recalled, over a series of regressions, a long life as a Zulu warrior who had fathered fourteen children. She knew minute facts of nineteenth century Zulu hunting methods, customs, and intricate war strategies known only to a tiny elite group of Zulu historians. That, and all of the past life regressions I've conducted and read about are the reasons I think sexist and racist attitudes are the epitome of ignorance. Souls seem to cross lines of race and gender as freely as you change socks. Oh, Homer, I'm thinking it will give me time to review my notes if we can wait until tomorrow to continue. Is that possible? I'm on my own schedule here."

"OK, Ms. Nasrene, I guess I can put my curiosity on hold 'til then."

"That really was stunning!" Di said, "None of my regressions ever yielded up anything as extraordinary. The most exciting thing I encountered was a brief life as a kitchen helper for a wealthy family in 14th century Russia, but I died of a horrible disease. Just how do you feel?"

"My darling, I feel like I've been living inside a tiny room, and now I've stepped through an invisible door, and I'm standing on the Milky Way with planets and stars, whole galaxies whizzing by, while in the back of my mind I'm saying again and again, 'Damn, I've lived before!' Ceeoni, I couldn't imagine what was happening to you last night when you first entered the Manor, but now I know you had a peek at something I've become sure of." He added, "So we know I was Miss Letty, or I think I was Miss Letty, and we have an idea you also lived at Starcross, maybe at the same time! You're the only person here who has never been regressed. I can't wait to see who you were, Miss Cee."

"Uhh, sure, of course—" she murmured, avoiding his probing glance.

Homer, realizing he had been ignored, politely changed the subject,

"It's all been decided, Nasrene, we're taking you home to the Starcross Lakes Estates with us. We've got a houseful of rooms, spectacular food and good old fashioned Southern hospitality."

"I most definitely accept that offer, thank you, but I'm so thrilled by the extraordinary Miss Letty, I would pay you. I've heard of past life recall like yours, but I never had a client who was so concise and, I think the word is 'methodical,' during regression. Di, have you got something I can put on until I get over to Emory tomorrow?"

"I brought most of the Magic Closet with me, which means I have several 'somethings' I'm sure will fit you." For some mysterious reason, Di's Magic Closet contained clothes in nearly every size. Ceeoni had asked her many times what was she doing with so many sizes, only for Di to mumble something about not being able to pass up a bargain and, after all, most garments could be altered.

As everyone was moving toward the front door, Ceeoni's watch read 1:30am. She was quite content that no one was paying any attention to her. Her thoughts were swirling through her head faster than Homer's galaxies.

Homer answered a loud ring of the doorbell that blasted through their silence. Detective David Saxon ambled in, obviously tired, but dashingly attractive in an olive green trench coat.

"David, come on in. Where's R.C.? I thought he was with you."

"Yeah, Homes. I saw the lights and your car, and I knew you'd want an update. R.C. has been with me most of the evening but he's at the hospital now."

"Hospital?!" Homer shouted.

"Yeah, they let him stay 'cause he raised a fuss and refused to leave."

"What? For God's sake, what happened?"

The gray of Homer's eyes had turned to stormy charcoal. Ceeoni's heartbeat quickened. She searched David's face for a clue, but he was in his flat police mode.

"Well," he said, "The not-so-good news is that we found Adam Delayno. Seems that he'd been stabbed several times."

Ceeoni gasped. She sat down in the chair behind her with her fists clenched tightly together in her lap, trying to hold back a feeling that her stomach was sliding up toward her throat. Di glanced in her direction, and Ceeoni, seeing the glance, straightened, strengthening her resolve not to let the craziness of this situation overtake her lifelong common sense.

"He must've been left for dead because it appears he was hit with something heavy before he was stabbed," David said, then added, "In a few words, Mr. Delayno is alive, but he's in a coma."

The small voice inside Ceeoni's mind whispered, 'He's alive!'

"Delayno's wounds aren't severe enough to be life threatening, but he's lost a lot of blood."

"Where was he found?" Di asked.

"In the woods, adjacent to the theatre—actually, between here and the theatre. He was very lucky something prevented him from being more seriously wounded. Funny, the doctor said his coma is probably only temporary. We're trying to discover how he got into the woods in the first place, but we're reasonably certain Delayno was attacked by the same person who attacked Minette Coulter and killed Basil Cassidy. All three victims were all struck from behind first."

"When can we see him?" Ceeoni could hear her anxiety and tension in the sound of her own voice.

The Sane Ceeoni had heard it too, and answered, 'He doesn't know you! In this era of master stalkers who terrorize and sometimes end the lives of public figures, the last thing he needs is an overwrought total stranger hovering over his bed.' Ceeoni blinked to dispel the surreal voice in her head. From their unspoken language evolved over a lifetime of friendship, Di shot her the familiar 'What??!!' expression that Ceeoni pretended she didn't see.

Homer rescued the moment, "Ah, yes, Ceeoni, since Adam was assaulted while under contract to us, we are obligated to make a courtesy call, but it's nearly 2am. We'll go to the hospital in the morning. And I thank you, David. I knew you guys were on the case."

"I can't take credit for this one. It was R.C.'s idea to search the woods first. As a matter of fact, he emphatically insisted. I admit it was way down my list to look for Delayno in that area. I can't figure out why he was attacked, unless he was about to be kidnapped and it was aborted."

"You could be right about that," Homer said, "his international fame and money would make him a good candidate for a sizeable ransom. And while we're on the subject, it occurred to me that Basil Cassidy might have been killed by someone who mistook him for Adam."

"Good call. We're considering every possibility." David whipped out his dimples, "I have a dream that in a perfect world, the clouds will part, Delayno will awaken before the Atlanta Journal Constitution goes to press, and he'll immediately finger the assailant who will confess all the crimes the minute we pick him up, then you can get on with your theatre, and I can get some rest." Laughter eased the strain that weighed heavily in the air.

Ceeoni's mind drifted to the bare facts of the past few days; a killer is stalking Starcross—a killer who had already committed a savage murder, may have sabotaged her brakes, viciously attacked Minette and caused Adam's disappearance. Where will this murderer strike next? And why? The reality of it all made her very uneasy, indeed.

x x x

Sunday morning, Ceeoni awakened to the sound of Di bustling around the room, being as quiet as she could as she arranged and rearranged clothes. Her bed was covered with different outfits.

"Good morning! It's about time you greeted the sunshine. Now Nasrene can choose from a wide selection. It's all here, sizes nine and eleven, casual to killing."

Ceeoni propped up on pillows, "I can see what you mean about Nasrene, she seems like a very special person."

"I knew you would agree once you met her. She has such beauty of spirit."

"Is she from Los Angeles, too?"

"Yeah," Di answered, "She said she was born at that hospital they tore down a few years ago, Queen of Angels."

"Oh, yeah. Is she married?"

"No—she's a true workaholic. She's never been married. Nasrene and I always tease each other about waiting for our Soul Mates, but I don't think Nasrene could settle for anything else. As a naturally gifted psychic with skills in past life therapy, I believe her man will have to be the real deal, you know, someone with whom she has a true karmic bond."

"Well," Ceeoni said, "I think for those of us who wouldn't know a karmic bond from a savings bond, most relationships are a case of mistaken identity, 'Oh, excuse me, but I was praying and hoping you were someone else, or I thought you had a little more depth of mind', not to forget the Biggie, 'I thought you loved me'. It would be great to be psychic, able to spot the misfits and phonies from the beginning."

"Girl, wouldn't you? If Nasrene had ever embarked on a series of mistaken identity tangents like the rest of us, I'd be surprised. She plowed straight through UCLA, earned degrees in psychology and parapsychology, without taking time for the senseless ca-ca folks get themselves into. I have to keep reminding myself that all my mistakes were necessary karmic lessons!"

"Sounds like Nasrene's had a heavenly life with less embarrassing memories, rationalizations, regrets and apologies, huh?"

"All due to Nasrene's very rare blessing that most people never experienced, and that is her Mom who is a true psychic."

"Really?"

"Her mom only reads for people she feels she can help," Di said, "and she never charges for a reading. Nasrene said her mother taught her to wait for a spiritual connection before she gets involved or commits to anything. I've visited Nasrene when her Mom was there, and when meeting her I had the feeling she knew every single one of my secrets, but it was OK. It's hard to express. There's something about her that made me feel secure, like the universe is a safe place after all. She taught me that nothing and no one is ever lost in the Kingdom of God."

"What? People can get lost to evil, can't they? I mean, say for example, all the world's killers, crooks, and generally disruptive types, like that girl Homer spoke of in Miss Letty's time, uh, Roxanne?" Ceeoni ventured.

"Well, according to karma, a corrupt Soul may live many lifetimes, suffering and dying in his destructive beliefs, until he learns to love others and himself. 'The wages of sin is death.' I don't believe that's a false statement, our sight is short, we just don't see the wages in most lives. The choice is always up to the individual Soul. 'It is done unto you as you believe,' so if you believe in good, you do good, and good is what is done unto you. It's all there in the Bible."

"Hmmm—OK, but what about Hell?"

"What worse Hell could there be than to have to meet the same challenges again and again? To have to reap what is sown? To keep earning the wages of whatever those sins may be, and dying in those sins over and over again? Until when? Until the Soul has finally learned to cease and desist destruction of every type, and chooses to love, and that includes even the smallest lessons."

"Di, I've heard you say stuff like that in the past, but now I know. I mean, I really know! I've had a tremendous revelation here. I've seen my Soul's survival for myself, even though I don't know who I was. I apologize for not taking past life regression, reincarnation and karma seriously, but I thought it could only happen to those special psychic people, like you or Nasrene and her Mom."

"Yahoo!" Di cheered, waving a green silk scarf, "The answer to prayers! I wanted so much for you to know what this freedom feels like. Since you and I grew up without mothers, we had to develop a working philosophy to help overcome obstacles, on our own. I think it's important that we know that this world, this world of appearances isn't all there is. This world is only the tip of the iceburg. So much of what we see around us is unfair or doesn't make sense, but when we can see that we're all really eternal spirits having a human experience, it makes the pain in this world easier to take."

"You know, having a Mother could've made a difference, especially in our early years, but no mother could've given me this feeling. To know that something in me is eternal, to actually have memories of living a past life—Di, it's freedom itself."

"Now we've gotta' get your tail into regression to see if you go back to nineteenth century Starcross. There's a reason why Homer chose you. He said he knew you were the one."

Ceeoni left to turn on the shower, but Di wasn't finished. She called after her,

"You don't seem too eager to be regressed!"

Ceeoni didn't answer.

"OK, OK, I guess you have your reasons. We'll work that out. But getting back to Homer, I'm glad I was free when I met him—totally free. To quote Norma Rae, 'There was nobody else in my head.' In the past, I was making romantic choices based on the old appearance/hormone connection."

"Like everybody else in the world," Ceeoni shouted through the cracked bathroom door, "But how in the Sam-hill-hellfire can you know the difference? What's happened with you and Homer comes under the Big Miracle category. The rest of us have to bump around until the relationship shows it's true colors."

"Waiting a while to commit seems to be the best answer to that one except, even then, Mr. Universe could be Bubba the Bigamist, Carl the Crackhead, Don on the Down-Low, and don't forget Jack the Ripper."

"Di, we have a pretty good idea Homer isn't the Ripper, but how does it feel knowing his Soul occupied a woman's body?"

"Ha! The same way I felt when I found that I'd occupied a boy's body. I've seen only slices of a few of my lives during various regressions, but in this one life I was a happy kid on a farm, maybe around the middle of the nineteenth century, and my name was Monty."

"Oh, I remember. You mentioned that a few years ago, and I thought you had lost your mind for real! But now I think you need to be regressed again yourself. Since you and Homer seemed to recognize each other, I'll bet you were someone close to Miss Letty."

"Yeah," Di grinned, "I can hardly wait!"

"Di?"

"Mmmm?"

"What if, uh, what if someone you thought you knew, someone you trusted, was regressed, and it was discovered that this person had been a murderer, like Jack or Jackie the Ripper?"

"Oh that's easy! I'd get him before he gets me by attacking with a lethal weapon—" As Di said that, one of her bunny slippers came flying through the partially open bathroom door, just missing Ceeoni's head.

x x x

Di settled on a sleek navy crepe pinstriped suit, checked out her stylish reflection in the mirror, and went to find Homer. Ceeoni dressed slowly, reflecting on the mountain of new information that would take months for her to assimilate. She slipped into a long-sleeved periwinkle dress made of a luxurious silk blend. The way it fit gave her the confidence to face anything the day had waiting for her.

The weather was a perfect 74 degrees on Homer's patio, where they ate Weber's perfect brunch under a wide tan and white striped umbrella. Weber had outdone himself; grits, eggs with cheese, bagels, lox, baked chicken breast, spinach quiche, fluffy biscuits, steamed apples with cinnamon, juice, and his wonderfully rich coffee.

Putting down her fork with a sigh, Di said, "Homer, I'm gonna' have to bail out of these big meals. Eating like this, I'll weigh 300 pounds in a few weeks."

"There'll just be more of that fine brown frame to love," Homer said with a wink.

Diana gave Homer the 'get back vampire' sign of the cross.

Nasrene, agreed, "Yeah, we gotta' stop saying we're gonna' stop, and get involved in the Do, but it's so easy to give in to Weber's temptation."

"On that note," Homer announced, "We might as well take the temptation all the way! Our first stop will be the Starcross Restaurant for dessert and to catch the Sunday Open Mike Jazz Jam, featuring the best music in the South. After that, the hospital visiting hours should be in full force. I just spoke to Detective Saxon, and Adam's brother is on his way to Atlanta. Oh, by the way, the Starcross brunch is really nice, but the food is better at Weber's Kitchen."

Weber flashed a pleased smile at the compliment, as he helped Ceeoni and Nasrene clear the table.

They walked into the crowded restaurant in the middle of a lyrical guitar solo that Ceeoni recognized, 'Funny Valentine', one of her favorite songs. The lush rendition filled her thoughts and gave her a feeling of peace. Beautiful music always reached Ceeoni's mood centers. She didn't hear anything else until the last note of the song drifted away. They followed Kevin, the sophisticated Maitre D', who sat them at the only table left. She let the music wrap her up in its multi-colored fluidity. She tasted every texture until the vocalist finished the Rogers and Hart masterpiece.

The singer came over, and introduced himself, "Mr. Dinsmore, my name is Eric Nightengale, do you have a request?" Homer whispered something into the clean-cut young man's ear. When the set began, the blind pianist was introduced as Howlett Smith, a composer from Los Angeles who set the mood with two lovely original tunes. This Sunday jam turned out to be a rare treat. The guests were romantic male balladeers, the likes of which she hadn't seen 'live' since the 80s.

Guitarist Pete Fox introduced the guest vocalists: Eddie Walker, who sang a lush, plaintive '*Come In From The Rain*'; and George Smith, who brought the room nearly to tears with '*If She Walked Into My Life Today*' from "Mame". His warm voice caressed the words, as Ceeoni wondered why the song made her feel so sad. She didn't know a single man she would want to walk back into her life again.

Minette waved slightly when she saw them, but the crowd was keeping her busy. Wearing a tailored pale yellow raw silk hostess gown, she seemed to be everywhere at once. Her expertise was evident in the way she directed the staff in between meeting and greeting customers.

"Is the place always this crowded?" Di asked.

"Yep," Homer chuckled, "And a lot of the credit goes to Minette." Diana tossed a cool glance in Minette's direction, that Homer didn't miss.

"Minette has her ways," he said, "but I hired her 'cause she came in here while we were building, handed me a knockout resume, and described what she'd do with the restaurant. She has a military background, having served in Desert Storm, but what sold me was the fact that she had managed one of my favorite restaurants, Cunningham's, in Dana Point, California. I let her hire her chef and staff, Weber and I field-tested the recipes, and she's been going at it 24/7 ever since. Excuse the corny way of describing the truth, but the South side was starving for a good restaurant."

"Is she, married? Divorced, or?" Di sounded only vaguely interested.

Ceeoni knew she wasn't disinterested at all, and Homer's perceptive answer was a shining example of a response to a lady's subtle signal for reassurance. He looked down into her eyes as he explained,

"I was impressed with Minette's resume, and I have a real appreciation of her dedication and background, but for some reason, I was never interested in anything else."

Diana leaned over so that only Nasrene and Ceeoni could hear.

"Maybe we can do some more past life regressions to see if Minette's cold Soul fits into this drama, and if so, where?"

Ceeoni agreed in silence. Minette did have an unusual kind of energy emanating from her persona, possibly because of a yen for Homer and/ or his money? Or what?

The band played an arpeggio, and the vocalist announced, "This is a special dedication to Diana", before singing the beautiful Etta

James classic, "At Last." Homer pulled Di close to him, with her head resting on his shoulder. After years of trials and tribulations, Di had finally been blessed with a love she never dreamed possible. As the last notes of the song died, Ceeoni felt as happy for Di and Homer as if her own heart had found it's home.

Diana's early life had begun with an abusive father and an incoherent alcoholic mother who had frightened and scattered their three children to the four winds and the kindness of strangers. When Ceeoni brought Di home every day back in elementary school, Eddie Jones correctly read the situation and immediately accepted her as another daughter. She was only seven years old, and nobody seemed to care about her comings and goings, her schoolwork, or whether or not she had clean clothes or a decent meal. Her two younger siblings were already in foster homes when her parents caused a head-on collision with a car carrying a family of four that no one survived.

With red swollen eyes, Diana came to school the next morning as if nothing had happened, and she followed Ceeoni home that afternoon, as usual. Eddie Jones, with the newspaper article about Di's parents rolled up in his blue mail carrier's jacket, knew he was the one who had to talk to the little girl about the accident.

"Di, you know I told you guys that God is always watching over us, don't you?"

Diana sat in the Jones' Leimert Park living room, with her tiny hands folded in her lap; her enormous eyes, as old as the ages, bore the weight of too much pain.

"Yes," she whispered, dropping her head, while tears poured down her cheeks. Eddie pressed on.

"God sometimes makes decisions that we don't always understand."

"I don't—I don't, I don' wanna' go with my Auntie," Diana sobbed, "I wanna' stay here with you!"

Ceeoni never forgot Eddie's stammered reply.

"Well, it's not up to me, Baby, we'll just have to see—"

Suddenly, Di screamed, "God took them away 'cause they were bad!"

"No, no, honey. They weren't bad," Eddie said as he hugged the thin form. "They, they just couldn't figure it out. Life is harder for some of us. Always remember that they loved you, in spite of their problems."

He made arrangements for Di to stay with the Jones' on the weekends, and summers. The Aunt turned out to be a busy distracted sort who, after having fulfilled her basic obligation to her brother's child, was glad to let Di spend most of her time with the Jones family. Di shared Ceeoni's room, and helped her get over the fact that her older sister, Sarah, largely ignored her. Ceeoni was happy to have a real sister, as well as a hand with the cooking and cleaning. Di healed fast and became a happy, inquisitive child who helped them both grow up stronger and more capable than they could have had they grown up alone. Eddie used to joke and say that Di and Ceeoni were raising themselves, but they knew better. They knew it was Eddie's well-balanced, understanding love that fueled their steady flight into maturity.

CHAPTER THIRTEEN

R.C. sat outside of Adam's hospital room wearing the smile of a whole tent-full of happy campers. He stood and squeezed Nasrene's hand as they were introduced.

"So happy to meet you R.C.," she said. "Detective Saxon told us Adam's in a coma."

"Oh—I'm not so worried now," R.C. rubbed his eyes, saying, "His coma is quite an unusual state, but in spite of it, the doctors believe that he's just fine. I've been here all night calling friends and family. Adam's brother keeps calling for regular updates, but there isn't much to tell anybody, because they don't know what's wrong with him."

"What do they think caused his injuries?" Homer inquired.

"Of course, no one knows for sure, but he's a very lucky man because he sustained a blow to the back of his head, and a series of stab wounds on his back and shoulders, but he has no serious trauma, no seizures, and only moderate swelling. They took a CAT scan and he has no blood clots, no broken bones, no internal spinal fluid build-up. He required a few stitches on the back of his head; the blow opened a large gash there. He did lose a lot of blood between that and his stab wounds. He required more stitches to close two of the wounds under his shoulder blades, but that's under control, no major organs were involved. Physically, he could get up and go home, and his strength is building rapidly. The part that makes no sense is the coma. Dr. Sakaya says there's no physiological reason for it, according to all of the neurological and medical measurements.

"I've been talking to him, playing his CDs and his favorites from other artists. I've been singing, reading the sports page, poetry, and everything else I can think of. He hasn't moved a muscle, but

I believe he will. I'm just glad we found him in time before he lost more blood, or infection set in."

Homer pushed the room door open, asking, "R.C., is it OK to go in?"

"Sure, he's in perfect health, although he's probably a little sore. The staff here is great, they stabilized him in record time, now they're waiting for autographs. Since he isn't in any danger, the Doctor gave permission for any stimuli to be applied that may possibly jog his memory."

"So little is known about coma," Di said. "Each case is different. People have responded to a familiar voice, or held an object or smelled favorite foods. Anything meaningful to the patient could trigger an awakening."

Nasrene spoke to R.C., "I've never had the pleasure of meeting Adam Delayno, but I am a licensed hypnotherapist, and I also practice past life regression therapy."

"Wow! Really? I've read quite a bit about that, and I know a bass player who goes to seminars where he says he's experienced several of his past lives."

"Great! Any familiarity with my profession is refreshing. I don't meet many people who are aware of hypnosis, or what can be healed through hypnosis. and through past life regression. Anyway, Mr. Ponder, I'd like to try to reach him through hypnosis. I don't know if hypnotic suggestion has ever been attempted while the subject is in a coma, but I'd like to make a run for it."

"Call me R.C. and c'mon in here," he teased while ushering her through the door, "I know Adam Delayno better than I know my own brothers, and during those late night, half-tipsy, we'll-save-the-world conversations on planes, buses, boats and trains, he's always expressed keen interest in hypnosis and mind exploration. I know he'd be open to it."

Everybody shuffled chairs, and got comfortable, while Nasrene took the chair beside Adam's bed.

"Many people fear hypnosis," she said, "but I can assure you it won't harm him, and it might bring him back. Will somebody please lower the lights?"

Placing her chair a discreet distance from Adam, Ceeoni shifted in her seat in order to have a full view of his face. Unexplained nervous spasms shook her insides. His long, spread fingers, still and somehow helpless, rested on each side of his body. She wanted to touch him. Breathing deeply and steadily, he seemed too big for the bed. A floaty sense of unreality took the room away, and Adam was all she could see. Her gaze traced his wonderful features; high cheekbones, his full, beautifully shaped mouth, and his heavy eyebrows that arched over closed eyes, fringed with silky lashes. She couldn't stop looking at him. R.C. clicked on Adam's recording of Stevie Wonder's love song, 'Too Shy To Say' and the song's melody and lyric seeped into her mind. 'And I can't go on this way, feeling stronger everyday—'

Through the invisible door to her unbidden emotions, she tried to sort out the stirrings she felt just hearing Adam's music, or his name.

Nasrene spoke in a matter of fact, friendly tone,

"Mr. Delayno, Adam, I'm Nasrene Asher, and R.C. gave me permission to talk to you. I hope you and I will be friends. I am a therapist trained to uncover and remove blocks in the unconscious mind. Your recordings are among my all time favorites. I'm going to awaken you now, because you have to come back to keep playing and writing. The world needs your music. Your music heals and brings great joy to a multitude of Souls. You are one of those chosen to pass Music of the Universe out to the world."

No response. Nasrene began the process again, suggesting that he will awaken. She repeated the suggestions again and again, only to meet Adam's unresponsive silence. Everyone in the room focused on the softly shadowed scene. Ceeoni wondered if this could possibly do Adam any good.

Nasrene hesitated for several minutes, before she spoke again,

"You are going back in time, back to another time—back to a time that directly relates to the events that have happened in your life during the past few days."

Nobody moved. For a brief moment, Ceeoni was surprised that Nasrene had switched to the past life regression techniques, but on second thought, the idea was to try to reach him using whatever means possible. Right then, he was out of reach; his consciousness lost in a place beyond the scope of modern medicine.

Nasrene repeated herself several times—then she slowly completed the regression, speaking carefully, "Can you tell me your name?"

Everyone was startled to hear Adam reply in the small voice of a very young child,

'Mah name Elijah, 'n ahm uh slave.'

x x x

Adam's voice was no longer the smooth baritone with husky depths that had thrilled her in media interviews and throbbed up and down her spine during Friday's concert. It was disconcerting to hear the hesitant, frightened little boy's whisper coming from Adam's splendidly mature physical form. No one in the room moved during Elijah's testimony.

Elijah said the year was 1849 and he was close to his eighth birthday. Now he had very important things that must be remembered, all the time. His Mama would explain the new rules to him over again, telling him that he had to remember, but he would forget and his Mama would be mad. She didn't get mad enough to tell his Daddy, because they both knew his Daddy would tan his hide. Elijah didn't mean to forget; it would just happen.

The Big Rules were:

Never, ever talk back to any white person, for any reason.

Do not speak unless you have to speak. Sometimes a white person will try you, and if you don't say anything, they'll leave you alone. If you have to answer, answer in as few words as possible.

Never speak fast or loud.

Never look a white person in the eye unless you are told to do so. Keep your head down, and say 'Yes ma'am', and 'No, sir'. Always work hard. No playing until Sunday, Christmas and the day after harvest.

He was curious about everything, and he asked questions whenever they occurred to him, many times in a voice loud enough to be heard by the overseer, who would warn his Mama, 'Verna, keep that boy quiet up there!'

Karma Rising

He loved his parents very much, but he had only a dim understanding of consequences, danger, or the proper way a slave was supposed to behave. He didn't have any idea that something he could do would cause trouble for his parents.

Elijah and his Mama and Daddy had come to Starcross from their home, the Baldwin Plantation, when Miss Sybil married Massa Bramwell, but this Starcross place didn't feel good. He'd heard tell of the whippin' post from cabin gossip, but he never saw one because there was no such thing at Baldwin. But here, a whippin' post stood in the barn. The sight of people with fresh shredded bloody sores among long festering welts, the voices screaming amid the whistling cracks of the lash snapping in his ears at all hours of the night, terrified him. He would awaken in a cold sweat, crying, and only his Mama's gentle prayers could lull him back to a restless sleep.

His Mama prayed that her family would be sent back to Baldwin like Mr. Baldwin said they could. At Baldwin, families were encouraged to stay together. Activities and rest time were a part of their lives, and food was varied and plentiful. His Mama said the new Massa had a devil, like all the rest of the slaveholders. They didn't care if the slaves were overworked, underfed and torn up from the lash. The Baldwin slaves had never been whipped, but Mistuh Baldwin had stayed only one night, and now he was far, far away.

Elijah made every effort to do as he was told. There was an enormous amount of work, and Massa Bramwell would turn up at the most unexpected times, looking to see if anybody was slacking. A few times, Massa nearly caught Elijah talking to his friends instead of working, and once, Massa soundly thumped him on his head as Elijah hid behind a tree in a forbidden game. Elijah knew how lucky he had been to get off with a single thump. His heart had almost stopped when he saw Massa, but the big man must've been in a hurry, he just took a swat at Elijah, and kept on riding by.

The slaves were always tired, even the strong ones who had never known the whip. His Mama said the food, corn meal mush and greens, with a small portion of fatback now and then, just wasn't enough. Elijah saw this as another way his little life had changed to a miserable existence.

After they had been in this strange place for only a few weeks, Miss Sybil and someone named Miss Letty made sure some new food was sent to the slave food lines. They said Massa didn't like it one bit because more food cost money, but Miss Sybil had backed up Miss Letty by threatening to talk to Mistuh Baldwin about it, although they could tell Miss Sybil acted like she feared Massa as much as the slaves did. Elijah's Mama said that Massa gave in about the food to keep Mistuh Baldwin from coming around to visit. Hominy and beans were added to the slave tables. He wasn't hungry all the time anymore, but he wanted to go back to Baldwin. He wanted to go back home.

Back at Baldwin, Elijah had been one of the boys who cleaned the stables and helped out with the horses. The best thing at Starcross was that he was still allowed to help his Daddy, Niles, and his friend, Phineas in the stables on Sundays.

Everyday, he was happy to get to his family's cabin in the evening so he could just be himself. Most nights, he was too tired to play. He would lay on his pallet and dream of his life at Baldwin and how he had felt when he lived in a place where he worked hard, but it wasn't scary. He was tired of remembering the rules, tired of his sore, bloody hands that had no time to heal. He was tired of having to watch out for Massa, who would creep up and sit on his horse under the drooping tree limbs, watching and listening for any sign of laziness. Massa Bramwell moved around so quietly, Elijah never knew he was there until the cold-eyed man was right up on him.

All the slaves knew that the slightest infraction was met with harsh reprimand. The offender was punished according to how many times he'd offended in the past, along with extra lashes for the latest crime. If after the whipping, the slave was still conscious, he was sent stumbling back to the fields, and no one was allowed to tend his wounds or help him with his share of the work.

Elijah was confused by how much the picture of Jesus, hanging in the bare room upstairs in back of the church, looked like Massa. The slaves could go there for Church on Sunday where Miss Sybil would read the Bible, and sometimes they would sing. Elijah was afraid of the picture of Jesus. It looked like Massa was staring back at him. His Mama said she had a feeling in her bones that the Massas

Karma Rising

just wanted the slaves to be scared, so they made the picture of Jesus look like them. She said nobody knows what Jesus looks like and, if he did look like a man, Massa Bramwell would be the last man in the world Jesus would look like.

No slaves escaped for the first few weeks they lived at Starcross, but soon, slaves began to disappear without a trace, which caused Massa to get meaner and meaner. Every time a slave ran away, it got worse. Massa would go out with some of the neighbors and overseers to try to find them, but they never brought anybody back. He hired two more overseers, and watched and listened, and held more beatings to get information that nobody would give him, if they could. The patrols would stay out all night, but still slaves came up missing from Starcross and surrounding plantations, confounding the hunters. They posted sentries, questioned everyone, and injured many in their search for the truth. His Mama said they were blessed that no one had been whipped to death, so far. Elijah's voice wavered, and a tear slid down his cheek; suddenly, he cried out in a half sob, 'Nobody know how dey gits away! Nobody know!'

The forlorn sound of his childish whimper caused Ceeoni to grip her own hands tightly to suppress her naturally instinctive desire to cross the room, put her arms around him and hold him.

Nasrene immediately began the awakening process, saying, "You are leaving this lifetime now, you feel no pain and no desire to react to the experiences of that lifetime. The pain is getting smaller. It is shrinking, shrinking, down to the size of a grain of sand, until it completely disappears."

Nasrene continued, applying the suggestions in gradual steps, "You will remember everything. When I reach the number '5', you will awaken fully alert, fully refreshed." She counted to five, but there was no response. She repeated the sequence. When Adam still failed to respond, she suggested that he return to the state he was in when she began the session.

Another tear ran down Adam's cheek as he took a deep breath, and obviously relaxed.

"Don't be alarmed," Nasrene said, "Usually, tears are apart of the healing process."

She turned off the tape recorder, and the loud 'click' seemed to snap everyone out of a common trance. Homer sighed and leaned back in his chair saying, "So Adam returned to Starcross, like I did last night, and his name was Elijah Baldwin. Elijah Starcross was the name of the slave who inherited Starcross, and left the property to a former slave named Phineas Baldwin. Damn! Where is the meaning or connection in these pieces?!"

"What?" R.C. asked, "What do you mean?"

"Oh, yeah, I forgot you didn't know. Nasrene took me through a past life regression, and I went back, well, back to, I actually saw myself, and I—"

Waving away Homer's hesitation, R.C said,

"Look, my friend, after what I just saw, my understanding has been stretched to include more than I could ever imagine. Please continue."

"OK," Homer answered, "I had visions of nineteenth century Starcross, and I, I was Miss Letty! I talked about being born here in 1782, and dying here at the age of 92, and like Adam's, my voice changed. The fact is, I saw what I saw. They were my memories, R.C. It sounds much more complicated than it was. They were simply my memories."

"And I had a profound deja vu experience when I first walked into the Manor," Ceeoni added, "I knew exactly where everything was located in that house."

"This is astounding!" R.C. said, "Adam was alive, right here, and Homer was alive? Alive! Only they were different, different people? Over a hundred years ago? And Ceeoni, you're apart of this too! Have you been regressed?" She shook her head. "When are you going to be regressed?"

Everyone's eyes were on her. Searching for words, Ceeoni had no time to identify what she was feeling; her mind was blank. She bit her lip. Nasrene, reading her tacit frustration, changed the subject.

"Then we need to discover how the information from that time relates to current events, only at this point, we have such sketchy information. I'm amazed at the easy flow of the testimonies. I've never encountered such clarity! It's certainly beyond any I've ever read about. You know, a lot of people fear past life regression because they think they wouldn't be able to handle the pain of the past. In spite of the suggestion to view the past as if watching a movie, there are people who still react and the therapist should be aware of that fact. Some have reported all sorts of experiences in that frontier that is forever under exploration, and our understanding of it is constantly expanding.

"Past life therapy allows the Soul to find what the Soul believes to be the source of the pain, where it is examined, reduced, and then discarded. A classic example is the client who was deathly afraid of cats. During past life therapy, she regressed to a lifetime as a Christian who had been killed by lions in the Roman sports arena. Believing that to be true released her from her fear. And she was also relieved of the unreasonable rage she'd carried all her life, until she realized the source of her anger."

"Well," R.C. asked, "What was it? Why was she enraged?"

"Because her deeper mind recalled being killed simply for someone else's amusement."

"Now that's enough to make anybody real mad," Homer commented.

"The best part is that she now owns a cat. Regression works. It is definitely faster than psychotherapy and certainly worth the effort, although no one really knows why."

"OK," Diana said, "During Adam's regression, when you gave him instructions to go to a life that relates to today's events, he went to nineteenth century Starcross and he sounded as if what he had to say was another piece of what Miss Letty was talking about. Nasrene, I was wondering if Adam's Soul could possibly have chosen to remain in limbo, deliberately?"

R.C. snapped his fingers. "Bingo!" he shouted, "I was wondering the same thing!"

"I'm as much in the dark here as you, and I'm no medical doctor," Nasrene said, "but I would guess that Dr. Sakaya's diagnosis of Adam's coma is correct. His condition has no neurological or medical basis and I've never heard of anyone doing what he just did while in a coma. The first thing I thought is that there is a powerful metaphysical force at work here."

"It sounds incredible, but could it be that Adam needs to tell us something?" Homer asked, "Something that can only be told by probing the past through past life regression?"

"Yes, yes and yes!" Nasrene waved a fist, "You two plowed on during your testimonies, with no digression, purposefully, and that's the best description. Purposefully." She stopped and jotted something down in her Journal. "I'm trying to get everything recorded. This case is bound to bust open the record books."

R.C. touched her shoulder, "Would Adam's doctor know anything about this?"

"I've decided not to share my findings with Dr. Sakaya, neither do I plan to mention the subject. Some physicians don't respect any school of thought outside of their formal training, in spite of unassailable evidence. I wouldn't want to risk possible intervention that would prevent us from continuing."

"We've got to keep going," R.C. said, "I believe it's important to Adam."

The nurse who came in the room to check Adam's IV introduced herself as Evelyn Michaels.

"Please push the call button if there's any change or if anyone needs anything. I'm monitoring his vitals from my station, but my guess is that Mr. Delayno is as healthy as he'll ever be. He's going to get up from there and be playing the piano before you know it."

"We believe that, Nurse Evelyn," R.C. said.

In search of a vending machine, Ceeoni squeezed past the nurse to the quiet hallway, at which time the Sane Ceeoni took over. 'Well, we know for sure that Adam and Homer lived at Starcross at the same time. Why are you avoiding the subject of regression every time it comes up? It doesn't look like past life regression hurt them any. Why didn't you answer R.C.'s question? What are you afraid of?' She chased her supercritical factor away along with any thought of past life regression.

Ceeoni rolled the cartful of vending machine munchies into Adam's room while Nasrene was discussing the work of the great psychic, Edgar Cayce, who was known as the Sleeping Prophet of the Twentieth Century. Di had mentioned him quite frequently.

Karma Rising

"Cayce died in 1945," Nasrene said, "Once he discovered his rare psychic abilities, he spent the rest of his life diagnosing and treating illness in people located a world away from the couch where he lay in a hypnotic trance. His arsenal of remedies included exercises, castor oil packs, vitamins and dietary corrections, all of which have proven more and more effective as new discoveries emerge. Cayce left thousands of well-documented files that are open to the public at the Edgar Cayce Society headquarters in Virginia Beach, Virginia.

"Included in these Cayce files are the transcriptions of over two-thousand 'life readings.' When Cayce did a life reading for the first time, he was shocked that he had told a patient how a past life experience was affecting her present life. Since he was always out of touch with what he had said during his trances, imagine his surprise when he learned he had told another client that she had walked with Jesus.

"Cayce could send his Spirit around the world or back through time, and forward into the future, which, by the way, is being done frequently nowadays. You would think that more reincarnation research would be in progress since doctors, dentists, psychiatrists, psychologists and hypnotherapists have observed their patients unintentionally, as if by accident, regress to other lifetimes during other types of treatment. Only in recent years has past life regression been regarded as a viable tool to diagnose and treat a wide variety of conditions in a few places. And it doesn't matter if it's 'real' or not, people insist that they've experienced this phenomena, they believe it, and have amazingly accurate details of that past reality."

Homer spun Di's chair around, with her in it, so that she faced him,

"Wait just a dang minute, Di-Di! You never said how you feel about my Soul having once occupied a woman's body."

"Sweetheart, I was telling Ceeoni about that this morning; I feel the same way I felt knowing I'd occupied a boy's body. No-thing." She nuzzled his cheek, "But I'm glad we're in the bodies we're in now!" Homer hugged her with exaggerated raised eyebrows, making everybody laugh.

"Get used to it," Nasrene chuckled. "Like I said, the Soul is androgynous; these bodies are chosen to teach us a thorough understanding of the Circle of Life. I think that when Jesus told us that we are eternal souls, nobody believed him, and there are some people who haven't had a past life experience, may never believe it, ah, but those of us who have seen these past visions, we know, beyond a shadow of a doubt—we know."

CHAPTER FOURTEEN

After chips, nuts and candy were washed down with awful machine coffee, R.C. made sure that the staff wouldn't intrude by advising the nurse's station that they were about to observe an hour of meditative silence. Nasrene was free to try to reach Adam again. She turned on the tape recorder and began the relaxation techniques. Adam didn't respond to any of her awakening suggestions. When she suggested that he was going back to a time that relates to recent events in his life, Elijah's child's voice suddenly returned, giving everyone a bit of a jolt.

'Yasum'

"Elijah?"

'Yasum'

"Where are you?" Nasrene asked.

'Starcross'

"Do you have something to say?"

Elijah began to speak slowly, saying that he had turned eight, which meant he was a bigger boy now. Some slaves didn't know their birthdays but he could write his, June 6, 1841. He knew all of his letters and numbers because Phineas was teaching him to read. Phineas was teaching all the children although at Starcross, it was forbidden. Miss Sybil had taught Phineas to read, and back home, nobody thought anything about it when he taught the others.

Since writing tools were unavailable and the utmost secrecy had to be kept, Phineas used the common method of drawing letters in the dirt at his feet, whenever there was no one around. As a result, Elijah and many of the slaves could write some words and simple sentences. Phineas had more freedom than the other slaves. He was the only person Miss Sybil trusted to drive her carriage. He could repair any breakdown, and he knew everything there was to know about horses. Miss Sybil told everybody that Phineas talked to horses and they talked back to him, and Elijah believed it. The horses would do things for Phineas that Elijah didn't know a horse could do. They came to him when he called, and they danced, prancing and tossing their manes as he sang. Phineas said that everybody can learn from a horse.

The trouble began on a beautiful afternoon when Elijah was helping his big friend, Phineas, wash down Miss Sybil's carriage. It was a fine four-seater, big and black and shiny, with red velvet seats and red velvet window covers that had fuzzy red balls swinging from the edges. Phineas polished one of the wheels until it gleamed. 'Lijah, ah reed de Bible all da way fru tree time,' he held up three fingers, 'En each time ah reeds it, ah loins suthin new.'

'Wha do it say?' Elijah kept on polishing hard, trying to get his wheel to sparkle like the one Phineas was finishing.

'Oh, it say many, many teengs,' Phineas answered, 'It say bout da ways peeples gits in trubble, en how wen dey trusses in God, dey allus wins. It say ta have fait, eben wen you cain see.'

'Ah wants ta reed it fo m'sef sumday,' Elijah answered quietly. Phineas stopped polishing. 'Lijah, reedn is bout de mos impotan teeng ya kin loin ta do. Teengs is gon be diffren, en it won be long.' Enthusiasm glowed in Phineas' face and he worked faster as he talked about what he thought the future held.

'Dis slave teeng ain gon las foh ebber, iss tarrn da cuntry apar. Wen ah drives Miss Sybil, ah reeds da paypuhs wen ain nobodah lookin'. De Naut don lak wha gon on down heah. De Sout got slaves foh nuttin en da othas has ta pay uh man foh de wuk he do. Iss been gon on foh ovah two-hunn'ed yeahs, en ah knows it cummin ta uh enn. Ah don know how oh wen but ah knows. Lijah, one day ya gon be free, dat why ya gots ta know how ta read!'

Suddenly, from out of nowhere, Massa Bramwell had snuck up and was standing next to Phineas, and he was mad. Elijah stopped still. Phineas and Massa were very tall, and from Elijah's eight-year-old point of view, and he was big for his age, they were giants, blocking out the sun. Phineas looked Massa straight in the eye. Massa glared at Phineas, with an anger that glowed hard gray like the time the pond froze over and turned to icy glass. They stood like that for a long time.

Phineas didn't move a muscle. Massa's rumbling voice growled slowly, 'Phineas, ain't no slave supposed to be bothering about books or trying to learn to read. Now, I heard tell of a few, but they were the exception. The majority of y'all couldn't learn something that complicated. Anyway, there's punishment for any slave caught with a book, and I know you don't want to get this boy in trouble, do you? Do you?'

'Naw Suh', Phineas answered, never lowering his eyes.

Talbert Bramwell turned away, seemingly satisfied. As soon as Massa was out of earshot, Phineas relaxed. 'See, Lijah? Fust, dey teeng ya dum caus dey brung ya heah in chain, but my Pa say, 'Ya may have chain on ya hans, but ain' no chain on ya mine.' He pointed to his head. 'Don ya fogit dat, Lijah!'

Elijah was very impressed seeing Phineas stand up to Massa like that, but he couldn't help thinking that it was a gift from God that Massa didn't hear Phineas say he had read the Bible all the way through three times.

Whistling happily as he finished his side of the carriage, Elijah's stomach sank when he saw Miss Sybil's crazy cousin, Roxanne, come from behind the shed. Phineas nodded to her, and led one of the horses away. Uh-oh. Elijah found himself alone with her. Elijah thought of her as the Devil Girl, because his Mama said she was born evil from the inside out and she was growing up to mean nobody no good. She looked real funny to him with her pale white skin that revealed bluish veins in some places, and her popped, almost transparent eyes that stared in a scary way. She had no eyebrows. The light yellow hair was wrapped in thick braids around her long narrow forehead. She smiled slightly at him, stretching her too-wet thin lips to show small pointy teeth. Her square prominent chin added to her ugliness, and he knew from his earliest memories that it was best to stay away from her. Back at Baldwin, he had seen her wring a friendly kitten's neck for no reason that he could understand. She was always hiding in shadows, watching the slaves, at the oddest times and places. Still polishing, Elijah moved further away from her to the opposite side of the carriage.

He looked back over his shoulder to see if she was still there, and was relieved to find that she was gone. But he was wrong. He heard her call from the carriage shed, 'Hey, boy, come here!' At first, he acted like he didn't hear her. 'Hey! I said come here!' She said, loudly.

He waved to her as she stood inside the shed door. 'Hi do, Miss Rockann' She was growing impatient, 'Dammit, Elijah, come here!'

He slowly put down his polishing rag and ventured as close to the doorway as he could without moving within her reach, but she took a quick step forward and snatched him into the shed by his shirt. To his horror, he saw that the small building was empty.

She grabbed his arm and twisted it up behind him, 'Oww-owww!' he cried.

He was a big strong boy, nearly as tall as she was, but he was unprepared for the fury of her attack. Even if she hadn't twisted his arm, she had the advantage because he didn't dare fight her.

'Shut up, and don't ask me how I am! 'Hi do Miss Rockann' she mocked him in a high-pitched imitation of his voice. Nobody could save him now. Save him from what? What did she want, anyway? Still applying pressure to his twisted arm, she backed him up against the wall and hissed into his ear, 'You be quiet, and do what I say, you hear?' Through glazed, half closed eyes she stared at him while pushing her warm fleshy body hard up on his. She began to move, slowly, rubbing back and forth against him, and her breathing got faster. He was terrified. Her high voice breathed in his ear, 'I heard what Old Phineas said! I heard it all, and I'm going to tell that he can read! I'll tell, I will! And Talbert will beat both of you with one of his big, long whips, within an inch of your lives!'

Elijah knew she was right. If Massa found out Phineas could read, not even Miss Sybil would be able to help him. Phineas would be whipped so badly, he'd probably forget everything he ever knew.

Elijah had no choice except to comply with her wishes, whatever they were. She seemed to be looking right through him, in a funny way. A trickle of spittle ran out of the corner of her half-opened mouth, down her chin to land on his shirt. Her grip on his arm was excruciating, and she was rubbing against him faster. What was wrong with her? He had seen the boys and girls chasing each other around the cabins in the evenings, playing lighthearted kissing and hugging games, but this wasn't like that. This was hurtful and ugly. She was almost like a Mistress, and he didn't want to cause trouble by disobeying her. He had more work to do and his stomach didn't feel so good. He had to say something quickly. He blurted, 'Ah'll do it! Ah'll do what you say!'

He wished she would get away from him, and turn his arm loose. The abnormal position was sending shooting pains up to his head. He tried to pull his body back from her rubbing against him, but she tightened her grasp, and whispered in between gasping breaths, 'Steal the key—to—the—stable—for—me, and—you—better—do—it—soon—or—I'll—tell!' Cold fear ran up his spine as a drop of salty sweat burned his eye. He blinked back tears. Suddenly, her eyelids fluttered and her whole body shook like she was shivering on a cold day. She sighed, giggled and as her arms went limp, Elijah jerked away from her soft body and her empty eyes. He ran from the shed as fast as he could; her thin laughter and parting threat chased him like sharp arrows piercing his head and his stomach.

'You better get it soon, slave boy!' she screamed. He kept running until he was halfway across the field to the comfort of his Mama's side, while Roxanne's mirthless cackle still boomed in his ears.

x x x

He didn't know what he was going to do. He'd never stolen anything in his life, and the thought of it made him physically ill. He didn't know how he would go about finding the key, or how he would muster the courage to actually steal it. His Daddy groomed the horses, but he didn't have a key. The stable was always locked right after sundown, and in the morning the grooms would have to wait for Massa or one of the trusted overseers to open the door. His heart sank when he remembered that Massa and the overseers were the only ones with access to the stable. Elijah was miserable.

He was afraid to tell anybody. Every day he watched for an opportunity to see what they did with the stable key, and every day Roxanne watched him. He knew she was biding her time, waiting for a chance to get him alone again.

Elijah had to pass the stable on the way to the field, and he made it his business to peer inside to see if the key was kept there. A few days later, his eyes fell on a key on a big ring, hanging by the door. It was too high for him to reach, but it was there. He figured that this key was probably the source of his agony; the key to the stable, the stable that was off limits to all the slaves, especially the children.

Now that he knew where it was, the problem was how to get it. His appetite decreased, he slept in fits and starts at night, causing his Mama to ask him if he felt well. No, he did not feel well. A week went by, and he hoped Roxanne had forgotten about the key, until he saw her standing across the field, following him with her dull, unblinking stare. Whenever he saw her, he was reminded of the Haints and Spirits that haunted the ghost stories the old folks told around the fires at night.

Days passed, and Elijah became more frustrated with his dilemma. Roxanne's demand weighed heavily on his every waking moment, so much so that he walked around in a confused daze. He was able to avoid her, but eventually, his luck ran out—she managed to corner him next to the water trough under the low branches of a big oak. He'd had a cup of water up to his mouth, when he felt arms snake around his neck. Before he could react, Roxanne jerked his head backward with all her strength. His eyes bulged, he sputtered, spitting water over her arm. Coughing and gasping, he struggled to get his breath. She pushed her face into the side of his neck. He smelled the odor of sour sweat. Her wet lips left spit in his ear, and her thin voice vibrated with anger, 'You better get me that key or I'll do it! I'll tell, and I goddamn well mean it' He felt her slimy tongue lick his earlobe, then her mouth sucked the side of his neck before she clamped her teeth down on the tender flesh there. At the same time, her probing fingers slowly felt and squeezed his crotch, pinching hard. He couldn't hold it any longer—he screamed.

'What's that?' the overseer shouted as Roxanne disappeared into the nearby bushes. Elijah doubled over in pain, but he wiped away tears, and forced himself to answer the question in an almost normal tone, 'Uh, nuttin, ah thot ah seen uh crawluh.'

Git ter yer work, boy,' the man grunted, before he turned his horse back in the opposite direction. Elijah felt the skin under his

Karma Rising

ear. The bite didn't bleed, but his fingers traced thick swollen welts in the shape of little sharp teeth, and he could barely walk from the agony of her sadistic pinch.

Days later, everybody had gone on ahead down the path from the field to the cabin but he lagged behind, having told anybody who inquired that he had a mis'ry in his leg. He was still in pain and lost in worry over his nagging problem as he limped past the stable. It would be dark soon. The stable was usually locked by then, which is why he almost didn't notice the door was ajar. He checked behind him. No one was following him and the stable was empty except for the dozen or so horses that had already been put up for the night. An occasional snort and bump from the stalls broke the autumn night stillness. He couldn't see clearly. Dim light from a single lantern cast a fluttering glow that surrounded the key in an incandescent halo that played up and down its length. The sight of it hanging there before his eyes made him dizzy and he had to concentrate in order to focus on the barrel and what he knew he had to do. In his entire life, Elijah had never been as frightened as he was at that moment.

His heart threatened to leap out of his chest, but he knew he might not get another chance like this. He had to act fast. He ran in and carefully placed the lantern on the packed dirt floor. A wheeze shook his already ragged nerves, causing him to gasp, 'Uh oh!' But it was only a horse. He pushed the heavy barrel a few inches and climbed up on it with wobbly legs, but he couldn't reach the key. He was certain his every move could be heard all the way to the big house, but he got down and pushed the barrel again. Climbing back up on the barrel, another surge of hot fear sucked the air out of his lungs and although he had to strain and stretch his fingers and he nearly lost his balance pulling the key off of it's nail, success was his, at last! With the key in his hand, fortune was still on his side. No one saw him, and he saw no one on his frantic run to his cabin, holding the metal so tightly in his pocket, it made a deep imprint in his sweaty palm.

Elijah and his Mama were in the field the next morning when Melbie, a young girl of about 15 whom Elijah thought was pretty, ran to them bringing the sickening news that his Daddy, along with three other grooms, had been whipped and sent to work at Wayne

Starcross' south Georgia plantation. His Mama sat down suddenly on the ground, her legs had given out from underneath her. With her trembling hands over her mouth, she stared into empty space while silent tears poured over her gnarled and calloused fingers. Shocked, he huddled, shivering, up against her until the overseer galloped up the row and drove the small crowd that had formed back to work.

Knowing that his Daddy was still alive made Elijah happy, but tears would start at the thought that he'd hurt so many people and, because of what he did, he might never see his Daddy again. Verna tried to calm him, saying that her prayers had been answered, at least in part, since Niles was out of Massa's reach. Verna believed her beloved was in a better place because Phineas said that Wayne Starcross was a fair and just man.

Elijah almost spilled the truth right then and there. He almost told her he had taken the key, and it was all his fault, but he was too ashamed and afraid. Guilt and fear swam around in circles behind his eyes. Massa's head overseer gathered everyone in the field and announced that a new patrol would be added the next day to make sure nobody stole a horse. In his heart, Elijah knew Miss Rockann had a reason for wanting that key and he was afraid no patrol could stop her. Elijah's head ached, and his mouth was dry, as if it was stuffed with cotton bolls. At suppertime, he took a shortcut past the outhouse instead of going to the food line; his roiling stomach couldn't stand the smell of mush and greasy fatback. He was half-running on the footpath as fast as he could. He hadn't seen Roxanne all day and that wasn't a good sign. His attention was captured by a bright orange and black butterfly bouncing along, flying near his face, going wherever butterflies go as it starts getting dark, when a pale, almost ghostly arm shot out from behind a tree and grabbed him. He had no time to put up strong resistance; she easily flung him against the trunk, and held out her hand.

'Where is it?' she demanded.

'Uh, ah—back uh ouah cabin, unduh uh bush.'

'Go get it! Now! I'll be right behind you, and if you're lying to me, or planning to run, you know what I'll do!'

Every time he looked back on his way to his cabin, all he saw through the trees were lightning bugs, flashing their mysterious little candles. Where did she go? He needn't have wondered. When he reached the tiny patch that was his Mama's garden, Roxanne was already there, frowning, her arms folded, waiting impatiently. She let him dig up the key, then she snatched it from him. In the dusk dark, her snide, slow smile and the tone of her peculiar voice made him uncomfortable. She drawled, 'Now that's real nice, Eee-li-jah—but you still got to do what I say, or I'll tell. Don't forget, you ain't nothing but a slave.'

He'd just gotten up from his knees, and was kicking dirt back into the shallow hole when the familiar sick feeling welled up in his bowels. He couldn't believe what she just said. But he'd under estimated her determination to inflict some sort of physical pain on him. She swung her foot fast and hard, so that the toe of her shoe slammed into his shin. He lost his balance, fell forward and, failing to catch himself, rolled over on the ground. Holding his swelling leg, he stifled his cries and rolled again to dodge her next swift kick. Ignoring the pain, he leapt to his feet, gasping for breath, prepared for only-God-knew-what, but she laughed and strolled away, swaying and singing,

'You better do what I say, Elijah black boy, if you know what's good for you.'

That Indian Summer night of his eighth October, he found out what Roxanne wanted with the key to the stable.

The tragedy happened after midnight, after everyone was in bed. He'd been sleeping badly since Roxanne had started her frightening intimidation, and he missed his Daddy. The cabin felt empty without the secure knowledge that Niles slept noisily across the room.

Searing pain in Elijah's body added to an eight-year-old's inability to cope with grown-up problems. He tossed around on his straw pallet, until he found a position that didn't put pressure on any of his sore parts. He finally drifted off into a light sleep, only to be awakened by a sharp horse's scream that bolted him upright in the bed. He strained to listen, but heard only the pounding of his own heart. Was Miss Rockann trying to steal a horse? Why did the horse make that scary sound? From a distance, muffled voices floated on the air. He listened carefully, wondering where the voices were coming from. He loved the horses. He hoped Miss Rockann wasn't hurting a horse. As sore as he was, he got up and, favoring his injured leg, he pulled on his brown shirt and pants, then slipped out the door. His Mama was sound asleep and snoring softly in her usual state of total physical exhaustion, and probably wouldn't stir until sun-up. Shaking inwardly, he headed for the source of the angry voices that reminded him of the nameless terrors in his most hideous night dreams.

In the hospital room, tears streamed from Adam's closed eyes at the same time Elijah's voice cracked in an anguished sob,

'You know wha happen! You was dere dat night!' He said no more, but tremors continued to shake his body.

Nasrene quickly brought Adam out of that time, but again, her attempts to awaken him were futile. She proceeded with the pain reduction suggestions, turned off the recorder, then stood up and stretched.

"He isn't going to say anymore now, and I know it isn't a good idea to try to force anything during regression. It must flow from freely from the regressee, so to speak. Now, wonder who in this room was present that night."

"Ceeoni?" Di searched her friend's face, "Do you think Elijah was talking to you?" Ceeoni didn't think so, but then again, she wasn't sure.

"Well," she said, "Elijah obviously recognized one of us here."

Nasrene, leaning against the windowsill, looked up from the notes she was taking.

"With so many people around Adam's bed, it's hard to know to whom Elijah referred. His eyes were shut, but actually, I thought he might've sensed that Homer was Miss Letty. Right now, my deepest concern is the effect of the intense emotional trauma he's reliving. If his memories are too painful, he may refuse to be regressed or he may refuse to regress to that particular place or to that lifetime again. If Adam's coma is due to overwhelming emotional dregs from that life, a coma, which was probably brought on by the shock of being brutally attacked on his 1997 return to Starcross, it is possible that if the trauma isn't exorcised, he could remain in limbo. If that's true, I pray he has the emotional courage to see it through in spite of the agony it's causing him."

"Oh God," R.C. groaned, "Nasrene, you aren't saying he could actually stay this way, do you?"

"Who knows? I've never seen or heard of anyone doing what he's doing. We all heard what he said. Because of whatever happened to him when he left his Mama's cabin to go investigate the noises, he was unable to continue, so those events caused him to retreat back into the comatose state. Like I said, it's obvious that the infected psychic lesions from that lifetime must be healed and, hopefully, we can help him."

"Nasrene," R.C. said as he crossed the room to give her a bear hug, "hey thank you for what you're giving him, and all of us. I have no other choice except to trust that a greater power is leading the band, as always, but, My Dear—you must have a share in this." She met his questioning gaze, "Why do you say that?"

"Well, when Elijah said one of us was in the stable that night, I believe he was talking to you."

CHAPTER FIFTEEN

"We don't know who was in the stable or what occurred there that caused Elijah's profound reaction," Nasrene said. "Hopefully, we'll find out, but I'm not surprised that he recognized someone in this room. As we've suspected, I'm sure there's a grand plan here. It's obvious the answer is entangled in a maze of the old Starcross secrets, and apparently, some of us hold the buried keys. I'm hoping a clue will turn up quickly that will relate these past events to our murderer. And, I agree that one of those nineteenth century Bad Guys is the present-day killer. Now, we need to discover if one of us has Roxanne's Soul, or the Soul of an overseer, or Miss Letty's dear son—"

Ceeoni and Di spoke simultaneously, "Massa!"

Their laughter broke the residue of tension generated by Elijah's piteous distress.

Homer slapped R.C.'s high-five, "Is Massa a piece of work or what?"

Ceeoni grinned, but the question repeated in her head, 'Dammit, Ceeoni, who were you?'

"God forbid that I was ever that blind, not even during the Dark Ages," Nasrene continued, "but then, we've all been blind in one way or another. Our Souls have learned different lessons in each lifetime. Like I said before, I believe learning is the only reason we're in these fragile bodies. Man has the illusion that he, or something else, has power that can, at times, go beyond God's power, or challenge the power of God. I think man has only a sort of temporary custody. Man's dominion affects what little change he can bring about in what little he thinks he sees. Mankind can move around and build things that aren't permanent. In the unfolding of time, nothing, especially the things that man does, is permanent. The only real change man can affect is within his own Soul. Man has very little power over the true picture, like the old tip of the iceberg—in reality, much more exists beyond our power and our eyesight."

Homer paid rapt attention, "OK, if learning is the reason, what are we supposed to learn?"

"It's been the hardest of man's lessons, eluding us as much today as it did in the ancient world. Simply put, we are to love God, ourselves, each other and the earth, because it is all one."

Di winked at Ceeoni, with a silent 'See there?' Before Homer or anyone else could respond to Nasrene's statement, there was a knock at the door and Minette Coulter pushed it open.

"Hi. I just came by to see if there's anything I can do. I know Mr. Delayno probably has tons of calls and letters. I thought I might be able to help."

R.C. pulled up a chair for her. Diana nodded, and busied herself rearranging an already perfect floral arrangement. Minette did the see-how-my-lovely-but-charmingly-unruly-hair-keeps-falling-into-my-face head toss. Ceeoni tried hard not to hold it against her. Minette tossed the hair back that had fallen over her eye, for the third time.

"I served in Desert Storm as an army hospital dietician and I've seen a lot of guys in comas. How is he?"

The golden 'T' zipper pull on the jacket of Minette's mustard boucle mini-dress identified it as a designer piece from Tuesday of Beverly Hills, a designer Di and Ceeoni knew. On Minette, the dress had the look of couture. Minette perched on the edge of the chair and peered at Adam's still form.

"You know, coma is one of the mysteries of human physiology. I've heard of people staying in a coma from durations of a few minutes to an entire lifetime." She crossed her perfect legs and added, "If you're waiting for him to wake up, you could be waiting for a while. He doesn't look so good to me."

Ceeoni, bristling at Minette's remark, snapped, "We're staying positive, having faith that he's healing and believing that he'll be as good as new, soon. His doctor says his wounds are superficial."

Minette shot a haughty glance in Ceeoni's direction, and fished her keys out of her bag.

"Well, that's admirable, and certainly all you can do. I should be going. R.C., I can juggle my calendar no matter where I am, to make room for a few hours on the phones via call referral. Just let me know."

"I understand by the grumbling I hear from the nurses' station that more calls are coming and the aides I hired are extra busy," R.C. said, "We may have to take you up on that."

"Hey Minette," Homer volunteered, "I'll walk you to your car."

With her biggest smile revealing flawless veneers, Minette threw the wayward hair back again and cooed,

"Homer, I faxed last week's receipts to the accountant and I think you'll like the numbers."

As they left, Di stuck out her tongue at the closing door. Ceeoni tossed a candy wrapper at her friend.

"Now, now, Dianna, how very, very un-spiritual of you!"

Ceeoni said a silent prayer for Adam, while one of his CDs supplied accompaniment to her jumbled emotions. The song his piano embraced was Thelonious Monk's 'Round Midnight'. The music danced in her head. She couldn't resist humming along with Adam's thick rippling chords, 'So let love take wings some midnight, round midnight, let the angels sing for your returning—'

The perplexed little voice inside her head stepped on the tender moment—'What in God's name are you doing here, humming love songs about love returning at midnight, while you sit next to a man you've never met, praying for his recovery?'

Ceeoni kept humming until her new little voice gave up.

Homer came back into the room accompanied by a tall elegant woman who wore a deep turquoise jersey suit, a matching wrapped turban, and a brilliant smile.

"Package for R.C. Ponder!" Homer yelled. R.C. jumped out of his chair and reached for his wife.

"Juno!" They held each other in a rocking hug. R.C. had said his wife was born in Senegal, raised in London, educated in Montreal and was teaching first grade in New York when they met. Juno's height, carriage and facial features reminded Ceeoni of runway queen Naomi Campbell. No one would ever guess that this sweet young girl was the mother of eight children.

After introductions all around, she gently kissed Adam on both cheeks, then turned a questioning gaze to her husband. R.C. answered the unspoken question in her eyes,

"Go ahead, Sweetheart, talk to him. Maybe you can jog something. You've always been one of his favorite people."

Juno took the offered chair, and held Adam's hand while she talked.

Her classic British accent sounded casually conversational, "Adam, Oh, Adam, it's so good to see you, and we are grateful to God you weren't seriously injured. I brought the three little ones with me, for your approval. And I have a very special message from your namesake, for your ears only. Now that he's almost fifteen, Adam Jr. says you're the best person he knows to help him with his jazz piano improvisations, and I can't wait for you to hear him play!

"I've been thinking about the way we all met—New York City, in the dead of winter. You were starting the promo tour for your second CD. I was taking my class on a field trip to Rockefeller Center. I was on my way to the subway followed by twenty-three first graders bundled in scarves, earmuffs, caps and mittens—they looked like walking laundry baskets. All the wondrous magic of the Christmas season had tied Manhattan up in bright red ribbon, trimmed in glittering silver and gold tinsel. Snowflakes, big fluffy balls of weightless cotton candy, fell in blinding profusion.

"You and R.C. were coming out of Atlantic Records and I heard R.C. say, 'I don't care where she's going, man, I'm going with her' and you were trying to stop him. I can hear you now, you said,"—Juno did a funny, near-accurate imitation of Adam's deep voice—'Man, that lady don't wanna be bothered with you! Look at all those kids she's got! Man, somebody's got to feed those kids. Now, you know that lady's too busy gathering groceries to hang out with you!' You had the kids giggling and laughing. When we got to the subway in the next block, I was terribly disappointed to see that you two crazy guys were gone. R.C. and I have talked about that day many times. He said visibility was nil, traffic stopped you, and I turned in the opposite direction. Actually, I had an odd sense of sadness when I realized you weren't still behind us. I remember thinking it was too bad we lost each other, although at that time, I didn't know why.

"You can imagine how shocked I was six months later when I came out of the front door of my school, and you and R.C. stood there, each clutching a dozen roses. I couldn't believe the happiness I felt. Remember what you said? You said that since you'd been back in New York, you guys purchased fresh roses each day and you followed R.C. to 16 elementary schools before he found the one where I was teaching! With that method it could've taken months. He said he never considered the possibility that I might be married or involved with someone.

"We were inseparable from then on, but I couldn't go on the next tour because of my school contract. I forget where you guys went, but when you returned, R.C., you, and whoever your girl was at that time, Millie somebody, were all waiting in a limo in front of the school, complete with a minister friend of yours. What was his name? Ah, yes, Robert Williams. We ran around New York getting the license, the flowers and the rings, and we kept Reverend Williams with us for the entire three-day waiting period. How that man could eat! We demolished some great restaurants in those three days and, in between meals, Rev. Williams would stop for big bags of McDonalds's. You said you'd rather pay his rent than feed him. You and R.C. kept singing a song you wrote together that had the title, 'R.C. better marry Juno today, before a slick bogus dude comes to steal her away.'

"R.C. and I were married in Central Park on an unforgettable summer evening with everybody holding candles. R.C. hired the chef from The Four Seasons, some theatre actors and musician friends of yours got together with your band and put on a concert, right there on the grass, that lasted into the night. Joggers, the police, and the homeless celebrated with us.

"Our big surprise from you came after the wedding. You gave us airline tickets, but nobody would tell me our destination. It was crazy! We wound up in the plush honeymoon suite of the wonderful old

Jefferson Hotel in Richmond, Virginia; complete with pink marble columns, and our own personal staff to wait on us for a week.

"Remember when the first Ponder baby was born? The fact that R.C. could be there calmed my fears, but neither of you has ever told the truth about how you got to London from L.A. No planes had been able to land at fogged-in Heathrow for days. You must wake up and tell me how you got there. You know, after all these years, I'm really tired of the 'We hitched a ride on the stork' story.

"The morning after little Adam was born in Tokyo was pretty special, too. We got smashed on the champagne you smuggled into my room, past those starched, inscrutable, thou-shalt-not nurses. We almost got away with it, too, until one of them kicked a bottle that rolled out from underneath the bed. She called her boss and they were so indignant. You took the opportunity to answer with the only Japanese you knew, you told a totally unrelated joke. I think it was, 'Why did the chicken cross the road?' When they started laughing, R.C. just happened to have stashed several more bottles of bubbly with the stray bottle, and it was a very good thing more babies weren't born that day because everybody, even the nursing mums, joined in the party. I still sing that lullaby they taught us.

"Oh, Adam, my dear friend, there are countless moments that will always live in my heart, and there is an entire squad of Ponders needing all the wisdom we can offer. Come back to us—you have so much more to do—" Juno's voice trailed off, as she dabbed her eyes.

Ceeoni had read that Adam Delayno was childless, and that his marriage had ended in divorce, but now she could see that the Ponder children were a part of his life and he had been there with them from the very beginning. The big scorching question crossed her mind again, 'What's he doing running around loose, unmarried? Is he committed to someone and they haven't legalized their union, like Oprah and Stedman? And if he has a significant other, wouldn't she, or he (He?—Gasp!), have shown up by now?' Di's theories were beginning to rub off because a possible answer wafted from her mental ethereal wings and materialized on her center stage, 'Maybe it's the soul mate thing, silly. Maybe he's like Di, Homer, Nasrene and so many others who refuse to settle for less.' She knew so little of Adam's life outside of his bio. It was stupid and frustrating to try to sort through one supposition after another.

She'd learned many a hard lesson about assuming; wishfully attaching desired characteristics to a person or a situation that existed only in her very own private dream box.

An especially embarrassing memory had added to the strain of the finalization of her divorce. Di had insisted that they take one of those five-day cruises from L.A. to the Baja Peninsula, based on her conviction that ocean breezes would banish Ceeoni's end-of-a-marriage blues. Diana didn't call the ensuing confusion a lesson; she cussed and fussed and said it was downright-lowdown-deliberate-deceit on behalf of the party of the first part. Ceeoni saw it as another ill-timed mistake that just missed evolving into something difficult to live down.

The first night out on the cruise, they were having cocktails on deck under silver stars when a handsome man sat down beside her and started a conversation. He seemed interested in her, this San Francisco mortgage broker. Kenny, Kenny Hutchinson. With his dark, craggy features and a cool, quiet seductive way of speaking, he reminded Ceeoni of satin sheets. Di spent the next day tweaking one of her TV scripts and bemoaning the fact that Ceeoni's new friend was the only good looking man aboard, if you didn't count the cabin boy. Ceeoni spent the next day basking in the attentive wining, dining and flattering Santa Ana wind of Kenny's charisma.

Through in-depth conversation, she and Kenny discovered that delightful place where individual interests and aspirations seemed to magically blend. She checked out his food preferences and made mental notes of menus to prepare for their divine little dinners at her place, or his. He looked into her eyes and kissed her with passion and promise on the second night, but on the following morning, his high-maintenance lady friend joined their table at breakfast, fully recovered from her bout of *mal de mer*. She turned out to be as friendly and charming as he. Di suggested tossing them both overboard, but the Sane Ceeoni beat up on her with the bare fact, 'Why didn't you just ask the man if he was traveling alone? And what's the matter with him, that he didn't immediately offer the whole truth?'

She swore out loud to God, herself and Di that she would never assume anything in a potential affair of the heart again. After that, she was more careful, but years later, here in 1997, persistent thoughts of Adam Delayno had commandeered her senses in a spectacular way that had no reason or rationalization.

The time in Adam's hospital room had flown by. Nasrene said she was hungry. Juno and R.C. said they were going to the Manor to spend the evening with their children and the nanny. Everybody gathered belongings, and pushed chairs against the wall, but Ceeoni moved slowly. She was finding it increasingly more difficult to walk out of the hospital room and leave Adam alone. She realized it wouldn't have taken much coaxing for her to accept the only other alternative, to simply sit by his bed and to hell with whatever he might think of her, a total stranger, when he awakened. Her heart skipped a beat at the whispered thought, 'If he awakened'.

Di intuitively wrapped her arm through Ceeoni's and steered her toward the door.

"Hey girlfriend, that gold number Minette was draped in was one of Tuesday's, wasn't it? I think I started to buy something like it last fall."

Tuesday had costumed shows at the Inner-City Cultural Center while Ceeoni was there and recently Tue's creations had started showing up in major stores.

"Yeah, I recognized it. I think my burgundy suit is made from the same fabric."

Talking about clothes was a surefire method of brightening many a somber occasion, and soon, Ceeoni couldn't resist smiling.

R.C. turned out the lights and closed the door behind them. As everyone walked ahead, Ceeoni put Di's discussion of boucle on hold, to run back into the room and turn on the bed light, so that Adam wouldn't be in the dark.

x x x

Settling into Homer's car, he asked Juno,

"So, Ms. R.C., how was your ride over?"

"Really good. The children slept all the way and when we arrived, Weber made sure everything was hassle-free. We had all sorts of luggage and toys and odd-shaped packages that he juggled with a great deal of patience. We got comfortable in a jiffy."

"Weber also filled the Manor refrigerator, and I think you can trust his good taste."

"Oh, Homer! We thanked Weber and you many times when we discovered the full fridge, with labeled, prepared meals. We warmed a marvelous spinach lasagna for lunch."

"Well," Di quipped, "We've gotta' hurry up and wean ourselves away from eating with Weber. We're haunted by mental pictures of trying to squeeze into gigantic muumuus, while he strolls around in those sleek silk gis of his, flexing his lean sinewy muscles, and laughing at our gluttonous inability to resist."

"R. C. and Adam are just like my kids," Juno laughed, "they can eat whatever they want and never gain a stone. You can count me in the bailout, but only after the stash is gone!"

"Meanwhile," Homer said, "If there's anything you need, just give us a call."

"Thank you so much, but what I need now is bed rest, and lots of it."

R.C. broke in, "Please, please pick me up in a couple of hours. You can believe that Juno, the kids and Nanny-Ada will be asleep in no time. Juno needs more sleep than the little ones. She's been known to drop off while in the process of uttering a sentence. I can see myself, insomnia and all, climbing the walls with nothing but the telly."

With her head resting on her husband's shoulder, Juno closed her eyes and muttered,

"They say taking frequent spontaneous naps is a mark of bloody genius."

Homer pulled into the circular drive in front of the Manor, and three beautiful and extremely exuberant children, ages two-and-a-half, four and six, spilled off the porch. The three jumping, giggling, shiny-eyed mixtures of Juno's and R.C.'s features with heads full of sandy curls, ran to the car and R.C. could hardly get the door open as they screamed and scrambled to get to their Dad.

"Oh," he said, "I missed you, and I missed you, and I missed you!" Their happy laughter formed nearly tangible clouds of joy.

Judging from the lines of cars, the Starcross Restaurant was packed. The night view from there included several estates and a snaggled skyline view of downtown Atlanta, oddly sparse for a major city.

"Homer, is there more of downtown than can be seen from this angle?"

"Cee, my dear, let's just say Atlanta is a city-in-progress. So far, what you see is all there is. Our downtown can't compare with the concrete canyons of New York, yet, but we're steadily building. And speaking of building, how do you like the restaurant's new top floor veranda?" To the left of the Greek revival facade that was nearly identical to the Theatre and Manor, the glow of tiny lights and candles could be seen through tinted glass. "What a romantic place for lovers to dine under the cosmos!" Nasrene said. She sighed as she shoved her bag onto the floor of the car, "I guess it would be impolite for me to ignore the fantastic surroundings and review my notes in between bites, huh?"

"I know what you mean," Homer answered, "I can't resist the temptation to mentally turn the last few days over and over, like a Rubik's Cube. I can only imagine what everyone else is feeling."

Inside, Minette sat holding court at the bar with two obviously enchanted young men. Within minutes after the group was seated, a waiter appeared with two bottles of Cristal,

"Champagne from Ms. Coulter's private stock, with her sincere compliments."

Raves for the creative cuisine went up around the table: crabmeat strudel with lime butter, free-range chicken in white wine sauce or lobster with artichokes, spinach Florentine, buttered carrots, Georgia peach mousse and coffee with brandy were served with expert efficiency.

"Whatever Minette's background," Ceeoni said, "she sure knows how to rock that kitchen. Where's the chef from?"

"New York. She and Minette discovered that they worked well together and Minette brought her along when we opened."

"Homer," Di cooed, "You are most definitely the ultimate ladies' man, even your chef is a woman!"

"Hi everybody!" Minette caressed Homer's shoulder, while pulling up a chair next to his. "Do you mind if I join you? How was everything?" Ceeoni thought, 'Now she knows dinner was great. I guess that's what she's supposed to ask.'

Minette slid into the chair without waiting for an answer to either question, then she proceeded to go through the hair tossing ritual. Ignoring Diana's sigh and everyone else, she looked through her long curly lashes at Homer,

"I'm so glad you came by. I was about to page you because I've got to run up to New York to see about my great aunt. She's had a mild stroke, and she's all alone. I want to make sure she has someone staying with her. I should be back by Thursday or Friday."

"I'm sorry to hear that. Although it won't be a happy occasion, you're long overdue for a break. Kevin can handle anything that comes up. Are your menus ready?"

"Uh, huh," she answered, "Aren't they always? Kevin will only have to make sure they check the produce every day. The vendor knows what we want, and the shipment should arrive everyday by 8am promptly, or they owe us a free order." Minette kept her eyes riveted to Homer's.

"Does Kevin know this?"

"Yes, and I'm sure I can trust his judgment." Di appeared to be oblivious to their conversation, but Ceeoni knew she was evaluating every word and every inflection, and was carefully weighing the silences in between. Ceeoni also wondered how long it had taken Minette to acquire her southern drawl, since she was from New York. Minette threw her hair again and actually batted her eyelashes. Di cleared her throat. Ceeoni didn't dare look in Di's direction. Di had a way of raising one eyebrow that could always cause Ceeoni to lose her composure to uncontrollable laughter.

"Good," Homer said, "Then it's all settled. Be safe, Minette, and let me know if there's anything I can do. Oh, do you have a ride to the airport?"

Minette nodded to Homer, and made a big show of rising gracefully from her chair. She, waved two fingers toward the table, tossed her ever-tossed hair, and sauntered away,

"You kids have a wonderful time!" she called, leaving the air charged with the fragrance of White Diamonds, which had just become Ceeoni's least favorite scent.

Detective David Saxon, having dinner with an attractive lady in one of the intimate booths against the wall, waved to them. The blonde at his side wore a pink concoction that revealed a great deal of caramel-hued skin. He whispered something in his companion's ear before he came over to their table.

"How's everyone this evening?" David inquired. Homer stood and shook his hand, "Dave, would you and your friend care to join us?"

"No, no thanks, I wanted to take a minute to keep you abreast of the progress we're not making. I'd love to be able to report a breakthrough in the case, but unfortunately, nothing new has occurred regarding Basil Cassidy or the attempts on Minette or Delayno. We're following what few leads we have." Ceeoni sipped her coffee. An awkward moment hung over the table as David hesitated, still standing uncomfortably.

Di came to his rescue, "Look, it's still so soon. Basil was murdered on Thursday, Minette was attacked on Friday, Adam was assaulted on Saturday, and today is just Sunday evening."

"Yeah, David," Homer said, "She's so right. Give yourself a break. This killer is elusive because he's either very lucky or very clever and, more likely, a little bit of both. I know your team is sifting and resifting minute variables, and soon you'll discover some important detail that the killer overlooked—still, there's got to be something, and I know you'll find it."

"Well," David laughed, "As Don Cornelius would say, 'You can bet your last money, honey', we will!"

"What I'm really curious to find out is the motive. Why, in God's name, would anybody want to do this stuff?"

"Homer, the chief and everybody downtown are losing sleep wondering the same thing." David must have felt his date glaring at his back, because he politely took his leave. There was nothing more to say. It was obvious the police were as perplexed as everybody else. Leaving the restaurant, Diana took Homer's arm. "So, how do things run while Minette is away?"

"Oh, I don't know. She's never been away before. She's been putting 12 to 14 hours a day into the operation, but I believe if we do what we've been trained to do, we'll be OK. Plus, Weber and I can keep an eye on things. He'll watch the kitchen, and I'll keep Kevin and the receipts together."

"You certainly have an unruffled attitude," Nasrene remarked.

"I guess I do. I've taken a lot of guff about it, but I believe in doing the best I can in any given situation, then I let the rest take care of itself," with a grin he added, "After all the stuff going on around here lately, I now realize I learned that from Miss Letty!"

CHAPTER SIXTEEN

Ceeoni felt the familiarity tug at her Spirit as Homer turned into the Manor drive-way. It was a feeling she was learning to expect and enjoy. R.C. answered the door, with Juno behind him, lovely in pumpkin satin lounging pajamas. R.C.'s smile lit up the foyer.

"You're right on time," he said, "the kids are asleep, and Ms. Juno is already yawning."

"Hallelujah!" Juno cheered, "Thank God you finally came for him. He's driving me crazy, pacing like a lion in a cage. If there's no improvement in Adam's condition soon, R.C. is doomed to fly into small pieces."

"Bingo, my love. Would anybody care for anything? We're very well-stocked."

Everyone settled into the luxurious green living room while glasses of juice and water were passed around.

"R.C. told me about the past life regressions," Juno said. "You know, that is probably one of the most fascinating subjects in the world to me."

Nasrene had been leaning back in her wing chair, but when Juno said that, she sat up,

"Oh, really? Would you be interested in allowing me to guide you through a regression?"

"Yes, I think I would. I've always believed in reincarnation and, this may sound crazy, but what created my interest was the identification I've had during the period around the American Civil War. There I was, a child in England, having dreams of a time I'd never heard of. Reincarnation is the only explanation for my having dreams of the Civil War, before I learned anything about it. I've always wanted to come to Atlanta—" She glanced at R.C., who looked at her as if he'd never seen her before. She smiled a little smile in his direction and added, "I wanted to see if Atlanta was like my dreams. I've always hoped to discover why I had those dreams."

"I believe that sometimes God speaks to us in dreams," Nasrene remarked.

"R C., I never told you about it, and I don't know why. Maybe I didn't want you to think that I've got bats in the belfry."

R.C. Ponder pulled his wife out of her chair, sat in it, and then coaxed her to sit down on his lap. With a fist in front of her face he said,

"Well, friends, we'll now hear a few more words from Juno Ponder. OK, 'fess up, speak into the microphone please, you've come this far; you might as well tell us all about those childhood dreams."

"Oh, don't tease! That's exactly why I was reluctant to talk about it."

"OK, OK—All husbands must learn to apologize. I know this is no time to make light of things like that. We've all had our minds opened wide this week."

"It's hard to explain my dreams, they were like collages, collages of a big fire, soldiers in blue and gray uniforms, and loneliness; I remember feeling deep wells of loneliness. The dreams became more vivid as I got older, or maybe because I became more familiar with them."

"Juno, could you see who you were?" Nasrene inquired, "Could you see yourself?"

"No, I only saw fragments. I wondered if I'd been influenced by a girl I knew at school. I was her only friend, not because she was from India, but because the other kids thought she was crackers. She was the first person who talked to me about reincarnation, saying it was a fact of life in her country. They believe Souls can reincarnate into animal bodies."

"I don't share that belief," Nasrene said, "I think Souls evolve through lower life forms, but once the Soul has evolved to a human form, it remains in the human experience, learning human lessons, until it no longer needs a body."

"What a theory!" Ceeoni said, "Then, could it be possible for some human forms to contain Souls that are not yet evolved to the human level?"

Nasrene laughed, "Some people believe that, and in light of how we treat each other, it seems like it happens frequently, doesn't it?"

"Well," Di quipped, "that would explain why some people seem so inhuman."

Homer fell on one knee, barked, and grabbed Di's ankle, she screamed, and he growled, "Who isn't human?"

"Wait," Juno, laughing, waved her arms, "Wait! Wait!" But laughter had her teetering precariously on R.C.'s lap. "This is supposed to be a serious discussion!" Steadying herself, she said, "I know a poem, well; it's a piece of a poem titled "A Creed," written by a Poet Laureate of England, John Maesfield. I memorized a part of it."

While climbing back up on his chair, Homer pretended to search around, "I thought I left some human dignity around here, somewhere."

R.C.'s exaggerated frown and his mumbled, "I didn't know you knew any poems," brought on new laughter. Juno kissed her husband's forehead and asked,

"You Ready? The yeas have it."

Her classic accent transported the quotation from the softly lit living room to London's Victoria and Albert Hall,

"I hold that when a person dies
His Soul again returns to earth
Arrayed in some new flesh disguise
Another mother gives him birth.
With sturdier limbs and brighter brain,
The Old Soul takes the road again.
Such is my belief and trust
This hand, this hand that holds the pen
Has many a hundred times been dust,
And turned as dust, to dust again.
These eyes of mine have blinked and shone
In Thebes, in Troy, in Babylon—"

Her last words trailed off into a whisper, leaving the room in silence. Homer went to the window and stared out at a blazing purple and rust colored sky providing a striking backdrop for an inflamed setting sun.

"Juno, can you recite that again for my records?" Nasrene asked. "Why, yes, of course," Juno answered in the middle of a yawn, "Oh, please excuse me, you know, I'd almost forgotten I knew that. May I take a rain check on the past life regression? I'm zonked, and I would loathe the idea of attempting something so important while in a state of numbing fatigue. After thinking about past lives since childhood, I can imagine a past life regression will be a life-changing experience for me and I want to be alert. Meanwhile, is it possible for me to observe a session?"

"How about now? Most people say it does change their lives, and it shouldn't take too long. All I need is a volunteer."

Nasrene looked directly at Ceeoni, who was quickly trying to think of a good reason to decline, when R.C. threw his kufi into an empty chair.

"Yes and Yes!" he yelled, "This is just what I've been waiting for!"

It was Juno's turn to look at her spouse as if she'd never seen him before. R.C. flopped down on the sofa. As soon as everyone was settled, Nasrene turned on the tape recorder and began the relaxation suggestions,

"You are now going back to a time that is affecting the events happening in your life today. What is your name?"

R.C. opened his mouth and spoke, in a light near-whisper, 'Verna, Verna Bal'win.'

"What year is it?"

'Dis 1849, but ah shudden be heah wit ya'll! Ya'll uh stranguhs!'

"What's wrong?"

'Massa, he beat me real bad. He say ah, ah poda say nuttin' no mo ta nobody.'

"Verna, do you believe in Jesus?"

'Yasum.'

"Then you know Jesus is protecting you. It's alright to talk to me."

Verna began timidly, then her voice became stronger as she told them that she and her husband, and their son Elijah, had come to Starcross from the Baldwin Plantation. She said Mr. Baldwin had always been good to people because he was born that way. His wife had died after their only child, Sybil, came into the world.

Mr. Baldwin built ships, and planted a small crop of cotton and peaches, so when Miss Sybil got married, he was able to send most of the Baldwin slaves to Starcross. There was a blacksmith and his assistants, a laundress and six assistants, a seamstress with three assistants, four maids, six cooks and kitchen help, carpenters, seventy field hands and their children, along with Phineas and six grooms who kept the carriages and horses. They were well fed, well trained and efficient.

Miss Sybil's cousin, a strange girl of twelve years, helped out with the sewing. Verna was a field hand and her husband, Niles, was a groom.

Verna saw right away that the new Massa wasn't like Mr. Baldwin. The new Massa had a streak of meanness a mile wide. From the first day, and for the first time in their lives, they felt fear and apprehension. She knew most slaves lived in fear, and she knew how lucky they had been to belong to Mr. Baldwin.

After they had lived at Starcross for a few weeks, slaves began to escape, and the whippings started. There was hell to pay. Massa poked around trying to find out how several slaves got past his patrols and watchers, but everything he tried didn't get him any information. Soon, Verna's friend Melbie told her there was a way to escape, but Verna didn't want to know who or how. It was too dangerous to know. She longed for her old life if she had to be a slave, but her secret wish was to be free. She longed for freedom for herself, and her family, and she longed for there to be no more slaves and massas and hate and beatings.

Melbie told her she better keep Elijah from being alone too long because crazy Roxanne had her eye on him, and it could mean white woman trouble, 'which wuz the wustest kine' for her handsome young son, even though he was only eight years old.

The next morning after Melbie said that to Verna, Melbie and her lover, a slave who brought milk every other day from a nearby farm, ran away without a trace. That afternoon, the short, fat, red-faced overseer with rotten teeth, rode up to her with a smirk on his ugly face, 'Let's go, Gal!' he growled.

The sound of his voice scared her, 'Go? Uh, yasuh.' He wheeled his horse around to follow her, as she walked slowly.

'Walk up now, move it!' he yelled.

Her fear escalated with each step. She knew he wanted her to walk faster so he could watch her body. While trying to stop her hips from bouncing, she prayed 'dear Jesus, let nothin' be wrong'. Scalding tears started up in her eyes. She knew where they were going. She knew because she had been seen speaking to Melbie the day before Melbie ran away. And as terror seeped into every nerve in her body, the gaping door to the whippin' barn loomed up dead ahead, like the gate to hell.

Behind her, the man breathed in fast, short excited gasps. He dismounted and pushed her roughly through the barn door. Cold sweat trickled down her back. The slamming door behind her closed all the light out of her mind. She felt a sinking sensation, as if she had fallen into a black hole and her real life didn't exist anymore. She couldn't stop the trembling that had taken control of her legs. Massa's rumbling voice suddenly came at her from several places out of the darkness.

'Somebody helped Melbie!' he roared, 'Who was it?'

'Ah, don know, Massa, suh.' Her own voice sounded muffled and distant to her ears.

'You were the last one seen talking to her!'

'Ah—ah—'Right then, even though fear ripped through her veins, she prayed that Melbie and Jesse had run like the wind to a safe place where this hateful man could never find them. 'Ah don' know, suh.' Her eyes adjusted to the dim light, and suddenly she was shocked to see Massa standing so close to her she could have reached out and touched the whip he twitched in his hand. Her stomach heaved, fear rushed to her head and she suddenly swung both arms to run—which way is the door? But the overseer caught her easily.

He pressed his body against her to restrain her flailing, when at the same time his hard body pressed against her buttocks. His foul breath filled her nostrils.

Talbert's loud order was immediately obeyed, 'Let her go, goddammit, or Jeb, you're next!' The man backed off, with a sly little slip of his hands down to grope her hips. Another man was in the room, a young overseer she recognized. Massa persisted, 'Take off all her clothes! Not you, Jeb!'

Her teeth rattled as the other man took off her dress but left her underpants.

'Everything!' Talbert bellowed. 'I want her to feel every bit of it!'

The man did as he was told. She had never experienced being chained or tied up. When he tied her hands, the combination of being naked in front of strange men, falsely accused and hog-tied, brought her fear and outrage to a place where panic exploded. As he tried to lift her hands up high to secure them to ropes already in place at intervals on the post, all she could do was scream and scream, hysterically, 'ahhhhhhh—' The first strike knocked her to her knees. Massa's whip cut through the delicate skin across her shoulders. It traced a stinging path that curled around her waist and licked her naked thighs. She felt her skin open in places, felt her blood and urine running in many rivers down her legs, heard herself screaming, 'Jesus, Jesus, oh Goddd—ohhhhGodohGod—ohGod—'

x x x

As R.C. thrashed and kicked, Nasrene quickly applied the suggestions for pain reduction. Juno sank down to the floor beside her husband and tried to hold him. Within a few minutes, he calmed down and Nasrene completed the suggestions. He sat up slowly, protesting,

"Hey, I'm OK. Actually, I'm OK. I'm ready to continue."

"Continue?" Nasrene asked

"I'm just fine. I've been thinking about regression so much, I believe I was psychologically prepared for anything my Soul would encounter."

"Why would you want to go on?"

"Juno, I don't know, there's something—"

Nasrene waited a few minutes before starting the recorder and giving R.C. the regression suggestions. As everyone expected, Verna returned,

'Ah shudden be heah!' she anxiously whispered, 'He cud come back ennytime!'

Nasrene soothed her fears again. "Massa is gone for the day, Verna, and he won't be back until tomorrow. It's OK to tell me what happened."

Verna said she couldn't figure out why Miss Sybil loved that Talbert Bramwell so much. 'Miz Sybil a strong un, but she sho skeert o' dat man wen she fine out how he wer. Cud be lak Miz Clemmie say, 'Ah piece o' man bettuh den no man a'tall,' but ennywon kin see de livin' hell in dat man.'

Verna said she thought Miss Sybil was waiting for her baby to be born and trying to make the best of it, although everyone could see that Massa's cruel ways and his staying out all night made her miserable.

'You know dat funny-eye cuzzin Miss Sybil brung heah?' Verna's voice dropped lower, 'She gittin wusseh n wusseh! But oh, Ah shudden be heah! Ah ben heah too lon! Massa he sen' mah Niles away cuz o' de missin' stable key, and deys washin me too! Massa, he whup mah Niles bad en sen him away—n'—n'—Melbie say Mis Rokann be followin' my Lijah! She keep dem dead eyes o' hern dead on my boy. She try ta git 'im in trubble. Ah knows she try ta git 'im n trubble. Ah knows! She follow'n Massa, too—ah knows, she plannin suthin!'

"What? What can you tell me?"

'Ah seen her sneakin' roun da stabel! She plannin suthin'—she try'na hurt my boy! Ahm gots ta go! Ahm stayin' too long! Ahm gots ta go!'

Verna's sobs grew more hysterical. Nasrene quickly took R.C. through the usual stages, awakening him. Homer helped him up and added a thump on his back, "R.C.! Man, oh man, you were Adam's mother!"

With a wide grin, R.C. took his kufi Juno held out to him, and replaced the hat at its usual angle.

"Verna told us she had a premonition of trouble involving Elijah, Roxanne, and the stable," Homer said, "but there doesn't seem to be a solid 'hookup' yet, so we don't know what it means." He glanced at his watch, "Hey, it's just 7pm. Let's switch reels. R.C., do you feel good enough to go check on Adam?"

"I feel better than I've ever felt in my life!" He hugged Juno, "I still can't get over it!"

"Me neither, ducks, but you and Adam share such a natural affinity, it makes sense. Watching you become someone else was amazing, and extremely disconcerting."

"For all these years," R.C. said, "I marveled how it was that Adam and I were instant friends. There was never an argument that amounted to anything, never a problem that we couldn't work out. I've always known he understood me, and he knew I understood him, from day one. Juno, my love, I want you to experience this, and considering your dreams, you were probably here, too, maybe at the same time."

"I agree. After what you went through, I'm sure my dreams have some ties to all of this."

"My curiosity is really itching, Juno," Nasrene said, "Just say the word. This is history in the making, and I'll be here with bells on my recorder."

Ceeoni listened carefully. Her inner voice quietly offered the suggestion, 'Maybe Juno is Roxanne?'

Covering a yawn, Juno began to gather up glasses, "Oh, 'scuse me, I need to sleep and think. But I'll be ready for my past life trek tomorrow. And don't forget to tell Adam I love him!"

x x x

At the hospital, Adam was as he had been when they saw him last. Dr. Sakaya nodded and zoomed past them out through the doorway. They arrived to find the nurse changing Adam's IV bottle; her agitation obvious in her uncoordinated movements. R.C. reached out and steadied the small tube protruding from the bottle, to assist her. "Hey there, Nurse Evelyn, are you alright?"

She nervously attached the bottle to its holder. "Thanks, Mr. Ponder, we've just called the police!"

"What?" Homer slammed his chair down.

"Yeah, I came in here to check his IV, and noticed there was too much fluid in his IV bottle. I knew it was supposed to have been nearly empty. There was more liquid than it should've been!" She paused to take a deep breath, "I knew right away something was terribly wrong! Then, the thought hit me, 'Oh Lord, somebody's added something to that bottle!'"

Her brown eyes were round circles of astonished indignation, "I hurried up and yanked that needle from his arm, called the doctor, and saved the funny bottle for 5-0."

R.C. spontaneously hugged the feisty nurse.

"Good girl. You probably saved his life. I thank you, and I know he'll thank you himself when he gets up outta' that bed."

Ceeoni's knees threatened to buckle, but she made it to a chair in time.

Opening his cellular phone, Homer punched the dial and shouted into it, "David? Dinsmore. I hope you check your messages regularly. We're in Adam's room at Crawford Long. The staff here has reason to believe Adam's IV bottle was tampered with. I'd like to request twenty-four hour protection for him. If there's some reason why this can't happen right away, please let me know. The Chief and I started school together, and she owes me a favor in exchange for all the times I let her kick my butt in sandbox."

Ceeoni watched Adam's face for any change; any sign he'd been affected at all by the unknown substance in his IV, but he looked exactly the same to her unpracticed eye, very handsome, and very still.

Dr. Sakaya, wrinkled, slender, and energetic as always, breezed back into the room so fast that Ceeoni looked to see if he was on roller skates.

"Ah, who is the next of kin to Mr. Delayno?"

R.C. raised his hand, "I am."

"Oh, yes," The doctor said without missing a beat. "Mr. Ponder, as far as I can determine from his blood work, his condition is unchanged. Thanks to the alert nurse, it appears that he didn't get enough of whatever was in the IV to cause any further damage.

Please continue to talk to him, play his music and bring people who could possibly trigger pleasant memories. I'm leaving orders that he can have visitors until midnight. Actually, we won't mind at all if someone wants to spend the night, now that we know he's still in danger. The police have the bottle."

"We're in the process of arranging police protection for him now," Homer said

The doctor, on the move, called over his shoulder, "Good! We don't need any more death stalking these halls."

Homer and R.C. had gone out for coffee. Di and Nasrene stood by the window, talking quietly. For a long time, Ceeoni had been fighting the urge to touch Adam. One touch. She stretched out her hand toward his. Just one little touch. His long, beautiful fingers appeared poised to take a keyboard by storm. Tiny beads of warm perspiration started a slow race down her forehead. The sane Ceeoni was always in a 'Have you lost your mind?' mode, and today was no exception, but she didn't listen. The words 'sanity,' 'normal,' and 'average' had lost their meaning in her life, plus they didn't work at Starcross anyway. A single touch wouldn't hurt.

She didn't even know why she wanted to do it. Her outstretched fingers made gentle contact with his, and at that moment Adam sighed a long, loud sigh. Shocked at the sound, Ceeoni jerked her fingers back.

"What'd you do, stick him with a pin?"

Ceeoni, too startled to reply to Di's question, sat frozen, staring at Adam's face.

Excitement trembled in Nasrene's voice,

"Wait a minute!" She sat down and hurriedly pulled a fresh tape from her bag, "That sounded like a good sign to me. Ceeoni, hold his hand, he might be ready to come back! Human touch may be what he's been needing! Let me see if I can reach him."

CHAPTER SEVENTEEN

Homer and R.C. passed the coffee cups while Di described what had just happened. Everyone hurried to settle down, after which Nasrene's relaxation suggestions led to her usual attempts to awaken Adam. And as usual, Adam remained unresponsive. Ceeoni continued to hold his hand, but nothing seemed to affect him until Nasrene switched over to the regression sequence, and as soon as she finished, Elijah's child's voice, strained, and emotion-filled whispered,

'Ah'm scairt.'

"What year is it?"

'1849'.

"Where are you now?"

Nasrene asked again, "Where are you?"

'Outside, near da stabel.' He broke down into sobs, and Nasrene stopped and reduced the pain. Ceeoni was struck by the enormous amount of agony balled up inside one Soul.

Elijah said he followed the wavering dim light glowing from the stable window. He knew he would get whipped half to death if he got caught, but the moon was hiding behind black clouds casting deep shadows, and he prayed he wouldn't be seen. The closer he got, the better he heard the words the voices were saying. He crouched down under the window and slowly raised up just high enough to see inside.

Furiously angry, Massa Bramwell saddled his horse. His back was turned to Miss Roxanne, who wasn't properly dressed. The thin yellow gown she almost had on was hanging off her shoulders, exposing a thin something underneath that was way too big for her. The sight of her woman's fullness and her colorless skin shining through the sheer material amazed Elijah. She had no business down here like that.

'What the hell is this supposed to be? Some kind of damn fool ambush? What are you doing in here? Cover yourself and get back in the house! I should've known all the time you stole that key!' Massa's voice sounded loud and menacing. He turned to face her, 'Now hang the damn key on that nail and get the hell out of here!'

Lifting a defiant chin, Roxanne placed both hands on her hips, 'I won't! I won't! I'll take a horse and follow you!'

He very carefully spaced his words, 'Hang up the God-damn key Roxanne, and get your dumb ass back in the house. You have exactly one minute to hand over that key!'

Expecting to be obeyed, he turned his back to her and continued to adjust the saddle. Roxanne shook her head from side to side, strands of her straggly hair remained in her face.

'No, No! No! I don't have to do what you say. You know why? You don't want me to tell my uncle what you been doin' to his precious Sybil and his precious slaves!' Her voice rose to a shrill shriek, 'And do you wanna know what else I know? Do you?' She had Massa's attention. He kept his back to her, but he stopped adjusting the saddle. 'Cousin Sybil is gonna have a black slave baby, that's what!!' she screamed, 'And I know why! Sybil's mama was a slave, that's why! And that makes your nasty old black baby nothin' but a slave! And guess what else? Your old hag Mama is settin' 'em free, right up under your stupid nose! They have a hidin' place! Your damn old slaves didn't just run off on their own. Your Mama and that ugly black maid of hers are settin' 'em free! And you don't know nothin'—you don't know nothin'!'

He stood stone still, as if he hadn't understood the meaning of her screeched tirade. Triumphant, Roxanne, took deep shuddering breaths, her pale eyes gleamed, as she hesitated, expectantly waiting for his reaction.

What did she mean, a black slave baby? Elijah wondered. 'How could that be? Miss Sybil was white and Massa was one of the whitest people he'd ever seen. And anybody knew Miss Letty couldn't set no slaves free. Miss Letty couldn't even ride a horse and no slaves could fit into that little open wagon she and Avajay drove around.'

Massa still hadn't said a word. Roxanne's eyes narrowed. With each heaving breath, her fleshy breasts and stomach shook. Massa moved quickly, whirling around to face her, yelling,

'That's a Goddamn pile of crazy Goddamn lies, and I'm gonna whip you 'til your own Mama won't know you!'

He reached out fast and caught her in both arms. His boots slipped slightly in the hay and when he stumbled, she laughed her high-pitched snicker and tried to embrace him. He reached to tear her hands away. The move infuriated her, and she screamed, 'You better listen! You're just a big fool!' He tried to pry the key out of her clenched fist until she sank her teeth into his chest so hard, red blood seeped through his white shirt. He grunted, and reached for his wound, which gave her a chance to wriggle from his grasp, as she backed away from him, talking fast, 'You don't wanna hear the truth! I'm tellin' you! I know all about it!'

Slowly, Massa walked toward her. Elijah believed that he was probably going to kill her this time. Roxanne backed further away as she kept talking,

'My Momma saw the whole thing! Uncle Baldwin, Sybil's Daddy, was sniffin' round the slave cabins after a Negress. My Momma told me how he gave her everything, and didn't care what nobody thought, not even his wife. My Momma said his wife died of a broken heart, what with that big slave bitch lordin' it over everybody! And it was a good thing she didn't live long enough to see that black bitch give birth to her husband's child!'

Talbert and Roxanne turned toward the creaking sound of the opening stable door.

'Who gave birth to whose child, Roxanne?', Sybil Baldwin Bramwell asked as she stepped into the flickering circle of lantern light. Nearly as tall as her husband, and nine months pregnant, she had gained a great amount of weight. The sky blue ruffled nightdress she wore was the biggest garment Elijah had ever seen. Sybil was never beautiful; her nose was short and up-tilted, and pregnancy had widened her already large face. With her thick hair fanned out around her cheeks, and her small brown eyes shining and bucked in anger, she was a frightening sight. Roxanne didn't flinch. She made no effort to pull the yellow satin robe around herself. Her eyes sparkled in happy surprise, and she spoke in a cajoling whine,

'Why, Cousin Sy-bil! Dear, dear Cousin! Why oh why don't you just go on and tell your husband the truth?' Her smile was a sarcastic sneer that didn't change, although Sybil kept walking toward her.

'What truth??!' Sybil choked in a near sob, 'And what are you doing with my robe and underclothes? Why are you down here in the middle of the night, with my husband, half-dressed? What's going on here?' She repeated herself, screaming, 'What's going on here??'

Phineas, who always kept an ear open for the horses, silently joined Elijah at the window, with a 'shhh—quiet' finger up to his lips.

Roxanne's mood changed abruptly. She danced on tip-toe in a slow circle, twisting the gown around her feet and half-singing in a childish soprano, as if explaining something to small children.

'See, cousin, it's common knowledge your Momma was a black slave.'

Astonished, Sybil cocked her head the way an animal turns to listen.

'I was just tellin' Cousin Talbert that your baby there is a slave baby, Sy-bil,' Roxanne said, 'Why, everybody knows when you have a slave Mammy like you did, all your babies are gonna be black!'

Sybil screamed a long. 'Noooooooooooo!' Blood rushed to her twisted features. Her eyes filled with tears,

'My Mother was Spanish! Talbert, remember my Daddy told you my Mother was Spanish, from Spain?! That's why I went to school in Spain! Daddy wanted me to learn the ways of my people. Daddy said—my Mother was—she was—she—'

Talbert's eyes, hard and glazed on his wife made Elijah think of how he would examine an insect he intended to squash. Roxanne threw her head back in one of her hysterical laughs, sucking air in snorting gasps.

'What? You mean you didn't know? You didn't know? Cou-sin Sybill! All this time I thought you were tryin' to fool Talbert! But you really didn't know? You didn't—?'

The only sound Elijah heard was Sybil's agonized groan as her face cracked; tears flowed while her lips moved to form words. She clutched her stomach with one hand and suddenly lunged at Roxanne, snatching a handful of the flimsy sheer material,

'Take off my gown!' she screamed as the girl ran past her. Roxanne simply shrugged off the gown, then stepped lightly over the little pile of fabric, while laughingly relishing the game. Sybil fell to her knees sobbing coarse sobs, bending over the shred of white lace she held to her swollen body.

Talbert went to her, whispering to her, attempting to lift her. Elijah looked around and found himself alone at the window; Phineas wasn't beside him any longer. He didn't remember what happened next. His mind became a jumble of blurry disconnected noises and colors that swelled up louder and brighter. He closed his eyes tightly and covered his ears, too afraid to see and hear anymore. The sharp smell of hot smoke burned his nostrils. When he opened his eyes, panic in his chest fluttered like the blazing fire before him.

Inside the burning stable, Massa carried Miss Sybil, who looked like she was asleep, and so heavy Massa staggered, slowly moving around the fire blocking his path; fire that caught onto everything faster than Elijah's startled eyes could follow. Elijah saw Phineas run past Massa to release the trapped horses that thumped and neighed frantically in their stalls. Roxanne, wearing only a short shift, ran outside. By this time, slaves, alarmed and fearful, had heard the noise. They hurried, bringing water, trying to put out the fire that was burning too fast to be quenched. Elijah ran around the front and saw Roxanne close the stable doors. A flash of silver betrayed the key still in her hand. He thought she had run out of the stable to save herself, but why had she closed the doors when the horses and the people were still—?

Then he realized she was laughing, frantically fumbling with the key in an effort to lock Miss Sybil, Massa, Phineas, and all of the horses, inside. Elijah was shaking all over and although he knew somebody had to do something, he didn't know what to do.

'Oh God, please—' Trembling, he got to his feet and ran to stop Roxanne, but Avajay rounded the corner of the stable and reached Roxanne before he did. She caught Roxanne's arms from behind, causing Roxanne's eyes to pop in alarm. The gleeful smile faded just before Avajay spun her around, and punched her hard in the face with her fist. The stable key plopped to the ground as Roxanne fell backward, out cold. Avajay stepped over the sprawled body and hurried into the burning building.

In the confusion, Elijah cried for the horses, and he cried harder when, with Avajay leading the way around the panicking horses and burning obstacles, Massa and Phineas carried Miss Sybil's huge body out, and placed her under the oak tree.

She looked so odd lying there in an awkward position, with one leg twisted underneath the other. Massa dropped to his knees beside her. He reached around to cradle her head, and pulled his hand away quickly. Staring at his hand, he carefully inspected the dripping blood that ran down his arm, soaking his shirtsleeve. Phineas knelt beside Sybil with tears running down his cheeks. Avajay knelt at Sybil's feet, and gently straightened the twisted one that was missing a blue embroidered slipper. Sitting on the grass, Massa gazed at his bloody hand as if it didn't belong to him. People coughed and choked in the haze, and rushed to keep the panicking horses from stampeding and trampling children and old people. Elijah knew nothing could stop the fire that was blowing wild in the strong wind. Filled with overwhelming emotion, he felt the hot fire on his cheeks, and wondered if he would ever feel like himself again.

Avajay's sharp command jerked him away from the roaring flames, 'You there, bring a container of water, and hurry!' Elijah ran the few yards to the trough, and filled the only thing he could find, a metal pan with no handles. He ran back to her, wobbling, spilling some.

'Now,' she said, 'Hold it over that pile of smoldering saddles to warm it a little, yes, hold it with this rag, I don't want you to burn your hand.'

With a pair of scissors from her pocket, she cut the skirt of Sybil's blue gown into large pieces. 'Quickly, Phineas, go fetch a lantern from the blacksmith's shed.' Since he couldn't see well in the thick acrid smoke and ashes, Elijah went about what Avajay told him to do in a dreamlike state. He jumped at the sound of a great noise, and cringed as the stable collapsed in on itself, leaving a pile of smoking, charred remains where the large building had been. He had seen dead people before. It dawned on him that the reason Miss Sybil looked so strange was because she was dead. He couldn't believe Miss Sybil was dead. He began to tremble. He heard his own whimpering, but he couldn't stop it. Avajay called to him again,

'Come sit close to me, I need your help.'

He sat beside her as he was told, and she covered his lap with the layers of the cloth. She closed Sybil's staring eyes and raised what was left of the blue nightgown until it was over her head. He was glad that her face was covered, but her huge legs and torso were exposed. Avajay washed the massive middle of her body with splashes of water from the pan he held. Before he had time to register his shock at the gruesome sight, Avajay quickly, silently cut the flesh of Sybil's stomach open. Her scissors seemed to have life of their own, sawing inch by inch through splashing spurting blood. Her deft movements became a bloody blur. He couldn't imagine what she was doing. Suddenly, she pulled a wet, wriggling infant from the dead body. She turned the baby girl up by her heels and slapped her bottom. The tiny baby gasped, choked and wailed. Awed, Elijah stared with wide eyes as Avajay placed the baby on his lap, cut the slimy cord of twisted gray skin attached to her navel, and wiped the little one clean with a dampened piece of the blue cloth.

He examined the squirming bundle of humanity he held. The miracle of this perfect little baby, emerging from a stomach, overwhelmed him. He wondered how she got in there. She didn't look like a slave baby to him, slave babies were brown and this baby was a light pink color. He disregarded Roxanne's ravings; she was crazy and didn't know what she was talking about, anyway.

Avajay arranged the material around the baby to keep her warm. It seemed natural for him to enfold her protectively while he looked into the most beautiful face he'd ever seen. He didn't care one way or another about babies, but this one had stopped her squalling, and was studying his face with round light brown eyes, like she knew him. He was mesmerized, exhausted, and too afraid to move a muscle, afraid to disturb her, afraid to hurt her or start her up crying again. He sat stiffly, unwilling to even wipe away his burning, itchy tears.

The commotion had died down; torrid heat from the fire had dissipated, and a chill cooled the air. People slowly went back to their beds. The horses were finally calm and tethered.

He watched two slaves carry Miss Sybil's blanket-covered body away while Phineas and another slave led spitting, cursing, struggling Roxanne back toward the Big House. Massa didn't seem to notice anything at all; he got to his feet and lurched aimlessly around the burnt wreckage without ever once even looking at his newborn daughter.

Unaware of his own state of shock, Elijah cuddled the baby and hummed a tuneless little song while Avajay talked to Darnella, a slave who had given birth two weeks before. The baby's eyes held their unwavering focus on his face. With Darnella at her side, Avajay leaned over to him and asked gently,

'Elijah, did you see what happened in the stable?'

In his mind's eye, images mixed up with blood, and fire, and screaming laughter blended into a senseless nightmare. He couldn't answer. He didn't know what to say. He couldn't remember. Avajay sat down on the grass beside him,

'Did anyone else see what happened? When I got there, Roxanne was trying to lock the stable doors. What did you see?'

He tried to remember, but his mind was enclosed by a wall of red tears. 'Ah don' know, Miz Vacha—'

Avajay patted his shoulder, smiled her thanks, and gently took the baby from his suddenly empty arms. The wet nurse, Darnella, followed her as she spoke conversationally to the bundle she carried,

'Come with me, little Soul, you have much to do. You will know great happiness and great pain, and the world will be a better place because of your presence in it. Miss Letty will be so pleased that you've arrived safe and sound.'

Elijah showed signs of emotional overload; he trembled and appeared distressed. It was obvious that further probing would be futile. Nasrene carefully reduced the pain and suggested to Adam that he would remember everything that happened. She asked Elijah one more thing.

'Is Miss Avajay in this room now?'

'Yeh, Miz Vacha, you heah," he replied.

Nasrene swallowed, 'Elijah, do you mean that I am Avajay?"

His voice was a barely audible tremulous whisper, 'Yasum.'

x x x

After Nasrene gave Adam the final suggestion, she hesitated for a few minutes before breaking the stunned silence in the room.

"Well, well," she said, "I can't say that I'm surprised."

She might not have been surprised, but everyone else was.

"I'm familiar with a few of my lives, but it seems that I had one here at Starcross, just like everyone else."

"And," Di interjected, "you were highly evolved spiritually then, also."

"Since we've all lived many lifetimes, with many more to go, a Soul might turn up anywhere," Nasrene laughed, "still, I'm anxious to learn more about Avajay."

"Elijah was the only one who might have seen Talbert kill Sybil, but he was too little to withstand the horror of that night," Ceeoni said.

R.C., visibly upset, jerked out of his chair and strode across the room,

"Look, we don't know if any of this is doing Adam any good or not, do we?"

"R.C., we know something from back then relates to today," Nasrene said, joining him at the window, "The universe has opened this rare pathway to the past, and I believe we'll find everything the Souls of nineteenth century Starcross seem determined to tell us."

Swinging around to face her, he blurted,

"I mean, I can appreciate the incredibly wonderful things we're learning about eternal life, ourselves and each other, but what about Adam? What about him? He's showing no signs of coming back to himself! Maybe all of this is too much for him! Maybe we ought to just leave him alone. Maybe the regressions are stressing him out, maybe we ought to let him heal naturally."

"We can't give up now," Nasrene took his hand, "most of all, if Adam's been carrying that great load of misery in his Soul, getting it out is doing him a world of good. Catharsis is the essence of healing."

R.C.'s face wore a pained expression as he wrapped his outstretched arms around her,

"Oh, I know, I do. I'm just chomping at the bit for him to get his butt up from there. I've never seen him disabled, incommunicado, so damn far away!" He kept his arm around Nasrene and rubbed his eyes with his free hand, in a classic gesture of fatigue.

"I think we all should just try to get some rest," Nasrene sighed. "Let's just go. We can't solve anything tonight."

Back at Homer's, Di stayed downstairs while Ceeoni bid everyone 'goodnight' and sought solitude. Throughout what felt like a long and sleepless night, her thoughts wandered around in the empty corners of the 'What-If Department, Among The Clouds of Speculation'. Was Adam really reacting to human contact when she touched his hand? Or was his deep sigh purely coincidental, an indication of awakening neurological activity that would've happened anyway?

CHAPTER EIGHTEEN

At breakfast Monday morning, Nasrene announced plans to go to her apartment at Emory University for her luggage. Homer had gone to get the newspapers, and Ceeoni had spent the morning on the kitchen phone, rearranging the theatre schedule. Jake had agreed with her decision to postpone saxophonist Gerald Albright's dates, for the purpose of keeping the Starcross dark for a full three weeks. The talent managers and agents she'd been able to contact were cooperative and understanding. Everyone asked her to convey well wishes to Adam and his family. She'd approved changes in the ads for the *Atlanta Journal-Constitution, Creative Loafing* and the college and university papers, to be implemented by the staff.

She had left Di schlepping sleepily around their suite in search of the perfect thing to wear. Di and Homer had stayed up until past the wee hours. After tossing and turning, the last thing Ceeoni remembered was seeing 3am on the clock. She had no idea what time Di had gone to bed.

She reflected on the enormity of what had come into their lives in such a short time. Within a few days she had come to realize that no matter how preposterous it seemed, Starcross was an enchanted place where the past and present overlapped, as if time had never existed.

Homer stormed into the kitchen and wordlessly threw several copies of the newspaper on the table before he poured himself a steaming cup of Weber's fragrant special blend. Ceeoni slid a paper from the stack. Oh! Starcross was all over the AJC! Basil Cassidy's murder and life history, Adam Delayno's bio, the kidnapping and assault on Adam, his present condition, and a rave review of the Friday night opening concert. There was a history of the Starcross Theatre, complete with an allusion to the "curse," which the locals said was put on Starcross by the spirit of the anonymous charred bones that had been found on the property. And if all of that that wasn't enough, there was a feature on Homer's life, the restoration of the theatre, and the building of Starcross Lakes Estates, as well as the feature on Ceeoni in the Arts Section. Aghast, she wondered if there'd been any other news in Atlanta over the weekend.

"Veggie brunch burger, anybody?" Homer asked as he bit into the sandwich in his hand.

"I was a veggie kind of girl before I saw 'Babe'," Ceeoni replied, "but I've had breakfast, thanks."

Diana made a grand entrance in a dramatic black watch plaid knee length pants and coat ensemble, "I'm ready to go, whenever and wherever we're going!"

Homer cuddled her close, and fed her some of his burger. "Yum!" she squealed,

"Where can I get some more of that?"

He gestured toward the covered platter behind him, "Weber makes them himself out of his famous secret ingredients." Di, chewing a mouthful mumbled,

"Homer, Darling, I could get used to these."

"See there," he said, "this is the delicious stuff that gives me the energy to hang out with you half the night and build houses by day, which I must go do now and which, I might add, will help me forget about that damn paper over there."

Wearing his ever-present silk Gi, Weber brought in a tray of juices. This day, the Gi was shiny black.

"Homer, I forgot to tell you. I took Minette to the airport last night, about 11:30, in time for the Delta redeye to Kennedy."

Behind him, Nasrene waved her farewell, "Well, I'm off. Web offered to drive me, but I don't how long I'll be. I've settled for Web's very fine and, hopefully, very accurate map to my destination. Thanks for the use of the car, Homer. Oh, and by the way, if you knew my sense of direction, you'd keep me in your prayers."

"Just call if you get lost, the phone is in the console," Weber said.

Homer answered the ring of the kitchen phone. What was said on the other end caused him to bang the receiver down, hard. Throwing his burger into the sink, he moved fast for the door, patting pockets for his keys, he called over his shoulder

"There's a fire on Starwood Drive, who's going with me?!"

Nasrene, already at the door, yelled, "A fire??"

Ceeoni rushed to get her kicked-off alligator pumps back on, while everybody scrambled toward the foyer. Outside, fire engines bleated their alarm sirens, smoke billowed up over the patio, darkening the view, and stinging their eyes.

The fire was just around the corner. Homer got there before the engines rounded the curve to the house. Suffocating heat and smoke filled the air. Parked across from the burning house in an empty field, they stood, noses covered, and watched the devastation. The fire was burning fast; it looked like flames had already demolished most of the building.

Ceeoni maneuvered around the firemen unraveling hoses to pull a brochure from the curb container—6 bedrooms, 6 marble baths, 8 fireplaces, marble foyer and dining room, library, gym, pub, tennis court, 14-foot ceilings, boat door, garden tubs, 2 Corian kitchens, in-door/ outdoor pool, guest house, waterfall and six-car garage. It would have been a wonderful place to live.

The normally even-tempered Homer Dinsmore was mad as hell, "Nobody can tell me this isn't arson! We've never had a fire! In nearly 30 years of building, there's never been a fire!" The anger and frustration in his eyes resounded in the louder than usual gruffness in his voice. Starwood Drive was a tangle of firemen who shot at the flames with high-pressure arcs in an effort to save some parts of the 6500 feet of luxury, but it was soon obvious that the fire had won.

"Oh, Baby," Di leaned her head on Homer's broad shoulder, "I wish there was something I could do."

"You already have, Di," he kissed her cheek, "You already have."

"I've been thinking about last night," Nasrene said. "It seems the regressions have led us to consider a pertinent possibility, that this Soul, the one who probably set fire to the stable in 1849 and was responsible for Sybil's death, is the same Soul with us today. Roxanne? Or Talbert? Or? It's strange that a fire would occur now. I mean, is the killer repeating himself?"

"OK," Homer groaned, "But where in the hell is he or she? We don't really know a lot about the killer in the past, but if he's doing the same things now that he did then, he's still good at covering his tracks."

"Yeah, Homer," Nasrene agreed, "and whoever it is, you can believe this Soul is totally enraged. He's shown he's prepared to do anything to destroy the theatre, and/or the entire Starcross Complex, and nobody would have a clue as to who or why.

"I'm grateful for Adam's coma because it may be the key, the only way we can unlock the killer's present identity is by probing the past by way of past life regression." She turned to Ceeoni,

"I hope you'll agree to past life regression soon. Your deja vu experience most definitely ties you to Starcross, apparently you were here around the same time."

Knowing she wasn't ready yet, or if she would ever be ready for past life regression, Ceeoni smiled slightly, and again, Nasrene left her alone.

"Well, all I know is what's done is done, and this house looks like a total loss. It'll have to be rebuilt," Homer sighed.

"Mr. Dinsmore?" asked one of the firemen, "What about insurance?"

"Oh, we have plenty of that," he said aloud, then half-mumbled to himself, "One damn disaster after another is quite enough!"

"C'mon, Homer, the professionals will finish up. We can't do anything," Di said.

"No," he said, "We can't do anything about this house, but we've got to do something. We're all in danger. I know our perpetrator has enough imagination to do plenty more damage."

Sitting next to Homer in the car, Di swung around to face the back seat.

"Nasrene, then the goal is to discover if Talbert or Roxanne killed Sybil Baldwin, and whoever that Soul is now, that person is the Starcross killer?"

"I don't know, I just don't know. There isn't enough evidence."

"Is it possible for a person to be doing these things without realizing it?" This question had been bouncing around in Ceeoni's head, and she finally saw an opportunity to ask it.

"Oh yeah, many psychopathic personalities are out of touch with their crimes; they attribute the 'bad things' to an alter ego, or they'll create multiple personalities. There are cases where the other personalities have separate identities whose activities, even allergies and medical conditions, are unknown to the patient."

"Whoa! Even medical conditions?"

"Sounds impossible, Ceeoni, but it's true, I've seen a severe asthma attack disappear the instant another personality takes over."

"Double Whoa! But, ah, well, is it possible for a person to lie or conceal information during past life regression?"

Regarding Ceeoni with curiosity, Nasrene answered,

"Hmm, I'm only guessing, but I would think so. People can be evasive and cunning, even when regressed. I believe that the regressions we've seen in the past few days were painful, but I've heard of cases where the past life visions or recall were terrifying, and people responded to that energy in many unpredictable ways. Here at Starcross, we've all rejoiced at the thought and we marveled at the irrefutable evidence of past life memories, so far, but some people are paralyzed with fear. And, as far as our murderer is concerned, we can't really assume it's Talbert or Roxanne. I said that because it could be either of them, but it could also be someone we haven't met. The only thing we can be sure of is that there's a reason why the past life regressions flowed so freely from each Soul, with each one telling their part of intertwining occurrences."

"And remember," Di said, "We had all been instructed to go to a life that relates to today's events. Now, I've been wondering, have other people shared knowledge of past lives?"

"Oh, I've heard of a few. I've read where two or three people shared past life memories, and there were fifteen people in California who discovered, through a series of regressions, that they recognized each other from a shared past in 19th century Georgia, but what's happened here is completely new to me."

Ceeoni was still mentally digesting the possibility of someone committing crimes that he or she couldn't recall and could lie about it, even during regression, when Homer hailed David Saxon speeding to the fire.

"Hey, Dave! You need to see me? We're on our way back to my house." With a trace of his dashing smile, David U-turned and, by the time they arrived, he was waiting for them in Homer's driveway. Nasrene, map in hand, spoke to the detective before she took off for Emory in the Black BMW, while everyone else went inside.

David sat back in one of the Moroccan leather chairs comprising a conversation area to the right of the doorway, and waited for everyone to get settled. To the left, a large teak coffee table sat between a pair of elegant black brocade sofas that faced each other in front of a two-story high, black marble fireplace. Several rugs and chairs matched the zebra patterned sheer drapes that covered a wall of glass with double doors to the patio. Tribal shields, masks, spears and statuettes from Kenya, Ghana, Mali, Nigeria and Benin all comprised the bold motif that fit Homer's personality. Weber said no designer had touched it; Homer had collected every odd piece and allowed his enthusiasm to create an atmosphere of exotic comfort.

"Homer," David said, "I don't know what's in your stars, Buddy, but you're catchin' Holy Hell. We've ascertained that the fire broke out before 9:30 this morning, and burned for a while before the alarms went off. Your crew was a few streets away, working on another place on Starcrest Drive, and naturally, nobody saw or heard anything. So, where was everybody?"

"I worked on the kitchen phone from about 9am," Ceeoni volunteered. "Di was getting dressed and Homer was out."

"Right," Homer said, "but I was back by 10:30 and I ran into three people we both know, the Shannon twins and Mimi's husband, Alonzo."

David rubbed his eyes, "Oh, OK—I spoke to Juno and R.C. already. They're on their way over to meet you here."

At the mention of their names, the ring of the doorbell announced the Ponders, who joined the others in the living room. Two hours later, after everyone accounted for their time and stated their morning's activities, David got up to take his leave, saying, "Well, I guess that's all for now. Have a pleasant day. Oh, Ms. Jones, may I have a word with you?"

Ceeoni led the way, "Sure, I'll walk you out." When they reached the foyer, David took her hand, "Ceeoni, let's just go do something.

We're all in need of some R & R. Why don't we take a walk, have lunch, get drunk—go to a hotel and lay up—"

Ceeoni wasn't offended, but she wasn't flattered, either. That wasn't the way to start anything, even if she wanted to.

"Well—I've only just arrived here. I need to wait until some of the air is cleared of squeaking doors and bumps in the night. I'll be more able to unwind and think when we're not stumbling through one sinister mystery after the other."

David pretended to fall against the wall, holding his heart. Before she could resist, he pulled her face to his and bent to quickly kiss her lips. With a small smile, he quipped, "Hey, Lady, you just don't know what we're missing. I've got a real thing for you. I don't know when I've felt something this strong, and I—"

Genuinely taken by surprise, David's spontaneous kiss was still warm on her mouth, when the doorbell rang. What Ceeoni was about to say as she turned away to let Nasrene and her rolling bag in, was lost in the moment.

"Hey there," Nasrene said, "Where is everybody?" Ceeoni pointed to the living room. David persisted as soon as Nasrene was out of earshot,

"Ceeoni, SweetCakes, can we get together soon? Please tell me that's what you were about to say to me?"

"David—uh, we'll talk. I'm just not—"

"Ceeoni, please, please don't give me any of the stock excuses!"

"Look, everything has happened too fast for me since I decided to take this job. If something doesn't settle down soon, I'll be stark raving crazy and only fit for my very own padded cell at Milledgeville."

David was holding one of her hands with both of his. He squeezed the fingers he'd captured. "Oh, you know about Milledgeville?" he asked, adding a dimpled grin.

"I read that it's the second largest prison-hospital complex in the country, and it's not far from Atlanta."

"Right. It's always held a large number of America's criminally insane, ever since it opened in 1842. Back then they called it the Georgia State Lunatic Asylum. One interesting fact is that when it opened, all the attendants were slaves—I guess caring for the deranged patients was too much of a dangerous and filthy job for the white ruling class."

"What a distressing name, Lunatic Asylum." The little voice in the back of her mind whispered, 'That's where they took Roxanne.' She unconsciously shook her head, as if having a sudden muscle spasm. He tried to pull her closer, "Are you OK?" he whispered. She nodded, but resisted his tug at her hand.

"Oh, Ceeoni, I'm sorry if it disturbs your sensibilities, but 'lunatics' was the common word for people who were mentally unbalanced. They eventually removed the word 'lunatic' and renamed it the Georgia Central State Hospital and it's still standing today. You sure you're OK?" he asked.

"Ah—yes, it's just that the idea of a hospital for the criminally insane is chilling. I can imagine all the lost souls who must've lived tortured lives there." She still felt the cold that seemed to linger in her bones longer than usual. Anxious to be alone to try to sort out her thoughts, Ceeoni gently extricated her trapped hand, but Detective Saxon was still in pursuit.

"Miss Lady Sweetness, don't you trouble your purty lil' head none—" He intoned in an unexpected and very accurate John Wayne impersonation, and she couldn't help but smile. He took that opportunity to reach for her hand again, but she opened the front door.

"Try and get some rest, Detective," she said.

With a parting dimple demonstration, he sighed, winked at her and spoke softly,

"Like I told you, Beautiful Lady, I can wait indefinitely for something truly special—I'm a very, very patient man—"

She knew she would eventually have to let him know in no uncertain terms that she didn't want anything to do with him.

CHAPTER NINETEEN

At the hospital, everyone got comfortable in Adam's room except R.C., who paced the floor, talking to Adam's still sleeping form,

"You know, if it weren't for Juno and the kids, I could stay right here in this room!"

"We all know that," Juno interjected, "I'm glad I'm here to keep you from harassing the staff."

"Juno, you know just sitting around has been difficult for me." R.C.'s words tumbled on urgently, "Since I met Adam, everything has been in high gear; touring, recording, getting married, the births of our children, juggling the momentum of meeting deadlines, putting out the fires of life's dramas, trying to stay on schedule and spend time with my family. It's been one big, beautiful circus, the best and highest of highs. We couldn't stop! Hell, who wanted to stop? I know if Adam had his way, he'd be practicing right now. It feels so weird to suddenly hold still, waiting!—not knowing when he's going to wake up, or how he'll be if he wakes up! Not to mention the logistics! His attorneys are taking over some of the business Basil Cassidy handled, and I'm taking up some slack on that end too, but there's all this stuff only Adam can do."

Nobody interrupted R.C.'s ranting, knowing that his frustration had to be expressed.

"For starters," R.C. continued, "We're supposed to begin a major tour the end of next week: two weeks of European jazz festivals, then on to Japan, followed by one week in Vancouver. After that, Florida, New York, then back to England. How am I going to tell these people something meaningful when I don't know what the hell I should say? Plus, within the next six months, he's got a film to score, a new CD to finish and a Cadillac commercial. Damn, Damn, Damn!"

After R. C. slumped in the chair next to Juno's with his head in his hands, Juno said,

"Look, he's going to be just fine. We've got to believe that. The best thing we can do is have faith. Now I know your bloody impatience rarely has time for faith, but we don't have anything else, and certainly, nothing works as well."

"Nasrene," Ceeoni asked, "I've been wondering, are there any other references in the Bible that would indicate reincarnation?"

"Oh yes, I can think of several. One interesting passage, among many suggestive of Soul survival, is when Elizabeth, the mother of John the Baptist, was pregnant with John. When she met Mary, who was pregnant with Jesus, in Luke, Chapter 1, Verse 44, it says, 'John leapt for joy in his mother's womb.' I think that means that John was an aware Soul, waiting to be born, who recognized the Soul of Jesus. If John hadn't been sentient and possessed of psychic abilities and/or prescience before he was born, then that wonderful recognition could not have been possible. People say that in 'Bible days' the 'Holy People' could do things we can't do today, but in St. John, Chapter 14, Verse 12, Jesus said, 'He that believeth on me and the works that I do shall he do also . . . and greater works than these shall he do . . . 'This is saying to me that we are all capable of miracles beyond the physical. The incident with John tells me that he not only recognized Jesus before they were both born, but he knew Jesus' earthly destiny, was expecting Jesus, and was joyous at Jesus' arrival. If you read the Bible in the light of reincarnation, you'll find many more passages that give you an idea that Souls survive death. One of the Psalms says, ' . . . in my flesh I shall see God.'"

"Well after what I saw and felt as Miss Letty," Homer said, "I know how totally seamless it is for me to still be me, even when I knew I had been Miss Letty."

"Most people who have been regressed feel the same way, as if the past life vision is a part of themselves that they'd forgotten," Nasrene commented.

"But, wait a minute, couldn't John have known Jesus in heaven? What would suggest life after life here on earth?"

"Homer, John had precognitive knowledge of earthly things while still in the womb, it doesn't state how he knew." She pulled open the bedside cabinet and handed Homer the King James Bible," Here, read some parts for yourself and see what you make of it."

"Where should I start?"

"Take a look at Ecclesiastes Chapter 1, Verse 10."

Homer quickly leafed through the pages, saying, "Oh, this is where it says 'there is no new thing under the sun.'" In a theatrical voice that soared toward Heaven like a preacher's in the pulpit, he read, "Is there anything thereof it may be said, See this is new? It hath been already of old times, which was before me. There is no remembrance of former things."

"That was beautiful," Di breathed, "I would love to hear you read two of my favorites, St. John, Chapter 5, Verse 24, and Chapter 8, Verse 51?"

After flipping pages, Homer read, "I say unto you, He that heareth my word, and believeth on him that sent me, hath everlasting life, and shall not come into condemnation; but is passed from death to life." He paused just a moment, finding the right line, "And the next one, you said is verse 51? OK, it says—'if a man keep my saying, he shall never see death'. And I can't leave out my favorite, John 3:16."

"Bing-o," R.C. said quietly. "For God so loved the world that He gave his only begotten son, that whosoever believeth in him, shall not perish, but have everlasting life."

"I believe Jesus came to give the world a clearer vision of a vast truth that isn't easily within man's ability to grasp." Nasrene's eyes locked briefly with every pair of eyes as she talked, "When the Bible says, 'lean not unto your own understanding,' I think we're like the blind men and the elephant, our understanding is so piteously limited. And God Jehovah, Yahweh, Jah, Allah, or whatever you choose to call God, is unlimited. The word 'Name' means, in the way of—or in the nature of, the way it works. Praising God's name I think means to raise up awareness of the certainty of eternal life and goodness in our consciousness, in spite of each Soul's earthly lessons.

"When deciding what to believe, we must know that what God can do and what God does, is far beyond our tiny ability to imagine.

I think that is the reason we must develop 'the faith of a child.' We all know how a child has a marvelous faith, until he sees the world's realities. True faith is believing in, and holding to God's eternal goodness as the only reality, even though our eyes see destruction and death. If life is eternal, then that destruction and death is only temporary."

"While we're on the subject," Homer said, "There's something else that interests me. Jesus talks about people in their graves hearing his voice on the Day of Judgment."

"Well," Nasrene answered, "Remember, the near death experiences so many people report? These experiences have been reported by people all over the world for ages, and they are the nearest anyone has come to dying. Some say the visions of Heaven, or of one's entire life—or of departed loved ones, are due to oxygen deprivation, and because the person comes back, he wasn't really dead. People who have actually been through a near death experience know better, for their lives are completely changed after encountering a 'Being of Light' or simply a Light that radiates complete and total Love. Could the Being of Light be Jesus? Some people think so," Nasrene said. "But, to answer your question with more food for thought, maybe Jesus, or the Light of Pure Love comes to each of us at death, one at a time, as in countless near death experiences, rather than all Souls on a single day."

"Well, you would think more Souls would remember that feeling of total love and would be more loving in the next lifetime."

"Yeah, Homer," she sighed. "Our human experience is based on what we choose to believe, even when our hearts know better. I recall Edgar Cayce wrote that the Souls who believe in the power of evil are still with us. He called them the 'Sons of Baal' because they melted down their jewelry and made a golden bull they called Baal, then they conducted an orgy while Moses was receiving the Commandments on Mt. Sinai. They believed the material, or 'mammon,' was all there is. Cayce said the 'Sons of Baal' are the same Souls who removed as much reincarnation from the Bible as they could in order to leave that which seemed in line with their own limited understanding. Possibly the idea that man's Spirit transcends death, and gets many chances to learn, was beyond their comprehension, which is still true today. Cayce said the same Souls are born again and again, determined to manifest permanent evil, death and destruction in the Eternal Kingdom, which, according to Jesus, is not possible if one only believes in the power of God. Besides, if one believes that God has a reason for everything, then, there is a reason why people have memories of past lives, as well as having many types of out-of-body experiences, and other evidence of Soul Survival. I'm reminded of the Biblical statement when God says, 'Behold, I make all things new.' I believe that the phrase, 'All Things', includes humanity. Which begs the compelling question, 'How can man fail to be inspired by a totally regenerating universe?—Totally!"

"Oh, yes, yes, and yes!" Homer clapped his hands. "The idea of reincarnation has liberated me and answered so many of my questions. I've spent my whole life wondering why bad things happen to good people."

Suddenly, R.C. left his chair, went to the window, stopped, and quickly turned toward the bed, his olive green robes swirled around his arms raised in an all embracing gesture.

"Adam! Adam, wake up, My Brother! There is so much to talk about. You're not going to believe how beautiful this is!"

x x x

After R.C. settled down, the click of Nasrene's recorder announced Nasrene's quiet voice proceeding with the now familiar relaxation process. Adam remained as unresponsive as ever, until the regression sequence was completed. When she asked,

"Where are you now?" the answer came immediately.

'Starcross Manor.' His voice had changed; the tonality sounded more mature than it had in the earlier sessions, but it was obviously Elijah's voice.

"What year is it?"

'1853'

"How old are you?"

'12'

Elijah said the four years since the tragedy had passed uneventfully. He worked hard everyday, and tried to get over the guilt he felt when he couldn't remember what his Daddy looked like. And he tried to get over the pain he felt when he remembered that Massa had whipped his Mama so bad, all she could do for several weeks was half-crawl, until the gouged rivers of shredded skin on her back and the open, festering welts encircling her upper thighs had stopped oozing pus.

He also tried to get over his haunting dreams of the horrible night of the fire. After the stable burned down, they had all gone back to bed, but Roxanne's screams and laughter could be heard through the night.

The next day, Avajay had Phineas and two other slaves build a cage up around Roxanne's bed, clear up to the ceiling. She yelled, chewed at the wooden bars, spit, vomited, and threw waste at the maids who took care of her, until the people from Milledgeville came to take her away. Phineas said Milledgeville was a place where they kept people like her who weren't right in the head. Everyone at Starcross watched them lash her hands and tie her to the rear of the wagon with a rope around her waist. She screamed, drooled and laughed as she walked behind the cart. Elijah never forgot how Roxanne's pale eyes stared blindly into space. All of Elijah's brightly colored, noisy memories of 1849, imbedded at the forefront of his thoughts, came rushing back time and time again as if it had all just happened. He didn't know how to make his memories go away.

Yet there came a day when he went inside the Manor House, where he had never set foot, beginning a journey that softened the sharp pain of his childhood and changed his life.

He remembered that a burning sun was high in the sky the morning he tripped and fell against a sharp rock in the field. Shocked, he staggered to his feet, holding his eye as blood gushed through his fingers. He couldn't seem to get his balance, and when his Mama looked up from her work and saw his face covered with blood and his inability to steady his legs, her screams alarmed everyone within shouting distance. Avajay, driving by the commotion in the one-horse carriage, stopped, and without hesitation, ran into the field and pressed her hanky to his gaping, ragged wound. She almost dragged him to the house, with his Mama following behind, sobbing. He was taller than Avajay and his Mama, but dizziness came over him in waves, and the two women ended up supporting his weight part of the way to the kitchen door.

In the four years he'd lived at Starcross, he'd never seen Miss Letty up close. This day she met them at the door of the big house, wearing a pink dress that rustled and floated in rhythm with the bouncing snow white ringlets on top of her head. Slave gossip had said Miss Letty was a cripple whose illness made her so feeble she kept to her bed most of the time, but she didn't look at all sick to him. Frowning, she swung into action, calling for servants to bring clean rags, water and her special salve, before beckoning them to follow her through the kitchen doorway. Divine food smells filled his nostrils and, in spite of his shooting pains, the delicious scents of unknown delights reminded him he was very hungry. Miss Letty led them, Elijah still supported by his Mama and Avajay, through a short hallway. He opened his one good eye and wondered if he was in heaven. He was surrounded by a pale pink and deep rose room, with sheer dusky rose draperies hung gracefully from the high ceiling to thick pink rugs. Cabin gossip hadn't prepared him for this unimaginable lush opulence; it was hard to believe people could actually live in a place like this.

Miss Letty gestured toward one of the big shiny pink chairs, but he didn't want to sit in it for fear his coarse, dirty field clothes would spoil it. When he hesitated, she insisted, and pulled a chair up in front of him to attend to his injury herself. He remembered the Big Lessons, one of which was, 'Always keep your eyes down when a white person is near.' But there were dazzling sights to see, long pink tapered candles in gleaming golden holders, fresh pink roses and white gardenias spreading their perfume from painted bowls and vases, and delicately carved tables with chairs covered over in a material made of silver flowers. It was impossible for him to avert his good eye as he had been taught.

Avajay stared at him over Miss Letty's shoulder. Finally, he closed his eye against her watchful scrutiny. They said Avajay had been with Miss Letty since she was fifteen years old, as her constant companion and nursemaid. A thick braid of black hair hung past her waist. Her skin was blacker than any slave's, but everybody knew she wasn't a slave. She rarely left Miss Letty's side. With long flowing robes draped around her small form, anyone could see she had come from somewhere other than Georgia or the Motherland. Avajay had a mark in between her large dark eyes that Phineas said all the people in her country had, but he didn't think they were born with those marks. Phineas said she could read the future and chart the journey of a man's Soul. Some of the slaves, and especially the children, avoided her, but Elijah was never afraid of her. He felt comfortable under her sharp gaze, although he didn't know why.

While Miss Letty gently cleaned his wound, he tried hard not to cry out. He wanted Miss Letty to see that he was a brave and grateful boy. But the pain and shock, coupled with the unfamiliar sights and smells, overwhelmed him; the room revolved quickly. He closed his eye, and opened it again, just in time to catch the room spinning out of control. He felt himself falling, but couldn't stop himself, and he fainted, blood, dirt and all, into Miss Letty's lap, against her pink gown.

Through a fog he heard Miss Letty talking to his Mama,

'See there, Verna, I told you he'd only fainted. Another inch and that rock would've gone clean through his eye. Bring him back in two days, about this time, and I'll change his bandage.'

'Yasum, we sho'ly graful, we sho'ly is,' his Mama said. He hadn't heard her sound so at ease since they'd come to Starcross, except in their cabin. Someone had propped a soft pink pillow between his head and the arm of the chair. He was wishing he could stay in those beautiful surroundings forever, when his attention was pulled to a large, gold-trimmed piece of furniture in a corner of the room. He wondered what it was. Elijah sat up and felt his head expand with a dull throbbing ache, but knew he should apologize for the blood and dirt staining the front of Miss Letty's dress.

'Oh, ahm sorry ah fall on ya—'

But she smiled and waved her hand, 'It's not important. Just try to keep from busting your face open again.'

He tried to return her smile, but there was a bandage wrapped around his head, and his face felt stiff and puffy. He fixed on the object of his fascination, wondering what it was. He didn't see the look that passed between Avajay and Miss Letty.

Avajay left and returned with a tray of sandwiches made with sage roasted chicken and a large pitcher of cool lemonade. Elijah had his first astonishing tastes of those succulent treats while he listened to his Mama and Miss Letty chat about the twin babies born to Gussie and Turk the week before. Miss Letty passed the plate around and encouraged them to eat as much as they liked. He chewed slowly to make it last longer, but he kept his eye on the object in the corner while Avajay kept her shadowed dark eyes on him.

Too soon, his Mama thanked Miss Letty again while moving quickly toward the door, with a tight grip on his arm. He knew she lived in fear of Massa's displeasure, and illness or injury was no excuse to be away from the field during work hours. Verna prodded him to move along, but he forgot about his mother's urging and Massa. Elijah stopped abruptly in the center of the room. Verna hit him with a painful blow to the ribs with her elbow, but he stood his ground.

He pointed to the four-legged, shiny whatever-it-was, and blurted out, 'Wha' dat?'

His Mama was shocked by her son's audacity, but Miss Letty didn't blink. Instead, she smiled.

'Why, it's a pianoforte, child.' Then she asked him in a half—whisper, 'Would you like to hear it?'

Her words, 'hear it' and her slightly teasing tone surprised him. Hear it? He had to hear it? What was there to hear? His thoughts went blank for a few seconds—oh, please, please let me hear it! Finally, he answered in a small voice, 'Yasum.'

He took a tentative little step toward it. Did it talk? Whistle? Sing? Maybe there was a drum inside, like the little drums Dini made for the slave children to play with.

'This one was built in Philadelphia, especially for me,' Miss Letty said. 'Until Talbert was born, I played many pianos in the capitals of the world, for kings, and heads of state.' He didn't know what a Capital or a Head of State was, but he nodded solemnly.

With the grace of a much younger woman, Miss Letty sat down on the bench in front of the mysterious thing. She lifted a panel that covered the front of it, and placed her fingers on the row of little rectangular black and white blocks, with each finger resting on a different block.

Not having any notion of what to expect, he waited in trembling silence. Miss Letty's fingers pressed the blocks, and he heard the most glorious sound. It was as though heaven had opened. Miss Letty played several chords, and Elijah lost all sense of being anywhere except inside of this new wonder that filled his entire being.

Excitement caused his heart to beat faster. His Mama and Avajay watched Elijah's face. Miss Letty didn't miss his emotional response to her playing. Her eyes moved to catch Avajay's. This time, he saw the almost imperceptible nod that passed between them, but the only thing that mattered to him was that Miss Letty smiled at him again and asked,

'Would you like to try it?'

He didn't feel his feet move him across the room. He looked at the blocks, that he later learned were keys, before he delicately touched one with a slender brown finger. He wasn't sure if he chose a good one, but he liked the sound. He eagerly slid onto the bench Miss Letty had vacated. He put both hands on the keys and immediately the thought came into his mind that each tone came from a different key, and the black keys made different tones from the white ones. Deep in concentration, he played a very close approximation of a chord Miss Letty had played. More chords followed, each more clear and concise than the last. It was as if the places to put his fingers were already together in his head, like the familiar places in dreams, waiting in smiling repose for this day to arrive. He could hardly contain his joy. Dizzy with discovery, his heart filled and ran over with this grand feeling, brought on by the exquisite music he now knew he could never live without. Elijah forgot about his pain and his closed eye. He saw his Mother's confusion in her eyes that darted from Miss Letty and back to her son's fingers coursing their strange patterns on the keys. Elijah knew his Mama was pleased that he was doing something really special, but he sensed her fear as thunder in the distance. When he played a combination of notes that delighted him, he laughed out loud, and over his shoulder he heard Miss Letty whisper,

'Oh Dear God!—you're the one—it's—you—!'

The double doors that led to the great hallway opened silently, and a glowering Talbert Starcross Bramwell entered the room unsteadily, still wearing midnight blue formal clothes from the night before, complete with lace cravat and cuffs, beard stubble, muddy boots, and a self-righteous, semi-inebriated belligerence. At 6'4" and over 400 pounds, he was a red-eyed, disheveled picture of the wages of excessive appetites, griefs and hatreds. Elijah remembered that when he'd first come to Starcross four years before, Massa Bramwell hadn't been so big, but Phineas said that since then, rich food, drink, and caring for nothing but greed, lust and meanness had made him look like the fat devil he was. Every time Elijah saw Massa or thought about Miss Sybil, it would all come back to him, like a sore in his heart. Two days after the fire, Mister Baldwin's carriage had arrived at Starcross with his horses dripping lather from riding hard all night. Elijah remembered that Avajay had taken him to speak to Mr. Baldwin, who asked him very gently, 'Elijah, what did you see through the stable window the night Miss Sybil got killed?' Elijah had stood unafraid, but nervous because it was no use, he couldn't remember. He told Mr. Baldwin what he had seen, but he couldn't tell him how the fire had started or how Miss Sybil had died. Mr. Baldwin stared out the window and didn't ask him anything else. Mr. Baldwin had left for Baldwin Plantation the next day, taking with him his daughter's body, the wet nurse, and the baby girl Massa had never looked at.

 Standing there in the dead silence that had entered the beautiful room, Elijah remembered how Massa seemed to sink into a boiling rage right after the stable fire. Every now and then, a slave would run away, and all Massa's patrols couldn't stop them. Slaves wouldn't talk to each other for fear of being seen with someone who was about to escape; they knew if Massa could find a reason to hold a whuppin', he would beat a slave for hours. Henri, who stole a bucket of peaches, lost an eye when the whip split it wide open, and he almost died. They'd heard tell of slaves being killed on nearby plantations, and his Mama said it was a wonder that mad dog of a Massa hadn't killed some underfed slave at Starcross. Phineas said all the slave owners were like Massa. He said the wrong a man does eats him up from the inside, until it shows on the outside, on his face, for all the world to see.

Massa's bellowing voice brought Elijah's spinning thoughts back from his painful past.

'Get the godamn hell back to work!'

The tense little group around the piano stared at the towering, feared figure who had instantly filled the warm space with his cold fury. Elijah knew his Mama was afraid for herself, but he knew she was more afraid for him. He had to do something. He employed the only defense he could muster, remembering his Daddy's words, 'If sumbody up en ya face bout ennyteeng, ack lak nuttin' evuh happ'n, foh as lon' as ya kin.' Elijah's stomach was in his mouth as he got up from the piano bench, and keeping his eye averted, he followed his Mama, who slowly backed out the door they had come through. He half expected Massa's whiplash to chase them, scooting along the floor to coil itself around their necks and drag them back.

Partway through the kitchen, they heard Miss Letty's voice ring out, no longer the soft voice of a woman past sixty, this strong voice bounced off the walls,

'Talbert, you seem to have forgotten that this is my house! I've been helpless to stop your God-awful beatings and the slavery that turned this beautiful land into a dungeon for innocent prisoners, but the day hasn't dawned when I won't help an injured child. He nearly knocked his brains out in your field of blood, trying to do the work of two men. Now, I can't fight you your way, but I can make damn certain you'll never get Starcross! Never! Not even over my dead body!'

Verna and Elijah reached the other side of the garden just as Massa's basso roared something that they were too far away to make out. But at the sound, his Mama urged him on. He was running as fast as he could, considering that each time his foot hit the ground, the impact jarred his throbbing face, and blood leaked from under his bandage. In spite of it all, he ran, holding his face while regretting having to leave the pianoforte, and the unexpected treasure he'd found waiting just for him, inside.

Elijah's voice trailed off. He simply stopped talking. Nasrene bid Elijah goodbye, and began the suggestions. When suggested that Adam would awaken, he was silent, as always.

"Adam? Adam? Can you hear me?"

Nasrene repeated the question, and took more time with him than usual, but he didn't respond. She concluded the session and turned off the recorder, leaving everyone in the room pondering what they had just heard.

CHAPTER TWENTY

"Now we know Adam brought his musical genius from a past life," Nasrene concluded. "Actually, I've read that all innate abilities come from talents developed in past lives and that the Soul picks up new skills in every lifetime."

"It dawned on me," Di said, "that Roxanne being committed to an insane asylum at such a young age, and being taken away from all she knew, would certainly be a major motive for revenge. I mean, anyone would be mad at whomever they thought was responsible."

Barely listening, Ceeoni was tearing through the corridors of her mind in search of a reason she had mentioned Milledgeville in casual conversation with Detective Saxon. Coincidence? Nothing at Starcross was coincidence. She'd learned that there are no coincidences, anyway. The group gathered their belongings and left the room, while discussing the case.

"You're right, Di," Nasrene agreed, "revenge would be a very strong motive. Hmm—I wonder what ever happened to Roxanne? She was only twelve, and I can imagine an insane asylum in those days was a horrific experience for anyone at any age."

Ceeoni's voice sounded a little too loud, even in her own ears. "Maybe—uh—maybe she learned the error of her ways; people do, you know. She may have been sorry for Sybil's death that was caused by her attempt to seduce Talbert in the stable that night."

Ceeoni ignored Di's puzzled glance, but Nasrene calmly addressed Ceeoni's 'what if'.

"Well, something else that may be of interest is that if the Starcross Slasher turns out to have Roxanne's Soul or someone else's, I would guess that she or he is a psychopath who is incapable of remorse or regret."

"No regret?" Homer asked.

"No regret—Na-da," Nasrene repeated, separating the syllables distinctly.

Ceeoni couldn't imagine intentionally doing harm, let alone feeling no regret.

"Whoa," Di said, "Now there's a concept to ice a body's blood. No remorse, no regret? God knows I'd hate to be on his list, and unlucky enough to meet him off in some of these spooky back woods around here."

"Brrrr," She put her arm through Homer's, saying, "Jesus! Here we are, not knowing if he's a she, or she's a he, and not knowing where he might be next and, I mean, he could be mad at any or all of us. Searching for a solution is frying me brains, but let's put it to rest and grab a bite. Join us for dinner, Juno?"

"No thanks, we're going to the Manor to dine with our children."

"Homer, my love, can we see if Weber has anything to eat in the house? If it's OK with everybody, I'd rather not eat out."

Homer kissed Di's forehead and opened his phone.

"Hey, Web!" he boomed. "Di and I were just thinking how wonderful it would be if you had something whip-up-able in the frig? Oh? He did? OK, we'll be there in a few minutes."

"Well, something may have turned up, at last. David left a message. He said he has some important information on the case, and he'll catch up with us. And by the way, Ceeoni, he said your rental car was free of prints, but there was no brake fluid in the car, and there were no leaks, so they believe your brake fluid had been deliberately drained."

Ceeoni climbed into the back seat of the Rolls, not at all surprised. It was what she had suspected all along.

x x x

They enjoyed Weber's delicious repast of smoked turkey, steamed broccoli, baked sweet potatoes in rum-raisin sauce, corn and pepper salad, mango bread, cheeses, and wines, served out in the open air patio beside the blue waterfall.

"Homer, how can you go to restaurants with Weber around?"

"See, Di, you need to know how this works; we have to let him decide when and how he wants to run the house and the kitchen. We go to restaurants to keep from wearing out our welcome."

Ceeoni felt her tension easing in the genuine warm atmosphere. Of all the places she'd been, she felt a kinship to this group of people like none other. She was apart of Starcross, without a doubt. But what part? She re-examined her reluctance to try past life regression. In her persistent mental search to figure out what role she might have played in 19th century Starcross, none of the pieces known to her seemed to fit. She hated to admit, even to herself, that regression was the only way to find out for sure.

The rear of Homer's house flowed and blended into a glorious symphony of huge oak trees, pines, magnolias and dogwoods; rose bushes and azaleas, dramatized by dark blue and green lights that turned on at sundown. A soft wind created subtle movement in the deep shadows formed behind the waterfall and underneath the greenery. Inside her head, the Sane Ceeoni quipped, 'Yuk, look at all the places someone who meant harm could hide, unseen behind that jungle-lush foliage, until it was too late!' Ceeoni yanked herself off the treadmill of her disturbing thoughts, and turned her attention back to the conversation.

"Oh, Nasrene," Di said, "When we were talking about near death experiences, I forgot to tell you that I still have your copy of *Saved By The Light*."

"That's yours, Di. I always give them away."

"What's that about?" Homer asked.

"It's a man's account of being struck by lightning and visiting Heaven. He had been prounced dead, and he awakened after twenty-eight minutes. The author, Dannion Brinkley, has written books, and he lectures extensively describing his extraordinary visions."

Nasrene added, "And, *Embraced by the Light*, by Betty Eadie, as well as *Life After Life*, by Raymond Moody, along with many others, describe similar accounts that have changed lives in wonderful ways. Another interesting fact is that the judgment some people experience during an NDE simply consists of one question asked by the Light. That question is, 'When in your life did you behave unlovingly?' Maybe the answer influences the lessons in the next life."

"OK," Ceeoni asked, "How would you explain the fact that when the 'God Part' of the right temporal lobe of the brain is artificially stimulated, anyone can have a near death experience?"

"Who knows? I certainly don't," Nasrene said, "but if the Soul is energy, a mass that actually can and does enter and leave the body, I've read a theory that the area you mentioned is an indicator, a sort of gateway, that registers this energy or Soul mass as it passes from the body. They say that this Soul energy passing from the body is what created the image of the man on the Shroud of Turin. Some people believe the man was Jesus. Also, the image on the shroud was reversed, like a photo negative. For centuries, details of the man's features weren't visible until photography was invented, and FYI, the man on the shroud has no navel.

"In NDEs the Soul is sent back into the body, as if it left the body prematurely or unintentionally. Many times, the person is told that it is not his time, or he is given a choice to go to the Light or go 'back'. Could it be that when that area is stimulated, no matter how it's stimulated, the energy mass that is the Soul is brought to the gate? Metaphysicians believe that this energy mass/Soul can never be destroyed. People report marvelous experiences that are remarkably similar at the Soul's encounter with what I believe Dr. Martin Luther King, Jr. spoke of in Memphis the night before he was killed. He said, 'I've been to the mountaintop and I've looked over, and I've seen the other side.' I think he had a vision of something real, something that is described in the Bible. I've often thought of NDEs in the light of the Biblical expression, 'the Kingdom of Heaven is closer than your hands and feet, closer than breathing . . .' Could an NDE simply be a glimpse of that ever-present reality?"

"All right, Nasrene!" Di said, "I wonder how anyone can attribute NDEs to pure imagination when the personalized characteristics of these episodes include descriptions of people who died before the dreamer was born, right down to clothes, jewelry and distinctive mannerisms, even descriptions involving contact with people yet to be born!"

Homer answered his ringing phone, "Juno! Well, yeah, I'll ask. Hold it a moment. Nasrene, Juno says she's ready to attempt past life regression."

"Now?" Nasrene's eyes lit up.

"Now, or whenever it's convenient for you."

"Yes!" She reached for her bag.

Struggling with the wrong-side-out sleeve of her jacket, Di called,

"Wait, you can't go without me!"

During the short ride to the Manor, Ceeoni made valiant attempts to shut down her inner questions, fears and new sensations. She closed her eyes and visualized scenes from some of her favorite plays, an exercise guaranteed to disconnect her frayed, overblown circuits. Tonight, as the houselights dimmed in her mental Theatre of the Stars, a musical was in order. 'Ah, 'The Wiz!' In the beginning, a beautiful dancer, the Tornado, straddling the rooftop of a spinning little house, whipped up a wild wind that swept Ceeoni, right along with Dorothy and Toto, far away from the madness and confusion of Starcross, to hang with the Hip Wizard of Oz—who, little by little, transformed from Andre DeShields into Adam Delayno.

x x x

Ceeoni volunteered to accompany Juno upstairs to tuck the little Ponders in, who were already bathed and dressed for bed.

"They do tend to behave better when company's around," Juno said. "Nanny Ada's out with a cousin who lives in Midtown. I always let her have evenings off after she's been with these three all day, although she's one of the few adults who can function well after a day with three toddlers."

The kids were so cute with their British accents, rattling on all at the same time. They looked to Ceeoni as if they'd grown some in the last two days. When she said so, Juno agreed, sadly.

"You notice how fast they change? I tell all my friends to enjoy their children, because they aren't children long. We can't get over how quickly our older ones became extremely independent, and totally fascinated with their own activities."

"I know you're proud of them. What're they up to?"

"Oh, R.C., the oldest, is sitting for his university entrance exams soon, and he plays guitar in a London retro rock group. Adam jokes that they're really playing 60's Rhythm & Blues, but they think they've discovered something new." Ceeoni laughed, and Juno counted on her fingers, "And, let's see, Adam is in 10th form, and plays Jazz piano; we have a daughter who is a talented cartoonist, just starting ninth form. Oh, our very quiet oldest daughter, a violinist, is in music school, and can barely tolerate any music that isn't classical. We have a nine-year-old son, who eats and breathes football, that's soccer to you Yanks, and 'The Footies' in Australia. They're with me Mum, and Nanny Ada's sister, who have the energy to keep up with them."

"I bet they're a lot of fun!"

"Yeah, when they can skim off a few minutes for us—"

The kids finally gave up on their high-energy tumbling and bouncing, and allowed Juno and Ceeoni to bundle them into their beds. Juno turned on the nightlight, "Get quiet now. Papa will be up to hug you goodnight."

Ceeoni wandered into the next room. The peaches-and-cream color combination in the sitting area was familiar to her, although it was a bit disconcerting to recognize that the 18thcentury Chippendale Baroque silver candlesticks and the peach and beige Aubusson carpet appeared to be nearly exact copies of the ones she knew had been there, whenever she had been there. It occurred to her that Homer must be very relieved to have discovered Miss Letty. He'd probably thought he was losing his mind in his quest for the perfect pieces of furniture. The view from the large window overlooked the rear garden. To her right, down through the glass roof of the atrium below, the antique piano that had made her feel so sad when she opened it, gleamed in the soft light. She knew it was the one Elijah had played in 1853.

Interrupting Ceeoni's musings, Juno asked,

"Do you have any children?"

"No, not yet; my marriage ended in divorce."

"Oh, I'm sorry, I didn't know."

"It was a long time ago, and I'm very happy there were no children. You know, Juno, I used to believe in the biological clock, but after this week, I'll never give it credence again. People say they hear the ticking of this clock, when in fact, we're really responding to a Divine Plan. Now I know I wasn't supposed to have kids then."

"Oh yes, quite! Nothing like giving birth eight times to give one a sense of karmic destiny," she laughed, "which has added to my curiosity about past life regression. I'm really looking forward to it. Hey, when are you going to be regressed?"

Ceeoni hesitated, "Uh, I, I plan to do so soon." She abruptly changed the subject, "By the way, Juno, how do you like this house?"

"Well, truthfully, I've lived in old, old houses all my life. These wonderful antiques only remind me how much I prefer new houses and new furniture, like the Starcross Lakes Estates; brand, spanking new and quiet. In England, the houses are so bloody old; they creak, squeak, whisper and hold conversations with you at all hours of the night."

Ceeoni smiled and knew in her heart she would never mind living in this house, and hearing everything it had to say. Juno waited politely for Ceeoni to continue.

"Juno, well, it's none of my business, but is Adam, is he, well—?"

"You want to know about his marriage, and children; or rather, the absence of same."

Surprised at Juno's intuition, she nodded. Juno grinned and winked, "It's fairly obvious that you fancy him."

Ceeoni dropped her eyes, "I admire his music, not to mention that killer smile," she added rather wistfully, "which are the only things I know about him for sure. I guess as far as a distant fancy goes, I'll take my place among the ranks of women all over the world."

"Ah yes, they adore him, and he adores them. I've seen them come and go, but," she glanced at Ceeoni appraisingly, "there's something about you that is very, very different.

"Anyway, Adam's marriage wasn't good for him or his wife, and R.C. and I must take some responsibility because we introduced them. She was, I mean, she is physically beautiful. She taught school with me in New York, and R.C. and I thought we were turning Adam on to a girl who would be perfect for him. We were all very young, but I think Adam had lost interest in one-night stands early on. He was tired of women throwing themselves at him, and his wife was such a contrast to the 'band fleas' that follow musicians, bands, athletes, and even politicians around the planet."

"Hey, band fleas is a great description," Ceeoni laughed, "How about stage lice? I've seen them stick themselves to an actor or artist in the theatre simply because, like Mt. Everest, he's there, and he's famous, or has been famous, so he can't help but be visible. Now, bear in mind the star can be an absolutely disgusting, abusive person or one who doesn't bathe regularly, or take care of his teeth, but he can have his pick from the crowd of devotees."

"And don't forget the quintessential old 'playa,' with the time warp polyester wardrobe, ill-fitting toupee or too-dark dye job whose girls keep getting younger and younger. And it doesn't mean a thing to him that these girls are clueless about the impact he's made in his field—they're right up in the front row of this legend's performances, clapping off-time, as artistic subtleties zip right over their air-filled heads. And he's got the nerve to think his friends are jealous!"

"You'd think he'd be embarrassed," Ceeoni quipped.

"Or he's in the springtime of his senility, and he's too far gone to be embarrassed!" Juno added, "But you know, I think a man has got to have an overblown ego to start with, before he can go to those extremes later on in his life. Adam doesn't have that sort of ego. He's never been the kind to instantly bond into intimacy. It seemed he wanted to be committed to someone. That's why we were glad when he married, but we were too inexperienced to realize what it meant to Adam that she hated nightlife, people from different cultures, or those who didn't fit her small-town, close-minded criteria of class and distinction, and, she was tone deaf. At first, she tried to hang with Adam. She tried to stay up late, and she tried to sit through those devilish concerts and jam sessions, but it didn't last long. It's strange Ceeoni, but you and Adam's Ex bear a slight resemblance."

"What? Oh, heavens, Juno! You know I've never met him. I wouldn't want to remind him of unpleasant memories, when—we do meet."

"No, I don't think you'll remind him of anyone. You have a rare quality that comes from within. R.C. calls it charm, and there's no substitute for it. It saddens me to see so many young women without a sense of that special trait."

"Why, thank you," Ceeoni mumbled.

"Aside from their talent, charm is the reason why women like Oprah, Whoopee and Maya Angelou inspire admiration and confidence in others. I think charm is a natural approach to human interaction; one that radiates strength of character along with a gentle consideration for others. Lila Delayno never heard of it, and after a while Adam realized her spirit consisted of wonderful genes wrapped around rigid fears and inflexible attitudes. I think he knows that he needs a woman with balance, humor, and a zestful approach to life."

"Where is his ex now?"

"She lives quietly, married to a minister, with two children. Adam made peace with it long ago. R.C. believes Adam is waiting, perhaps, searching is a better word, for the great love, the Grand Paramour."

It was as if Juno had reached into Ceeoni's innermost desires and pulled out the Big One. "I guess everybody's hoping for that," she answered in a small voice.

Concern crossed Juno's face, "Yeah, but some people never find it."

"You love him very much, don't you?"

"Ceeoni, Adam is the brother I never knew, the father I never met, my oldest son, and next to R.C., the best friend I've ever had."

R.C., breathless from running up the stairs announced,

"Hey, they're ready for you, Kiddo. I'm going to kiss those little round faces. Don't start until I get there!"

CHAPTER TWENTY-ONE

In the Manor's green living room, Juno sat stiffly on the couch while Nasrene turned the lamps down low.

"Now, get comfortable. There's nothing to be nervous about. This kind of relaxation is a natural state, and I think you'll enjoy it very much."

Careful not to muss her chic geometric haircut, Juno stretched out on the green pillows R.C. had placed for her.

The suggestions began. As expected, in answer to Nasrene's request that she regress to a time affecting her life today, Juno went to the 19th century, but not to Starcross.

"What is your name?" Nasrene asked.

A cultured male voice, honey-coated with a southern drawl, rolled off Juno's tongue, 'Jasper Baldwin.'

Everybody looked at each other. Juno had been Sybil Baldwin Bramwell's father.

"Where are you?"

'The Baldwin Plantation in southeast Georgia'

"What is the year?"

'1860'

"How old are you?"

'I'm seventy years of age'

Jasper said that until his father died in 1800, Baldwin had been a rich peach farm, worked by slaves, but he had no interest in farming. By the time he was nineteen years old, he was newly married and had used money left to him by his grandfather to buy into a small shipbuilding business. He was born to be a builder of ships. In the 1820s, all around him planters were starting to take advantage of the emerging King Cotton era, made possible by the widespread use of the cotton gin that had been invented in the late 18th century. The' gin' or engine, separated cotton bolls from their tiny, sticky green seeds at the rate of fifteen bales a day, a job that would have taken fifteen slaves two years. Before the gin, cotton was hardly worth the effort.

After people discovered what the gin could do, newcomers poured into the South, buying land and slaves, to get rich growing cotton. Jasper said that cotton didn't interest him, and he refused to force his father's slaves into the hardest labor that way. Most slaveholders lived in mortal fear for their lives after purchasing a work force and beating them into submission. He was proud that the Baldwin slaves had lived decently all their lives, but he was more proud of his sleek seaworthy ships that earned great amounts of money.

It all started one hot summer day in 1813, while he was in Savannah on business. His wife, Nettie, who never wanted to accompany him, preferred to spend her time planning strategies geared to pushing herself a few rungs up the local prestige ladder. Parties meant nothing to him; neither did his wife's relentless social climbing. He concentrated on his work, and stayed away from the house as much as possible.

He'd never been attracted to slave auctions, but he found himself asking his driver to stop when they approached a slave block on the waterfront, where he watched the auctioneer bring up a female slave for sale. Jasper sat in his expensive carriage, out of the humid Savannah sunlight, and tried to see the woman's face who was being led up the stairs for the crowds' examination. The sinister rattle of chains scraped his ears. Though off in the distance, he was impressed by the woman's bearing. She carried her shackles with quiet dignity, as a monarch would carry a scepter and train. Excited, he stood on the coach step for a better view. Over a sea of frilly parasols and top hats, he saw the most magnificent human being his eyes had ever beheld. Her six-foot rounded figure was easily two inches taller than he, with the face of an ebony angel. He was awed by such beauty and grace, and he knew instinctively it was his duty to protect her. Her presence created a long and furious bidding war, but he was determined not to lose her. Impatiently, he doubled the highest bid, ending the volleys, allowing him to purchase the first and only slave he'd ever bought. The auctioneer's toothless British clerk cackled,

'She be a tricky, foit'n black bitch, she be, Sah, they soy ha 'ole famly doid on t' crossin' sep fo one sistah. She be sold todye coz' ha mastuh soy 'e better sell ha for 'e 'aftah kill ha. Ha name be Isis, and Oiy saiy, Sah, ha mastuh soy she cawn't e'en drop no suckas, Sah. Tween you 'n me, if ya don' moind my soying so, Sah, ya pied way too much for ha stubborn, sorry arse!'

Jasper said he later learned that Isis' former master had repeatedly beaten and raped her, but Jasper sensed that no amount of punishment could kill her soaring spirit or bend her to any man's will.

Alone with Isis in his carriage, she refused to look in his direction. He ignored the clerk's warnings to 'keep ha choined.' He removed the shackles himself. She shrank from his touch and kept her eyes averted while rubbing the swollen, festered sores the metal had scored on her wrists. She didn't speak at all during the eight-hour trip to Baldwin, and she wouldn't touch the buns and fresh pears he offered her.

He talked to her, telling her a little about some of the people she would meet at Baldwin, her new home, but when she didn't respond, he wondered if she knew English.

Isis wouldn't eat at all the first week, which caused her to become visibly thinner. He gave her the best vacant cabin he had, and added little accessories that he hoped she would like. He sent women with food, who also tended her wounds, and he asked others to stop and speak to her. A week later, he was relieved when Phineas told him she had shyly joined the supper line. He sent Phineas' wife and the dressmaker to Isis' cabin to coax her to select fabrics for dresses and underpinnings. The women put up a great to-do. They 'oohed and aahhed' and made the decisions, while she only nodded slightly. He looked in as they were finishing up, and left for the shipyard happy just to have seen the trace of a pleased expression on her face, although she still hadn't spoken a word to anyone.

As he was leaving for work one morning, days later, he found her standing by his carriage, carrying a basket of laundry. Beautiful in a plain tan cotton dress, with her thick coarse hair pinned back under a tan bandanna, she gave the impression she was waiting for him, but he couldn't read her somber face. She turned away suddenly, as if she'd changed her mind, but he caught a glimpse of the same little smile he'd seen on the day of the clothes fittings. He was grateful for that much.

'Good morning, Isis, you look very nice today.' Accustomed to her silence, he kept walking.

'Thank ya fuh ya kineness, Mistuh Ballwin.' It was the first time he heard her husky musical voice. She moved away quickly, before he could respond.

His heart leapt in his chest. She began to wait for him in the evening, and each day their friendship grew. They talked about everything. Her intelligent understanding of complicated issues caused him to tell her about his ships, and his problems.

In their talks, she was awed by the world he showed her through his eyes. Up until the time Isis came into his life, he had been young and impressionable enough to have believed the myth that slavery protected ignorant blacks from exploitation by Northern factories and other unscrupulous employers. Isis made him aware of the fact that most slaves were only ignorant of the European language, customs and inventions. She didn't understand the general one-to-the-other bond of trust that supported the well-organized and legal exploitation of people who couldn't fight back, as a desirable and honorable way of life. Jasper said he prays God will forgive him his stupidity. He taught her to read and write. He had made an agreement to free his slaves after they'd learned to read and when they turned twenty-five, but few chose to leave Baldwin, the place of their birth.

He couldn't help falling in love with Isis and, no matter how disgusted his slave-owning associates were, all that mattered to him was the time he could spend with her. Being with her made him feel alive. He knew of many slave masters who would never admit their attachment to their women of the slave quarters, but the mixed children of those alliances were everywhere, in plain sight, especially in the South.

Jasper said that his wife, who already treated him with disdain, reacted with outrage at seeing him with Isis. Nettie Baldwin had come from a family where cruelty to slaves was expected. His humane attitudes toward blacks had been a main bone of contention in their young marriage, from the start. She would tell anybody who would listen about his gross behavior, embellished with her own imagined details, but she failed to mention the fact that she'd turned her young husband out of her bed a few weeks after their wedding night, four years before Isis came to live at Baldwin. Jasper had married Nettie hoping she would become more attuned to his ways, and with experience, he'd hoped she would overcome her aversion to him. After several years passed, he realized nothing could improve the situation. In fact, he faced the truth, which was that he found her vain and ignorant, and he disliked her almost as much as she detested him.

When he met Isis, he knew that as long as she was in his heart, no one else could ever reside there. At the time, Isis was at least 38 years old, 15 years older than he and his wife, but she had an ageless capacity for joy that ensnared him in its shining brightness. He happily turned his back on his beautiful but embittered wife who had never been a wife to him, to enjoy Isis' rare insight, humor, and the loving warmth of her sensual enthusiasm.

Isis said she was accustomed to hatred from whites, but Phineas told him that the moment his carriage would leave the Baldwin gates, Nettie would heap an astonishing amount of backbreaking tasks on Isis, with a vengeance. Isis didn't complain, but he didn't know how to stop it, short of taking Isis with him when he left.

The tension mounted. He could see the fatigue in Isis' face, and even though the situation had gone on for only a few weeks, he couldn't allow Nettie to continue to mistreat her. Before dawn one morning, he took Phineas and his family and Isis on a trip to Savannah, sensing they all needed some time away from Nettie. Plus, he was having trouble leaving without her, knowing that she was being misused during his absence. When they returned late in the evening, his wife, standing in the lane with both hands on her hips, met their carriage. He recognized her rigid posture, and the crazed furor in her eyes.

Before Phineas could bring the team to a full standstill, she snatched the coach door open,

'So Jasper, you've been out with your big black whore! You're going to get rid of that good for nothing lazy bitch, do you hear? Do you hear me? There are laws against what you're doing!'

Nettie moved fast in an effort to climb into the coach but, Jasper anticipated the move and jumped down to face her. He instructed Phineas to take Isis and his family to their quarters, while he restrained Nettie.

Small, and fair, Nettie always turned beet red and salivated uncontrollably when she worked herself up into a frenzy. Suddenly, she attacked, clawing at his face to gouge his eyes. He held her fast, but she cursed and kicked at him as he wrestled her into the house. With her fighting, it was all he could do to coax one of the doctor's powders down her throat. A chaser of whiskey never failed to keep her sleeping quietly well into the next day.

That evening, he went to Isis' cabin, alone, for the first time. He wanted her to know she wasn't obligated to stay at Baldwin, only to be abused by Nettie's hatred. He wanted to let Isis know she could go if she chose, and he would arrange for her safe passage to the North. She opened the door, and although she gestured for him to come in, he felt awkward and clumsy. He was surprised at the still, otherworldly atmosphere he encountered when he entered there.

The interior of her cabin was an oasis of peace. She'd made covers for the bed and chairs out of an old blue quilt that had belonged to his mother. Two small lanterns cast a glow of quiet serenity, softening the dark plank walls. He was reminded of the expensive, gaudy red and gold opulence Nettie had haphazardly draped all over his family home, which had begun to feel like a gilded black widow spider's web.

Then, he remembered why he had come. He tried to put the words together that could take her away from him,

'Isis, you don't have to stay. I can—'

But she was walking toward him, holding him with her eyes.

'What I mean is, I'll help you get away from the South, I'll,' he stammered. She stopped so close to him, he could reach out and touch her. He ached to touch her, but he was afraid of frightening her. Within his line of vision, a small hanging mirror showed him her lovely face, wearing a trace of the smile he had dreamed of seeing again. His own reflection revealed a man whose plain, flushed features were aflame with a love few hearts would ever know.

'Shhhh,' she whispered, as she stepped out of the tan dress.

Every minute spent with her was not enough, and it wasn't easy. Nettie watched them like a hawk. He knew she recognized and begrudged him his undeniable happiness. He employed the utmost discretion, but soon, Isis became pregnant, in spite of her belief she couldn't conceive, and she developed troublesome symptoms early on. Nettie's sharp eyes saw the slave midwife going into Isis' cabin and guessed the truth, which gave her more to rant over. Then, for no apparent reason, Nettie became oddly quiet. She even smiled at Jasper once. A few weeks passed in relative peace, until he took an unavoidable trip to South Carolina. Planning to stay away for three days, his business concluded sooner than expected, and he was able to return to Baldwin a day early. He drove his horses faster as he approached the gates of home, and almost collided with an unfamiliar wagon turning into his driveway. He hailed the driver,

'Ho, sir, do you have business at the Baldwin Plantation?'

The dour-faced passenger tipped his dusty black top hat,

'Yas suh! I'm here to see Missus Baldwin!'

'I'm Mr. Baldwin. Please, Sir, may I be of service?'

'My business shouldn't take long, suh. I've come to pay for and collect a pregnant Negress.'

Jasper's anger was instantaneous and intense. He was stupid not to have suspected; nevertheless, it was a blessing he'd arrived when he did. One hour later in the evening, and—Smiling, he walked over to the wagon, and fished into his purse, 'Please sir, forgive the imposition,' he said, 'but the Negress of whom you speak is no longer on the premises.' He handed the man a gold coin. 'I hope this will adequately compensate you for your unnecessary journey.'

The thin slave merchant's scowl was replaced with a wide, gap-toothed, leering grin when he saw the coin in his hand,

'Why, yas suh. Thank you, suh. No trouble at all, no, suh. You and the missus feel free to call on me any time, anytime you want to do business. Yas, yas, suh!'

Jasper saw Nettie before she saw him. Surrounded by perfumed candlelight and bouquets of fresh flowers, she posed on the gold parlor chaise lounge, obviously expecting someone she considered important. She wore one of her favorite yellow gowns, a silk and lace ruffled affair, reserved for very special occasions. She looked up, fully expecting the presence in the room to be the maid announcing her guest. At the sight of her husband, her faded blue eyes bucked in angry dismay,

'What are you doing here?? Today isn't Thursday!'

She looked past him nervously, licking her lips and glancing at the gold mantle clock. He didn't answer her question, but poured himself a snifter of brandy that was set out with the silver tea service, surrounded by a platter of finger sandwiches.

'Care for a tot, Nettie?' he asked, as he raised his brandy toward his lips.

She strode across the room and violently slapped the glass out of his hand,

'Goddamn you to Hell, Jasper Baldwin! He should've been here by now! You stopped him, didn't you? You stopped him! You were outside at the time he was supposed to be here!'

He ignored her, wiped his wet hand with one of her dainty napkins and poured himself another drink,

'Nettie, in over sixty years, no one has been sold at Baldwin, and I don't intend to let it happen now.'

With his face turned away, he felt her close the gap between them. 'You slave-loving son of a bitch!' she screamed as she swung at him, but this time he didn't attempt to restrain her. Dodging her blows, he lifted the partially filled crystal decanter with his free hand, and aiming for one of her treasured imported Italian gilt mirrors, he threw it hard over her head toward his target. Wide-eyed, she watched the heavy bottle spin through the air. Her hands covered her open mouth as the container demolished the mirror, shattering glass into tiny flecks and chards that sprayed everything in a glittering shower, laced with splatters of fine Napoleon brandy. The only movement in the room was the tears of rage coursing down her cheeks, until he raised his arm to slowly sip his brandy.

'Nettie, I've been gentle with you, but if you think you're going to come at me like always, I swear, I'll fight you like a man.'

She opened her mouth to speak, but he spoke first, 'We never should've married.' he said. 'Hell, for that matter, we never should've met! Isis isn't the problem. The problem has always been just you and me. We never loved each other, not even a little bit. When I married you, I didn't know one woman from another. I just wanted a warm body in my bed, and God knows I was wrong, and God knows I've suffered for my sin. You married me because I offered you a way to become Mistress of a great house, an escape from the wretched one-horse garbage dump your family calls a plantation. You would've followed a stranger if you thought he could save you from that vermin and maggot infested pile of poverty. I can't imagine what you expected, but after our wedding, when you acted like I'd half-killed you, I should've sent your tail packing right then. You're either too selfish or too damn stupid to realize any nineteen-year-old wealthy man like me would've had a willing woman in his bed the next day.'

Jarring claps and booms of a fierce Georgia thunderstorm rolled overhead, shaking the rafters and windows. He ignored her stare of unadulterated hatred. He knew she would kill him if she could. Clouds covered the sun. Lightning crackled and flashed, streaking across the room, as if the ceiling had opened. Wordlessly, Nettie raised the voluminous hem of her gown and ran for the front door; flowing yellow silk billowing and bounding behind her with every step. Her high-pitched, bone chilling scream could be heard above the wind that howled in the chimney, as her floating skirts made it seem as though she flew off the last two porch steps, out into the storm.

Jasper ran behind her, certain that within a few minutes, he'd bring her back, soaked, kicking and screaming. The rain obscured his vision. He threw off his saturated coat that slowed his progress. Frustrated and drenched, he called her name. Phineas and several others must have heard his voice because they joined him in his search. They sloshed through mud, shouting to be heard over the loud thunder while straining to see through the cold deluge that slammed into their eyes and stung their skin. Soon, he stumbled over Nettie's body sprawled, face down, her forehead cleanly split open by her fall against the gray marble border of the two-foot deep garden pond, now overflowing with blood red rain.

He had no emotional room left for her, not even to grieve. Nettie Starks Baldwin was buried under the Oaks, in the year 1817.

Isis' difficult pregnancy ended in stillbirth. The beautiful little boy was interred on the other side of the plot from his wife's fresh grave, out of respect for Isis and their son. He believed the heavy physical tasks Nettie had imposed on Isis contributed to the death of their firstborn, and had an irreversible debilitating effect on the state of her health.

Jasper knew he couldn't compensate for the loss of the child. When Isis wasn't anywhere around, he knew to look in the cemetery, where she would sit by the little grave for hours. Sometimes he would go and silently sit on the ground beside her, and wonder if anything in the world would make her smile again. He remembered that he'd learned of her only surviving relative, a sister who had been sold off the ship to a horse farmer in Virginia.

He became determined to find her, and find her, he did. His secret inquiries and negotiations to bring Isis' sister to Georgia were completed by mail, and when he went to collect her and her children, he told everyone he'd return in two weeks. Weather conditions stretched his journey into a month, but Cleo was extremely happy at the prospect of reuniting with her beloved sister, and her two small children were pleasant and bright. Cleo's owner exchanged the three of them for three of Jasper's purebred horses, a stallion and two mares. Jasper could tell that the man thought he had gotten the better of the deal, but Cleo's owner would've been shocked had he known Jasper Baldwin was willing to give far more than three thoroughbreds in exchange for the little slave family.

Isis, Phineas and his wife, and several children waited excitedly to welcome him home. One of the most beautiful moments of his life was to see Isis' face when her younger sister eagerly jumped down from the coach, and ran up the stairs to cover her with tears, laughter and long lost kisses.

He cherished every day of the three wonderful years he and Isis had together until she became pregnant for the second time. He watched in horrified disbelief as her perfect body wasted away over the nine months. It appeared that she probably wouldn't survive childbirth. He tearfully apologized to her many times, but he knew her illness had nothing to do with pregnancy. When he was ten years old, he'd seen his mother die, and when he was eighteen his father had fallen to the same ravaging disease. He'd walked the grounds all night the first time he'd smelled the same foul odor of death on Isis that had permeated his parents' rooms in their final days. The pain Isis endured was as unrelenting as his parents', and he had to make peace with the inevitable, it was just a matter of time.

Heaven gave them a wonderful gift when Isis survived the birth of a healthy daughter they named Sybil, after her mother, Syterre, and his mother, Billie. There were days when her pain would subside, and she'd have enough energy to hold Sybil and talk to him. When the baby was a month old, he'd spent another night up with Isis, biting back tears when she screamed in agony, trying to get her to keep down a few thimbles of broth, changing bloody sheets, and assuring her it was no sacrifice. He felt helpless and angry with a God who wouldn't heal her, or allow him to take her place. Before morning light, exhausted, he curled up beside her thin form to hold her for what was to be the last time. Cleo and Phineas awakened him that afternoon, as they tried to pry her cold, lifeless body from his desperate grasp. He hadn't realized Isis had been dead for hours in his arms.

x x x

Jasper continued his testimony, saying that his baby daughter, Sybil, was the light of his life. She reminded him so much of his Isis, but soon, he knew she had to get away from the South, or bear the onus of being black.

She grew tall and beautifully proportioned like her Mother, with a light olive complexion and a glorious mass of wavy brown hair. She could easily have been mistaken for having Spanish blood, which is why he told her that her Mother had been born in Madrid. Jasper made arrangements for Sybil to attend an exclusive school in Spain, and to teach English there after she graduated.

When Sybil returned to Baldwin, still unmarried at the age of 29, Jasper discovered that her willful and demanding traits, although 'ducky' in a little girl, were quite distressing in an adult, although he knew her haughty exterior belied her good heart. His worries increased after Talbert Bramwell changed her life overnight by asking for her hand in marriage. It concerned Jasper not only because Sybil could be difficult, but also because her mixed blood could manifest in her children. He couldn't tell the young couple the truth. He concocted the madness in the family story; knowing that even though they agreed not to have children, they probably would, and all he could do was pray, pray that their offspring would be as fair-skinned as Sybil.

In the years that had passed since his beloved Isis' death, Jasper buried his grief in long hours at the shipyard. Cleo ran the house well, and their needs were few. When Sybil and Talbert married, Jasper added most of the Baldwin slaves to his daughter's dowry, to give the young couple a good start in business. Although the Bramwell family was wealthy, and in the cotton era, credit was freely offered for the purchase of cottonseed, equipment and slaves, a superior workforce would ensure their success.

Everyone at Baldwin breathed a sigh of relief when Sybil insisted on taking 12-year old Roxanne Baldwin to Starcross with her. Nettie's cousin's orphaned daughter had come to Baldwin at the age of three, but over the years the girl's behavior had shown that she was an odd child. She fought and intimidated the other children, and was caught peeping in windows and torturing small animals. She especially hated Jasper. He'd grown increasingly stymied, not knowing what to do about her. He'd told Sybil all about her, but Sybil was enchanted with Roxanne's uncanny sewing ability and insisted that she would keep the strange girl busy, while seeking a fitting suitor for an early marriage.

In October 1849, the agonizing news of Sybil's death, brought by a late-night messenger, cut through his heart like a hot knife, but he was forced to make some fast decisions before he could indulge his pain and sorrow. The first thing he had to do concerned Roxanne. Since no one at Baldwin or Starcross knew how to care for someone in the state Miss Letty's message described, he knew it fell upon him to have her committed to the Milledgeville Lunatic Asylum. In spite of Roxanne's youth, Jasper had no choice.

Secondly, he followed Miss Letty's and Avajay's advice that the newborn, Clarisse, would be better raised up in the loving Baldwin home, away from Talbert, the father who didn't want her.

'Cleo and I were overjoyed to raise Clarisse; to have a little part of Isis and Sybil all over again.' Jasper said softly.

CHAPTER TWENTY-TWO

Jasper's quiet voice had stumbled over his last words. Nasrene recognized the signs of his fatigue, and applied the pain reduction suggestions, adding that Juno would remember everything. After Juno was awakened, R.C., with tears in his eyes, rushed to take his wife in his arms, a sudden move that startled everyone. Juno also appeared to be sobbing, but then they seemed to be laughing at the same time, as they held each other in a rocking embrace. Nobody understood what was going on.

"Hey," Nasrene broke the odd silence, "Are you two OK? I mean, you weren't together in that lifetime, but I would venture to guess that you were together at other times. I once had a couple who were clients, they—"

Juno waved her hand, "Oh, no, it isn't that. I guess you could say we're stunned."

"You see," R.C. said with a smile while wiping his eyes, "Our oldest daughter, the quiet one who plays violin? Well, when she was very little, about three or so, Juno and I were teaching her how to write her name. I wrote G-L-O-R-Y, and said, 'Glo-ry.' But she frowned at us, took the red crayon out of my hand and wrote, I-S-I-S, in big bold letters. I didn't know she could write any letters, and so I inquired at her playschool. No child there could write and no child there had that name, but now, oh God, Juno, she's been through bloody hell."

"Bingo," Juno whispered, and the little voice inside Ceeoni's head echoed, 'Bingo.'

"So, Juno, how do you feel?" Nasrene asked.

"I feel liberated! At the same time, I had a sensation of surrealism, like that strange shift in perception you sometimes feel in dreams, where the most preposterous situations seem normal and familiar, until you wake up and say to yourself, 'I just dreamed I was on a Supersonic airliner flying around in someone's apartment, and it seemed like the natural thing to do."

"That's a typical reaction," Nasrene said, "It dissipates gradually, once our emotions accept a concept of an endless universe, and the certainty of our endlessness in it. Most people envision their lives through a very narrow finite prism. When those illusionary boundaries are removed, it does take some getting used to."

"Look, Nasrene, I don't know if it means anything, but I believe Nettie Baldwin and Roxanne Baldwin were the same soul," Juno said, "Jasper knew them both and felt their similarities."

"Yes, it does mean something, and you're probably right. It explains Roxanne's determination to destroy Sybil's chances for happiness by trying to seduce her husband. Remember, Sybil was Isis', the hated Isis' daughter, Sybil was Nettie's husband's lovechild who was born in spite of Nettie's scheme to overwork and sell Isis."

"Oh, yeah," Di added, "and that explains why Roxanne confronted Sybil and Talbert in the stable with hurtful information, in an attempt to destroy their marriage. Then she tried to lock them in the burning building, which might have caused Sybil's death and could have killed the baby, Clarisse. So now," she sighed, "that same Soul is back, wreaking havoc on Starcross again."

R.C. counted on his fingers, "Let's see, Roxanne was twelve in 1849—" Ceeoni filled in the date, "Which meant she was born in 1837, and Jasper told us Nettie had died in 1817."

"Plenty of time to be reborn," Nasrene said. "We're getting a closer look at how the Souls of the past interacted. Eventually something has got to emerge to help us hook it up to 1997. Everybody think, and keep searching your memories for clues."

Homer and R.C. looked at each other and laughed, "Man, if you've been wracking your brains as much as I've wracked mine, between the two of us, we would've found the killer long ago."

"Homer, I don't think wracking is gonna' get it. After turning all the facts over in my head, I'm just sittin' here with no sleep."

Karma Rising

"And after all that lack of sleep," Homer groaned, "Neither one of us has come up with a damn thing."

Ceeoni ambled toward the window and parted the pale green sheers to look outside, "Homer, you said Detective Saxon will catch up with us? I can't wait to hear his new information." She quickly pushed the darker green drapes aside, "Hey!—C'mere a minute. Isn't that David's car?? I wonder why he doesn't come on in."

The car David had been driving, a late model beige Chevrolet, sat at the end of the Manor driveway, as if it was about to pull up to the house. The headlights were on, but the car wasn't moving. R.C. and Homer peered through the window, then took off out the door with Ceeoni and the others following. The car doors were locked, but inside, Detective Saxon's partner was slumped over the wheel, his face turned toward the passenger side. Part of his skull poked through pulpy, bloody brain tissue that had oozed onto his shirt collar. The only way anyone could tell that the dead man was David's partner, was the distinctive shock of curly red hair that covered the half of his head that wasn't bashed in. Diana screamed. Alarmed, Ceeoni knew something was wrong but she couldn't see over Di's head. Ceeoni was the last one to realize that the man in the car was dead. She squinted her eyes. The sight of another bloody corpse jolted her nervous system into uncontrollable trembling, and she had to breathe deeply to keep from fainting. A knife, about a foot long, with an ornately jeweled handle, protruded from the left side of the man's neck.

She fought off a wave of nausea announced by a sickening roll of her stomach, knowing that she'd seen that knife before. Her emotions intertwined into hazy knots, as she ran through doorways and hallways of her mind to remember where—?

Homer drew Di, Nasrene and Ceeoni away from the gory scene as he called the police, after which he said,

"Well, it appears as though he was stabbed through the window. All the blood on the passenger side of that car makes me afraid for Detective Saxon. Whatever could've happened here, and where is David?"

Ceeoni remembered that Adam had been missing until he was finally found alive, and she wondered if Detective Saxon had met the same fate, only this time the killer's plan hadn't been disrupted. Within a few minutes of Homer's call, Atlanta's Finest began a search of the grounds for Detective Saxon.

The police questioning was over, and Ceeoni tucked herself into one of the green wing chairs and tried to remember why the knife that killed the detective seemed somehow familiar. So many questions, so few answers. She'd been in Georgia since Thursday, and now, four days later, she found herself trying to sort out two, and maybe three, murders, an attempted murder, her tampered brakes, an arson, and her feelings for Adam Delayno. She knew she couldn't think straight. Sparse facts and guesses chased each other in circles. Did someone kill Detective Saxon because he'd discovered something important to the case? Why was David's partner killed? And where had she seen that knife? The police blocked off the area where the car was found, and took the corpse and the car to check for DNA, hair fibers, and other possible clues.

"OK! That did it!" Homer shouted. "We've gotta' do everything we can. Juno, go get the kids! We're all gonna' stay at my house. I knew the day would come when I'd need three guest suites. I want to keep everybody together so I'll know where you are at all times. This town is full of hotels, and I've got other places you could stay, but that wouldn't put my mind at ease!"

"Yipeee!" Juno cheered, "I thought you'd never ask! This old house moans and groans all night. Nanny Ada says the children haven't slept all that well. R.C. says I'm the only person in the known universe who can sleep with a murderer running loose, but even I've been waking up now and then, which is unusual for me, unless a child is crying. I knew I couldn't completely unpack, anyway, since Adam's stuff is due to arrive soon. I'll call Ada's cousin and have Nanny Ada join us at your place, Homer."

R.C.'s family was soon moved from the Manor to Homer's Starcross Lakes estate. As they relaxed in Homer's unique living room, the grandfather clock struck nine.

"Hey," Nasrene said, "it's still early. Why don't we go see how Adam is doing?"

Di, the forever hangout partner, began a search for her shoes that, as usual, had been kicked out of her field of vision. "Tonight's the night, and oh, the time will be right," she sang to herself.

"Keep that thought, Di," R.C. said, "When Adam was first diagnosed, I explained to Dr. Sakaya that Adam Delayno is a knock-down-drag-out-hope-to-die-super-serious-lifetime-card-carrying night owl, and he, of all people, will be more likely to open his eyes after the sun goes down."

Stifling a yawn, Juno excused herself, "Forgive me, you guys go on," she said, "my suite is sheer heaven, and that bed is calling, plus, the children will be up early."

"As if we didn't know," R.C. grinned and kissed her cheek, "I do feel better with you and the Moppets over here."

"Unless the killer is some sort of supernatural alien," Homer said, "Weber can kick the average ass, which makes this establishment a poor choice for anybody to come up in here with mayhem on his mind."

"I'm taking a pot of Weber's special blend, thank you," Di called on her way to the kitchen, "That hospital swill tastes like the bottom of a trash can."

'Why the mascara?' Ceeoni asked herself as she freshened her makeup. 'Because Adam may wake up?' Her little voice inside answered, 'Well, why else, silly?'

x x x

They identified themselves to the guard sitting outside Adam's room, and signed in. Inside, Nurse Evelyn greeted them while she changed Adam's I.V.,

"How's everybody doin'?"

"Great!" R.C. answered, "How's the Chief?"

"He's in excellent health and he's getting better looking every minute," she laughed. "We've had to fight the nurses to keep them from standing around in here gazing at him. And, may I add that the whole thing about these patients being outta' touch, is a bunch of bull. I just got a spirit message, loud and clear, that he needs some real company. He needs to hear folks he knows rather than a troop of giggling hospital staff."

The room had filled up fast with flowers. Homer and R.C. helped the nurse load a utility cart with as much flora as it would hold,

"Nurse, please feel free to spread the flowers he receives among the patients, and save the cards and addresses for me?" R.C. asked.

"Sure! The patients and staff will be glad to get them. Fresh flowers, you know, growing things, always lift people up. Oh, and R.C., your idea to register Mr. D. under a phony name is working. A lot of newspaper folks have been inquiring, but they haven't found him yet."

"What name did you use?".

"Nasrene, I didn't want to choose a name that would be a tip-off, like Yamaha, Roland, or Steinway, but then I decided on Elijah Starcross. I think once he knows the whole story, he'll appreciate the irony in that."

He turned on Adam's CD, "Like a Lover". The title tune hammered out a lush Latin groove, decorated with heavy percussion and strings that whispered and caressed as it penetrated Ceeoni's emotions. She closed her eyes and let it pour over her.

"Nurse Evelyn," R.C. inquired, "have you ever heard this CD?"

"I have very little time to listen to anything. I'm a single mother, and I'm going to school for my masters." She gestured toward the bed, "This is his CD?"

The thick plants and flowers provided a setting for the sensuous drums transforming the hospital room into a steamy island hideaway. Nurse Evelyn, a plump, young member of the hip-hop generation, would probably never turn the radio dial to a jazz station. When the cut was over, she sucked air through her teeth,

"SSSSS—I don't know why, but I didn't think he played anything like that!" Speaking to Adam she said, "Ex-cu-uuze me, Mr. D., I didn't know you were absolutely smokin' hot!"

"We'll get you tickets to any and all of his concerts here," R.C. said. "We'll let you know the dates. After all, you saved his life. Give me your number, and we'll send a limo for you and your posse."

"Now you're not gonna forget, are you?"

"Forget?" He scowled at the question, "Not in this life. Don't you forget!"

"I'll be ready! All I need is a week or so advance notice, so I can do the whole thing, you know, nails, threads and hair all hooched up to get my freak on."

Ceeoni didn't dare look in Di's direction, but she did hear Di repeat, "Freak on?" loud enough for Ceeoni's ears only.

"I had them put the bag of cards and letters in there," Nurse Evelyn said, pointing to the closet.

Ceeoni asked, "What do you do with his cards and letters?"

"I keep a record of everything, but I only give him the ones I know he'd be interested in. C'mon Ceeoni, walk with me to the vending machines. I'm gonna' need some help."

She followed R.C. down the hall as he said, "I'm expecting Adam to make a significant change once his brother gets here."

"Oh?"

"Adam is very close to his brother. They have a strong bond from having been two little guys who had to grow up fast, depending on each other. I'm hoping Adam will feel his brother's presence."

"What's his brother like?"

"Oh, he's cool. He's very much like Adam, except he's an academician, but he's streetwise, too. Adam is an artist, period. Boring things like business details are a great big mysterious drag to him. The late Basil Cassidy, Adam's brother Samson, and I were able to function as a three-pronged anchor for Adam's success. Adam consults with Samson on legal matters and purchases, he consults with me on major career moves, and he consulted with Basil on business and tax issues."

"Is Samson married?"

"No, he and Adam haven't been so lucky in love. He tells this story frequently. I'm not telling you anything he wouldn't tell you himself. He was engaged to the same lady twice. The first time was during college in Detroit, but she married another guy when Samson went to law school in California."

"Ouch! Mercy! And after that went down, they decided to get married again?"

R.C. borrowed a snack cart, "Yeah, but by then, she had two kids, which was OK with Samson. He stays in touch with her kids, still. Anyway, her marriage had crashed and burned, and after Samson had passed the California Bar, guess who showed up? Now, Juno and I were bruising through the unhappy aftermath of Adam's divorce. All we could do was hurt with them, because we couldn't be of much help. So, this second time around, Samson could afford to spread all the stuff to make life easier, you know, the ring, the house, the joint accounts, etc., but when he won a scholarship to study international law in Amsterdam for six months, it was all over."

"All over?"

"Yeah, she called him, long distance, to break their engagement and then she married someone else before he got back home."

"Oh, how awful!"

"That's what we thought, but we realized it just wasn't meant to be. We also thought Samson would be devastated, and he was messed up for a while, but he didn't sink to an emotional Skid Row low, if you know what I mean. Juno said on the second time around his intended's flighty, or better said, nonexistent sense of loyalty finally woke him up."

"That could make a person decide they're not so much in love, after all."

Near the nurse's station, he found coffee cups, paper cups and a pitcher of ice.

"There're gettin' the royal treatment today," he laughed.

Every time Ceeoni entered Adam's room, she half-expected to see him sitting up, awake, and fully recovered. She tried to visualize what he might say. A few crappy movie lines marched across the silver screen of her mind. She asked herself if she really wanted to be present when he opened his eyes, and risk discovering that he was the kind of person who could utter something like, 'Where am I?' in a trembling soap opera whisper. If so, it would have the effect of ice water on her hot fire of infatuation.

CHAPTER TWENTY-THREE

Ceeoni eagerly sat close to Adam's bed and took his hand at Nasrene's request. She asked R.C. to take the other. Gently holding his long, warm and beautifully shaped fingers, she imagined those hands passionately exploring her sensitive skin. She mentally slapped herself, and turned her attention to Nasrene's suggestions. Adam didn't stir or respond. The regression stages came next. When Nasrene asked, "What is your name?" A confident adult male voice, smooth and soft as deep black velvet, answered,

'Elijah Baldwin Starcross.'

Ceeoni noticed he didn't use the name, 'Bramwell,' probably to avoid identification with Talbert.

"What year is it?"

'1874.'

He was thirty-three years old.

Elijah said that when he was thirteen, Miss Letty had moved the precious pianoforte into the upstairs back room of the church that sat in front of the Starcross Manor. Every night when he'd finished his work and Talbert had turned his attention elsewhere, Miss Letty taught Elijah the rudiments of music, and privately joked about how much of it he instinctively knew. Eventually, he earned permission to play the piano, after Miss Letty explained to Talbert that Elijah was a musical genius. Talbert didn't like it, and he didn't give a fig about music or genius, but Elijah was an obedient hard worker. Soon, Talbert forgot about it. Phineas' lessons had taught Elijah to read, and Miss Letty brought him books, all sorts of books. He enjoyed reading books written by black authors; poems from the black Russian, Alexander Pushkin; a Phyllis Wheatly collection; "The Count of Monte Cristo" and the "Three Musketeers" written by Alexandre

Dumas, and articles from the newspaper, "North Star," edited by the brave human rights activist, Fredrick Douglass. Miss Letty made him promise to never let anyone know that he'd read those articles advocating equality.

His secret reading made him aware of the history of the Abolitionists' Movement and the white people who had dedicated their lives to ending slavery.

Among many, he was amazed to learn of Henry Ward Beecher, abolitionist minister; the fiery John Brown, and Illinois journalist Elijah Lovejoy, who was shot in 1837 for his anti-slavery newspaper. He had long talks with Phineas, who understood the roots of slavery, and the effect on the country. Growing up, Elijah had believed that everyone except Mr. Baldwin and Miss Letty adamantly and unquestioningly accepted the premise that blacks were three-fifths human and, therefore, inferior, which had been purported by the United States government since slavery began. The Abolitionists' Movement intrigued him, still, he thought slavery would never end.

Elijah figured that Talbert was aware of the fact that he could read, or maybe he thought books were in the church for Miss Letty to amuse herself while he practiced, or he simply hadn't noticed. Elijah was still very careful to keep his personal books hidden in the cabin he shared with his mother. He practiced at odd hours, sometimes in the middle of the night, using music that Avajay had ordered by mail from various publishers. He couldn't wait to practice music by Chopin, Beethoven, Bach, and Mozart, along with works of more obscure composers. His appetite for more books and more music was voracious; he devoured everything he could get his hands on.

On a red letter day in 1860, when he was nineteen, Miss Letty took Elijah and his Mother to see Thomas Green Bethune, "Blind Tom" as he was called, whose fame was spreading throughout the North and South. Elijah was allowed to sit outside the big house at the Bethune Plantation in South Georgia, and listen to a concert played by the eleven-year old slave known as the Musical Marvel.

Born blind, Tom had been playing classical pieces since the age of four, and by the time he was eight, he was playing concerts for large audiences. He could play anything after hearing it once. That day,

Elijah learned that another slave other than himself had been gifted with an extraordinary knowledge of music.

That was also the day Elijah realized that although he enjoyed showing off his talent to people who didn't believe a slave could play the piano, the music itself was necessary to the human spirit, for the listener, as well as the player.

Avajay discovered that Oberlin College in Oberlin, Ohio, was the first accredited college in America to admit blacks. She was also most gratified to learn that Oberlin's music department was especially respected. She said Oberlin was made for Elijah and through Avajay's and Miss Letty's efforts, Elijah was accepted in 1861. Anxious for him to have a formal education, Miss Letty also wanted him to socialize and share his music and his intellect with appreciative, like-minded people.

Avajay predicted that the Civil War, although far from Georgia in its first year, would escalate and spread to Atlanta, contrary to popular belief. Elijah said he was overjoyed and apprehensive to be accepted at Oberlin. However, with the war going on, it was a wrenching decision to leave Starcross with its small group of elderly residents essentially unprotected, but he had no choice except to comply with Miss Letty's and Avajay's insistence.

Phineas wrote to him at Oberlin, assuring him that the handful of former slaves, including his mother Verna, were able to keep the place up because Miss Letty had stripped the Manor of all luxuries and had hidden the valuables for safe keeping, according to Avajay's instructions. They'd closed most of the rooms, and limited their living space to a small area on the main floor. Talbert, weighing over to 500 pounds by Phineas' estimate, waddled around in an angry alcoholic haze, threatening to allow himself to be conscripted into the Confederate Army.

Phineas thought it was comical that Talbert never questioned the source of his daily supply of imported wine. Avajay had included stacks of cases in her huge hidden stash of canned fruits, vegetables, herbs and teas. She had started compiling her stash two years before the war began.

Fortunately, Starcross was situated in a remote area separated from Atlanta and the main roads by rough miles of dense forest. Phineas' letters described life at Starcross and the devastating effects of the war. Although off the beaten track, Starcross saw the horrors of wounded soldiers and looters who found very little there to loot. The Starcross Ladies tended wounds, fed hungry soldiers and destitute families, and regularly faced desperate souls who stole all their visible food at knife or gunpoint. They even buried two Confederate soldiers, who died there.

A letter from Wayne Starcross with news of his father's good health lifted Elijah's spirits considerably. Still, worry became a part of his life as the War Between the States raged on.

Oberlin opened up a whole new world for Adam. His artistry was sought after and appreciated. He met other artists, educators and human rights activists. He gained a deeper understanding of how fortunate he was to have had such rare individuals, Miss Letty, Avajay, Phineas and Mister Baldwin, in his life. He developed the ability to identify self righteous ignorance in those who embraced oppression, which helped him loose his spirit from the shackles of unforgiving hatred.

His school also bore the distinction of being the first co-educational institution of higher learning in the United States. Suddenly, he was meeting women, black and white, who found him attractive, and shared his love and his knowledge of music. He enjoyed the company of several of the most beautiful and learned of his newfound friends. He began to perform concerts in Philadelphia, Boston and New York, and became more experienced and certain of his performance ability.

Elijah said that he took longer to graduate because of the war and his concert schedule, but he was in no hurry. He enjoyed earning money for the first time in his life, and he relished his new freedom, his new friends and his popularity. He attended and performed at private salons, where liberal intellectuals and artists of all colors congregated to share anti-Confederate stories of heroism and bravery.

An exceptional incident early in the war became the talk of the town. A slave, Robert Smalls, stole the Confederate ship, 'Planter' by quietly sailing it, with his wife and children, away from Charleston, South Carolina, into Union territory where he presented it to the Northern forces. In spite of Union triumphs, Elijah was haunted by his deep concern for his parents and Starcross, as the war drew closer to Atlanta.

Phineas wrote that Avajay had insisted that Wayne Starcross and his family abandon their plantation, and by so doing, they escaped a looters' raid that burned his mansion down. With Avajay's help and Wayne's cooperation, Elijah financed his parents' reunion. Through a friend met at Oberlin, Verna and Niles were relocated to their own small farm across the Canadian border. This area, Puce, Ontario, he later learned, marked the official end of the slave escape network, the Underground Railroad. During those secret negotiations, he wasn't surprised to discover that Oberlin College had been a station on the Railroad.

In the fall of 1864, the papers blared news of the bloody battles that moved closer and closer to Atlanta, as General W.T. Sherman pressed his massive army forward. True to Avajay's prediction, Atlanta, a city of a little more than 9,000 was taken by the North. Sherman's taking of Atlanta did not bring about the desired Confederate surrender, however, and true to his threat, Sherman's men set fire to the city. The northern soldiers removed metal railroad tracks to stop the South's supply trains. In some cases, the metal was heated and bent around trees to prevent rebuilding the railroad, a process called, 'Sherman's Necktie'.

Elijah received no communication from Georgia for weeks after the burning of Atlanta and, knowing that most of the city was destroyed, he was frantic with worry. Stories of brutality in the wake of the northern victory and occupation, kept him poring over the published lists of civilian casualties. He knew there were fatalities that went unpublished due to the rough terrain, winter weather, and the sheer numbers of conquering troops. He didn't know if any of his letters were getting through, and his anxiety increased as the weeks went by. All he had to hang on to was Avajay's prediction that the people at Starcross would survive. He prayed that her prediction was accurate.

Elijah was elated to receive a letter from Phineas assuring him that his parents had been safely settled and everyone was well, proving another one of Avajay's predictions to be correct.

During the war, thousands of slaves escaped and joined the Union Army to free themselves from bondage, while others had blindly followed their Masters into the Confederate Lines. All in all, over 180,000 black soldiers served, and many died during the Civil War. Slavery was legally abolished in 1865, which meant that over four million slaves were legally free. Still, the depressed economy and intense racial prejudice caused conditions in the South to be worse than slavery.

Although the South was occupied by federal troops to assure peace, waves of freed slaves migrated north, seeking greater freedoms. Many others stayed in the South searching for lost relatives. Elijah's freedom was in his music, and he knew that no matter what, Starcross always called to his heart when it was time to find his way home.

He graduated from Oberlin in 1867, and graciously declined Oberlin's offer to remain on staff in the music department. Instead, he accepted a contract from a Philadelphia promoter to tour a chain of concert halls in England and Europe, which marked the beginning of a mutually profitable professional relationship that lasted the rest of his life.

When he returned to Georgia in 1868, Miss Letty had finished rebuilding the parts of Starcross Manor that had been burned during the war. His precious piano had been saved. But the fighting had left much of the South in shambles. Everywhere, there were burned out houses, buildings, bridges, roads, railroad tracks, and even fields, partially or completely destroyed. The South was busy rebuilding; engaging in a hustle and bustle of renewal, but Elijah could see the old hatreds towering like a pile of rotting filth in the center of a flowering garden.

That following year, Miss Letty opened the 600-seat Starcross Theatre she'd built over the old church. She gave Elijah a two-room apartment suite upstairs in the new theatre, next to a room that was to be used as a general office, where he could practice undisturbed. He worked with her on the theatre booking schedule, thereby helping to make a lifelong dream of hers come true. By that time, she was 86 years old, with enthusiasm and energy to rival several younger people. Phineas, who was about her age, and Avajay, fifteen years her junior, always tired sooner than Miss Letty. Elijah imagined that all

Talbert's bleary eyes could see of his Mother was a pink taffeta blur of rustling perpetual motion.

The theatre was successful from the beginning. Atlanta was growing in all directions. Elijah's sophisticated knowledge of plays and artists was the reason their presentations were enthusiastically received. He led a fulfilling life, spending most of his time touring, and during his off time, he traveled to his parents' Canadian farm.

In January, 1874, Elijah said he was upstairs in the theatre office packing music in his cases in preparation for a six-month concert series. It was one of Georgia's coldest months, and he'd spent a busy evening sorting through music, and keeping a blazing fire burning in the fireplace. As he worked, he hummed a difficult passage from Chopin's Etude Number Three in E Major. The room grew warmer, and Elijah took off his jacket, and eventually his shirt. His well-muscled torso developed a sheen of perspiration from the exertion of collating heavy stacks of scores.

Still humming, he stood over the piano to play the passage that had been running through his mind. He sat down and went over several bars very slowly, then again, a little faster. Deep in concentration, with his back to the door, he wasn't aware someone had entered the room until the sudden draft caused the candles on the piano to flicker. Behind him, he heard a high, thin feminine voice say,

'Now that sounds real good. I could listen to you play all night.'

He swung around and faced the elegantly dressed woman who had invaded his privacy without knocking. He didn't recognize her immediately. He stood, a slender, but powerfully built figure in formfitting black breeches. The slight frown on his handsome features deepened. The woman continued to smile at him,

'Oh, my, my how you've grown, Elijah,' she drawled.

Embarrassed, he reached toward the chair to retrieve his shirt, a movement that flexed his muscles in the fire's glow. The woman's colorless gaze widened at the sight of his rippling flesh. Although a wispy yellow veil covered her hat and face, he didn't miss the gleam in her eyes and the slow sensuous way she licked her lips. He was trying to be polite, but there was something unpleasant about that gesture and the singsong rhythm in her pronunciation of his name, 'E-li-jah'. He never liked guessing games in the first place.

Laughing at his confusion, her hollow giggle set off a distant alarm in his heart. The white blonde curls descending from underneath the jaunty hat, the weird laughter; the voluptuous figure, heavier than it had been, all combined to jog his memory.

Although he was over six feet tall, a familiar chill of childish apprehension caused an alarm in his head to ring even louder at the recognition of his old nemesis. He stared at her as the years rolled back, fresh and sharp in his mind's eye, as if it had all just happened. His thoughts sank into the smothering darkness that contained his childhood fears. Visions of her as she had been nineteen years before came to the surface of his awareness, intact. Her blackmail, her hot breath on his cheek, her mindless cruelty; the blood, death and screaming destruction flashed across his mind. He felt again his terror on the night of the fire that although buried, would always remain with him. This strange woman who was certainly no stranger still smiled seductively at him. He heard his own raspy whisper break through the clanging silence,

'Ah, Miss Roxanne—'

A single tear ran from the corner of Adam's right eye. Nasrene quickly began the suggestions that by now, everyone knew well, ending the session.

No one stirred. Ceeoni tried to hide her own intense reaction to Elijah's testimony. She could feel the deep grooves her nails had carved in her palms, and taste the soreness in her bottom lip, suddenly salty with blood from biting back sobbing tears.

CHAPTER TWENTY-FOUR

The frown on Adam's face faded as Nasrene gently dabbed his eyes. "Hmph!" Diana sputtered, "So Roxanne returns! Of all the nerve!"

Unaware that R.C. had silently opened the door, Nasrene said, "I know what you mean Di, but I believe divine healing is taking place in everybody concerned. The past life regressions are revealing karmic patterns and, whether we like it nor not, Roxanne seems to be a key to a maze of 19th century dynamics that could lead to the killer's identity."

"Well, she's walkin' on the outside of my good side," Di huffed. "Seems like she caused all their problems from the start, now she turns up again, about to stir up some more crap!"

"Too bad we can't jump back in time and change the course of events, like they do in the movies," Nasrene sighed. "Whatever they did to each other has already been etched in stone."

R.C. had admitted a bearded replica of Adam Delayno, who remained in the doorway listening to everything Nasrene said. Nasrene must've felt someone looking at her. She raised her eyes, and discovered his gaze. They stared at each other. His wink broke the spell. In a flurry of activity, she began gathering her tapes and recorder.

"Hello, Everybody!" Samson said, hugging R.C. "Say, man, I got here as soon as I could! Where's my baby, Juno? On what part of the planet are my kids hangin'?"

R.C. beamed, "Samson, Juno is here, man, with the three youngest. You haven't seen the last two, have you? I've got photos of all of them. You won't believe how they've changed!"

"I can't wait. It's been a real drag to spend so much time away from my family." Looking closely at Adam he said, "I never thought we'd be getting together under these terrible circumstances. How is he?"

"Man! It's been rough!" R.C. realized that he hadn't introduced the stranger, "Oh, I'm sorry everybody. Meet Samson Delayno, Adam's brother."

The resemblance between the two brothers couldn't be denied. Both in their mid-thirties, with similar broad-shouldered physiques, they shared nearly identical facial features. Samson's hearty laugh and straightforward manner made him instantly likeable. Ceeoni wondered how much Adam's personality was like his brother's.

He sat in the chair on Nasrene's right and regarded Adam with tender concern.

"We believe he's just fine," R.C. said, "Well, the prognosis is that he could wake up any moment. He has no neurological damage that can be detected with MRI, or anything else. We think we know why he's chosen to stay that way, but we don't know for how long—"

"Chosen?" Samson exclaimed, "Chosen to stay that way?! Oh I don't think Adam would ever choose to stay like that! His energy wouldn't let him just lay there. R.C. you know him as well as I do! His nickname is 'Thunder.'"

"Maybe we should say there appears to be a metaphysical, rather than a physical reason for his coma, but we'll fill in the details. Be prepared for mindbenders," Nasrene commented.

"Samson," Homer asked, "have you already checked into a hotel?"

"Yeah. The Airport Hilton. I took a cab over."

"Well, we've been the targets of some maniac's murderous rampage and, at this juncture, we're completely in the dark. We think the police are, too. As of tonight, the lead investigator on the case is missing and his detective partner was murdered."

"I know about Basil Cassidy. You mean there's been another murder, on top of the attempt on Adam?"

"Right in front of Starcross Manor! Man, it's been a fast and furious nightmare. This is just Monday, and everything has happened since last Thursday, at the Starcross Theatre, the Starcross Manor and the Starcross Lakes estates. Oh, Samson, I'm Homer Dinsmore. I restored the Starcross property, and built the Estates Community."

Samson shook Homer's extended hand, "Homer! Homer, all right! Good to meet you. Say, what do you think could be a possible motive for these crimes?"

"Your guess is as good as mine. Suddenly, pow-yow! We found ourselves in the middle of a crime wave, but we'll tell you how it went down. Let's stop by my place for a snack, then we'll show you Adam's house."

"Yes, Starcross. I'm anxious to see this place Adam's so excited about. He's traveled the world for years and I've never known him to be fired up over a house. Excuse me a minute, I've gotta' tell him something." He sat on the bed, and whispered into Adam's ear.

"We can leave the room if you like," Nasrene offered.

"Oh, no, stay." He sniffed, and spoke to no one in particular, "You know, Adam made me, literally made me, go to school, and he's three years younger. The two of us were the only family we had, and it was Adam who kept me together by insisting on our constant communication during the years we were in separate foster homes. He even paid for my college education. He always said one of the reasons he was glad he started making money early in life was to be able to help me and the people he cares about."

"Bingo," R.C. interjected, "My kids are part of a trust fund Adam established. He had Basil put the whole thing together so that a part of his writing and publishing royalties are reinvested into the trust every year."

"It's a good thing Basil did," Samson laughed, "because Adam would've given it all away." He placed his hand over his brother's, "I'll do anything to see that whoever did this to him is brought to justice. He means everything to me."

Di introduced herself, "Samson, I'm Diana Underhill. I'm visiting my friend, Ceeoni," she paused slightly before adding, "and Homer. How long will you be staying in Atlanta?"

He lifted her hand and kissed it, "Ms. Divine Diana, I took an indefinite leave of absence from work."

"Sounds marvelous, to be able to take off."

"Well now I can. In all the years I've been there, I didn't dare take more than a day off."

"Really?"

"Yeah, since Adam plays weekend concerts, I've been able to go somewhere with him on a Friday evening over to Monday, but I haven't taken a real vacation. I think that's why they told me to take as much time as I need, and I intend to do just that."

Nasrene interjected, "Sometimes a vacation is like sleep, a vacation can knit up the raveled sleeve of care."

"True, but during the first years after I'd earned a full professorship, I didn't have time to check out my sleeve. I think I had a suspicion that my position might not be there if I stayed away too long." His smile was so like Adam's, Ceeoni's heart skipped a beat.

Nasrene stepped forward and held out her hand, "Hello Samson, I'm Nasrene Asher." Kissing the offered hand, Samson said, "Enchante, beautiful lady."

Nasrene watched him intently while fiddling with the handle of the Hermes bag over her shoulder. Samson held her hand a split second longer than good manners dictated. Ceeoni couldn't believe her eyes,

'Why Nasrene,' she thought, 'I do believe you're nervous!' Di's slightly raised eyebrows signaled that she'd noticed, too.

Nasrene introduced Ceeoni. When Samson's lips brushed her fingers he murmured,

"My pleasure, lovely Ceeoni," but his eyes drifted back toward Nasrene. Ceeoni remembered Nasrene's unattached status as she followed them out of the hospital.

"Samson," Nasrene asked, "What's your area of specialization?"

"Criminal Law, Loyola University, Los Angeles. By the way, Nasrene is a wonderful name."

"Thank you. I was told it means the glow on the face of the believer."

"Now that just gave me warm pleasant chills. Do you live in Atlanta?"

"No, I came here two weeks ago to complete a research project at Emory University. I teach courses in parapsychology at UCLA."

"UCLA? Parapsychology? Wow! You must tell me everything you do there. Now that I know where you are, and I just happen to live only five minutes from Westwood, possibly I can visit some of your classes. At your invitation, of course."

Nasrene hesitated, "Oh—yes, I'd—be honored."

"Very well, Nasrene, we have at least two things in common already."

"Two things?" she asked.

"Yes, we both teach in Los Angeles, and I have a keen interest in subjects associated with your field. I believe UCLA has received a great deal of notoriety because of the eminent parapsychologist Dr. Thelma Moss."

"Right!" Nasrene said, "Her work is a constant source of inspiration."

Samson's light conversational tone became serious, "I overheard you talking about past life regression; in fact, I listened carefully to what you were saying when I came into Adam's room. Are you involved in that in some way?"

"Samson," Nasrene turned to face him, "it's like we stepped into another world when we came to Starcross, all of us. Maybe you, too. We've been privileged to get a wide glimpse of something that has eluded most of mankind, and something that goes far beyond the mayhem of the last few days."

"Which is?" he asked. Nasrene hesitated again before answering, "Immortality."

"Did I hear you correctly?"

"The survival of consciousness after the physical form dies. But I'll begin at the beginning as soon as we get settled somewhere. I have to collect my thoughts, and I do that much better sitting down."

"No fair!" he laughed.

Nasrene gave him a playful little nudge, "Samson, it can't be encapsulated!"

"OK, OK, I'm at your mercy!"

Homer tipped the parking attendant as Samson whistled and walked slowly around the front of the sleek silver automobile.

"What year is this?"

"'59 Silver Cloud. I found it all wrecked up in an auction back in '83. It was my congratulatory gift to myself after the Starcross restoration began to take shape."

"It's cherry, Homer," Samson said.

"Yeah. I have a friend, a retired mechanic who brought it back to me looking like this, and he keeps it up. In those days, I didn't know my hair was going to match the color of the car so soon." He added, "By the way, we're all staying at my house, Juno and the kids, everybody—and when you find out what's been going on around here, you may want to join us. The attacks have no rhyme or reason, although my police friends tell me that all crime has a reason whether we know it or not. Since we don't know where, when, who or why, you may be safer with us. Shall we go get your bags?"

"Well," Samson answered slowly, "since you put it that way, I'll be happy to be your guest, if it's no imposition."

"My friend, you'll find that I'm not a person who intentionally puts myself in a position that is an imposition."

x x x

It was nearly midnight by the time Samson was checked out of his hotel. During the ride, Nasrene started to relate the recent events since Basil Cassidy's murder. She finished up in Homer's living room over a late night snack of cheeses, fruit and crackers.

Opening a bottle of Penfold Australian chardonnay, Di asked, "Who's having wine?"

Homer reached under the bar and pulled up a very large shaker, "I'm a Martini kind of guy myself."

"Now you're talkin'!" R.C. laughed, "Let me give Juno a call. If she isn't out like a light, I know she'll want to see Samson. Web, what's the number to our suite?"

"Press seven."

Nasrene sat close to Samson on the sofa and asked, "Any questions?"

Samson was obviously an active, careful listener.

"As a matter of fact, yes, I do have some questions." His approach was reminiscent of a sharp trial lawyer's collection of testimony. He asked each one what their outstanding impressions had been during past life regression and nodded in understanding when Nasrene said that she, Di and Ceeoni had yet to be regressed.

R.C. leaned forward and spoke in an awed half-whisper, "Samson, Juno's Soul was a male slave owner, and I was Elijah's mother. Only—Only Elijah's Soul is now—Adam."

He searched Samson's eyes for a reaction, but Samson was on a fact-finding mission.

"I'm especially interested in the intertwined relationships," he replied.

"Man," R.C. said, "All of us are in a kind of mass energy hype scene, or an old *Twilight Zone,* or the universe is trying to tell us something. What's as extraordinary is that each one of us spoke of all these little facts about our lives in the 19th century that everyone else corroborates, and each one adds bits of new pertinent information. Right now, it's like a puzzle, a big jigsaw puzzle, with key pieces missing here and there."

R.C. waited, "Well?" The room was still, waiting for Samson's reaction.

"I learned early on that a great energy guides my life," Samson said. "Watching my brother play the piano when he was just a little guy taught me that he was a part of something grand, something larger than most of us can conceptualize. When I was nine years old, and Adam was six, I could see this Spirit working through my brother, but I couldn't imagine anything working through me. I remember feeling that I was living in darkness and I wouldn't ever be able to reach the light. At that time, for whatever reason, and I had them all; malnutrition, pain and anger, for starters, and—I couldn't read.

"People don't understand how hard it is for a child to see properly when he's worried, scared and hungry. In a child's eyes, the problems are all there is, and everything else fades into a blurred, distant background. I didn't understand that anything else existed outside of my problems. They were already giving Adam music lessons because he had already exhibited his genius. Ah, but what I didn't know then was that this great energy works for anyone. My brother, at that tender age, was perceptive enough to realize I was catching hell because I couldn't read. He told me that he'd decided to teach me himself.

"We sat down with books, and I guess I was motivated, too, because within a few months, I was reading everything. Up until then, I think people thought I was retarded. Hell, I thought I was retarded! When I told them Adam taught me to read, nobody believed it. After all, he was only six, but he knew how to get it across to me. And did I catch up! I went crazy. I read just for the exercise, and I needed to prove to people that I could read. I carried a book with me just in case I'd get a chance to read. You know, I was always ready to whip out my book. Just a few months before, I hadn't found a miracle in my life. Suddenly, my spirit was released from its constricting box, and I began to excel academically. Adam and I became known as The Delayno Brothers, respected up and coming extremely cool mini-celebrities in the 'hood', who also knew how to fight, which is of prime importance when you're almost seven and ten years old. I said that to say that I believe in miracles because my whole life has been a miracle."

Ceeoni sipped her wine, enjoying the conversation, impressed with what she'd learned of Adam's early life, and a little boy's compassion for his older brother.

"Well then, have you any more clues?" Samson asked as he moved a little closer to Nasrene. She shook her head. Samson looked from R.C. to Homer.

"OK. So where do we go from here?"

"Something's got to connect, but so far," Homer answered, "our information is just plain skimpy."

"Since we found ourselves in the middle of this drama, nobody's had much sleep, except Juno, the kids, and Ada, the Nanny," Di sighed. We've been awake over 20 hours out of every 24, running on sheer adrenalin."

"Right," Homer added, "I've even seen Weber, at the most unusual hours, staring out the windows, which isn't at all like him. This murderer has us all wired up and edgy as hell. I haven't had time to tell Web the rest of the details, but I know he feels the vibe. It's not every day we have a houseful of people running around half the night."

"Maybe I can add something here. Nasrene, what do I have to do to get you to guide me through a past life regression?"

"What?" Nasrene asked as she looked into Samson's eyes. Samson smiled at her and repeated himself. Di's eyebrow shot up when Nasrene giggled and displayed difficulty locating her bag at her feet. Samson got on one knee and pulled the bag from under the side table, then caressed her fingers a little as he handed it to her.

"You know, there's something familiar about all of this. I recently recalled dreams I had about plantation life when I was very little. It was always the same house, which led me to believe that it stemmed from the feeling slavery created in all black people. I figured I was empathizing with my ancestors. I thought about those dreams for the first time since I was in elementary school when Adam told me he'd finally found the home he'd always wanted, a Greek Revival mansion in Georgia. I wondered if I'd been dreaming about Adam's future, but now I'm wondering if I was dreaming about the past."

Samson abruptly swung around and smiled at Nasrene, "Let's do it, Gorgeous. I'm ready to see if I've lived before."

CHAPTER TWENTY-FIVE

While Nasrene repeated the relaxation suggestions to Samson, Juno came in quietly and eased herself down on R.C.'s lap. To Nasrene's question, "What is your name?" Samson answered in a soft gravelly tenor, totally different from Samson's rich baritone.

'Phineas Ballwin.'

"Where are you?"

'Stahcruh'

"How old are you?"

'Dis 1849. Ah wer bon on da Ballwin Plantashun in Ballwin Sprang, Jawja, roun' 1791, ah, ahm 47!' he replied proudly.

He said he liked living at Baldwin, 'Ah knows ef duh Lawd seed fit ta mek me a slave, ah wer lucky en mos' ta be bon a Ballwin. Ah wer jis un l'il oldah en Mistuh wen he marra up wif he skinny l'il po whi trash wife, en ah wer by he side wen he fall all ovah hesef fo dat big firey slav gal, Isis.'

Phineas said Mr. Baldwin wanted his slaves to learn how to read. Mister Baldwin cautioned Phineas not to let others know he could decipher letters. The fact that reading was forbidden was the first reason. The second reason Phineas' knowledge was dangerous for him was that many white people didn't know which end of a book to open and sheer jealousy could get him beaten or killed. Phineas kept up his narrative, saying,

'Aftuh Isis leev dis wurl, ol' Mistuh greev en he greev. Soon, he git busy en he spoil Miz Sybil lak he spoil huh Mama.' Phineas said he remembered driving Sybil to a children's party when she was about seven, and all she talked about for weeks afterward was a boy named Talbert Starcross Bramwell.

When Sybil came back from Spain, at the age of 29, she had turned into a fine looking woman, in spite of having inherited all her Father's worst facial features. If anybody looked close, one could tell she was 'uh high yalluh' but with all her fancy clothes, nobody remarked about that, even if one looked close enough.

Mr. Baldwin wanted only the very best for his Sybil. Phineas said he could see that even though Mr. Baldwin had many reservations, he felt that maybe it was prophetic that the tall handsome stranger who walked into Sybil's life at the New Year's Ball, was the boy of her childhood dreams; arrogant, rich, and demanding her hand in marriage.

It saddened Phineas to see the light fade out of Sybil's eyes not long after they moved to Starcross. Talbert turned out to be cold, distant and mean, and his bride found herself alone most of the time while her husband drank and ran around. There wasn't anything anyone could do to help her. There wasn't anything anyone could do at Starcross except work from sun-up to sundown and pray for a change.

Phineas lived alone. He was the only member of his family to move to Starcross with Sybil. Phineas' wife and his three children had stayed at Baldwin. Late one hot August night, he'd been at Starcross for only a short while, when an unexpected knock came at his cabin door. Startled, he hid the Bible he'd been reading under his pallet, and opened the door to find Avajay waiting.

'Miss Letty wants to speak with you, Phineas.'

Her big dark eyes fixed unblinkingly on his face. He blew out his candle and followed the tiny figure wrapped in a flowing white gown. Her long braid, like a silken rope, swung from side to side with each step she took. He loved his wife, but he thought Avajay, with her silent dignity, her dark lips, and her black, black skin, was the most beautiful woman in the world.

She led him up the lane to the church, a walk that was too short because he felt good walking almost beside Avajay. Miss Letty met them at the back room door, and led the way up the stairs, where she closed the door, locked it and smiled at him. The room was bare except for tables and chairs, same as always. As she walked over to him, he backed up closer to the fireplace.

'Phineas please sit down' She said softly.

'Yasum, Miz Letty.'

'You must never tell another living soul what we're talking about tonight, you hear?'

He averted his eyes, like he knew he should, and squeezed into a little chair.

'Yasum,' he mumbled.

She sat down in the chair next to him, and gripped his hand. He'd never seen Miss Letty close up like that before. He couldn't imagine what she wanted with him or her reason for holding his hand tight like that. His heart started beating faster. Even the best white folks could sometimes turn on you without warning for no reason. The intensity in her voice made him more uneasy.

'Phineas, Phineas, don't you be frightened, please, and most of all, please trust me. And look at me, for God's sake!'

He looked her right in the face. Miss Letty tightened her grip on his hand.

'Avajay tells me you're brave, and you can be trusted, and she's never wrong,' Miss Letty said.

Oh. He smiled inside knowing Avajay thought well of him. But what did Miss Letty want? Her eyes bored into his.

'And Phineas, Avajay tells me you can read.'

He could feel his stomach sink toward his knees. His eyes moved to Avajay's.

'Miz Vacha,' he asked, 'Wha mek ya teeng dat?'

How could she know?

Miss Letty shook his hand a little. 'Phineas, please, we're in desperate need of someone who can read. Tell me it's true.'

Avajay, standing against the wall, never took her large dark eyes off of him. Long minutes passed. He heard a voice in the back of his mind urging him on, 'G'wan. Sho em.' With his free hand, he picked up the hymnal on the next chair and opened it to a page.

'Dis say 'Mazin Grace' wer wrut by a slave ship cap'n name a Tom Newton, whil he wer outta sea, wif slaves en da hole. It say aftuh da Lawd speak ta him, he cudden be no cap'n no mo. Dis book Carrell en Clayton, Vahginnie Hahmanny, aighteen tirdy-one'

After he set the book down, Miss Letty's wonder-filled stare made him feel more uncomfortable, but he didn't avert his eyes. He was proud that he could read. There was another long silence. He was surprised to see a tear roll down her cheek.

Wiping the tear, she sniffled a little and said,

'That—was very good, Phineas. Phineas, I'm asking if you'll work with us to help slaves escape to the North.'

Samson jerked suddenly, startling everyone in Homer's living room, as Phineas said,

'Greagawdahmydee! Dat how dey ben gittin away!' He stopped talking.

"Phineas," Nasrene prodded, "Can you tell us any more?"

Phineas' voice, stronger now, answered, 'Yasum. Den Miss Letty say undah Gawd, all peepls poda live, en wuk, en git pay, en raise dey chirren same a ennybody. She say she wuk wif peepls sennin slaves ta freedom! She say, 'Will ya hep us?' Tree time!' Phineas said he didn't believe his ears. On the sofa, Samson held up three fingers and repeated, 'Tree time she say!' Then he slowly stretched out his arms as Phineas almost whispered,

'Ah feels sumpen riz up en me lak uh gian oak tree wif grea branches, en leafs blowin' en da win.'

He said didn't know how to tell her he was ready to lay down his life.

He returned the strong grip she still had on his hand—he looked straight into her eyes and said,

'Ah be mydee pleas, Miz Letty, mydee, mydee pleas.'

Phineas continued, saying he found out how they had been going about their secret activities. They'd been doing it for years, but Miss Letty and Avajay told him it had been easier before Talbert turned Starcross into a cotton plantation, before so many people were watching what everybody else was doing. Phineas was able to secretly teach most slaves to read street signs and maps a little before they left, which assisted their survival wherever they might end up.

One of their biggest problems was Roxanne.

'Dat gal got nuf fedders en huh hed ta fill up da well!'

But she wasn't very smart, and they were able to get around her. They knew that Sybil kept Roxanne busy most afternoons. Miss

Letty and Avajay would begin most of their arrangements in the middle of the day, making a way for the escaping slave to slip away in the hours after everyone was asleep, in spite of Talbert's watchers.

Roxanne's sneaky movements were well known by Phineas, who kept his eye on her. Through their intricate system, Phineas could communicate where danger was at all times. He and Avajay could duplicate sounds that made a casual listener think he was hearing birdcalls. The refinements that Phineas added to their system, made their activities run smoothly.

Phineas said everything was working very well until the night of the fire. He began to shake his head quickly, in agitation

'The Fiah! Fiah! No, oh no, no—' he groaned, 'Ah, oh Gawd, ah cudden stop it! The fiah cot so fas!! It cot onto erryteeng—so fas!! Wern nuttin' ah cud do! Po lil Sybil, nevuh had uh chans, she nevuh had uh chans!'

"Did you see who killed Sybil?" Nasrene asked.

Phineas didn't respond.

"Did you see how the fire started?" she persisted.

'Lijah see. Jis him, jis Lijah.' Phineas said, his voice trailing off.

Recognizing his anguish, Nasrene began the pain reduction and awakening process.

x x x

Samson's eyes opened, and for a moment he appeared slightly dazed. Nasrene reached to help him up, but as he got to his feet, Samson put his arm around her instead, asking her, "Have you experienced this?"

"Many times and many lifetimes, but never like this, in tandem with others."

"Well, if it's alright, I'd like to go to the Starcross Manor."

"Sure," Homer answered, "are you O.K.?"

"Homer, my friend, you know those science fiction films where the heroes jump through a spinning vortex? Let's just say, if this turns out to be a parallel dimension, I won't be surprised. My mind and heart are filled with a whole flood of bright, technicolor memories, running at warp speed."

"We're on this starship together, ducks!" Juno said, slipping her arm through his.

"Baby girl! Give me some sugar!"

Juno reached up and kissed his cheek,

"I'm so glad you're finally here," she said. "I know Adam will improve now, and listening to Nasrene's tapes will help your sanity. You'll hear how all of us have been transported."

"I will Angel. My sanity is in need of a band-aid." Samson kept his arm around Juno, and pulled Nasrene closer into his embrace,

"If it's a dream, then so be it. I don't care what it is! I just know that it's a profound experience to be with you again, my dear friends."

"Samson," Nasrene said, "It seems you played a really pivotal role in the story, so far. We've learned that Adam's Soul—Elijah, went through quite a bit to protect Phineas from Massa's wrath to keep him from discovering Phineas' ability to read, and Adam has carried the repercussions in his Soul ever since."

"Nasrene, let me get this straight. You said that I, rather, Phineas, taught Elijah to read in the 19th century?"

She nodded as his eyes searched hers, "It's incredible, but Elijah's Soul returned the favor. As I told you, Adam taught me to read in this life, and you," he smiled, "you were Avajay—"

Homer jangled his keys, "Hey! I thought we were going to the house!"

Diana followed Homer out the door, grumbling,

"A person couldn't rest around here if a person wanted to!"

"Well, would a person rather get left?" Homer sang, gleefully.

Samson and Di sat in the front seat of the car comparing notes about their 19th century identities. It was almost 2am when they rounded the corner of the Manor driveway.

"Oh, these are the dogwoods!" Samson gasped, "Hey! Hey, this is it! I remember my first spring here, Jesus! This is it!—Prettiest sight I ever saw. I felt like these trees bloomed their heads off just for me. This is the very Lane I've seen in my dreams! Nasrene! This is it!—"

Suddenly, Homer slammed on the brakes and backed up fast. Samson had to catch himself to keep from falling forward into the dashboard. The tires spun as Homer turned the wheel, jerking everyone far to the right and kicking up gravel, he aimed the Rolls' headlights into the trees. He shoved the gearshift up into park, and left the engine running. The chassis rocked back and forth from the sudden stop, as he jumped out, yelling,

"Did you see that?"

"What? See what?" R.C. yelled, grabbing the door handle in an effort to get out of the backseat. His abrupt movement sent Juno sliding off his lap. Homer ran in front of the car, with Di at his heels. R.C., Samson, and Nasrene were right behind them.

Juno, climbing back on the seat, asked,

"What was it? What was that? Ceeoni, did you see anything?"

Ceeoni got out of the car, straining to see what Homer was chasing. Running fast, he disappeared into the woods with Nasrene and Di trailing behind him. Soon, R.C. and Samson gave up and walked back to the car.

"Did you see what it was?" Ceeoni asked

R.C. adjusted his Kufi, "Not a thing. Did you?"

"I didn't see anything either," Juno replied.

A few minutes later, Homer stalked out from among the trees. "Dammit, maybe I'm getting' paranoid, but did anybody else see a form moving in that direction?" He gestured over his shoulder.

Puffing to catch their breathing, Di and Nasrene joined them. "I know you weren't seeing things, because I detected movement over there, too," Di answered as they climbed in. Homer started the car and drove slowly, carefully watching both sides of the narrow driveway.

"What did it look like?" Nasrene asked.

"It might have been a deer," R.C. offered, "Weber thought he saw a deer this afternoon near the house."

Homer shook his head, "Well, if so, that damn deer was running on two legs!"

They rounded the last bend in the road, and Samson's eyes widened at the sight of the mansion.

"Ahh, there she is!" he whispered, "Now I know what a time traveler must feel like. Homer, you changed the front doors. Those gold handles aren't the original knockers. Well do I remember how

Phineas used to polish the silver crosses with four-point stars in the center."

"Yeah, I'd found the family emblem in different places around the house, but the door knockers were long gone. The doors had been damaged over the years. You know, I never imagined they were silver. Guess my guessing couldn't fool you, eh?" Homer chuckled.

Inside, Samson, delighted, recognized almost as many rooms as Ceeoni, and he had knowledge of where the outbuildings had been; the barns, smokehouse, and even the location of the blacksmith's shed and the stable that had burned down on that tragic night in 1849.

Nasrene's attention was focused on Samson, even when she was talking to someone else. In very subtle ways, he acknowledged her presence, with a nod of his head or a light touch. Unlike Di and Homer, who teased each other in a boisterous fashion, Nasrene and Samson's gentle consideration for each other was lovely to see. Of course. Avajay and Phineas had been devoted friends for the better part of a lifetime. Aha.

It was after 3am before Ceeoni could get to her suite and into a hot bath. Nasrene and Samson stayed in the living room with the regression tapes and a bottle of wine. Di and Homer were in the kitchen deep in conversation.

Ceeoni knew that meeting Homer was an event that couldn't have happened more perfectly for Di, had she written the script herself. Now that Di would soon be living in Georgia, Ceeoni knew she would miss her friends at UCLA, 'The Rev' O.C., and the studios where she pitched her scripts, but life and love had led Di to Starcross and an entirely new exciting path. Ceeoni smiled to herself knowing that she and Di wouldn't have to scope out each other's latest escapades by E-mail. Karma had kept the Dynamic Duo together, after all.

CHAPTER TWENTY-SIX

The next morning, everyone dispersed to various parts, leaving Ceeoni on the patio. Sun splashing on the lush colors in the yard highlighted the brilliantly hued blue birds, the flaming red cardinals, and the bushy tailed squirrels that carried on their morning activities, accompanied by a great deal of conversation. She hummed a few bars of "Spring Can Really Hang You Up The Most," and enjoyed the wonder of a November morning in Georgia that could feel so much like spring.

She answered her phone as soon as she could wrest it from her bag. Jake's voice, breathy and urgent, sent her nerves into high gear.

"Oh, Ceeoni, Ceeoni?"

"Yeah, Jake, what's the matter?"

"I'm at the theatre, and I've already called the police!"

"Police? Oh, God—what is it?"

"Every seat in the house has been slashed! Also, the furniture in the dressing rooms, the lobby, the offices, even your photos and posters. And the mirrors are shattered, glass is everywhere, drapes are cut. Damn, he even slit the carpet in a few places. Someone came up in here with a knife. It must've taken hours to trash the place like this! Ceeoni, our blessing is that he couldn't reach the lights, and he didn't take any time with the backdrops and cables. The piano will have to be refinished, good thing it was locked. It looks like it was hit many times with something heavy."

Ceeoni couldn't talk. Jake's voice softened somewhat.

"I've been trying to stay calm, but I keep imagining the great expenditure of hateful energy it took to tear it all up like this. And whoever did this must have keys. When I got here, it looked like peace-on-earth from the outside, then I turned on the lights and it knocked me to my knees. It's gonna take days to get this cleared away! I don't know when we can get the theatre up and running again!

"Ceeoni, I hope you'll call Homer; I don't want to be the one to tell him. Oh, and two employees have already left letters of resignation in my box. After this, we'll be lucky if we have a full staff left. I hesitate to verbalize the moot question, 'Will anybody ever buy a ticket to come near here?' Damn, people are going to believe this place is really cursed."

"Look, Jake, I know you can't relax, but wait until the police arrive, then go home. Somebody else can carry the ball the rest of the way," she added dismally, "I've gotta catch up with Homer."

She knew the theatre had been locked. It was a habit to lock up. She shivered, imagining the violation of the gorgeous venue. She waited a while before dialing Homer. He had to be told.

His psychic antenna as uncanny as ever, Homer answered his phone without giving her a chance to speak.

"Hey, Ceeoni," his voice took on that rare, subdued quality, "Something told me to stop by the theatre. It's hard to conceive how anyone could be so enraged! And in God's name, whatever for? The extent of the damage has us wondering if there were two vandals. Di can't resist picking stuff up, but I keep telling her we need to leave it so they can sift it for clues. The police, janitorial service, and the insurance company will be here soon."

"Homer, I—" Ceeoni began, but Homer, who was not fond of condolences, interrupted.

"You know I understand. Now here's something you puzzle solvers can gnaw on. I just learned that the knife that killed David Saxon's partner was a rare antique, set with precious and semiprecious stones, from 18th century Spain. Either the killer didn't know what he had, or the fact something like that could be very expensive, meant nothing to him. They think it's worth over $50,000, and it bears no prints."

The mention of that knife hovered like a chilling shadow over her heart. Her inner voice screamed in frustration, 'C'mon, Ceeoni! Where have you seen that knife?'

"Ceeoni," he asked, "are you there?"

"Overload, Homer—"

"That's exactly how I feel," he sighed. "Well, the police haven't made any progress with David Saxon's car, except the fact that the blood on the passenger side proved to be his. They've ascertained from the angle of the knife and the wound that David's partner was bludgeoned and stabbed through the window, and David's blood on the half-opened passenger side window suggests that he was also attacked through the window, as well, but it's all they have."

"David's blood on the passenger side means he's either wounded or dead. Why would the killer take Adam and Detective Saxon away? To torture them? Adam had luckily escaped whatever the killer had intended. Oh, Homer, what do we do now?"

"I wish I knew, but remember, I've lived with the Starcross dream most of my life. It's gonna take a lot more than this to turn us around. I know it's slowed us down, but it won't stop us."

"You have an enormous amount of courage, but the financial loss alone has got to have you reeling. I don't know if I had anything to do with it or not, but your troubles began at nearly the exact moment I arrived here."

"Hold it, Ms. Cee. We're insured all over the place, and, who can say, maybe it wasn't meant for us to open now. Don't fret. You brought me my Diana, Nasrene, and your sweet self, which adds up to more happiness than I expected I'd ever know. What's happened to us is worth more to me than all the money in the world."

She couldn't reply.

"Cee, are you there?"

"Yeah, me, too. Ah, can we check on Adam later?"

"Sure, I've gotta make a few runs, and I have to meet a truckload of materials coming to the Estates. Please tell everybody we'll be back about 2pm. Jake is putting together a list of damages that will enable us to converse intelligently with the insurance people, who'll eventually be getting in touch with you. Hey, don't get quiet on me. I'm not walking on air, but I know we'll be OK. I can remember what it feels like to have absolutely no resources, no nothing, and this doesn't feel like that."

She smiled at the smile in his voice.

"I feel better already. Homer? Would you please see about my plant, Violette?"

"Excuse me?"

"On my desk, you remember the little African violet, you know—?"

"Oh, yeah, your office door had been kicked in, everything had been knocked off your desk, but Di insisted on sitting your plant back up. It was on its side on the floor. Lost a little dirt. Still the flowers are alright."

She didn't know why that lifted her spirits.

"Please tell Jake I'll be over there as soon as I can, and thanks." But she knew just visualizing the damage to her theatre was all she could take for now.

x x x

Juno, R.C., Nasrene and Samson joined Ceeoni and Nanny Ada on the patio and helped explain to the three little Ponder kids that it was too cold to get into the pool. During Weber's wonderful brunch of spinach quiche, fruit salad and buttered potato slices baked in rosemary and parmesan, Ceeoni told everybody about the theatre vandalism and the lab results on the murder weapon, as well as the rare, ornate Spanish knife.

"Still no prints, and no real clues," she concluded.

"You know, Homer's speculation that there could be two people doing all the dirt is something that doesn't hit me right," Nasrene said. "I doubt that it could be two. It's rare for two people to share the sort of fury I feel here. I wonder if the search for Detective Saxon has yielded anything."

The obvious possibility that the detective may have been murdered continued to be left unspoken.

The kids romped and squealed in that surreal dimension of sheer bliss kids know so well. Cool, but mild weather allowed Georgia to show off her November splendor. Ceeoni understood how the children would want to splash in the waterfall cascading from the second-floor dining room into the far end of the pool. The tropical setting tantalized and invited even a timid swimmer, like herself.

Homer had explained to her how the waterfall was created. Water was carried by pipe to circulate beneath the floor of the second-story circular dining room. The white Mediterranean dining table and chairs for twelve sat on a raised Lucite island in the center of a pool of gently flowing blue waves. Six wide walkways of clear Lucite radiated out from the island to the curved walls of the large room giving one the illusion of walking on water. Though actually quite shallow, the rippling water against the dark cerulean tiles lining the pool created the illusion of endless depths. The water drifted under the Lucite walkway leading through the wide glass doors and under the patio, where it became the eighteen-foot waterfall that streamed down into the grotto.

After Ceeoni and Juno cleared away the brunch dishes, Ceeoni meandered into the dining room to marvel at its masterfully innovative design and absorb its healing peace.

Weber and Ada scooped up the kids for an afternoon of shopping, leaving Ceeoni, R.C., Nasrene and Samson to steep in contemplative silence.

Di came in ahead of Homer and threw the newspapers onto the living room coffee table.

"You know these people need a life!"

Well, if you think that coverage is excessive, wait until the vandalism report comes out," Homer said. "The CBS News at noon anchor just coined the phrase, 'the star-crossed Starcross complex', which doesn't strike me as so damn clever. Every minute our slasher is free to ravage us, the more difficult our recovery will be."

Samson broke the gloomy silence that followed. "Hey, maybe Phineas can add something meaningful."

Catching Nasrene's glance in her direction, Ceeoni realized Nasrene had been on the verge of again asking her to be regressed. She took off in search of a Perrier, acutely aware that she couldn't allow her fears to hold her back much longer. She probably had pertinent information locked inside her Soul. She owed it to everyone to volunteer for a past life regression. She shushed the little voice inside her head that began to sing to the tune of "Three Blind Mice," 'OK, when?—OK, when?—OK, when?—OK, when?'

Samson had relaxed on the sofa when Ceeoni came back to the living room. She quietly took her seat just as Nasrene completed the suggestions. As expected, Phineas returned right away.

'Hi do!'

"What is your name?"

'Phineas Ballwin.'

He started talking before Nasrene could ask another question, saying that two days after the stable fire in 1849, he'd had to hurry to build a containment for Roxanne, because she had to be physically restrained. Then he drove Darnella, the wet nurse and her two-week-old son along with Mr. Baldwin, who tenderly held his newborn granddaughter, back to Baldwin, following the wagon that carried Sybil's body. Baldwin's housekeeper Cleo, and her small staff of assistants had the nursery in lovely readiness. Tiny Clarisse already had everything money could buy, and more love than could ever be bought.

Phineas had helped his wife and an unmarried son and daughter settle on her uncle's farm in Michigan. His marriage had become one of distant love and respect; the kind of relationship some people develop after the children have grown. He thought of staying in Michigan with his family, to spend the rest of his life farming his own land and sitting on his 'own self's' porch, a free man, but he still had work to do where he was desperately needed. His wife was proud of the fact that Avajay, Miss Letty and many other lives depended on him, along with the brave people who made up their network. Even though he lived at Starcross he kept up with news of his family and news of Baldwin through letters and his coach-driving friends.

Turmoil grew in the nation, but nobody thought it would turn to all out war, except Avajay. Phineas learned that Mr. Baldwin wanted little Clarisse to experience the same sort of advantages as children of other wealthy families. Thus, in 1858, when she was nine, she was sent with a chaperone and two maids to be educated in Paris. Phineas was summoned to drive her, the maids and her English cousin, Mary Starcross, to their ship at Savannah.

His work with Miss Letty and Avajay kept him busy. He acted as go-between for Miss Letty and a group of Episcopalians, Quakers and other abolitionists, along with freed slaves, agents, conductors, and workers, who made up the Underground Railroad. Every other day, on his regular trips to the Coach Stop, he carried special messages, along with the mail. It was still a monumental task to keep Talbert Bramwell and his ever watchful watchers from suspecting anything, but Phineas had refined the elaborate system that Miss Letty and Avajay had developed, making it run as smoothly as one of his well-oiled wagon wheels.

Phineas read newspapers, Miss Letty's books and Elijah's letters that gave him a grasp of the legal, moral and economic arguments against the southern attitude, and he became familiar with the mounting hostilities on both sides that caused the North to eventually invade the South. People were surprised that the war escalated as quickly as it had. The North thought they would spank the gray pants off of Jefferson Davis' Confederates and send them 'advancing to the rear' within a few months, but that was a terrible miscalculation. When the war was finally over, more than 500,000 lives were lost.

The South, though outnumbered from the beginning, fought furiously. In spite of the fact that nearly half the Southern population consisted of slaves, and tens of thousands of them used the war as their opportunity to escape, the Confederates proved to be a formidable force.

The Emancipation Proclamation, enacted January 1, 1863, freed the slaves from bondage and added fuel to the secessionists' fierce hatred of President Abraham Lincoln. Phineas followed the course of the war carefully. He understood the human error, and the happenstance and strategies that created tremendous losses on both sides. Among the dozens of battles, from the Union defeats in two major confrontations at Bull Run, Virginia, right up to Sherman's capture of Atlanta, several turning points stood out in his memory. There was Lee's defeat in July of '63 at Gettysburg and, the very next day, Union General Grant's victorious ending of the 47-day standoff of the resistant Confederate stronghold at Vicksburg, Mississippi, where they said the Confederates had eaten rats to survive during the long siege. Late in '63, Phineas rejoiced at the North's eventual capture of Chattanooga, eighteen miles from Chickamauga, where one of the bloodiest battles of the Civil War had seen a Union defeat that tallied the deaths of over 35,000 causalities. Phineas, who had driven the Baldwin and Starcross coaches all over Georgia, realized that Chattanooga and Chickamauga Creek, Tennessee, were not that far away from Atlanta. It was just a matter of time before Avajay's prediction would come true, and Atlanta, the 'Jewel of the South' would be penetrated by the Union Army.

The frightening daily news caused even Talbert Bramwell to abandon his futile attempts to keep a cotton plantation functioning. As the skirmishes grew closer, and shortages of help and supplies grew, Talbert's employees either joined the military or left to be with their families. Soon, there was no one to help him hunt down runaway slaves, and he turned his hand to daily drunken discussions of surefire strategies guaranteed to save the Confederacy.

Battle after battle was fought in vain attempts to hold back the Union Tide, to no avail. In the face of the Northern forces' proximity and the Confederates' inability to prevail, Talbert, who still believed that the North could be defeated, nevertheless fled to a cohort's Florida sugar plantation to help plan a fresh assault on Sherman's 90,000-strong Northern army, from a safe distance.

'Massa lef' in da middle o' da night, lak da cowah he wer, wi'out lookin' back ta see if 'n he Mama ded or livin',' Phineas said, indignantly.

Phineas recalled those months before Sherman reached Atlanta as a time of great fear and chaos, but he felt redeemed. The day he'd prayed for, the day he knew was coming, and the day he was joyful that he'd lived to see, was upon the land. All around him, although poor and hungry, slaves, no longer in bondage, embarked on frantic searches for lost relatives. Some slave owners dispersed and abandoned their plantations, while others dug in, prepared to defend with their lives, their honor, and their property—their right to enslave others.

Phineas said he kept a torn newspaper reprint of President Lincoln's Gettysburg Address among the pages of his Bible. The short speech, delivered at the dedication of the military cemetery at Gettysburg, Pennsylvania, meant a great deal to him. He didn't understand all the meaning, but he'd preserved the scrap of paper because the words were precious. Miss Letty said the words were taken from the Declaration of Independence—'that all men are created equal.' Lincoln was his hero; the first president to recognize people of color by holding audiences with several Negroes, including Frederick Douglass.

Soon, in spite of the crushing defeat at Kennesaw Mountain, north of Atlanta, General W.T. Sherman regrouped the Union Army and pushed into the city, fighting the 177-day siege of Atlanta, inch by inch. During the night of September 1, 1864, General John B. Hood and his greatly outnumbered Confederate troops were forced to abandon the city. Mayor James M. Calhoun, carrying a white flag on horseback, surrendered, and Sherman's Northern forces occupied the throne of King Cotton, Atlanta.

Sherman cut supply lines from other southern cities and laid to waste whatever could be sold, traded or forged into anything that could be used to make war, in an effort to force the South to surrender. When he ordered all stores, factories and public buildings burned and called for the evacuation of the city, civilians were given a choice of which direction to go, North or South. Although the evacuation order was mandatory, of course, many stayed.

Phineas said that during the Siege of Atlanta, the noise of shells bombarding the city had made sleep impossible. Throughout those weeks, he closed his eyes for only a few minutes at a time. Sherman's fires were lit that November and from their vantage point on high ground, Miss Letty, Avajay, Phineas and a small group of the displaced who found themselves at Starcross, watched flames and smoke destroy their world. With ears plugged to block out the cannon blasts, they kept going to the windows to stare, mute, unbelieving and mesmerized, at thick night skies, blazing fire as bright as day.

Cotton, tobacco and other farm products, including food, were confiscated. The war clogged the roads with the straggling homeless and wounded. Starcross was away from the heavily traveled arteries, but those who wandered through the woods to Miss Letty were freely given what food, medical attention and temporary shelter Starcross could offer. Most days they fed hungry people until the vegetable soup from Miss Letty's cauldron ran out.

Phineas related that before the war, Avajay's predictions had led them to prepare their hiding place to store a great stockpile of preserved beans, fruits, vegetables, cases of wine as well as Avajay's carefully cultivated and dried herbs and teas. Phineas had built shelves upon shelves there to hold canned goods that would keep for years. They had added to their secret stash when they could, and only brought out a few jars for the cauldron Miss Letty put on every other day. There was no meat, no livestock, and the fish in the streams had been exhausted or contaminated. He covered their well, which was fed by an underground stream. They collected rainwater in barrels, and told everyone the well had already been poisoned.

The hiding place was their lifeline. After while, few people had anything to steal. At Starcross, only a few jars of preserves could be found but since food was as good as gold, sometimes looters stole that.

But even thieves hurried away from the elderly and sick in the big empty house in the woods.

'Vacha say we gon' be all righ', onna counna dat hidin place, thank the Good Lawd!' Phineas said.

x x x

Phineas began to breathe faster. Speaking in an agitated near whisper, he said that Miss Letty, Avajay and Phineas were alone at Starcross most of the time, when Sherman's March began. The army tore up the countryside as it moved, burning some plantations and leaving others. Every day, the fires came closer.

Sure enough, one rainy November evening, the crunching sound of hooves on gravel and a loud chinking chorus of metal stirrups and spurs announced the approach of a large group on horseback. Phineas had developed the habit of watching the lane and surrounding woods for strangers, a practice that had at least warned them of unexpected guests. At the sight of the company of Union soldiers trotting toward him, he set his lantern down, and with a deep sigh of resignation, went to fetch Miss Letty.

The superior officer, a short, fat pimply faced man, wiped rain out of his close-together eyes and squinted at her before he dismounted. Phineas heard the smirk in his greeting,

'Evenin', Mam, I'm Lieutenant Michael Shervington. Do you mind if I ask how many others are here on this property Mam?' His added 'Mam' was an insulting demand.

Miss Letty, in the doorway with Avajay close by her side, hesitated for a moment before answering,

'Only who you see, sir.'

'Oh, no! What a shame! All your slaves ran away?' His mocking attitude was met with Miss Letty's firm answer.

'I don't hold that a man should be abused, and bound to work without pay, Lieutenant.'

The officer glanced at Avajay, then caught his aide's eye with a private wink, as if he knew her statement was just another version of the desperate lies southerners were telling to try to save their properties from Union torches.

'Pity,' he yawned slightly while slowly removing his yellow doeskin gloves, 'But you have all been abusing that ethic for a few hundred years now, haven't you?' he snapped. 'No matter', he said. 'We will be partaking of your famous southern hospitality by lodging at your fine mansion for the night.'

Phineas said he knew that meant they would load up what they could find, before deciding whether or not to set fire to the house.

Samson paused. Nasrene waited a few minutes, then gently urged,

"Phineas, do you have more to say?"

Biting his lip and wringing his hands, Phineas groaned,

'Oh, Lawd, dis heah cud put uh enn ta erryteeng. Vacha say she cain see wha dey gon do. Oh LawdGawd!'

Nasrene calmed him down, and when asked if he could continue, he nodded.

Beginning slowly, Phineas said that facing those Union soldiers, Miss Letty was polite, Avajay was watchfully silent, and he, Phineas, kept his ears open while he sat on the porch rail, repairing an old harness that hadn't seen a horse since the war began. Miss Letty's nervous fingers plucked at her brown shawl.

'Of course, Lieutenant,' she answered. Her consent was an unnecessary formality. Everyone knew she had no choice in the matter.

'Your name, Mam?' He asked as he dismounted.

'Leticia Starcross Bramwell, but people call me Miss Letty.' The officer's near smile curled up into a sneer.

'Miss Lu-cy, what do, uh, did you grow here?' He slapped his gloves into the outstretched hands of the soldier at his elbow before striding up the steps.

'Food for the table and nearby farms, until—'

'The officer broke into her sentence, saying, 'This is a mighty nice big house your cotton bought for you, Mam.' His attitude caused her to pull herself up to her full five feet, four inches.

'Cotton had no hand it!' she said. 'My father and my husband were artists! This house was built in 1782 to be simply our family home. The cotton was planted against my wishes.'

The officer snorted, brushed past her and stalked into the house, as if he owned it and she was in his way. Phineas knew they would receive no mercy from this man, who probably didn't have it in him to understand that Miss Letty had told him the truth; her disdain for the profits of oppression surpassed his. The Lieutenant would never believe he was about to destroy a place where a daily fight for freedom had been waged since long before he or any of his fire-starters were born.

That night the residents of Starcross stayed in the stable with the Union officer's horses, while soldiers occupied the house, cabins and grounds. Acrid campfire smoke choked the fresh air and helped to keep them awake, in spite of the comfortably warm, sweet hay surrounding them. They listened to unfamiliar noises and conversations in northern accents humming throughout the night that blended into early morning sounds in the gray drizzly dawn. The sweet scents of coffee and porridge made Phineas yearn for serene mornings of the past.

The troops began to move out, marking the dreaded, inevitable hour. Phineas recognized Starcross blankets and kitchen pots hanging from Union saddles. He was glad they hadn't taken a liking to Miss Letty's cauldron.

Not knowing what to do, Miss Letty, Avajay and Phineas drifted to the courtyard in front of the house. Avajay stood still as a tiny statue, eyes closed, oblivious to the drizzling rain and the breeze that blew tendrils of long black hair around her face. Phineas knew she was praying. Miss Letty leaned on Phineas' arm as the Lieutenant gave hand signals to a group of soldiers who seemed to enjoy swarming through the front doors of her family home. Amid chaotic confusion, Phineas heard Miss Letty breathe,

'Thy will be done.'

After setting a dozen fires in the main house and out-buildings, the Union soldiers filed down the Starcross Lane. Certain that the little clump of elderly people huddled helplessly in the courtyard could only make feeble attempts at disrupting the conquering victor's fiery handiwork, the soldiers laughed and joked.

But being of advanced years didn't stop the group in the courtyard from swinging into action as soon as the last Union horse was out of sight. Flames licked from the upstairs windows, trying to catch onto nearby tree limbs, but damp weather prevented the moist leaves from turning the surrounding woods into a roaring inferno.

They drew water from the rain barrels, and Phineas pulled up the slats covering the well, but the destruction was spreading rapidly, and they had only a few containers. He cut the bucket loose that had been hanging by a rope in the well, although once it was filled, he was the only one who could carry it. Within minutes, he heard thundering hooves, coming close fast, but he couldn't see around the bend in the lane.

Horses? Tears and smoke fogged his vision, but he thought he'd heard horses! Suddenly, a double line of Union cavalry, galloping hard, bore down upon them. The men jumped from their mounts and, in the midst of their frantic rush, it crossed his mind that the army had returned to be certain their fires had caught well and were burning.

'Ah speks deys back ta finiss us off,' he said to himself. But then, he wiped his eyes, not believing what he thought he saw. Did the soldiers in blue uniform have brown skin? Brown skin!? 'Gawdamightyknows!' His eyes hadn't deceived him; the soldiers' faces wore expressions of concentration on their brown features, features set in all beautiful shades of beautiful brown skin! 'SweeJeezusgloreebee!' He knew there were colored troops in the Union Army, but he'd only read about them. He didn't think he'd ever see such a sight. He'd read that General Sherman believed colored soldiers were no good in battle. Of the thousands of troops invading Atlanta, he had read that blacks were deployed only as cooks, porters, and reinforcements for enemy lines.

Phineas folded his arms and, in an attitude of smug pride, he quipped, 'Ah guess Ol' Gen'l Shaman too busy ta read da papuhs bout da Co'nel Shaw Fitty-Foh Masatoosets at Fot Wagnuh!' Phineas smiled, adding, 'Sumbody need ta read dem papuhs to im!' Then, as if wondering out loud, he lowered his voice, 'But wha' all dem black soljuhs doin' down heah?'

He said hope and new strength sent him hurrying to secure the horses while the soldiers ran to extinguish the fires. Several of the four dozen or so soldiers headed back down the lane at Miss Letty's direction, he guessed to try to save the old church building. With blankets and the few containers they had, they all expended the depths of their efforts, but he soon saw that most of the buildings were ablaze beyond saving.

Choking, gasping and exhausted, Phineas moved to help them, but his knees buckled as a crackling column of smoking silver lightning touched the ground where his feet had been. Crouched on the earth, he looked up at the massive rumbling black cloud rolling overhead that suddenly dumped a sky-full of rain into his upturned face, drenching everything with a hammering, stinging gift from God that left Starcross dripping, steaming, charred and damaged, but still standing in the suddenly brilliant morning sun.

After all the fires were out, the Union soldier in charge escorted a bedraggled Miss Letty to the blue damask chair, the only piece of furniture left in the parlor that hadn't been sacrificed for firewood. Settling into the window seat next to her, the sergeant appeared to Phineas to be very young, probably no more than twenty-two years. Several soldiers reclined on the floor; Avajay sat on a little footstool against the far wall, while Phineas passed pans and chipped bowls of cool water from the well bucket. Nobody spoke for a very long time.

Miss Letty patted the Sergeant's hand,

'I don't know how to thank you for the kindness you showed us. It was a miracle from heaven you and your men were here when we needed you.'

'Well, that big Ol' Georgia rainstorm didn't hurt us any,' he laughed, 'but, actually, I should be thanking you, Ma'am.'

Avajay's eyes flew open. Miss Letty repeated what he'd said. 'Thanking me? Laws, whatever for?'

'Yes, ma'am. See, on the main road, on our way to reinforce General Sherman's right flank, we passed a large company on the march to Savannah. Now, we were moving faster than they were, and as we went by, I heard one of the soldiers bragging about how they couldn't resist burning the biggest house he'd seen around here. He described the two ladies, the mistress and a black slave with a funny mole between her eyes,' he touched a spot above the bridge of his nose, 'then it was like my memories all came back to me. I knew this place had to be up in here somewhere, and I knew they were talking about her,' he gestured toward Avajay. 'I put it together, and realized it was you.' Miss Letty and Avajay looked at each other, perplexed. The Sergeant's face broke into a wide smile. 'It was you who set us free!' He swung his arms in a sweeping movement. 'My whole family! You gave us pepper to spread on our heads and feet to confuse the dogs, and you told us the way to go. You taught us how to find the North Star.' He pointed to Phineas. 'And you showed us how to read street signs, and maps. I just graduated from Oberlin, and my sister, you remember Sissy? She's there, studying to be a teacher. I was little, but I knew this was the house. My mother and father tell the story in great detail. There's no way we could ever forget you and this place. We could never forget—'

In the stunned quiet, the Sergeant stood and came to attention. 'Sergeant Monty Cameron Birdlaw of General O. O. Howard's Fourth Corps of the Army of the Tennessee, at your service!'

Tears glistened in Avajay's eyes. Holding the torn gown, reaching out her free hand to him, she left her little stool. He met her careful, faltering steps halfway with a grown-up version of the way he'd laughed when he was five, muffling her whispered 'thank you' in his joyful embrace.

He dabbed the trace of a tear from her cheek and looked into her eyes.

'Mam, can you answer me one thing?" he asked.

'Yes?'

'You got any more of them apples and peaches in a bag?'

He hugged Miss Letty and Phineas, too, before he took his leave. With a smile, Phineas added, 'Gen'l Shaman gie Savannuh ta Presidun Lincon foh da Chrismus, Decembuh 21, aiteen sikdy-foh.'

Phineas recalled the mixed triumph and sorrow of April 1865, when the Confederate Capitol, Richmond, fell on April 3rd, and the next day, President Lincoln, led by black soldiers, entered the ravaged city. Lee surrendered to General Grant on April 9th, and five days later, on April 14th, Abraham Lincoln was shot to death at D.C.'s Ford Theatre.

The Civil War was over. At Starcross, they grieved and as they recovered, Miss Letty began to rebuild the Manor and decided to make her lifelong dream come true by building the Starcross Theatre over the old family church.

Miss Letty received a letter from the hospital where they had taken Roxanne. A Dr. Pendleton had written to inform families of Milledgeville patients that the hospital had been used as a Confederate infirmary during the war, and they'd experienced no war-related casualties among the residents. Dr. Pendleton's letter went on to say that a much improved Roxanne Baldwin had been an exemplary patient-assistant to the kitchen staff in his personal residence and was in excellent spirits.

Phineas stopped talking.

"Phineas, do you have any more to say?"

There was no answer. She persisted, "Can you tell me where the secret hiding place is located?"

Silence. She tried again, "Phineas, where did Miss Letty and Avajay hide their food and valuables?"

She waited a few more minutes, but there was only the ticking of a distant clock, and the sound of Samson's peaceful breathing, until Nasrene began the awakening process.

CHAPTER TWENTY-SEVEN

After awakening from his past life testimony, Samson sat up, smiling.

"Samson," Nasrene asked, "I'm wondering if your conscious memory can lead us to the hiding place? After all, you recalled where the old buildings had been."

"Phineas knows, of course, but the secret place must be buried in my deeper mind. I felt extreme fear when you mentioned it. Come to think of it, it must've been a tremendous burden to have hidden that knowledge for so many years. I can imagine we were incredibly careful to keep the location from being discovered. The slightest mistake would've created far-reaching repercussions.

"Before the war, we lived in an era and in an area where slaves were big business, a way of life that created the great southern prosperity. White human rights activists and abolitionists were reviled; they threatened the livelihood and, sometimes, luxury that slavery made possible. Indeed, slavery was a hot button that caused people to kill each other at the drop of a hat, even though most were too poor to afford slaves. Protecting their right to own slaves and protecting their land was the main reason given for fighting to secede from the Union, but before the land needed protecting, slavery was the overarching issue. Sherman's victory was the final straw that broke the Confederacy's back, the entire premise of which was traitorous, at best."

"You know," Nasrene said, "General Sherman himself was a paradoxical figure in many ways. He disregarded black soldiers, but I read that he was one of Henry Ossian Flipper's most enthusiastic supporters when he became the first black to graduate from West Point in 1877."

"Yeah, like Phineas said, 'maybe somebody read the papers to him!'"

Nasrene closed her journal and asked,

"To switch gears, does anyone recall ever having had dreams of some sort of secret place in the Manor or theatre?"

Everybody lapsed into silence, searching their minds for the umpteenth time, hoping for a forgotten clue to the location of the place mentioned in the past life regressions—a secret place, known only to Miss Letty, Avajay, and Phineas.

"Nasrene, I'll be willing to be regressed anytime you say. If I go back to Miss Letty again, she might be flexible enough to drop some clues."

"Thanks, Homer," Nasrene sighed, "Remember we all grew old, successfully keeping that location from the world. Over the years leading up to the Civil War, and during the war, we were elderly, alone and frightened. We were in constant danger, first from slave watchers, then, the looters and opportunists that roamed the countryside, and we had no way to defend ourselves. That hiding place had been a haven of survival for escaping slaves, and during the war, it became our key to survival, allowing us to stay alive and prosperous, as well as providing us the means of helping countless others. I'm casting around in my mind, trying to think of another approach to the regression questions because I believe nobody is going to just flat out give up that location. It meant everything to them for decades."

"We looked into every nook and cranny in the house when we searched for Adam," Di said, "and as you know, we found nothing."

"Well, I think there is something, and we need to find it, because—"

"Wait, hold it," Homer interrupted Ceeoni's comment, "I've been inside, outside and underneath the Manor and the theatre since 1975, sometimes several days a week, for hours at a time. Even then, I had a bit of unconscious access to Miss Letty's knowledge. If there's a secret hiding place, I would've found it by now, wouldn't I? I'm willing to bet the entrance to it was covered over when they rebuilt after the war, or who knows? Maybe it was destroyed during Sherman's fire, and Miss Letty saw no need to re-build it."

"Homer, did you find anything that might have been the remnants of a large space?" Nasrene asked.

"We did find unusual features in the structure, things we'd never encountered anywhere else, but nothing that would suggest a hidden chamber. I attributed the oddities to all of the damage and rebuilding it had been through, just like all these old places in the South."

"You know," Samson said, "the visions I saw during the past life regression were astounding, but now I see how things I was exposed to in my past life, influenced this life. For example, I chose General O.O. Howard as my subject for a high school paper, never having a clue as to where I'd ever heard about him. I had no answer when people asked why. I earned an 'A' for that report, mainly because the one-armed general was such a fascinating figure to me. I was inspired to really work hard on that report."

"O.O. Howard?" Nasrene asked.

"Yeah, O.O. not only commanded the right flank of Sherman's March, but after the War, he headed up the Freedman's Association that provided assistance to thousands of former slaves. Also, he was one of the founders of the black university that bears his name. It appears that past lives carry over into the present in strange ways."

"Anyway," Samson said with an air of dismissal, "concerning the secret place, the idea of a hidden chamber certainly holds the lure of intrigue, but I have to agree with the obvious. Wherever it was has been lost to history."

Oh, noooo!," Ceeoni howled, "We're overlooking the obvious! Where else would the killer get an 18th century Spanish dagger?"

"Of course! Oh, of course!" Samson blinked and slapped his forehead,

"The knife belonged to someone in the past who had been to Spain—" Ceeoni finished Samson's thought, "A person who had enough money to buy an expensive jewel-encrusted souvenir. Like, Sybil!"

"Yes!" Diana's excitement could be heard in her voice, "We learned that Sybil's things were left at Starcross after her death, and

Miss Letty probably stashed her stuff in their secret place along with the other valuables."

"Bingo!" R.C. yelled, "Then as you can see, the killer knows the secret place and, here we are, going through a pile of past life regressions that tie in with the present in some ways, but no one will reveal that key location. Elijah said they wrote him saying that Miss Letty had hidden her valuables, but that seemed to be all he knew. He hasn't mentioned that he knew of Miss Letty's underground activities, either." "Maybe he didn't know, "Samson offered.

"We've got to find that place!" Ceeoni said. "If the killer's found it, so can we. It may hold something, and," she took a deep breath, "perhaps my piece of the puzzle during regression will help. I—I think I'm ready—I may even be—"

"No way!" Di interjected, "Get real. I don't believe you have anything like that madness in you. I know you're not Roxanne."

Ceeoni said nothing out loud, but inside, her little voice asked, 'Who? Who was I?' Steeling herself for the past life regression, Ceeoni was saved by the ring of Homer's phone.

"Dinsmore!" he shouted. "He did? Thanks, we'll be right there!" Not one to waste any time, he started toward the door, reaching into his pockets for his keys.

"What? Homer?" Diana called after him, "What's happened? Hold up a minute. I gotta find my shoes."

"Oh, Baby, I don't know why you can't read my mind, Crawford Long, Nurse Evelyn said Adam moved a little. They think he may be waking up. So who's riding with me?"

x x x

The hospital clock read 3:20 pm when they arrived. Dr. Sakaya supervised as Nurse Evelyn and two nurse's aides rolled a cart full of plants from Adam's room. Nurse Evelyn said she'd go for coffee, while everybody located chairs. A CD of Adam's played, while Adam's left hand moved on the blanket, as if his fingers were depressing piano keys. Ceeoni recognized the song that was playing, "I Wish You Love," but Adam's fingering didn't match the notes they were hearing. If he was playing a song, it wasn't the song that was coming through the speakers. Was he playing a song?

R.C. sat by the bed and spoke to Adam.

"My brother, you've been on break long enough. Now it's time to get the band back on the bus. Only you can do that. Only you can lay the groove cold in the pocket. Aw, man!" He groaned in frustration, "Adam?" But Adam slept in the same position he'd held since late Saturday night, except for the steady repetitive movement of his left hand. R.C. seemed dismally disappointed when he received no response, but seeing Adam move, if only just his fingers, gave Ceeoni a lift.

The doctor confirmed her optimism while he adjusted the monitors.

"This is a very good sign. It shows a marked increase in neurological activity. Does anyone have a small portable keyboard that can be brought in? Since Mr. Delayno is a pianist, I'd like you to slip a keyboard underneath that hand in hope the sound will stimulate his awareness."

"Sure. He has several of them around the house."

"Good. Mr. Ponder, continue to play his CDs and anything else you know he loves. And please, everyone, talk to him, sing to him," Dr. Sakaya's arms waved in the classical conductor's arc, "reminisce!"

He zoomed out the door at high speed. Nurse Evelyn left a cart containing a pot of steaming coffee and a tray of assorted donuts, before taking off to answer a call.

Samson sat by the bed and took Adam's free hand in his, "Hey, Thunder, your first teacher, Miss Cora Lee, sends her love and prayers to you. I spoke to her the other day, and she wanted me to tell you she still don't take no mess off nobody.

"Back when you'd been taking lessons from her for only a year or so, I'd go with you to practice, and I'd hear you crying when she popped those fingers with a plastic ruler. I remember being quite ready to beat her up, thinking she was hurting you every time you got into your usual scrape over the sonatas and art songs she'd chosen for you to learn. Piano time was precious to you. Being just a kid, you only wanted to play what struck your fancy that day, as any seven-year-old would. Damn a discipline, you were ever ready to jam to everything you'd heard, from Motown to Basie, B. B. King to

Ahmad Jamal, with a little Gene Harris, Peterson, Brubeck or Philly International on the side.

One afternoon I did something you didn't like, and 'pow,' you hit me with Miss Cora Lee's ruler as hard as you could, and I saw it was too thin to hurt. Whoa! Were your chops busted! That's when I realized it was your pride making you holler like hell when she hit you. The look on my face started you laughing, and it got just plain silly from that point on. Miss Cora Lee came in and caught us knocking over chairs and chasing each other around the room with that ruler. Remember? She didn't utter a sound. She simply marched straight out the door and returned with a big hard yardstick, which she unceremoniously stood in the corner by the piano. Then she sat down, checked her watch, and glared at us. Ha! We hurried up and pulled our act together! Boy, neither one of us ever moved so fast, picking up chairs!" He chuckled, "And we never tried that again. We had big fun growing up, Bro. Without you, I don't think I would've made it. Life's standing still since you've been away—"

"Can I try?" Nasrene asked. He nodded and gave her his chair. She switched on her tape recorder.

"Adam, I am about to make suggestions to awaken you."

She gave him suggestions for a while, but he didn't respond. When she completed the past life regression suggestions, his left hand stopped moving.

"What is your name?"

A cultured, subdued baritone answered, 'Elijah Starcross.'

"Elijah, do you know why Adam is moving his fingers?" The question, repeated, received no response. Then she asked,

"Where are you?"

'In my room at Starcross.'

Elijah said it was October 1875. He'd spent the past few years dividing his time between his tours, visiting his parents' Canadian farm and Starcross, although travel for Blacks in America was insulting and demeaning, especially in the South.

He compared notes with his friend, Ella Shepard, music director of the 9-voice ensemble of former slaves, formed in 1871, who made up the Fisk University Jubilee Singers. She told him of the road horrors she'd encountered, nightriders, hate crowds, as well as the rigors of finding food and lodging. He'd kept up with the Fisk Singers' progress as they traveled around the United States and abroad. Their haunting performances of the secret Slave Songs, known as Cabin Songs, like 'Steal Away,' 'Go Down, Moses' and 'Swing Lo, Sweet Chariot,' never before heard in public, brought the singers international acclaim, the blessings of Queen Victoria, and funds to build and expand the struggling Fisk School in Nashville. For centuries, the Slave Songs had been used by slaves as signals to convey messages of encouragement as well as escape plans. Ella told him of an incident one night on a lonely road, when a band of the Ku Klux Klan, wearing, white sheets, with their torches burning, waylaid their coach. Terrified, they stood out in the cold air, silently praying, awaiting their fate. When the Wizard asked what they were doing on the road that night, they began to sing, filling the darkness with their beautiful voices. Ella said while they were singing the Wizard threw off his hooded mask and walked away in tears.

Elijah realized that he was fortunate that Phineas and Elijah's Oberlin friends always directed him to the safest accommodations and routes.

He said that he was shocked to see Roxanne stroll casually back into their lives at Starcross. The day she arrived, Miss Letty and Avajay had entered his quarters just as Roxanne gleefully watched an embarrassed and un-amused Elijah clumsily try to fasten his shirt. Right away, Avajay's eyes bucked in alarm when she recognized the woman in yellow. Candles and firelight bathed the room in a warm flickering glow, but Elijah's skin dripped with the cold sweat of anxiety. Of the three people there, he knew Roxanne's unpredictable nature best. His earliest memories as witness and victim of her devious and violent temperament were a part of the bad dreams of his youth. He stood by the piano and silently bid the Heavenly Father, all the Angels and Miss Letty to send Roxanne back to wherever she had come, and he could tell that Avajay shared his feeling.

Miss Letty avoided Avajay's and Elijah's eyes, pretending she hadn't read her old friends' distaste for this strange new development, as she said firmly,

'Everyone deserves to be heard.'

Still ignoring Avajay and Elijah, she focused on Roxanne.

'When were you released from the hospital?' she asked.

'Five years ago,' Roxanne answered in a high, childish whine, 'everyone was jealous of me because I got cured and I married my doctor! That was 1868. We lived in Milledgeville in his big pretty house until I—uh, his—untimely death. He left me all his money, but his stupid family saw to it that I never got it!' She dug through her gold satin purse. 'My husband's two sisters forged his signature and wrote a new will, without me in it. They took my house and turned me out with only these clothes on my back!' She dabbed her eyes with a yellow lace hanky and handed Miss Letty folded papers, which Miss Letty quickly read.

'I see,' Miss Letty said, 'This is an official marriage license between Roxanne Baldwin and a Kenneth P. Pendleton, MD. Well, it looks fine to me.'

'Actually,' Roxanne giggled in her humorless hollow soprano, that still struck apprehension in Elijah's bones, 'They all hated me! They were jealous of me because I'm beautiful!'

Roxanne pulled a small wad of bills from her bag, which she tried to put in Miss Letty's hand,

'If I can just stay here for a little while, I'll pay my way, and I'll work hard, very hard. Honest I will. I don't have anywhere else to go.'

'No—no, Roxanne,' Miss Letty waved the money away, 'that won't be necessary. I'm going to write to the hospital to ascertain if all is as you say, and—'

Suddenly, Roxanne burst into tears. Miss Letty automatically reached out to comfort the sobbing, shivering woman, who whimpered like a child.

'There, there—' She patted Roxanne's back and smoothed the veil over her pale curls.

Elijah realized that the combination of the official documents, the offer of money from a small hand that trembled ever so slightly, and the profusion of tears had softened Miss Letty completely. He was appalled. Even though Roxanne's outward appearance was normal, he was suspicious of her intent. Or was it possible she was cured? He knew nothing of people who had madness in the head.

'After the war, I did receive a letter from the asylum, assuring me of your stable condition,' Miss Letty said, 'and we could use some help. I've decided you can stay until I hear back from the Milledgeville hospital officials.'

Avajay blinked, and shifted her shoulders impatiently, but anything she was about to say was aborted by Miss Letty's sharp glance. He'd never seen Avajay register strong disagreement with Miss Letty before, but it made no difference. Miss Letty remained unfazed. Elijah's heart wanted to scream out to her not to take this chance. He wanted her to make Roxanne leave immediately without even spending the night. Phineas could take her to the Coach Stop. She had money, but no trunks; the only clothes she had were the obviously new garments she wore. Even if her madness was cured, Elijah knew something was very, very wrong.

Miss Letty started for the door and beckoned to Roxanne. 'You may have your old suite for the time being. I'm writing to the hospital now.'

'Yes, Mam,' Roxanne murmured as she lowered her eyes like a saint and followed Miss Letty from the room. But a pale, sly sidelong glance in his direction let Elijah know that Roxanne had finally gotten something she'd wanted for a long, long time.

He was aware that Miss Letty allowed her to stay out of the compassion that was natural to her. Miss Letty saw a thirty-six-year-old widow, alone in the cruel world, who had been cheated out of her inheritance by her inlaws. Also, the poor widow had spent her entire young life locked away in a ghastly lunatic asylum, all due to an unfortunate spell she'd had when she was only twelve years old. The door closed behind them, leaving Avajay and Elijah staring at it in dismay.

The ninety-one-year-old Miss Letty was thoroughly set in her ways, but she was no fool. She made good her promise to write a letter of inquiry to the Milledgeville authorities, which she read to them out loud before giving it to Phineas to be posted at the Coach Stop the next morning:

Georgia State Lunatic Asylum
Milledgeville, Georgia

Dear Sir or Madam,
As a potential employer of a former hospital patient, Roxanne Baldwin Pendleton, I will appreciate any information you can supply regarding her recovery and release.

Thank you,

L.S. Bramwell, Starcross Georgia

xxx

Elijah continued his testimony, saying that in the ensuing months, Roxanne proved to be a diligent worker. Elijah noticed that Roxanne, possibly copying Miss Letty's habit of wearing the same color clothing, always wore shades of yellow. It was a habit that he thought eccentric, as were other aspects of her behavior. Yet, not a hint of anything unusual happened, and they welcomed the extra pair of capable hands.

Talbert Bramwell had returned to Starcross as soon as he thought it was safe, and continued with his endless round of parties. Of course, after the war, his friends who were still alive and weren't severely maimed had come down in the world, but a fatter than ever Talbert carried on his social activities with a determined, pre-war zeal. He still acted as though he didn't see Roxanne, but she prepared refreshments and served and cleaned up after his guests, while silently staying out of his way.

Although up in years, Miss Letty's and Avajay's combined efforts pulled consistently large crowds to the Starcross Theatre. All was well, and Elijah left for New York in December of 1874, free of any major concerns.

He received Avajay's note informing him that on July 25, 1875, Miss Letty had expired peacefully in her sleep. She had never been ill. He was devastated, and although he knew that ninety-two vigorous years was a rare blessing, he would miss his dear friend. He finished his business, and took a coach to Canada to visit his parents before returning to Georgia.

Avajay had refused to drape the door with black ribbons and she didn't expect everyone to wear black, as was the custom when in mourning, because Miss Letty had hated that sort of thing. Miss Letty had redecorated the house the past Christmas in bright colors to encourage visitors to join in a celebration of life, but to Elijah it was the biggest house in the world without her. The cheerful silk draperies and new imported rugs in her favorite shades of rose, mossy greens and peach failed to lift his spirits.

Avajay's eyes filled with tears as she clung to him in greeting. He half expected Miss Letty to come from the kitchen, white curls bouncing and pink taffeta rustling in rhythm with every quick step, her grey eyes wide with enthusiastic curiosity. She would never let him rest until he told her details of his trips; the programs he'd played, descriptions of venues, the latest fashions, his reviews, and his personal critiques of his and his fellow performer's performances. He had always taken notes, and brought back foreign newspapers and theatre schedules for her. He knew how Miss Letty had embraced life and that knowledge eased the pain of missing her. Stuffing his grief into music, he played her favorite pieces on her old piano, Mozart, Beethoven, Chopin and cabin spirituals, all night, night after night, until his sorrow subsided, finally releasing him into sleep.

Weeks later, Elijah sat at his sunlit desk, noting the new additions of music halls and theatres on the itinerary of his upcoming tour to begin in December 1875. He answered the unexpected knock on his door that announced Wayne Starcross, who entered with his straightforward bearing and his right hand extended. The 5'5" attorney's face, a male version of his cousin Letty's, was also crowned with a shock of bouncing white ringlets. Built like a wrestler, and always impeccably attired, his viselike handshake caused Elijah to flex his fingers to check for damage.

He smiled Miss Letty's smile, 'Well, Elijah. How are you? And are your parents well?'

Elijah couldn't imagine the purpose of this visit, but he invited Wayne to be seated. Wayne smoothed the silk lapels of his black velvet jacket before handing Elijah a large envelope.

'Oh, don't let me get too comfortable. I'm certain I'd ask you to play for me, which would distract me from prompt attendance to my next appointment.'

It was true. Wayne rarely failed to coerce Elijah to play excerpts from his concerts.

'How was your trip?'

'Everything went fine, thank you. The audiences were generous.'

'As well they should. I hope to have the pleasure of hearing you play again soon, Elijah, but today I came to advise you of Mrs. Leticia Starcross Bramwell's last will and testament. Elijah, to discharge formalities and get straight to the point, it seems that she left everything to you.'

'I beg your pardon?' Did he say Miss Letty had left him something?

'Elijah, Elijah! This is yours, the house, the theatre and the surrounding land, which amounts to about 500 acres.' He lowered his voice, 'She wanted you to have it.'

'B-but sir, aren't there laws against former slaves owning property?'

'Yes and my cousin was well aware of those laws. I was given instructions to seek every means necessary to see that it doesn't fall into Talbert Bramwell's control. I'm prepared to stand by Miss Letty's wishes as much as possible. The Starcross Estate is now a part of a trust with Lloyd's of London, in your name, and by time the inevitable legal rigmarole is settled, everyone concerned will probably be deceased and this place will be a pile of dust.' His smile faded, 'I'll try to keep it secret, but these things are published and registered in public logs. What I'm saying Elijah, is Starcross belongs to you for however long I can keep the legalities of the trust tangled. It's up to you to stay out of the woods, and as far away from groups of snarling white men as you possibly can, probably for the rest of your days. And rest assured, snarling white men, outraged over your prosperity, will want to start the war all over again.' Wayne's half serious levity wasn't lost on Elijah. He knew that once the news was known, his life would be worthless should he be caught out alone, by the wrong people.

'Elijah,' Wayne said, 'Miss Letty and I are descendants of an old family. Our forebears came over from England on the Mayflower. No one in our family ever owned slaves until that pathetic ass-end of the lowest form of humanity, my Cousin Talbert, took it upon himself to finance his excesses with cotton, against his mother's wishes. I was too damn young and fearful of his insane wrath to even think of trying to stop him. Our family looked upon slavery as inhumane, and in moral opposition to the principles of Christianity and democracy we came to this country to establish. No Starcross ever believed it was worthy of us to prosper off the backs of men, women and children in chains.'

Elijah lapsed into a thoughtful silence while Wayne turned toward the door, saying,

'You know, I understand why she left it to you.'

Elijah, staring at the envelope he held, turned his attention back to the amiable man standing before him,

'Forgive me. It's so—'

'Oh, it's quite all right.I was saying that I know why she left it to you.'

The question in Elijah's eyes was accompanied by a quizzical raise of his eyebrows. The lawyer's steady gaze met his.

'Miss Letty knew that Starcross, Avajay, Phineas, and even Talbert, would be safe in your hands.'

Elijah shook the hand that was again offered and quietly replied, 'She was right, Sir.'

CHAPTER TWENTY-EIGHT

Elijah said he was always busy when he was in Georgia. His schedule allowed very little time for dwelling on the resentment that he knew would result from his ownership of Starcross. He wasn't naive. He was aware that opposition would be mounting all around him, once the news got around. For that reason, he felt blessed to be away from Starcross most of the time.

At first, Talbert was beyond disgusted. He seethed with anger, sulking in his room, too humiliated to host any of his famous parties. Elijah deliberately didn't move into the house, and didn't change his behavior in any way. Eventually Talbert went back to his old ways.

Elijah began to feel sorry for Talbert, whose ever-expanding girth was grist for the gossip mill. The challenge Talbert faced in his determination to dress in elegant attire every day was obvious. Talbert's charade of the 'the genteel former slave owner of class and distinction' was impossible to maintain after people learned of Miss Letty's will. Realizing that Talbert had squandered his cotton profits, Elijah, in memory of Miss Letty, quietly increased the sum left for him in an envelope on the foyer table every month. Talbert's only real claim to postwar southern gentility was the fact that he still had money, albeit a monthly allowance, a fact which inspired his poverty-stricken associates to swallow their pride and call at the disgraceful Starcross Manor at about the time Roxanne was about to serve supper, several times a week. Everyone pretended to ignore what they knew to be the truth about each other; that the frequent uninvited guests had enjoyed few solid meals since their last visit to Starcross.

Elijah had to admire Talbert's thick-skinned ability to associate with like-minded individuals who knew the Starcross Manor had been bequeathed by his mother to a former slave, but he felt no triumph presiding over the turned tables of Talbert's social dilemma.

Avajay and Roxanne had established a silent but efficient working relationship. Avajay, ever wary of the pale, vacant-eyed Roxanne nevertheless settled into an uneasy routine. Elijah was too busy to think about Roxanne or Talbert. His head was filled with music, practice, schedules, programs and preparation.

Late one fateful evening Elijah hurried to get back to Starcross from a visit to a music publisher near Jonesboro. The meeting had taken longer than he'd planned. He said that clouds drifted over the moon, and a few tiny hailstones whipped around his ears. His fingers, encased in black kid gloves, were numb, and he couldn't feel his nose. Taking a chance that he would be recognized by a hostile local was far more dangerous than it was to be a black man who appeared prosperous, or to simply be a black man out alone on a dark night.

The road was smooth, and his horse, Symphony, was the fastest horse he'd ever ridden. He was pushing the mare to her limit, when he saw he was soon to overtake a coach up ahead. He got closer and recognized the coach as one he had hired from time to time. Riding hard past the window, he caught a glimpse of a woman's face in profile, framed in the half-light; a face so lovely he nearly lost control of the reins. Like a spear of lightning, his rather cavalier interest in an array of beautiful women in several countries, diminished like raindrops in the tropical hurricane that battered his senses. He detected a fresh floral scent floating in the air. In winter. What was it? Lavender? Yes, Lavender. Within a fraction of a second, he could no longer see into the window and, too soon, found himself pulling up alongside the driver, Walter Duplesis, a Freedman from New Orleans.

'Walter, *mon ami!*'

'As I live and breathe! Elijah! You shouldn't be out by yourself on a night like this! The moon is hiding, and hatred lurks in unexpected places.'

Elijah slowed, against the will of his mount who tugged and sidestepped, but Elijah held her fast.

'I know, I know. I'm taking a shortcut to Starcross that no self respecting highwayman or roving diehard Confederate would dare follow, and Symphony doesn't need the light of the moon!'

He lagged back a bit and glanced over his shoulder in hope of catching sight of Walter's exquisite passenger again, but his line of vision was obstructed by the bright, swaying carriage lantern. The later the hour, the more perilous it was for him. It was necessary that he go his separate way immediately. Hoping to prolong his visit with Walter as long as possible, he said,

'I'll be leaving for Savannah and requiring your services within a few weeks.'

'Oui, monsieur. Paris?'

'Oui, et Allemagne, et Espagne!'

'And Germany and Spain! A fine tour! Just leave your departure date and time at the Coach Stop with Louis, and I'll meet you then, as usual!'

Symphony, knowing the way home, jerked, straining to be off. Elijah couldn't think of anything else to say. He had no choice except to relax his grip and allow the thoroughbred to have her head.

'Au *bientot,* Walter!'

The black horse snorted, reared on her hind legs and spun in a semicircle as her fore hooves danced in the air for a moment before she leapt into a gallop across the field.

'*Depeche toi,* Elijah, and keep to the shadows!'

In his quarters at Starcross, he built a fire and tried to practice while wondering about the lady of the coach. Who was she? It was certainly none of his business, she was a white woman, and this wasn't Vienna, London or even Oberlin, it was Georgia. He fell into a restless sleep, and found himself waking up several times visualizing the enchanting profile that had burned its contours into his memory. What was her destination?

In the middle of the night, Elijah was awakened from his light sleep by the creaking of carriage wheels passing under his window. Pulling back the drapes, he stared at the rear of Walter's coach lumbering its way up the Starcross Lane toward the Manor, and he knew, at that moment, nothing in his life would ever be the same.

Adam stopped talking. Nasrene waited to see if he would say more. When he didn't, she applied the awakening techniques. After the entire process was over and she had given him the final suggestions, the fingers on Adam's left hand began to move again in the same odd pattern. Homer put his arm around Di, "Now we know how Elijah inherited the property, which was of particular interest to me. It seems each one of us is able to see only a small section of the past life during regression. The rest of that life remains out of reach, except for little flashes here and there."

"Hmmm," R.C. said, "I'm curious about 'The Lady of the Coach' Elijah encountered." His eyes moved over to where Ceeoni sat.

"Yeah, me too," Nasrene agreed. "Maybe he'll tell us in the next regression. He said his life would never be the same. I think everything he said is important." She too looked at Ceeoni.

Ceeoni realized that Di was trying to catch her eye, but just then, Homer decided that speculation time was over. Taking Di's coat off the back of her chair, he asked,

"Well, is anybody as hungry as I am? I'm starving!"

"That's because love makes you hungry," Nasrene teased in a stage whisper.

Samson came up behind her and kissed her on the side of her neck, then nipped her tenderly with a growl, "If that's true, then I'm the hungriest man in the world."

Di and Ceeoni exchanged their 'I told you so' message in a glance, as Nasrene squealed in a gale of girlish giggles.

"My friends," Homer said as he headed for the door holding Di's hand, "tonight is a very special night."

"Why?"

"Because it's Soul Food Night!"

"Oooh!" Ceeoni said, "I've been looking forward to sampling Atlanta's soul food. I can imagine it's much better in the south than it is in California."

"Don't let our bogus reputation fool you. Some of the soul food chefs are perpetrating fraud, and if you could fly around some of these kitchens, you'd catch them opening cans of vegetables, and throwing them around the main dishes, without adding any seasoning except a load of sugar. Web would never do that."

"Does he make soul food once a week?"

"Nah, Nasrene, Soul Food Night is any night I can talk him into it."

On the way back to the house, Homer made a quick stop to pick up "The Lovers ", a famous Jacob Lawrence print he'd had framed at the Level II Gallery and Jazz Club on Marietta Street. It was his guests' first trip to downtown Atlanta, a changing area that still paid tribute to the past.

They stopped and bought Cokes at the Underground, a mall below street level, adjacent to the Coca Cola museum. The mall, a red cobblestoned re-creation of a few blocks of charming stores, restaurants and souvenir shops were as they had been before Sherman's fire—the heart of pre-Civil War Atlanta. They passed the CNN Center where construction of a super arena was in progress, replacing the old Omni Center. Adjoining Ted Turner's Omni Hotel, it sat across from the half-concrete Centennial Park that had been built for the 1996 Olympics. The streets were abuzz with international tourists, vendors and students from Georgia State and Georgia Tech mingling with workers going home from their downtown jobs.

It was after 7pm by the time they sat down in Homer's dining room to Weber's knock-down-kicking-back-gut-expanding-masterpiece of fried chicken, baked red snapper, green beans, potato salad, corn and tomatoes, candied yarns, corn muffins, and sweet tea, followed by homemade ice cream and cherry cobbler. Weber, carrying a tray of brandy snifters, took an elaborate bow at the resounding applause from the table.

"Web," Samson said, "I'd give you a standing ovation, if I could stand."

Juno took R.C's hand, saying,

"We're sending you several standing O's, Web, and as much as we hate to eat and run, well, I mean, to eat and stagger upstairs, we promised the wee ones we'd hang with them before bedtime."

"R.C.'s so bloody antsy," she added, "I'm sure he'll be right back!"

Everyone went into the living room, leaving Di and Ceeoni clearing the dishes.

"Ceeoni, my Sistah, has it occurred to you, as it has to everyone else, that you are probably the 'Lady of the Coach'?"

Ceeoni's heart hadn't stopped fluttering since she heard Elijah's testimony. Trying to hide her confusion from Di had never worked in the past, and wouldn't fly now.

"Di, I don't know. I don't know what it means! Everything is so strange and terribly familiar all at the same time, just like a dream."

"OK, Cee, we'll just have to wait and see, huh? I'll get off your case. By the way, Homer tells me that Weber had been a Ranger during Desert Storm, and he holds advanced degrees in karate, and oddly enough, cooking is just his hobby." The change of subject was just what Ceeoni needed.

"Karate, hmm? That's why he slides around here with his terrific physique encased in those jewel colored gis of his."

"Yeah," Di said, "I've come to the conclusion that he's showing off how you can look if you don't eat his cooking!"

"Did Homer say if Weber has ever been married?"

"It was sad. His wife died suddenly of a heart condition, after their three daughters were grown. He and Homer have been friends since college. Homer said that his wife's death took him to the depths of despair and his recovery was slow. It was his work with Dinsmore & Associates that gave him something to take his mind off of his loss. Now he's one of the company's board members, as well as one of the biggest stockholders. He enjoys watching Homer's back and feeding the hungry. Would you believe he dated Minette for a while?"

"Di, you're kiddin' me! Minette? I can't even imagine those two talking to each other, in spite of their having the food thing in common. He seems to be a warmer kind of spirit."

Well, on a lighter note, I'm vibing on us having our very own bronze Steven Seagal 'Under Siege' dude right under the same roof!"

"Ha! Except I have a feeling that Weber's cooking would cause Seagal to run out of the kitchen, bury his pots and pans, and hang his head in shame!"

Homer beckoned to them from the archway, and asked Weber to join everyone around the living room coffee table.

"Web, you've got to hear this! Look, everybody, the hell we've been going through the last few days may not be close to coming to an end, but today, Di and I arranged for armed security patrol teams to cruise the entire Starcross area, twenty-four hours, every day, until this madness is over. Maybe we won't be so damn easy to surprise from now on. I know this will help us all relax a little. I wish I'd remembered to tell Juno and R.C. about it—I don't want anyone to be alarmed should searchlights or footsteps appear where no lights or steps are supposed to be." Wearing silk close to the color of his tan skin, Weber relaxed against a pile of pillows on the floor and smiled his gentle smile, "Homer, with everything suddenly turning sideways around here, overnight, I've been preparing for the worst. I'm glad you told me about the patrol so that I don't accidentally blow a hole clean through one of your rent-a-cops."

CHAPTER TWENTY-NINE

"Ceeoni," Di said, "I think you'll be more comfortable on the sofa."

In Homer's softly lit living room, Nasrene waited next to the sofa with her tape recorder. All eyes were on Ceeoni, who slowly left the chair she'd chosen and parked on the sofa edge.

"Well—" Ceeoni felt the nervous perspiration on her forehead and upper lip, "R.C. and Juno aren't here," she stammered.

Nasrene handed her a tissue from the package in her bag,

"We'll tell them about it, and they can listen to the tapes." Ceeoni thought she saw an 'Aha! I gotcha' now' gleam in Nasrene's smile.

"Ceeoni, please don't be frightened. You've watched everybody's regressions and you've seen how easy it is. I'm curious about my own Soul's journey. I plan to regress myself later to see what is in my Soul that is affecting my life now."

"Can you do that?"

"Yeah, Cee, anyone can do that, but past life therapists have different methods of coping with the deep seated emotions that people can encounter, and there are various techniques to reduce pain or to completely nullify it. Care must be taken in case the visions are especially disturbing. Now, please relax."

Ceeoni knew she couldn't stall any longer. She couldn't weasel out of her past life regression. She didn't really want to get out of it. It was necessary. Rigid and uncomfortable, she mentally tried to sort out her reluctance to comply with Nasrene's quiet urging. There wasn't even any loud, unbidden advice from her peanut gallery of inner voices.

"Ceeoni," Nasrene said, "I know you're apprehensive, and rightly so. You are in an entirely new environment, surrounded by people you just met. You had an earth-shaking deja vu identification with Starcross Manor, and then, through everyone else's regressions, you learned about Roxanne, who was a psychopath and may have had some tie to you. Suddenly, you know you're an important part of what everyone experienced in the 19th century, but you don't know what part. Your entire life has changed within a few days. You've found yourself right in the middle of a murder mystery—complete with a determined, illusive, probably criminally insane stalker, you've been present in the discovery of two slashed bodies, and nobody knows why these crimes are being committed. It's enough to give anybody a nervous breakdown!"

Fighting back tears, Ceeoni's invisible barrier began to crumble in the light of Nasrene's perceptive insight.

"I believe," Nasrene said, "our Souls have all been in situations where we made grievous mistakes, but we've got to know that whatever we've done, divine salvation is forgiveness, which happens to be man's greatest stumbling block. God forgives all, but learning to forgive others and ourselves, is humanity's hardest lesson. Now, please lay back and allow yourself to relax completely. And, Ceeoni, I don't think you're Roxanne!"

With that, Ceeoni realized she had passed the point of no return. She nodded her consent, settled herself and closed her mind to everything but Nasrene's soothing voice.

Nasrene proceeded with the suggestion that Ceeoni regress back to a time that relates to the events happening in her life in the present. Eventually she asked,

"What is your name?"

Ceeoni's voice became a higher, lighter soprano that obviously belonged to a younger woman, with traces of a French accent,

'Clarisse Starcross Bramwell'

"What is the year?" Nasrene asked.

'1866'

"Where are you?"

'Home,' she answered with a sigh.

"Clarisse, where is home?"

'The Baldwin Plantation, Baldwin Springs, Georgia'

Clarisse said she was in her seventeenth year and had just come from Paris to visit her beloved grandfather's sickbed. Over the years, she'd kept up a lively correspondence with Grandfather Baldwin and her Grandmother Letty at Starcross that had helped her feel close to her family. Although she feared for her family's safety during the War Between the States, it was after the war when Grandmother Letty advised her of her Grandfather Jasper Baldwin's grave illness. Clarisse made up her mind to visit Georgia, but her stay would have to be shortlived in order for her to begin her studies at the Universite` de Paris in the fall.

The war had exacted a terrible toll on Jasper Baldwin. The magnificent Baldwin Plantation had been burned to the ground by a Union Army Captain, who, after housing his entourage there, concluded that Jasper was a prominent Confederate shipbuilder, and a major contributor to the war effort. Jasper certainly was a shipbuilder, but he felt no attachment to the Confederate cause.

After the fire, Jasper had developed a heart condition that left him confined to a bed in a hastily built cabin, surrounded by Cleo, his 80-year old housekeeper, and several freedmen who had been born at Baldwin.

Clarisse arrived just in time to spend two weeks with the gentle man who was her grandfather before he passed away. He had been so happy to see her. Cleo said she believed he'd willed himself to live a little longer so that he might be with Clarisse again. They spent every day of those last weeks talking, as much as they could. He told her the history of the Baldwin family, and how much he had loved her Grandmother Isis and her Mother Sybil. He wept when he spoke of the regret that haunted him knowing that some of his ships had been used for war, while others had been outfitted with manacles and employed as slave ships. He said his mistake had been in immersing himself in building strong and beautiful ships without caring much about who purchased them for what use.

During their last conversation, he'd grasped her hand with desperation in his eyes and begged her in his whispery voice, 'Clarisse, please tell me that you forgive me?' She would've forgiven him anything, although he didn't say what he wanted her to forgive.

'Of course I forgive you, Grand-pa-pa,' she said truthfully.

Many years later she would understand his unspoken reason for asking forgiveness. Satisfied, her grandfather fell asleep as she held his hand in the sweltering room. The noonday sun splashed through cracks between the cabin logs, adding bright golden stripes to the red flowered bed quilt that no longer rose and fell; Jasper Baldwin had drawn his last breath.

Grandmother Letty, Avajay and Phineas had joined Clarisse at Baldwin, and even though it was under such sad circumstances, she was glad to have spent those precious days with all of them. She shared a cabin with the two ladies and learned that living in a small area with a wide variety of aggressive insects was hardly better than living outdoors. The cabin was well appointed with furniture rescued from the fire, but it was cramped for space, oppressively hot, and the single window caused her to face the ashy rubble that had once been the proud home and graceful grounds of her childhood memories.

There was no question about her grandfather's interment; he was buried next to the grave marked 'Isis Baldwin, Beloved wife of Jasper, Mother of Sybil, Grandfather of Clarisse—Love Never Dies'. Clarisse, who then inherited Baldwin and the ship building business, put the business up for sale, and arranged for Cleo to move in with her widowed daughter in Savannah. She couldn't bear to sell Baldwin, but she couldn't live there. The dozen or so Baldwin freedmen agreed to stay with their families to build up and farm the land. Phineas' advice and knowledge of the area helped them get the arrangements made and tasks accomplished during that difficult time.

In the cabin after the funeral, Clarisse and Miss Letty folded a bundle of clothes and linen, while Cleo decided how they were to be divided. Avajay, sitting on another of the three small beds, sorted through a box of odds and ends. After Cleo left with a loaded basket, Clarisse opened a subject she'd wanted to ask her Grandmother Letty for years.

'Grand-ma-ma, why hasn't my father written to me? I've sent him many letters, and I appreciate the courteous messages you wrote me from him, but, he's never answered. I hope it wasn't because of some offensive thing I might've said in one of my communications to him. Has he been well?'

Miss Letty glanced at Avajay, who put down her busywork and gazed at Clarisse with an unreadable expression.

'Ah, well, my dear,' Letty said, 'I must apologize for not giving you a direct answer when you asked about your father. We deliberately evaded your questions, because we didn't think you should know your father's true disposition until you were old enough to understand. Now that you're seventeen, it's time you were told.'

Tears started in Clarisse's eyes. 'His true disposition? He's ill, isn't he? He must be—'

'My angel, your father isn't ill. I think I know what happened to him.' She sat down on the bed beside Clarisse.

'What's the matter with him? Is he an invalid?'

'Yes, well, no,' Miss Letty paused before she said, 'Uh, physically he's as healthy as a horse, and as a matter of fact, he eats and drinks like one, as well. There isn't anything physically wrong, Clarisse. What's wrong is inside. It's in his heart. He's mean, overindulgent and extremely overbearing. We believe he went through a crisis when he discovered his Father's dead body. I think he suffered from that shock and he got much worse after your mother passed.'

At a loss of words, Clarisse couldn't miss the sadness in Miss Letty's eyes. Her grandmother stood and took both of Clarisse's hands in hers and said,

'Whatever the reason, Talbert Bramwell has spent most of his life being as cold as winter snow, and you wouldn't like him very much.'

'How old was Father when it happened?'

'He was nearly eleven. Now, we were all grieved and shocked but Talbert was so young. I don't believe he ever really recovered from the horror of that experience. Clarisse, nobody ever expected a tragedy to occur. Life was just going on as usual. We thought nothing of it when Thurman worked late in the solarium, which he often did, and we assumed he only had a little cold. As it turned out Thurman's little cold was far more serious. The next morning, Talbee went to find his Daddy, and all I heard were shrill, hysterical screams, then silence. I sensed in the ominous tones of my son's terror that I was hearing the sounds of my life ending. I ran downstairs to find my dear husband dead and my son missing.'

'Missing?'

'Talbert had run away. We were frantic. I'd just completed the process of enrolling him in a South Carolina Preparatory Academy, and he was due to leave within a few days. He hadn't wanted to go to school at all, feeling that we were rejecting him by sending him away to school. His father's death added insult to injury in his eyes, and, Clarisse, it was the lowest ebb of my life—My Dear husband dead and my son missing. I walked in a sleepless trance, searching the house and the woods for miles around, day and night.

'A week later, I found Talbert inside a barrel in the smokehouse, unable to relate to anyone. He had gorged on smoked meat for days. He'd always been a willful child, but after that, he was impossible to control, and he didn't speak at all for several months. He would hide food he'd stolen from the kitchen and eat until he regurgitated, then eat again and again, day and night. Thinking that a new environment might help him, we sent him to the Academy the following year, but they sent him right back home. After trying many private teachers, I finally found one he was able to tolerate.' Clarisse began to cry, and Miss Letty cradled her in her arms. 'Look, Talbert is living his life the way he chooses. Pray for him, and have faith that God is always protecting even the most wayward of His children.' Clarisse wiped her eyes with the pink linen hanky Miss Letty offered.

'What an awful thing to happen to an eleven-year-old. Grand-ma-ma, he sounds so pitiful!'

'He is, child, but enough of that. You're such a beautiful girl, I'd imagine you'd be thinking about marriage' Clarisse dabbed her light brown eyes and smiled a little,

'There have been suitors who've called since I've been old enough to receive company, but there's no one special. Cousin Mary is forever arranging social affairs that include scads of young men.' They grinned at each other, and Miss Letty went back to her folding.

Clarisse reflected on what Miss Letty had said about her father, which she would carefully evaluate later, but she had another question gnawing at her heart.

'Grand-ma-ma?'

'Mmm?'

'Do you know what happened the night my mother died?'

'Yes, child,' she replied. 'There was a—fire in the stable the night you were born.'

Clarisse already knew that. She'd been told that her Mother had given birth to her, then she'd expired from injuries received in the fire. She needed to know more.

'Grand-Ma-Ma, what was my mother doing in the stable, nine months pregnant, at three O' clock in the morning?' Her grandmother averted her eyes,

'I only heard the noise, I wasn't there.'

'The fire started very quickly,' Avajay interjected, 'and the only person who saw what happened was a small boy, and he was too frightened to remember. We could only believe it was an unfortunate accident.' Avajay looked away and Clarisse realized there was something, some detail they weren't telling.

'Oops! I almost forgot!' Miss Letty said, digging into the pocket of her gown. She handed Clarisse a small intricately designed silver jewelry box, 'Here, these are for you.'

Although Clarisse knew the subject had been changed deliberately she was excited to receive a gift. She tucked her questions into the back of her mind and opened the box to find a pair of stunning black opal earrings, ringed in sparkling diamonds, along with a pendant on a double interwoven silver chain.

'Oh, thank you, Grand-ma-ma!'

'Do you like them, my Dear?'

Clarisse held an earring up and laughed at the way the slightest movement revealed the vivid blues, greens, reds and purples that appeared to turn on and off inside the dark background, as dancing sunlight ignited the encircling diamond prisms.

She laughingly kissed her grandmother's unwrinkled cheek before slipping the earrings in her ears,

'I shall wear them with my new black taffeta gown!'

Clarisse said Miss Letty led her to the small mirror over the washstand, draped the pendant around her granddaughter's neck and secured the clasp.

'The opals are magic, Clarisse,' she said, 'and one day you'll discover how wonderfully magic they are.'

Clarisse suddenly stopped talking.

"Clarisse," Nasrene asked, "Do you have anything else to say?"

In the silence that followed, R.C. tiptoed back into the room and sat next to Homer.

Giving up, Nasrene, had begun the final suggestions to Ceeoni when Clarisse suddenly responded,

'Yes?'

Startled, Nasrene stammered, "Cl—Clarisse?"

'Yes.'

"Where are you?"

'Starcross Manor.'

"What is the year?"

'Why, it's 1875!' Clarisse said, as if the year was common knowledge.

x x x

Everyone in Homer's living room realized that Clarisse had regressed to a time nine years after her first testimony. During the nine-year interim, her voice had deepened. It had become the voice of a grown woman, far more subdued than the youthful seventeen-year-old she had been only moments before.

Clarisse said she had graduated from the Universite` de Paris in 1870 and still shared the Paris flat with her English cousin, after graduation. That year, the Franco-Prussian War escalated. In 1871, new problems plagued the French in the form of volatile civil rebellion as the Communards, the troops of the Republic, fought for power in the streets, turning Paris into a pyre of death and disease.

Reflecting on that violent, bloody time, she wondered how anyone had survived. She and her cousin Mary tried to book passage to Georgia, but it was impossible. She and Mary volunteered in the overcrowded, understaffed hospital near their flat, where long lines of devastated humanity sought refuge daily. Any help at the hospital was desperately needed. Plus, in Clarisse's mind, Georgia was a darker place, the place where her mother had died mysteriously, her own father wouldn't welcome her, and her real home, the home of her heart, Baldwin Plantation, was only an ashy memory.

She had loved her Grandfather Baldwin, Grandmother Letty, Avajay and Phineas, and enjoyed their frequent correspondence. She especially enjoyed Miss Letty's fascinating, and sometimes hilarious descriptions of the theatrical performances and performers.

Throughout those turbulent years in Paris, Clarisse was troubled by frightening dreams. The dreams had nothing to do with her difficult daily life. Deeply personal, the dreams became more graphic as time went by. She saw herself living in a great house with a man, a man she loved, who always abandoned her. Every time she had the dream, she and the man would be extremely happy together. Then, in a flash, the scene would change, and all she could see was his wide shoulders and the back of his head as he walked away from her. She'd wake up in tears. She knew his face so well while she was asleep, but in the morning, she couldn't remember what he looked like. The dreams became dazzling in detail. She saw herself with people wearing strange clothing, but she couldn't remember their faces, either. Her nights were filled with pain and blood and a woman's screaming laughter, and Clarisse began to wonder if she was losing her mind.

In 1875, a letter from Avajay brought the news of her dear Grandmother Letty's passing. Clarisse's sadness, mixed with guilt for having stayed in Paris without visiting Georgia, caused her to write Starcross, expressing her profound grief and regret.

Avajay answered by return mail,

'Clarisse, your Grandmother loved you deeply, and she understood your heart much better than you'll ever know. Phineas and I will be overjoyed if you should decide to visit Starcross.'

The mystery of her mother's violent death was forever in the back of Clarisse's mind. Somewhere at Starcross answers may lie hidden. She had certainly found no clues to her mother's death in Paris. She had never seen either of her parents. Or the place of her birth. Yes, it was time to go back to Georgia.

Fate stepped in when her cousin Mary, twenty years her senior, shocked everyone by eloping with a government clerk, a coworker who was as prim and proper and pleasant as she. Clarisse decided to vacate the spacious flat she and Mary had shared with their French housekeeper since 1858. Her decision to go to Georgia solved a big problem for the happy newlyweds, for which they and the housekeeper expressed eternal gratitude.

Clarisse's note to Avajay saying she was planning a visit was answered in a single sentence, 'My Dear Clarisse, we've been expecting you.'

Cousin Mary Starcross, who had become quite dignified after becoming Madame LeBlanc, offered the same advice concerning propriety that she had when Clarisse had sailed to Georgia in 1866. 'It is considered improper for a young woman to travel alone!' Clarisse, unconcerned with antiquated custom, knew she would be just fine. Only one of her fellow passengers, a very old English lady, inquired after the whereabouts of her chaperone, but no one else seemed to care. The weather was cold but she was cozy warm in her new chocolate wool coat, trimmed and lined in sable, complete with a sable Cossack hat and muff. She slept somewhat better than usual during the crossing, but the same painful dreams continued to disturb her rest.

Soon, the ship docked in the bustling port of Savannah. She noticed that the women wore fashions that were a bit outdated by Parisian standards, which was the only explanation for the stares following her while she hurried to keep up with the porter who wheeled her trunks to the line of waiting coaches. The porter loaded her trunks onto the next coach, with the help of the coach driver.

The driver, a great freckled man with coarse red braids peeping from underneath his top hat, said his name was Walter, and cordially assured her in his French accent, that he'd been to Starcross many times. She settled down in the roomy grey velvet interior, anticipating the unknown. During the three-and-a-half-day trip, Walter stopped several times to rest and to change horses at coach stops along the way.

They had met no travelers after the sun went down on the third night. But soon, pounding hooves of an approaching rider on horseback caught up with her coach. Thundering past her window, his nearness startled her. For some reason, she was curious to see his face. The carriage lantern, protruding from the side of the vehicle, revealed a man who sat tall in the saddle and whose cape whipped around him in the wind. She stretched a bit to get a look at the traveler who had slowed his horse to speak to Walter, but the lamp was in her way, and what they said to each other evaporated in the creaking of the wheels.

Clarisse shaded her eyes from the bobbing bright light with one hand, to be able to see, as the man's cloak settled into a graceful arc over his mount's back. The rider rode side-by-side with her coach for only a few yards, and then the horse sidestepped in an impatient, dance-like motion that briefly turned the man's face in Clarisse's direction. In that instant, clouds moved away, allowing the glow of the moon to illuminate his dark handsome countenance. Moonlight outlined the perfectly shaped tightly curling hair that framed the expressive eyes and sharp cheekbones of his elegant face. His full mouth, graced with the trace of a smile, completed an image that caused her breath to catch in her throat. She didn't believe what she thought she saw. Shocked, she inhaled sharply in an involuntary gasp; her gloved hands clasped over her heart that accelerated triple time at this astonishing manifestation. Compelled to lean forward to look again, she saw the horse rear gracefully in a whirling equine pirouette. She heard the man's voice sail on the wind, 'A *bientot*, Walter!', in the wake of horse and rider's breakneck surge across the field and into the woods.

Clarisse couldn't control the sense of unreality created by the sight of the black horseman. The feeling that time was somehow out of step, sent throbbing confusion coursing through her head, where a dozen voices screamed the question battering the core of her being—Oh, God, Oh God—who is this familiar stranger and why does he haunt my dreams?

Clarisse said it was after 4am in the morning when the carriage turned up the dogwood-lined driveway to Starcross Manor. At last! The intoxication of being there was enhanced by the loveliness of the theatre and the house; far more beautiful than the pictures she'd formed in her mind.

Phineas helped her down from the carriage with a welcoming smile, 'We ben waitin' on ya' haf da nigh!' Avajay, a silvery braid swinging over her violet dressing gown and shawl, hurried with her lantern to greet Clarisse with a hug. Clarisse thanked Walter and followed Avajay, leaving Phineas and the coach driver unhitching the horses. 'Come in from the cold, my dear! Phineas and Walter are old friends and they'll be warming by a cozy fire within minutes. You must be exhausted after such a long trip. Are you hungry? There's hot chocolate, and cook's sweet buns. I've prepared the suite that was your grandmother's.'

Far too excited and curious to be tired, Ceeoni stopped on the porch to stare toward the right side of the circular driveway at the horse tethered there; an unsaddled black mare that raised her ears and stared back at her in seeming recognition.

Realizing that Clarisse hadn't followed her through the front doors, Avajay looked to see what had captured her attention. 'She's a real beauty, isn't she?' 'Yes,' Clarisse agreed, 'yes, she is. We passed a rider and a horse like that one on the road tonight. Who does she belong to?' 'Well, you may have seen him. Elijah arrived a short while ago, and Phineas was just wiping Symphony down. No one rides her but Elijah. You remember the musician Miss Letty spoke of?'

'Oh, yes—the pianist, the—the toast of Oberlin, concert halls, and Grand-Ma-Ma's pride and joy.'

'Second only to you, Clarisse!'

Clarisse smiled outwardly, but inside, she was trying to remember every single detail she'd heard about Elijah.

Inside, they crossed a green marble foyer and climbed the grand winding staircase, where paintings in gilded frames lined the wall. Avajay pointed out portraits of prominent historical figures that had been painted by Clarisse's grandfather, Thurman Bramwell, and the wonderful study of George Washington that had been painted by her great grandfather, Charles Starcross.

The next painting was a larger-than-life work of a tall, attractive woman, standing, wearing a flaming red Spanish lace ruffled dress, with a red lace mantilla flowing over her long, lustrous hair. The woman in red lace exuded enthusiasm, intelligence and vitality. Before Clarisse could inquire, Avajay said, 'That was Sybil.'

Transfixed, Clarisse, for the first time in her life, looked upon her mother's likeness. She marveled that she'd inherited Sybil's thick brown hair, slightly pouting mouth, and round, defiant chin. She'd often wondered what she would think if she ever saw a painting of her Mother, and now all she could do was try to find a handkerchief to dry her tears of gratitude, gratitude to see that her mother was the kind of woman who wouldn't burn to death in a stable without trying to tear the doors off first. Her intuition had always whispered that her mother's death was no accident. She had to find out more about the night Sybil died. Next to Sybil's likeness, a painting of the same size in an identical frame was of an extremely handsome Confederate Colonel in full dress grey uniform.

'Avajay, is that—?'

'Talbert Starcross Bramwell.'

Of course, sure enough, Clarisse said that she did have his deeply set eyes, only his were blue and—cold, and shadowed with, what? Pain?

'Oh, I didn't know he was a—' But Avajay's clipped response cut through her comment.

'Everyone knows your father was never in the military. Also, he doesn't look like that anymore.' Clarisse swallowed and made no reply, but her father's piteous charade strummed unexplored regions of her soul, careening her already mixed emotions from disappointment to sorrow.

Avajay entered the suite, stopping to light the bedside candelabra before stoking a dying fire in the white marble fireplace. Slowly, with anticipation, Clarisse inspected her grandmother's private sanctuary. She could feel Miss Letty's presence in the room's carefully chosen appointments and the elegant blending of shades of pink in luxurious textures.

'Avajay, how did those paintings and artifacts survive the war?'

'We hid them, along with other things. I'll have someone bring heated water, if you'd like.'

'Yes, that would be so nice.'

Clarisse removed her fur hat and turned to place it on the dresser, as a blond woman, her translucent gaze fixed on Clarisse with a glare of raw contempt, passed by the open door. At Clarisse's cheery 'Hello,' the women nodded faintly with a haughty lift of her square chin and proceeded slowly down the hall, her dressing gown flowing in waves with each step. Ceeoni shivered a little in an effort to shake off the passing woman's nearly tangible hatred. She busied herself hanging her wrap in the spacious 18th century Italian armoire, while trying to sort out the night's emotionally charged revelations. Suddenly, she had a few of the answers she'd sought all her life, along with unexpected new questions for which there might never be answers. That strange woman, the woman in the hall didn't know her. How could the woman show such searing malevolence for someone she didn't know?

Folding back the rose satin duvet, Avajay said, 'I took the liberty of laying out one of Letty's nightshifts and I'll have your trunks unpacked tomorrow.'

'Thank you. Avajay?'

'Yes, dear?'

'Who was the blond woman in the hall?'

'Oh, that's Roxanne Baldwin, your cousin.'

'My cousin?'

'On your mother's side. Roxanne came here in 1849, at the age of twelve, when your parents were married, but she, uh, left that same year. She returned to Starcross a few months before Letty passed, and Letty allowed her to join the domestic staff.'

Clarisse waited for Avajay to say something else, but Avajay kissed her cheek and bid her goodnight, before silently leaving Clarisse alone with her new impressions.

After a warm bath, she climbed into the big comfortable bed, hoping for sleep. Instead of resting, she tossed and turned through a chamber of nocturnal tortures, where a colorless-eyed creature lurked in the dark hallways of the house that she realized was Starcross Manor, and the man of her lifelong dreams had a face and a name.

CHAPTER THIRTY

Ceeoni turned away, as if she had fallen asleep, but her pupils darted from side to side under closed lids. Nasrene awakened her gently, and helped her sit up, "Now Miss Ceeoni, how do you feel?"

"Splendid, and splendidly mystified." Di hugged her, "Girl, us too, but I kept trying to tell you that you couldn't have been Roxanne. I had a feeling all along. You were all anxious for naught. And speaking of anxious, I can't wait to see what's going to happen next!"

Ceeoni couldn't wait either. She felt lightheaded with the colors and clarity of her detailed visions. Grinning, she swung her feet onto the floor. "Di—"

Nasrene refrained from stating the obvious, but the 'I told you so' in her smile was unmistakable, "Ceeoni, if you don't mind, I'd like to regress you again. I awakened you because I knew Clarisse needed a rest, but she's a talker, and she's very observant. If she knows the secret place, or anything else pertinent, she may lead us to it."

Homer handed Ceeoni a glass of water, "Hey, welcome home! After a mere 131 years, those earrings are back with their rightful owner, eh?"

"What earrings?" R.C. asked, "Did I miss something?"

"You heard the last half. Before you came back, Clarisse began by recalling her visit to her Grandfather Baldwin's deathbed right after the war, when she was seventeen. Miss Letty and Avajay met her there and Miss Letty gave her a set of jewelry, with black opal earrings. Well, what is so astounding is that I found the earrings in a trunk in Miss Letty's sitting room the day we finally gained entrance to that room!" He smiled in Ceeoni's direction, "For reasons that I just discovered, I gave them to Ceeoni."

R.C. whistled. "And a great big bingo! We all need time to recover from that. Meanwhile, can we make a fast run to Crawford Long before it gets too late? I want to drop off those keyboards."

On the way out Homer shouted into the intercom, "Web! We're going to the hospital, be right back!"

"There was something else," Ceeoni said as she caught up with Nasrene and Samson, "I felt an overwhelming sickening fear come over me when I saw Roxanne."

"Did you understand why you felt so fearful?"

"No. There was only a sense of, maybe revulsion. Oh, I'm not sure, but the strength of it stayed with me."

"Well, that was your first sight of her," Samson offered, "I remember how she looked, and I'll bet it was truly scary seeing those empty eyes of hers glaring at you from out of a dim hallway in a big old strange house."

They waited outside the Manor until R.C. ran down the steps with a pair of portable pianos that he stashed in the Rolls' trunk. Settling into the front seat, he expelled a burst of air. "Whoa! It felt funny in there!"

Funny how?" Homer asked.

"I don't think I'm being overly sensitive. You know how you feel when you know you're being watched? In a creepy way? We can all sense a negative atmosphere, but at times it can be undeniably dark. I remember one of the heaviest I've encountered was back in the '80s in a downtown Dallas restaurant, Ratcliffe's, beautiful place with a powerful vibe. They told me the Neiman Marcus chain had their first store in that building and it had also been a funeral home before they renovated. I've been in a many a house of death that didn't feel cold and clammy like that restaurant, or like the Manor felt just now."

Homer dialed his phone, "I'll bring that to the attention of our patrolling unit. There may be a reason."

"There's always a reason," Nasrene said, "and whatever it is, you can believe it's horrendous. Take Dallas, for instance. That's where Bonnie and Clyde met and lived; Doc Holliday practiced dentistry there before they asked him to leave, not to mention the Kennedy assassination. Anything might have happened in that Dallas building leaving only dregs of its energy, while the gory details are lost to the living."

"Nasrene, my love," Samson said, "I have a feeling that you won't rest until Starcross yields up all her buried secrets."

Ceeoni, musing over Clarisse and her encounters with Roxanne and Elijah, wasn't paying close attention to the conversation. She found a chair in Adam's room and, more than ever, enjoyed the sight of him. Her entire being soared, knowing that Elijah had been deeply affected at his first sight of the woman in the coach, the woman whose memories were her own. To her consternation, the sane Ceeoni's official authoritarian negations barged into her euphoria, 'Excuse me, but that doesn't mean Adam Delayno will feel the same way about you when he finds out about all of this. He may consider it ludicrous. Besides, he could be somebody you wouldn't want around, like those nice men you met who had a load of the right attributes, but none of them interesting. Or like the Ex-King of Your Heart, Dear Hubby Moraku the Masquerader, who rarely uttered a heartfelt word to you, or anybody.' Her thoughts chased each other until R.C. noisily flipped the piano case metal fasteners and extracted the instrument, bringing her back to the present, back to Adam's bedside.

Adam's fingers still moved in their repetitive pattern. R.C. placed the Yamaha under Adam's fingers so that his left thumb fell on middle C.

"Maybe he's writing a tune," R.C. suggested, "Adam starts writing in the key of C sometime, just to get the melody, and I quote, 'out of his head and into his fingers.' Later, he'll change it to a higher or lower key, depending on what sounds best to him."

R.C. turned on the piano, and it's loud, dissonant sequence of notes jolted everyone. He quickly turned the volume down as Nurse Evelyn came in with her hands over her ears.

"EEEEEUUU! That's awful! Mr. Ponder, my patients may have to be surgically removed from the ceiling!"

"Sorry," R.C. apologized, "It was unintentional. I wasn't thinking about the volume."

"Leave it to a pianist to send brain activity into his fingers before he can do anything else." The nurse peered over his shoulder, "Whatcha' doin'?"

Oh, we're putting one of these pianos under his hand, like this. Please do so, from time to time. The doctor said it will stimulate his awareness. You can also try different effects by pushing these buttons. Here, see?" He pressed a button and the notes Adam played sounded like a whooming organ, another button changed the tone to a harmonica sound, and another produced delicate bell chimes. He left the setting on a normal piano sample. "You can experiment with the different sounds."

"Well, OK," she giggled, "but I don't have to stay in here and listen to it, do I?"

After Nurse Evelyn took her leave, Nasrene pulled a chair up to her usual place beside the bed, and R.C. automatically turned the piano off.

"Thanks, R.C., maybe he's ready to come back."

Adam's fingers stopped their motion as soon as Nasrene began the regression suggestions. When she asked, "Where are you?" Elijah's voice, modulated and familiar, replied, 'In my quarters above the Starcross Theatre.'

He said it was the morning after the lady of the coach had dominated his thoughts throughout the long and sleepless night. He knew she was there, at Starcross. Without a doubt, the carriage he'd seen in the early hours was hers. Was she a relative or a friend of the Bramwells? He was tormented with dozens of speculations that banged around in his head with questions that would probably never be answered, because he had no right to ask. Anxious to ease this disturbing surge of unfounded excitement, he bathed and dressed in tan pants and a full-sleeved white shirt, then hurried downstairs carrying an armload of scores, to rehearse at the stage piano. It was the perfect place to practice. He enjoyed the hearing the theatre's razor sharp acoustics, while imagining pairs of critical ears occupying each rose velvet seat.

He played several chords and ran a series of scales that required his full concentration. The crisp, rich piano strains began to calm his ragged nerves. From where he sat, he could see the stage door that led out to the hallway. He stopped playing when the door opened and a vision in turquoise cashmere, the woman he had seen in the carriage, came toward him, her lovely face aglow, smiling. Bewildered and bedazzled, he sat with his fingers frozen on the keys.

'Oh, I'm sorry I interrupted you. Please—' she gestured toward the piano, 'continue.'

But he had regained his manners, and was on his feet. 'Hello,' he stammered.

Charmed to distraction by the way the color of her morning gown enhanced her light brown eyes and tawny skin, his own voice had sounded oddly distant in his ears.

'Forgive me, I heard the music. You play beautifully. I'm Clarisse Starcross Bramwell.' She held out her hand, but he hesitated. For a moment, he couldn't remember his name, but he remembered hers. Clarisse! Sweet Jesus! This elegant, full grown woman was the baby he'd cradled in his arms after he'd wrapped her tiny, kicking body in rags torn from her dead mother's blue nightdress.

He collected himself and broke the awkward silence, 'Miss Bramwell. Yes, I believe I passed your coach on the road last night.' He briefly clasped her proffered hand.

She stared at him for a second before answering slowly, 'Yes, I believe you did.'

'My name is Elijah, Elijah Starcross.'

'Starcross?' she asked.

Regretting that the brief touching-of-hands ritual was over, he backed away a step to maintain a polite distance. 'Your grandmother wanted me to keep the Starcross name. She said it looked dramatic on theatre marquees when she was performing.'

Clarisse laughed, an unexpectedly deep, hearty chuckle. 'She was an extraordinary person. How long did you know her?'

'My family moved here from the Baldwin Plantation when your parents were married. I was eight years of age. When I was twelve, your grandmother took the time to give me music lessons. I'm a professional musician because of her patience and generosity. She opened the door for me and my family to have a better life than we ever dreamed possible, and might I say that I miss her and your Grandfather Baldwin very much.'

'I miss them, too. Although I spent little time with them, we wrote letters regularly.'

'Oho! Then it is my duty to tell you everything I can recall about your grandparents, and my early, though sometimes foggy memories of Baldwin.'

Her eyes explored the contours of his face exactly as they had minutes after she was born.

'I would like that,' she laughed. 'I remember! Grand-ma-ma and Avajay wrote me about you! Now, let's see. You've been playing concerts in the north and in Europe. Now that I've heard your music, I can understand why they were enthusiastic about your talent.'

'Why, thank you, Miss Bramwell.' Extremely flattered, and unsure of what to do, he sat back down at the piano. 'Clarisse, please. What was the piece you were playing?'

'It's from a symphony in B-flat major by Franz Peter Schubert.' Her gaze remained fixed on his face. He tried to look away, but her eyes seemed to caress his. He admonished himself for such a bold assumption.

'I'm familiar with several of Schubert's works. Please, finish it.'

She folded into the chair beside him like a magnificent turquoise butterfly. He felt his pulse pounding loudly in his ears; he hoped she couldn't hear its boom. He willed away the tremor in his hands and played the piece from the beginning. A stolen glance at her exquisite face delighted him, for she was listening with closed eyes and the trace of a smile.

'Clarisse, if you like beautiful melodies, you may like this.' Happy to show off for her, he played Lizst's 'Liebestraum,' and was touched by the tear that made its way down her cheek. He found joy in how she laughed and clapped her hands when he played Chopin's 'Minute Waltz.' He had never played so flawlessly. The hours passed, with both Clarisse and Elijah having more fun than either of them had ever had.

At suppertime, since Elijah never ate at the Manor with Talbert, a tray was always sent up to the theatre. Sometimes Phineas or Avajay, or both of them, would join him for meals in his quarters. When he told Clarisse he never ate at Starcross Manor, she asked,

'Elijah, would you mind if I take my meals here with you?'

'Clarisse, of course I'd be honored, but you don't—' She raised a protesting hand. 'Look, I've been essentially on my own since I was nine years old. Cousin Mary was always away, and our housekeeper drank large quantities of tea sweetened with rum every day, from midday until the old dear fell asleep after supper. Therefore, I've been left to my own devices most of my life, and I'm accustomed to eating wherever I damned well please.'

Again, her eyes bored into his. He was supremely elated that she wanted to dine with him. I would imagine your presence would be sorely missed at table.'

'Oh, goodness! I can't imagine either one of those two caring where I take my meals. They're a cheerless lot, anyway. Breakfast today was my first meal at Starcross, and they didn't seem to know I was there, or at least I couldn't tell by the way they ignored me, and they ignored each other. My father kept his enormous face down in his enormous plate, articulating only an occasional grunt, while the very odd Roxanne served this enormous breakfast of swine, eggs, potatoes, tarts, chocolate and wine. Wine! Smothered by an enormous amount of mean, stony silence. Elijah, the enormity of it all robbed me of my appetite. I excused myself from the table and had a cup of tea with Avajay in the kitchen.'

She looked very small and vulnerable to him then. Her amusing description of breakfast with her father belied the isolation she must have been feeling. Days later, she told him she was happy to be there, and that she felt surprisingly comfortable living at Starcross. She said she had no plans to go anywhere else for a while. He didn't dare hope she wanted to stay because of him and, at the same time, he didn't know how to determine if that was true. As each day marched closer to the hour when he would have to leave her to honor his touring obligations, he continued to ask himself, 'Elijah, you fool, what could you possibly be thinking?' He theorized that her loveliness and the trace of sweet lavender that permeated the air even after she was gone, must be driving him to madness.

Clarisse didn't bring up the subject of her Father in their long conversations except to say she knew he was avoiding her. Elijah knew Talbert's stubborn disposition, but it seemed he was treating his daughter with the same unbending loathing he had shown the slaves. Clarisse said Talbert had only spoken one sentence to her since the day she'd arrived, 'Hello, I hope you had a pleasant trip,' before he abruptly walked away. She puffed out her cheeks and performed a hilarious imitation of her father's rumbling, gravelly voice, then she took a few steps with her back arched, arms held out and her stomach poked forward, in an amazing, nearly exact duplication of the slow, silent waddling walk that was Talbert's trademark.

Elijah laughed so hard, tears formed in his eyes, but behind the laughter he could see that her father's disdain was hurtful and confusing to her, and he wished with all his heart there was something he could do.

He thought of talking to her about the night she was born but decided against it. His memory of that night in 1849 was sketchy, and a touch of nausea still threatened his stomach whenever he gave more than a passing thought to it. He didn't think that what little he could tell her about the night her Mother died would assuage her grief over Talbert Bramwell's unreasonable scorn.

Whatever was wrong with Talbert had worsened after the stable fire. Elijah could never say to Clarisse that there were those who believed her father may have had something to do with his pregnant wife's death. Cabin gossip had rumored that the eruption in the stable had been so terrible, it had sent Roxanne, who was a bit daft to begin with, right over the edge, causing her feeble mind to snap. They said that even if Talbert hadn't killed his wife outright, he certainly could have saved her if he'd wanted to. Elijah didn't know. After 26 years of searching his mind, he still couldn't remember.

For weeks, Clarisse and Elijah spent every day together. She would sit and listen intently as long as he practiced, never fidgeting when he went over a passage again and again. She shared her love of the world's great literature with him, especially the Bible, and he entertained her with music he thought she would like.

She took quite an interest in the stories he told of his early life from Baldwin to Oberlin. He felt a need to tell her of everything that had ever mattered to him, but he hesitated to mention his inheritance. He reasoned that since Clarisse was the next of kin after Talbert, the very efficient Wayne Starcross should have informed her of Miss Letty's wishes, but Clarisse hadn't said anything about it. He began to feel burdened by what he was reluctant to say to her. After days of vacillation, he finally decided to bring up the subject.

They had never discussed slavery or its underlying ramifications. Clarisse treated him with the natural ease he received, and had come to expect from Europeans, which stood to reason as she had spent most of her life in France. Their conversations flowed easily from music to art to fashion to theatre to philosophy to poetry and to the mundane that made life funny, peculiar and awe inspiring. He had no idea how much she knew or cared about the political issues of the day, or the laws and conditions that bound the lives of former slaves, but he prayed that his inheritance of her family's home wouldn't damage their friendship, which had become his most treasured possession.

They ventured out with Phineas one perfect autumn day, on a pleasant walk through the woods to gather winter wildflowers. Upon their return, Avajay had thoughtfully left the little table in his quarters set with hot covered dishes and tall slender candles, to which Adam added wild blue violets to Clarisse's vase of Oxeye Daisies. After a supper of light, flaky whitefish garnished with snap beans, he toyed with his fork, while mentally trying out ways to open the conversation.

She sat across from him, wearing a demure, angelic soft white gown that failed to disguise the contours of her body, and contrasted with the earthy curiosity dancing in her eyes. 'What's wrong, Elijah?'

She had come to know his moods well, and he had learned that no evasion would work. In that respect she was like her grandmother.

He paused, and then plunged. 'Clarisse, Miss Letty left Starcross to me.'

'I know.'

She knew, but how did she feel about it? He shifted uneasily in the dark brown brocade wing chair. 'You knew?'

'Yes. Grand-ma-ma wrote to me and asked if I thought I would ever want to live in Georgia. I told her the truth. Knowing my Father has something against me, I couldn't imagine making my home here. She wrote back saying that since my Starcross cousins wouldn't be able to live here and attend to things the way she would have them, she'd decided to bequeath Starcross to you. She didn't know if Wayne could find a way to get around the legal barriers, but if he couldn't, he was instructed to sell it and divide the proceeds between Phineas, Avajay, you, me, and my father, rather than let all of Starcross go to the natural heir. Elijah, she told me her decision wasn't based on a kind of punishment-from-the-grave. She did it to be sure her 'Dear Ones,' as she put it, 'shared in her estate for as long as possible.' She knew if Talbert had control, he would never consider anyone else.' Leaning forward, Clarisse looked deep into his eyes. 'She said you were more than a son to her, and you would take care of us.'

Recalling almost the same words said to him the day he learned of Miss Letty's intentions, Elijah returned her penetrating stare until her unreadable expression caused his pulse to quicken. Overwhelmed, he pulled his gaze away from her hazel hypnosis to watch a thin curl of smoke rise over the wavering candle flame. As always, he tried to anticipate what she would say after looking at him like that, and each time, she surprised him.

Slapping his arm with her linen napkin, she said, 'Oh, stop being so uncomfortable! If you're concerned about me, don't be! I have enough income from the sale of Grandfather's shipyard to build a house just like this one, if I choose.'

Her mischievous grin reminded him of a precocious four-year-old's attempt to appear far too grownup to require a protector. He smiled into his sherry, enjoying the state of enchantment to which he ascended while in her presence.

CHAPTER THIRTY-ONE

Elijah continued his testimony, saying that since Clarisse's arrival, Roxanne had become more sullen, a feat he wouldn't have believed possible. The woman seemed ready to explode with resentment. He decided to send her away as soon as he returned from Europe the following spring. Even Miss Letty's tender heart wouldn't have allowed Roxanne to continue inflicting her unfathomable hostility on everyone. They had to put up with Talbert, but they didn't have to put up with Roxanne. Her peculiar behavior had always annoyed Elijah, but lately he had seen her robed figure pass slowly by the theatre at odd hours, her pale face peering through shadowy strands of wind-whipped hair as she glared up at his windows. Clarisse was given a frightful start one stormy night at the sight of Roxanne's rain-soaked figure standing as if in a trance, at the edge of the woods.

Although Clarisse made little to do about it, he knew that between Talbert and Roxanne, Starcross couldn't have been a pleasant experience for her.

Avajay spent most of her time overseeing the smooth running Starcross Theatre, where she and a small staff presented touring plays and concerts on Fridays and Saturdays. Phineas efficiently seated patrons and sold tickets, elegantly attired in a gift from Elijah, a well-tailored, black formal ensemble.

Elijah compiled a list of places to inquire where Roxanne might secure a position. He wrote to a friend from Oberlin who had asked him if he knew of a suitable companion for a bedridden relative. In his letter, Elijah described Roxanne's sulking, silent disposition and her exceptional domestic capabilities. He hoped he could find someone who would overlook her dour demeanor. To expedite the process, he included his agent's London address. Most assuredly, Avajay and Phineas wouldn't miss Roxanne, but soon, Talbert Bramwell would have to find a comparable servant to serve him and his God-awful, incessant drinking parties.

Elijah's days at Starcross were growing shorter. His plans were to spend Christmas at sea in order to arrive in England at the first of the year. He was torn. Each moment spent with Clarisse was sacred to him, and he didn't want to leave her. He constantly berated himself for the way he felt about her. He knew he had to quit thinking of her as a fragile baby one minute and the most desirable woman in the world the next. He knew he had to quit thinking of her, period. He had to get away. Maybe getting away would diminish the aching passion that was growing inside him. A mere accidental touch of her hand would begin a tense spiral of desire that threatened to take over and spin his senses out of control.

He asked himself if he should attempt to take her hand, ah, but she was white, and no matter how much artistic acclaim he received, he was a former slave. She was always friendly toward him, but he didn't venture to imagine it could ever be more than a friendship. He believed she appreciated having a friend in, what was to her, a foreign environment; a platonic friend with whom she could converse about her interests, a friend who knew not only the lights of Paris, but a smattering of French, as well.

Elijah was happier than he'd ever been, sadder than he'd ever been, sure of his heart, and far too confused to be certain of anything. He thanked God for his music, for in it was the only place he could hide.

The days passed blissfully, but too fast. In what seemed like minutes, the night he was to leave was upon him. At the rear of the theatre, Elijah said he helped Phineas and one of the grooms load the heavy cases into the carriage by lantern light. Elijah had taken down his last trunk and was looking forward to a last late supper with Clarisse when Phineas hailed him. Time was running out, and Elijah was anxious to savor every moment of being with Clarisse, but he stopped to have a final word with Phineas.

'Thank you for your help. I don't know what I'd do without you!'

'Ho, 'Lijah, you look lak you reddy ta wak out on uh staige.' Elijah, dressed for travel in a dark gray suit, long gray redingote and boots, wrapped his arm around his old friend's shoulder.

'That I am, but this time, I hate to leave. I know you you'll look after everything for me. Please see that one of the grooms rides Symphony regularly.'

'If 'n she let 'em,' Phineas chuckled. 'Ah sweah, dat hoss try ta ou'run da win'. She chunk riduhs offa huh bak wi' uh toss o' huh mane lak deys flies.' Phineas hesitated, searching for words. 'Ah, 'Lijah?' Although ninety-plus years, Phineas stood as tall, straight and strong as a man half his age. Except for a side tooth lost to a horse's kick, and a bald pate, he had hardly changed over the years. Again, the question of what had kept Phineas in Georgia crossed Elijah's mind. He'd supported his wife and his children from afar, and none seemed the worse off. Phineas' family had done quite well for themselves, running their own thriving stable business in Canada. Elijah couldn't bring himself to ask Phineas why he'd stayed, considering such a question to be intrusive, but he was grateful that Phineas had chosen to live at Starcross. The pocket watch, a gift to Elijah from the London Symphony Orchestra Conductor, read 8:30. He had less than three hours before he had to leave. But since Phineas rarely, if ever, wore such gravity in his eyes, Elijah waited and listened.

'Lijah, ah ben intendin' ta tak ta ya, en ah gess ah bettuh do it wile ah kin.'

'Yes?'

'Wall, Ah knows it wer uh long time ago, but ya membuh da nigh Miss Risse wer bon?'

'It's all I've thought about when I can tear mysef away from her beauty, and Phineas, I haven't told her I was there that night, yet.'

Phineas nodded with an understanding smile that faded into a concerned frown, 'Lijah, ya wuz liddle, but membuh wha Miz Rokann say cause Massa n Miz Sybil ta git so mad?'

'I think the horror of the fire, and the shock of Avajay delivering the baby that way, was too much for me. I guess I blanked most of it out. Why?'

A chestnut nuzzled Phineas' shoulder and he stopped to adjust the gelding's mouthpiece while patting his nozzle affectionately, 'Wall, 'Lijah. See—Uh—'

Keenly interested, Elijah followed Phineas as he moved slowly around the team, checking the hitches, still talking, 'Ya know, ya done gon en mek uh gud lif foh y'sef en da wuld. Me en Vacha ben read'n bouw how da peeples luvs ya music. Miz Letty wer right proud o' ya, en ah am too.' Elijah smiled his thanks, as Phineas suddenly changed the subject. 'Lijah, uh, ah kin see ya ben spennin uh lotta time wi Miz Risse.'

At that moment, Elijah believed Phineas was about to tell him to forget about Clarisse, and he was preparing to let his friend know he was thinking the same thing—that the best thing he could do would be to go away and never come back. He started to say so, but Phineas held up his hand. 'Son, foh ya meks up ya mine bouw ennyteeng, ya needs ta know da troot.'

'Truth? What truth?'

Phineas dodged the flick of a horsetail before he spoke. 'See, she don look lak it, but en da eyes o' de wuld, Miz Risse black as dis heah.' He pointed to his wrist. Elijah's heart stood still.

'Phineas? What—What?' he stammered, his eyes widened in surprise.

'Ya hud right, suh!' Phineas finished his sentence in a whisper, 'But ah don teeng she know! Ol' Mistuh B, he raise huh lak he raise Miz Sybil, lak she uh fine, rich white mistuss.'

Elijah wiped his brow. 'Phineas? Wha—?'

'Wall, iss wha Miz Rokann tell Miz Sybil en Massa en da stabell dat nigh. En 'Lijah, iss da rezzin Massa go all da way crazuh! Miz Sybil din ebben know. She din know! Dat night, Miz Sybil commens ta yellin, en das wen ah runs ta git da hosses. Wen ah gits ta da doh, ah sees da fiyah rare up, en—en—'

'Phineas. Phineas? How could—'

'Ah wer righ dere, 'Lijah, a'foh ya wuz bon, en ah seed da way it all happen! Miz Sybil Mama wer'n Spanish lak dey say. She wer un slave! Massa Bramwell, he din know, dat why he wer shook so bad. But, 'Lijah, ah don teeng he kilt Miz Sybil. Naw, naw,' he shook his head, 'ah sholey don!'

Elijah vaguely recalled Roxanne saying, 'Your precious baby is gonna be black;' but when the baby didn't have brown skin, he thought it was just some more of her mindless raving. Phineas laid a large calloused hand on his shoulder, saying,

'Lijah, sum peeples teeng one lil draugh uh black blud iss wuss dan uh wikkid cuss. Now, Miz Risse black, but she look lak she white, en it be hahd foh uh black man ta be wif huh, speshly down heah, speshly eff'n dat man go by 'da name uh 'Lijah Stahcruh.' He swung up into the driver's seat. 'Ah'll be righ back. Ahm gonna tote dis heah ta da Coach Stop. Ain hahdly no room foh ya butt back der now!'

Elijah shoved his hands into his pockets, and tried to catch his runaway thoughts. Phineas lowered his voice as he untied the reins. 'Lijah,' he said, 'Deys minny chirren o' da massa wif black blud, but dey livs en da white wuld, passin'. Down heah, dey wuz jis a minny black a dey wer white so ah suspeks deys minny fambluh have black blud by now, but sum don show it, so dey teeng 'why suffuh?' Den, deys sum, white a dey kin be, lak dat Ellen Craf,' he chuckled, 'Back en '48 she en huh husban' runs away. Dey skaped! She poda be a massa en huh husban' poda be huh slave. She wer werrin' man close, ebb'n uh top hat! She wer proud o' huh black blud. Yassuh! Seem lak sum is proud o' dey black blud. Now 'Lijah, ah knows Miz Risse lak ya, but effn she do fine out bouw huh blud, she migh na wanna be down heah in da slave cabin wif us!'

Phineas' last words echoed in his head, 'She might not want to be down here in the slave cabin with us.' Elijah said he didn't know what to say, 'Phineas, I—I—'

'Son,' He pointed to the sky, 'We cain see whu He know—only He know.'

'I don't think she likes me that way. We've just been friends,' to which Phineas replied with a smile and a cryptic, 'uh huh,' before he snapped the reins and pulled away. 'Hiyahhh, geedeyap!' he shouted, still smiling.

In a high state of nervous excitement, Elijah rushed upstairs, only to pace the length of the room several times before Clarisse knocked on his door. He tried to act normally, as though nothing had happened, but Phineas' revelation had changed his perception of what was possible in their lives. His mind desperately sought out ways he might discover if she could care for him, but he deemed all of his 'what-ifs' unsuitable. Would she care for him if she knew she was black? He could never be the one to tell her the facts of her lineage. If she didn't find out about her grandmother, would she reject him because he's black? If she did find out about her mixed blood, would she prefer to remain living as she had always lived—as a Southern white woman? Should he just kiss her and risk violating her trust and confidence? Oh God, no! Or should he wait and write his love for her in a letter once he was halfway around the world? Then, if she rejected him, at least he wouldn't have to face her.

x x x

Upstairs, Elijah wordlessly removed his coat, and lowered himself into the brocade chair. Clarisse sat across from him, serenely, as if an artist had deliberately positioned the slight tilt of her head, allowing shadows from the flickering firelight to outline the soft curve of her shoulders and the rounded fullness barely covered by her low neckline. While they listened to the crackling fire and their own thoughts, he indulged himself in one of many favored, forbidden fantasies, visualizing the two of them, laughing breathlessly, running to board the ship bound for the south coast of England together. Tonight.

Her eyes followed him, watching him pour the ruby claret into a pair of sparkling crystal glasses. Firelight and candle glow enhanced the golden tan of her skin; the tan he'd assumed was left over from the summer sun. The fire enhanced her topaz eyes, and played against the muted sheen of her sienna gown, creating a portrait he would eternally cherish in his heart. Although she hadn't stirred at all, except for the movement of her eyes, something about the way she looked at him made it hard for him to breathe. Fearing that his face would betray the searing hunger burning in his veins, he averted his gaze, cleared his throat and handed her a carefully written copy of his itinerary.

'Clarisse, I would like very much for you to write to me. I promise I'll correspond often, as well. I've included several addresses and the dates when I'll be in each location. You can always contact my agency, there, at the top of the page. They'll forward mail in case something unexpected arises.'

She gave him one of her slow friendly smiles. 'Thank you, Elijah. I will write often. I promise. Now, is there anything I can do to help you with last minute packing?'

He had finished his packing early in order to have as much time with her as he could. He shook his head, finding speech, at that moment, impossible.

He had eaten very little, and noticed that she hadn't touched her corn pudding.

'You weren't hungry?'

'N—no.' She answered quietly, sipping her wine without taking her eyes away from him. He knew she would miss the cordiality of their friendship after he left, but half his life would lie dormant until he saw her again. It seemed as though he could hear his watch ticking louder and faster.

Music was his therapy, his sanctuary, his church, his stairway to God. Playing the piano took him away from the physical world. When the music was over, he could return to the preposterous vicissitudes of reality after having glimpsed rarely seen wonders beyond life's harsh confines.

In search of the right composition, one that would exorcise the heavy sadness and confusion threatening to overtake him, he played random notes that led him into the opening chords of a Beethoven piece known as 'Moonlight Sonata.' The ethereal beauty of the music filled the air, masking her footsteps as she came up behind him. She leaned the weight of her body against his back and began to gently massage his shoulders. He felt her breathing quicken with every stroke of her satin fingers. Blood rushed to his head along the heated path she traced from his clavicle to both sides of his jaw line, and up into the hollows behind his ears. Her warmth was all over him. The chords he could no longer remember flashed before his eyes like jeweled dewdrops fading in the sunlight and unbelievable sensation of her nearness. His long denied love and need for her swelled with the joy of discovery, making him feel dizzy and suddenly, ecstatically, free. In one swift desperate motion, he abandoned Beethoven to stand and draw her up into his arms, covering her mouth with his, tasting her open sweetness. He took her face in his hands and thrilled at what he'd only dreamed he would see there, his own passion equaled and mirrored in her eyes.

With both arms around his neck, she held him, and caressed him, sighing softly against his lips as he ravenously captured her mouth again. His big, sensitive hands slid over her body, exploring the valley of her small waist, then slipping downward to probe and cup her firm, curving hips while pressing her tighter against him. She gasped when his lips simultaneously moved slowly and sensuously, kissing the lavender scented flesh between her breasts, just as the door opened and Roxanne Baldwin entered the room, her colorless eyes brimming with shiny excitement and triumph. Clarisse and Elijah quickly broke apart, embarrassed, struggling to breathe normally in their awkward discomfort.

His anger rushed to his head. My God, what was she doing? Had she been standing in the hallway all the time, listening, and waiting for this moment?

Roxanne strolled toward them, wetting her too-bright smile with her pointed, flicking tongue

'Well, well, well! Looks like the two slaves have found each other.' Savoring her advantage, she wiped perspiration from her brow with the back of her hand. 'Two little slaves together kissing, getting ready to make more little slaves?'

Clarisse stared, shock written in her eyes; her chest heaved with each ragged breath, but she said nothing.

Roxanne's thin, hollow laughter heated Elijah's anger, and inwardly he blamed and cursed himself for allowing this to happen, by forgetting to lock the door. But who could have known? Roxanne moved a few hip-swaying steps closer to Clarisse, and he knew if she came any closer, he would forcefully restrain her. Roxanne correctly read the fury in his face, because she halted her advance. He'd had enough. He took a step forward to physically escort her from the room, but Clarisse held his arm. 'Elijah, please—' she said. He reluctantly stood back.

Clarisse's voice, low, slightly hoarse, inquired politely, 'What are you saying Roxanne?'

'It's like this, rich missy prissy Bramwell,' Roxanne snapped, 'Your grandmother was a slave, which means your mama, my dear cousin Sybil, was the daughter of a slave, which makes you as black as dirt!' She laughed again. 'It's really funny. I've been surrounded by a stupid herd of slaves and slave-lovers all my life. That stupid old bitchy witch Letty, even left Starcross to him!' She nodded her in Elijah's direction, 'And don't let him fool you! The night your daddy killed your mama, Elijah was there! He knows a lot more than he told you!' she snarled.

Tears collected in Clarisse's eyes. He put his arms around her, not knowing if it was what she wanted. She clung to him, making a small noise that sounded like a sob. He could feel her shivering. She raised her eyes to his, and he knew he had to answer the unspoken question as best as he could.

'Clarisse,' he began, 'I, I think that's why your father couldn't be a father to you. He learned of your mother's mixed blood the night she died. I was watching through the stable window, and I know Roxanne was the reason it all happened. Roxanne was only twelve years of age, but she exhibited a grown woman's aggressive determination to seduce your father. She'd used a stolen key to wait for him in the stable to try to get him to pay attention to her, but he ordered her back to her rooms. Your mother found them, and that's when Roxanne told them about your grandmother Isis. Clarisse, I think your mother sincerely believed she was half Spanish. I was only eight. Had I been more mature, I might have understood it better.

'Unfortunately, I can't remember all the details. But the horror of it has remained engraved in jumbled chaos in my memory. I'm sorry, I don't know how your mother died, yet I'll never forget the way I wrapped you up and kept you warm the minute Avajay brought you into this world. Clarisse, mine was the first face you ever saw.'

Her knees were giving way, but his support kept her from falling. Roxanne snickered gleefully, assuming her arrows had hit their mark. Clarisse clung to him, burying her face in his chest. He didn't know what to do to ease her pain. He told her the one thing in life of which he was certain. He bent and whispered in her ear, 'Clarisse, I love you—'

Abruptly, she stiffened in his arms, and her tremors ceased. With a brief glance in his direction, she squeezed his fingers before she pulled away from him. He searched her face for some reaction and was astonished at the new resolve in the set of her features. He saw that this was no fragile magnolia blossom on the verge of crumpling into wilting hysteria, and Roxanne saw it, too. Clarisse, with narrowed eyes, turned toward the other woman as if preparing for attack. Her posture took on a subtle readiness, a quiet attitude of waiting, waiting for Roxanne to make the next move. The blond woman's pale gaze shifted from Elijah to Clarisse, and back again, measuring, attempting to gauge what damage the volleys she'd imagined to be powerful ammunition, had inflicted. Roxanne's attack would have hit a lesser woman like a cannonball to the stomach, but Clarisse was almost calm. There were echoes of Miss Letty's steely nerve in her stance, but there was also a fearlessness that was all her own, and he loved her all the more for it. Roxanne's crazed, high-pitched tirade burst forth from her then, reminding him of pus streaming from an infected wound.

'You can't be so high and mighty, you black bitch,' she screeched. 'Your daddy killed your mama because of what she was, and he was trying to kill you too!'

Tearless, Clarisse regarded Roxanne as if the perspiring, wild-eyed woman in the tight, yellow gown had just crawled out of a rotting corpse full of worms. Roxanne's sails had lost their headwind. Her well-planned and well-timed harangue should have had a more destructive effect. She had longed for Clarisse to be crushed by an explosion of all consuming pain. Even he couldn't have expected Clarisse to absorb the life-changing revelation with such outward equanimity. Obviously, Roxanne wasn't capable of understanding what had gone wrong. Her confrontational bombardment had worked so well before, in the stable

That night in 1849 came roaring back to Elijah's thoughts. He could almost feel the acrid stable smoke stinging his nostrils. He recalled how Sybil's world had been torn apart, piece-by-piece, with each word the twelve-year-old Roxanne had screamed, before something, or someone, had put an end to her life and nearly killed the baby she carried. Now that he was a man, grown, with new information, he realized the meaning of what he'd witnessed in the stable. He questioned if Sybil could've lived with the knowledge that she was the daughter of a slave. But what concerned him most was how would Clarisse feel now?

Her artillery depleted, Roxanne's conquest sank like a rock in the ocean of Clarisse's composure. With an uncertain self-righteous smirk and her large chin lifted, she strained to appear superior, but it was clear she didn't know what else to say. The only sounds in the room were Roxanne's ragged, agitated breathing and the soft rustle of Clarisse's taffeta skirts as she moved toward him, reaching for his hand. Ignoring Roxanne, she leaned heavily against him while he enfolded her securely in his embrace.

Elijah said that the ugly, agonizing scene had taken only a few minutes, but within that short period of time, integrity had glimmered through Clarisse's unshed tears, and a bright supreme strength emanated from the beautiful creature he once more held cradled in his eager arms.

Elijah's voice had become so quiet that everyone gathered around the hospital bed had to listen carefully to hear him. It was apparent he wouldn't be saying more in this session, but Nasrene asked for one final question,

"Elijah, do you know where the secret hiding place is located?" Her question went unanswered. Adam slept on.

After Nasrene completed the process, everyone silently reflected on what they had just heard. Ceeoni didn't share Elijah's recall of the incident. Still, she was completely shaken by his testimony that had deepened the mysteries and miracles intertwining these people who had lived at Starcross more than one hundred years before. The man on the black horse had been Elijah. She had loved him, and he had loved the woman she had been. She felt compelled to kiss the man who had Elijah's memories.

As she moved to gently touch her lips to Adam's cheek, Diana's account of Karmic Law came to the forefront of her mind. She realized that the ties between Clarisse and Elijah may have been balanced, with all debts paid, in which case they would pass each other as casual acquaintances or oblivious strangers—ships in the night. Or their love could carry over into this life, into this here and this now.

CHAPTER THIRTY-TWO

While riding back to Homer's, Ceeoni ignored Di's "Oh-wow-I-thought-so!" look that came with a raised eyebrow, because she was too wired to talk about Elijah yet. In addition to everything else she couldn't have anticipated, she'd started visualizing new bits and pieces of her life as Clarisse Starcross Bramwell. She had never been to Paris, yet she spontaneously recalled the beautiful flat she shared with the studious Mary Starcross. She saw images of herself attending to fetid, hopelessly infected wounds amid a hideous collage of reeking hospital filth and pain wracked screams during the burning of Paris.

"Nasrene?" she asked, "I've seen pieces of life in 19th century France, and I'm wondering if that's normal?"

"What's normal? This is all new to me, Ceeoni. I've read of a few similar accounts, but everything about the past life regressions here is groundbreaking. You seem to be especially prone to spontaneous memories of that lifetime. I know there are unusually valid reasons we're all caught up in this, but you, Homer, Adam, and the killer, whoever it may be, are the major players in laying this karma to rest. Remember, after Homer restored Starcross, hired you and got the ball rolling, it was your deja vu that brought us all together. I think discovering this place inside yourself, filled with the familiar and the forgotten, is expanding your consciousness. I firmly believe that encountering evidence of metaphysical phenomena is a purposeful gift from the Spirit, in order for the Soul to attain more highly evolved levels. I was very young when I was shown that what really matters is beyond the physical. Once opened, the inner vision continues to expand."

Ceeoni recalled Di's earlier statement, 'Get used to it,' and how fast it had become her mantra as she struggled with new realities.

Weber, clad in slinky olive green, met them at the door with news,

"Hey! They've found no prints anywhere in Adam's hospital room, other than that of signed-in guests and personnel. The I.V. bottle was clean, and there's no identification of the substance in the bottle yet, but the fire in the Estates was arson, without a doubt. Traces of gasoline soaked rags were found around the gas lines."

"Was the gas on?" Ceeoni asked. "Aw, yeah," Homer sighed, "Weather permitting, we always have the gas turned on to show houses with the fireplaces lit."

"Well," Di said, "Nasrene, I know it's late, but I'm buzzing with curiosity about Avajay. If you're willing and you show me what to do, I think I can guide your regression."

"Good idea Di. Let's do it. Let's see if Avajay will come back. I can regress myself, but if you insist, just give me a few minutes and I'll write it all down. You ought to know it by heart by now."

It was a little after 1am before Nasrene, poised on the edge of a zebra chair under the spacious room's single lit lamp, finished typing furiously on her laptop. The cozy fire cast gyrating shadows on the wall, creating a gamut of expressions passing over the hanging ceremonial masks' exaggerated features. Their seeming gladness, sorrow, perplexity, anger and terror reminded Ceeoni of the maze of conflicting emotions vying for domination of her thoughts. Rather than sit and stew, she got busy and helped Weber set out platters of fresh strawberries, pears, red and green grapes, peaches and cheeses.

"Hey, Web," Homer called to him as he was leaving the room, "As I told you, past life regression isn't a séance or a sacrificial voodoo ritual. Would you care to check it out?"

"Say, I'm glad you asked, but I wouldn't want to intrude on anyone's privacy." Di handed Weber a glass, saying, "I think we all agree that everything happens for a reason and we've learned that every Soul here is supposed to be here."

She raised the bottle of Schramsberg sparkling wine to which Weber grinned and held his glass out for her to fill.

"My arm is twisted! I have to admit that I'm very curious."

"OK, Di," Nasrene announced, "Here's the printout, and I'm ready."

At that, everyone settled close to the sofa where Nasrene had reclined. Diana flipped on the recorder and read the regression suggestions in a smooth, professional manner. The regression sequence complete, Nasrene simply began to speak in high-pitched precise English, interrupting Diana's first question and proceeding without allowing Diana to ask another.

"What is your—?"

'I am Avajay. The Grace of God has allowed me to sometimes see the past and the future; however, it is not given me to know when my third eye will be open and the path illuminated. My inability to anticipate a critical outcome has left a bittersweet memory of my life at Starcross.'

Avajay said she had come to Starcross led by a detailed vision of destiny she'd had when she was a girl of ten, living in the shack she shared with her parents and two brothers on the outskirts of Calcutta. The vision had revealed that the course of that lifetime would revolve around a young American musical artist whom she would meet in England.

The vivid vision had left Avajay entrusted with a list of explicit instructions. The American, Leticia Starcross, would have a granddaughter, who had to be born at the exact moment specified in Avajay's vision, in order to form an important link in the Grand Design. Avajay was assigned to join with Leticia to assist and uplift dozens of Souls. At the same time, Leticia's granddaughter and a Great Soul she would love would require protection from one who had pursued them throughout many lifetimes. This one lived and toiled in the service of Darkness and Death. Avajay said her vision had closed with three words of ominous caution, 'Watch your step'.

Avajay had been born into the lowest caste, the Dalit, considered unclean, and therefore, 'untouchable' by the higher classes of her native India. The Untouchables, subservient to the superior castes, have been relegated, sentenced for life, generation after generation, to the dirtiest, menial jobs and unimaginably deplorable living conditions. In keeping with her vision and against all the odds and laws of her caste, she was chosen, from her eighteen-hour day of scouring rows of public latrines, to work as a chambermaid in Southport, England.

Her new job at the Royal South Hotel caused her to wonder if she had attained Nirvana. Although on call, which many days amounted to a mere fourteen hours, she dusted strange, beautiful lamps and statues, swept and polished shining floors, tended fresh flowers, and changed perfumed bed linen that had hardly been used. She felt like she was on holiday. She found her starched, stiff white uniform confining, but the exotic table scraps were delicious. After sleeping on a floor pallet in a one-room shack with her whole family, her own little cot in the warm hotel basement lined up with those of the other maids, was an unheard of guilty luxury, while she waited for her divine destiny to unfold.

One morning in the year 1807, her attention was drawn to a woman registering as a hotel guest, alone. The American lady, beautiful in a deep plum cloak and bonnet, was doing her best to ignore the desk clerk's eyerolling, huffing, haughty disdain, reserved exclusively for those whom he considered to be beneath him. Avajay, pretending preoccupation dusting a statuette, didn't hear the guest's name, but she thought well of the lady's parry of the clerk's rude attitude.

The clerk ventured another sarcastic question dripping with leering innuendo, 'When is the gentleman, er, ah, I mean, the rest of Madame's party due to arrive?' To which the woman, refusing to be intimidated any longer, snatched up her room key and walked away without a backward glance. Avajay's heart rejoiced, 'Bravo, Miss Starcross, if that is who you are.'

That night, as Avajay rolled a cart of dishes from the lounge to the kitchen, the sound of music, executed with strength and fluidity, wafted from the closed salon. Peeking through the door, the sight of the American lady rehearsing at the harpsichord, set Avajay's pulse beating faster with the certainty that her destiny had, at last, arrived. So far, her vision's sequence of events had been accurate to the day, but she had to know if Miss Starcross would understand and accept, if the appointed path to the Greatest Good was to be fulfilled.

She waited until almost midnight before slipping from her basement corner, past the other sleeping maids. She tiptoed through the silent halls to tap lightly on the pianist's door.

'Yes? Who is it?'

'Miss Starcross, I am Avajay, the maid.'

'No thank you, I won't be requiring anything this evening.'

'Please, I wish to speak with you concerning a personal matter.'

A personal matter? Letty, wondering what the matter could be, invited the girl in to be seated. She took the chair facing Letty and met Letty's curiosity with a steady, solemn gaze. 'Avajay is a very pretty name for a lovely girl. What magnificent hair!'

'Thank you, ma'am,' she answered, smoothing the coiled braid at the nape of her neck.

'How old are you?'

'Fifteen, Mam'

'You speak beautifully. Were you born in England?'

'No Mam, but I study English every day.'

'Well then, Avajay. You wanted to talk to me?'

'Yes, Mam'

'You needn't lower your eyes, and please, you needn't call me Mam,' she said.

'You may call me—' But, before she could finish, Avajay said,

'You shortened your name to Letty, because you detest the name Leticia. You are twenty-five years old, and you live in Starcross, Georgia, in the country of America. I am to accompany you there to assist you in fulfilling your highest Soul evolvement. Your favorite color is pink, and you have never been in love. Your beloved governess and teacher entered the Spirit World last month, but you will meet her again in other lifetimes. Soon, you will marry, and you will be ecstatically happy. The happiness in this life will far outweigh the sadness.

'I am the embodiment of one of your Spirit Guides. I have guided other Souls in past lifetimes, but for now, I am to be with you to help you and the one who is to be your husband, in working for the cause of human freedom. This is a turning point for our Souls and the world. We must learn to meet our fears, or we are bound to re-live them.'

Avajay took a deep breath and focused on the amazed wide eyes that stared into hers. Letty's hands had flown to a place over her heart in a still, unblinking, posture as she mentally processed the shocking truth of the girl's words. Avajay knew that Letty immediately recognized the reality and gravity of the unspoken commitment required, and that she had only a moment to make the most momentous decision of her life. Letty, with a trace of tears standing in her eyes, leaned over and took both of Avajay's hands.

'My dear, I—I will be leaving England for the Continent in three months. Three months after that I will return to Starcross, and I will send you money for your passage to Georgia.'

'No, first, I must go to Calcutta to bid my family goodbye, for I will never see them again. Then, I will meet you in Austria after your final European concert, six months from now. If I am not there, everything will go wrong, which means we will lose this opportunity, and our Souls will be required to begin again. You must give me the eight hundred pounds sewn into the lining of your bag.'

Letty's stunned gasp was ignored, as the girl quickly took a piece of paper from her pocket. Handing it to Letty she said,

'Here are all of the arrangements; the hotels where you will be safe, and times and places where you will find secure transportation. As you can see, you will have to change some of the agency's plans, but you must follow these instructions to the letter, they are for your good and the good of many.'

Letty read the paper quickly. 'It's all here! Every stop on my tour! When did you make these arrangements?'

'Since I knew you would be in Southport.'

'How long have you known I would be at this hotel?'

'I have been waiting here for you for two years.'

x x x

Avajay said that six months later the conflict between Austria and France, blown to full proportions, made travel extremely dangerous, but Leticia Starcross enjoyed artistic carte blanche behind French lines. The center of Vienna was relatively safe, where the beautiful American artist performed for prominent officials and military of the French occupation. After one memorable concert, she accepted an extravagant bouquet and a series of standing ovations from a tiny enchanted patron in the front row, the self-titled Emperor of France, General Napoleon Bonaparte.

The night before Letty was due to leave Vienna, a midnight signal tap on her door announced Avajay, who hurried in and breathlessly rushed around the room, gathering Letty's things; throwing warm clothing on the bed. 'Quickly, put these on! Thank you for following the instructions. The guards expected your servant to arrive, and I was able to pass the checkpoints easily, unmolested.'

'But my coach doesn't leave until 7am, and that's hours from now,' Letty protested, while changing into the clothes.

Avajay silently fastened the latches on Letty's bag before opening the door a crack. Looking up and down the hall, she asked, 'Do you have everything? We must leave now!' At Letty's affirmative nod the girl took off, keeping to the shadows along the dim passageway. Letty hesitated for a moment before grabbing her coat and muff and running to catch up with the tiny figure whose black satin bonnet ribbons flew above her bobbing, bouncing cloak.

On their way out of the hotel, they gingerly tip-toed past two sleeping guards. When they reached the bottom of the ice covered stairs outside, the coach driver abruptly lifted Letty and Avajay, one by one, out of the blinding snowstorm up into the comparative warmth of the carriage, while grumbling in French-accented English, 'You took long enough to get here!'

The coach wheels rolled forward a few inches, causing Letty to bump into the handsome, well-dressed lone passenger already seated inside. She mumbled an apology to him, then whispered to Avajay, 'This is a mistake! Where are my trunks? I'm going to need my music! I left my trunks for tomorrow morning's departure!'

'I had them transferred to this coach. The 7am coach will be waylaid by a resistance squad, and all the passengers will be executed.'

In response to Avajay's whispered explanation, Letty shivered and moaned softly, as the coach lurched forward, picking up speed.

'Madam,' the young man next to her inquired politely, 'Please forgive my intrusion, but are you not feeling well?'

'I am quite well, thank you.' She couldn't help smiling into the kind, sincere face of the man beside her who politely tipped his tri-cornered hat.

'Oh, very good. I didn't expect such charming traveling companions. Please ladies, allow me to introduce myself. My name is Thurman T. Bramwell. I'm from New York and it is certainly a pleasure to converse in English again.'

Avajay said, 'Human destiny is not etched in stone. For the growth of the Soul, we all have choice. Good or bad, our choices eventually lead us to our highest levels, lesson by lesson. Letty bravely put her fear aside and trusted the Angels that sent me to her. The rewarding happiness we found at Starcross resulted from performing the dangerous tasks we all faced in releasing dozens of Souls from bondage. We were always terribly afraid, but we couldn't allow our fear to stop us, although we had to continue our work alone from 1827, for thirty-six years.

'After Letty entered the Spirit World, Clarisse and Elijah needed my advice, which was all I could do. Phineas was there, giving his loving strength and support, but we knew we couldn't interfere with the course of their love; we couldn't push them in any direction. It was entirely up to them to make their own choices, in spite of fear, as must we all.'

It was obvious that Avajay had finished her testimony, and probably wouldn't say much more. Sure enough, she stopped talking. Diana waited a few minutes to see if she would say anything else.

"Avajay?" There was no answer. "Do you know the location of the secret place?"

'No! Oh no! No! I could never tell! Never!'

Avajay's negation exploded in a breathy, urgent whisper as she tossed and turned her head in quick, jerky movements. She calmed down gradually during Diana's awakening techniques. Di closed the session with the usual suggestion that Nasrene would remember everything.

"You know," Ceeoni said, "since we've been led here to help identify the illusive killer, and to complete something or right wrongs from that time, I'm anxious to find out more about Clarisse's part in it. What I'm saying is that I'm ready to be regressed again, whenever you are."

"Great, Ceeoni! I'm glad to know that." Nasrene was reaching for her bag, "How about now?"

Settling on the sofa Ceeoni said, "After all, Avajay said we mustn't be afraid, but I can't help wondering what we're not supposed to fear?"

"Now how did I know that was coming?" Di answered, "And, if you wanna know what I think—I think fear was a factor in the unsolved 19th century Starcross issues, which means Avajay's warning is something we all must learn, to face life's scary stuff in faith instead of fear."

Obviously excited, Weber had been paying close attention. "Wait! Hold up a minute. What's happening here? What just happened?"

Nasrene explained, Homer added, Di and Ceeoni amended, R.C. and Samson clarified, and within a few minutes, Weber had heard condensed versions of their past life explorations, and how they felt about the incidents they'd relived.

"It's certain that these past life regressions are the most extraordinary I've seen or heard of," Nasrene said. "Feel free to review our tapes, Web. Also, there's such a great wealth of info about regression in books and on the Internet, I'm surprised more people aren't into it." Weber raised his glass in a toast. "Well, you've got me going. Please proceed! I'm anxious to witness another excursion into the unknown."

No longer feeling anxious, Ceeoni closed her eyes and relaxed, eager to comply.

CHAPTER THIRTY-THREE

Everyone paid close attention as Nasrene gave Ceeoni the regression suggestions. Once Ceeoni's relaxation took effect, Clarisse immediately returned.

"Where are you?" Nasrene asked.

'In Elijah's quarters.'

"What year is it?"

'1875'

Soon, it was apparent that Clarisse had regressed to a split second after Roxanne's bitter confrontation, on the night of Elijah's departure. Clarisse's quiet voice, a near monotone, belied the obvious tension in Ceeoni's tightly clenched hands as she said,

'Cousin Roxanne's ferocious countenance faded into a slack-mouthed, blank expression, as if her disguise of sanity had suddenly evaporated. She sauntered from the room, giggling in highly pitched, toneless ripples of private amusement; her mad laughter piercing my very bones with a sinking sense of foreboding.'

Clarisse continued, describing how she was disquieted by Roxanne's attack but she had been no stranger to the evil that men do. She'd known the feeling of living in fear when the 1870 Prussian War gathered force and eventually spilled into Paris. The following year, that war led to the catastrophic revolt of the *Paris Commune* and the *Communards'* burning of city buildings along with over 20,000 executions and other killings. For days into nights, hours on end, Clarisse attended the wounded, destitute and diseased, while praying for the dead and dying packed into every corner of the *Assistance Publique Hospitaux de Paris*.

During that time she'd faced dangers of all types. The Paris streets were filled with the German occupation, where bloody street fighting, looters, cut pockets and lewd propositioners flourished. She learned to dodge them all with agility while negotiating for food and necessities with shifty-eyed black marketeers in dark alleys. Living with a multitude of hideous realities in those years of death had toughened her spirit, so much so that Roxanne, Elijah or anyone couldn't help but under-estimate Clarisse's fortitude by a mile.

But at that moment, Elijah was her paramount and most immediate concern. He was leaving soon, and she didn't want to emerge from the sanctuary of his embrace. She didn't want to think on Roxanne's state of mind, or any circumstance of birth, not even her own.

Roxanne's accusation that Talbert Bramwell had murdered his wife and attempted to kill his own unborn child echoed a possibility Clarisse had pondered most of her life, a possibility that was, in her mind, the reason for her father's morose silence, and she didn't know what to make of any of it. She would pore over every minute detail of Roxanne's ranting later, but in Elijah's arms, she thought only of him. Should she tell him that long before she actually saw his face, she'd spent nights overflowing with dreams of loving him, and that every second, every breath she took, brought him deeper into her heart? Her love for him had overridden her common sense. It was too late to try to pretend to be coy. She knew he was fond of her—could that fondness be love? In the bizarre, exaggerated way of dreams, this day of his departure was what her nocturnal images had foretold. But just maybe, maybe the tearful outcome of those nightmares could be changed.

She felt his arms tighten around her. For the short time they had left, she needed simply to be near him, to mindlessly revel in his presence. She loved everything about him; his sharp intelligence, his easy grace, and the mysterious depths of his dark eyes, in which she knew she could drown. Her heart fluttered at the sound of his voice, and the way he looked as he leaned over the piano keys to study a score or to concentrate on executing a phrase, made her knees weak.

In the aftermath of the emotional tsunami she was feeling, she took several deep breaths to try to control her trembling,

'Clarisse? Are you all right?'

She didn't want to think. She just wanted to stay close to him, and he knew it. He gently guided her to settle beside him on the piano bench.

'Yes—I'm fine.'

Elijah's words fell softly, hesitantly. 'I can't imagine Roxanne being treated with any more finesse than you did just then. Please believe me, I promise you she'll be leaving Starcross as soon as I can locate a position for her. Actually, I've already made inquiries. I must do that out of respect for Miss Letty's principles. Your grandmother would never turn anyone away, especially a woman with no means of fending for herself—especially Roxanne'

'Roxanne? Why Roxanne?'

'You see, Roxanne spent her youth in an asylum for the hopelessly insane, all because of the—uh, hysterical spasms she had the night your Mother was killed in the stable fire. Your Grandfather Baldwin arrived as soon as he could, and made the arrangements for her hospitalization, then he took you away. You were less than a week old. Of course, Miss Letty kept everyone abreast of your progress, but she didn't think you would ever come back here. So, I believe when Roxanne turned up on the doorstep, your grandmother, in her way, tried to compensate for the years she had been confined, by taking her in. The hospital assured Miss Letty that Roxanne was doing well, but I don't think she'll ever be completely sane.'

'Oh Elijah, how awful.' She digested his enlightening explanation with a sigh. He squeezed her hand, 'Clarisse, I need to talk to you.'

'Mmmmm?'

Her barely discernible nod encouraged him to forge ahead. He began speaking slowly,

'As you know, I was born a slave. In spite of my freedom, and all that I've been blessed enough to achieve, I'll be a slave until I die, and even beyond the grave, according to most people and the segregated cemeteries in this country. I can only guess at what you might be feeling now. After a lifetime of looking on at the plight of an enslaved, helpless and despised group of people, I know it could be irreparably crushing to suddenly discover that you, yourself, are one of them.' He paused. Clarisse didn't respond to his cue, although she knew he was right. Silence now would leave too much unsaid for too long. It would be months before he could return to Starcross. She'd heard the urgent question between the lines of his careful statement regarding her emotional state, and she knew she had to tell him what was on her mind, but his nearness was making marshalling her thoughts impossible.

'Clarisse,' he probed, 'I like to think that had I been born white, I would never be one to accept the fallacious notion of supremacy, whether it be by birthright or divine right, or whatever pap cruel ignorance has invented to justify itself. Then again, possibly everything I've suffered, which, thanks to your grandparents, was nothing compared to the horrible indignities I've witnessed while knowing all of it could have happened to me, became the million and one reasons why I understand this truth. I'm proud of my people and the strength that has preserved us. Tonight, I saw such strength in you, as well.'

She wordlessly disengaged his distracting arms and his hands that warmed her skin. His eyes followed her as she moved to the window. In that moment, they were both aware that whatever she would say to him would have to be what he was seeking and what he deserved—her truth, from her heart, and nothing less.

A hard rain pelted the leaded glass, distorting the dim manor lights twinkling through the trees. The fat water droplets splattering and gathering into running patterns mimicked the ticking of hundreds of tiny clocks, marking time, reminding her that she would soon be parted from him. She didn't turn in his direction. Her voice, even and conversational, betrayed no inner turmoil.

'Elijah, I feel exactly the way I felt before Roxanne stormed in here. My mother's cause of death remains a mystery, but now I know a little more about that night. Naturally, I'm shocked that Grandmother Isis was a slave. Still, I'm partly relieved. I always thought that what caused my Father's chosen alienation was that he blamed my mother's death on my birth. But now I know it was far more complicated than that. Please understand I'm aware of how unimaginably insulting my life as a negress in 1875 America would be if it weren't for my family's sheltering prosperity, but all of it—m—my African blood that bestowed my 'peasant's complexion,' which my friends thought odd, but nonetheless envied—,' she sighed,

'It's beyond my control. I can't help what I am, and I can't change the events of the past. Perhaps unexpected feelings about this night will surface later, but right now, I feel only the agony of having to face the desolate days ahead—without you.'

Candles flickered as he crossed the room to take her roughly into his arms; the wavering flames enhanced the fiery light in his eyes. He kissed fresh tears from her cheek and held her, rocked her, his words muffled and slurred in the soft flesh of her throat.

'I tried so hard to stop loving you—I tried not to need you. I thought it was impossible—I tried to get you out of my mind.'

Overwhelmed by his dizzying confession, she clung to him, lost in him, listening to her own heavy breathing in concert with his. Taking up where he'd left off before Roxanne's intrusion, he pulled her even closer. With a sensitive touch, warm and caressing, he rolled her hips against the swollen rise of his body with a deliberate, unhurried knowingness. This wasn't reminiscent of the awkward, sloppy encounters with a few of her former suitors that had made her feel far too violated to allow further liberties. She relinquished all control to breathlessly let him have his way. Tantalizing kisses roamed her shoulder and traveled lower, while he unbuttoned the back of her dress and unhooked her lace bustier with one hand, allowing the sheer fabric to fall away from her round breasts. His lips explored, tasted and taunted the hardened tips, sending trickles of perspiration and tremors of aching longing inching down her spine. The trembling spread into her legs when she realized he was simultaneously loosening his own clothing.

He murmured her name. 'Clarisse, oh, my sweet Clarisse, only you can stop this. I can't stop myself—'

Her halting, half whispered reply came in short gasping rhythm with what his lips were doing to her. 'That night on the highway,' she breathed, 'I didn't understand why I had dreamed of you before we met. Tonight, you told me what my heart always knew—that I've loved you and only you—only you, from the minute I was born.'

He groaned as he lifted her easily, and dropping garments along the way, he carried her to the tapestry draped bed where the fire warmed the inner chamber in an undulating golden glow. On his knees, he covered her mouth with his own, drawing out and sucking her tongue, while his fingers explored crevices and valleys, awakening erotic pathways she never knew existed. Suddenly, struggling to catch her breath, before his embrace made her forget what she intended to do, she wriggled away from his sensuous snare and came to a kneeling position facing him. His agitated breathing slowed; although puzzled, he held still for her. She removed his black silk shirt; the last piece of clothing between them. A tiny gasp escaped her at the picture created by fire-lit shadows moving and playing on his flawlessly muscled skin. She was reminded of a magnificent mahogany statue she had seen in the Louvre. Consciously resisting the urge to touch him, she backed away a bit and took off her silver chain; the twisted silver chain with its dangling black opal ringed in diamonds, which she placed around his neck. She surveyed the result, with a smile of satisfaction. The shimmering pendant appeared smaller against his smooth, broad chest, but it seemed to belong there. Staring at her, he lifted the opal and kissed it. 'S'il *vous plait, ma cherie,*' he whispered, 'please hold still, let me look at you. I want to preserve this moment.'

His kisses still tingling on her skin had erased all traces of modest reticence. She was proud and pleased to have found favor in his eyes. She leisurely arched her back, pushed her heavy hair up with both hands and basked in the way his gaze devoured and adored her elongated dark nipples, feasted upon the sumptuous lines of her broad hips, and lingered on the slight pout between her thick thighs.

Elijah, with a grunt of lustful exhilaration, reached out for her, his long intake of breath through clenched teeth changed into low moans. In a maddeningly slow, silken motion, he took her lips again and again. Suddenly, urgency replaced tenderness as wave after wave of searing, pounding, pulsating sensation consumed them, and there was no longer any day or night or time or place or separation between this woman and the only man she would ever love.

From far in the distance, beyond the door to rapturous primal bliss he had shown her, his husky voice repeated, 'I love you—love you, God knows I love you, forever—'

She awakened alone underneath the heavy counterpane in his rosewood bed, and found her clothing draped neatly over the footboard. He had thoughtfully left a candle burning that had burned down to a stubby pile of smoldering wax. She bathed in the chilly water closet and dressed before a dying fire, but she didn't need heat. Her soul sailed on a tropical sea where Elijah was sun, and water and all the air she breathed. Dreamily recalling her new world of scorching passion and the tenderness of their parting, she slipped into her gown and nearly missed seeing the little note that fell from the sleeve. Written on onionskin in his large elegant scrawl, it read,

My Darling, how I wish you were accompanying me, but after this tour, neither Hell nor the fury of the Four Winds will keep me from your side.

Eternally Loving you,

E.

Days afterward, with the miracle of his love and his note kept close to her heart, Clarisse went about her daily activities wrapped in a cloud of pure joy. She was drawn to Elijah's rooms, where she kept his books and his precious piano dusted, just for the thrill of feeling close to him. She had no contact with Roxanne, a fact for which she was most grateful.

Clarisse said that the Christmas holidays passed quickly for her and the year 1876 began on a cloud of euphoria. Suddenly, Clarisse began to sob. Tears rolled down Ceeoni's cheeks, in between shuddering intakes of breath she said,

'I—I—wrote to Elijah every day, but time passed, and I received no reply, not a single letter! I believed he would write to me, I believed him, but weeks turned into months! And—Oh God!' she screamed, 'Just like my dream! Ohhh—ohhh—!'

Nasrene quickly calmed Clarisse, reduced her pain, and awakened Ceeoni. Di sat beside the sofa dabbing dark rivulets of mascara-stained tears from Ceeoni's cheeks with a dampened towel Weber handed her from the bar. Ceeoni answered Nasrene's concerned, "How do you feel?" with a weak little smile.

"Goodness!," she murmured, wiping away tears, "I felt incredibly sharp pain but it's over, I'll be OK."

"Hey," Di fanned Ceeoni with the towel, "Oh, long have I suspected that underneath that quiet exterior of yours lies an active volcano, bubbling hot lava, ready to blow, now Clarisse's testimony has removed all doubt!"

Waving away Di's teasing, Ceeoni took a sip from the cup of chamomile tea Homer held out to her, then closed her eyes in an attempt to dispel the gloom of Clarisse's anguish. At the same time her heart reveled in the glory of her 19th century love, a love like none she had ever imagined.

"Hmmm," Nasrene said, "So Clarisse gave her opal pendant to Elijah in 1875. Poor Clarisse, it must've been torture to have discovered the love of your life, and within hours you're separated from him, only to be jolted by the sickening truth, that, for whatever reason, he doesn't write or, well, maybe he can't. I hope nothing had happened to him."

Samson interrupted, frowning. "Say, R.C., all this focus on a pendant? You know?"

"Samson, my man, I was thinking the same thing—it's all coming together!—Ceeoni's earrings—I see—now I see—that's why Adam had to have it—"

"What?" Ceeoni asked, "R.C., what did Adam have to have?"

"The pendant! Adam always, always wears a black opal and diamond pendant. Come to think of it, he doesn't have it on now, and I haven't seen it since the concert Friday night." R.C. looked dismally down into his beer. "In all the excitement, I guess I didn't miss it when I collected his personal belongings. I forgot all about it—He calls it his lucky charm, and, damn, now I guess its gone!"

"Well," Nasrene said, "It did its job. Adam is lucky to be alive. Considering the way Elijah felt about Clarisse, it was natural that Adam's Soul would lead him to seek out a copy of that pendant from his life at Starcross."

"Hey, I'm a walking witness," Homer added. "Probably like my mad search for accurate replicas for the Manor restoration. And believe me, nothing but the closest to what I knew was right would suffice, which is why it took so long!"

R.C. quickly shook his head, "Yea Homes, only this ain't no copy, it's the real thing!"

"The real thing?"

"Adam's pendant isn't merely like Elijah's. I'm certain it's the same pendant, and Ceeoni's earrings, too! I know now that they actually belonged to Elijah and Clarisse! Ceeoni, in the back of my mind, I noticed that your earrings resembled Adam's pendant, but it's a common design I've seen so many times, I had no reason to make a connection."

"I guess we've all been too frustrated to see all the connections," Ceeoni said, "what makes you think it's the same one Clarisse gave Elijah?"

"Well, his pendant came complete with that peculiar twisted silver chain Clarisse described, and—"

Ceeoni remembered seeing the silver chain shimmering against Adam's chest during the Friday night concert. "But couldn't it have been a coincidence?" Ceeoni bit her lip after her slip into bland conventional thinking raised several pairs of eyebrows. "Wha—what I mean is, how could that be?"

Not one to miss milking a dramatic moment, R.C.'s intense glance swept each perplexed face before he slowly replied, "I was with him when he bought it in London, about two months after I started working for him. It was one of those once-in-a-great-while, crazy, spooky incidents that defies explanation, that is, until now."

"Wait, wait, please wait!" Di hurried to the bar, "Anyone need a fresh drink? I don't wanna miss a word of this!"

CHAPTER THIRTY-FOUR

Everyone waited, anxiously poised in rapt attention, waiting for R.C. to explain, but he took his own sweet time, deliberately ignoring them while adjusting his kufi to the perfect angle, in silence. Di responded by leading a chorus of 'Boos' followed by a barrage of tossed peanuts and chipped ice that sent R.C. collapsing into a chair with hands raised in surrender.

"OK, OK!" he laughed. "Since you put it that way—just don't stone me! Well, it happened in the Soho district after the all-day listening party the label had given in celebration of Adam's first album release. The company was thrilled that the recording's advance orders amounted to what is called 'shipping gold,' which was rare for a new artist. It describes sales that had already added up to over a million units, earning a Gold Record Award before the product even had time to reach distributors. Nowadays, it's a common occurrence. The party was held at the decades old Ronnie Scott's, a classic, world famous jazz club, that's still going strong, by the way, and it was the first star-studded event either of us had ever attended: Freddie Hubbard, The Rolling Stones, Cleo Laine, Oscar Peterson, Dusty Springfield, and giants from all areas of the music industry had come through.

"We were trying to be cool, acting as though we'd been the celebrated hosts of elegant soirees like that all our lives, while hoping the 'gee whiz' we were feeling didn't show. Adam's album playing over and over set a gala atmosphere that shimmered from early in the day until it started winding down around 7pm. Adam had presided over the festivities graciously, accepting and exchanging kudos with his usual humility and infectious wit, but toward evening he took me aside, confessing that threads of conversation were tangling up amongst the champagne bubbles, to which my thickened tongue and burning cheeks attested.

"What party amateurs we were then! I remember my relief when Adam turned down an invitation to continue the reveling at some earl's castle, and suggested we take a walk before we embarrassed ourselves. Adam and I had already engaged in ongoing dialogue concerning his career path, including the importance of appropriate public decorum. We didn't want to be seen trying to function in a state of semi-inebriation, to put it mildly.

"We mustered up what we hoped were dignified farewells and, leaving a handful of press, company execs, promoters, agents, and a few disappointed groupies behind, we took off, welcoming the head-clearing air and the opportunity to rehash the day's extraordinary events. We knew we could always catch a cab when we grew tired of staggering around.

"The London fog surpassed its density record that night, making deciphering my little street map impossible. We didn't know or care where we were, anyway. At the corner of a dark narrow alley, we came upon an antique jewelry shop and Adam stopped dead in his tracks so abruptly I could almost hear squealing brakes. His eyes fixed on an opal and diamond pendant resting on a red velvet pedestal revolving sedately in the window. Strategically arranged lighting revealed startling colors hidden in the black stone and permeated each prism mirrored and multiplied in its encircling diamonds, exploding in a spinning, glittering, nearly blinding display. Unmoving, with hands jammed into his bomber jacket pockets, Adam seemed mesmerized by the pendant. Now, since he didn't say anything, of course I didn't say anything either. Standing still in the cloying, chilly mist had become damned uncomfortable, but I knew Adam was either drunker than I thought, or he was unveiling a streak of theretofore unseen certifiable insanity. And, whatever it was, was serious. When he said, 'C'mon, let's go inside,' I was glad to get out of the weather, and curious to see what he was going to do.

"Greeting the chubby, formally attired young guy behind the counter, Adam went straight to the point, saying, 'Good evening. I'd like to purchase the pendant in the window—the black one on a spindle.' My mental double take told me the opal probably cost more than a few bob, but the man did say 'purchase.' I could imagine what a sight we were, two disheveled foreigners, reeking of champagne, one brimming with wild-eyed purpose, and the other, a semi-conscious sidekick, tromping unsteadily into his tidy store out of a foggy night.

"The clerk regarded us through heavily lidded gray slits that telegraphed unflappable British disdain as he carefully removed the necklace from the window, pedestal and all. He held it protectively against his pinstriped vest, displaying it, but at the same time he backed away from the counter as if to keep his treasure out of Adam's reach. A polite cough prefaced his nasal warning, delivered in a kindergarten teacher's condescending chide, 'Ahumpf! It is for sale, sah, but you must understand, it is quite expensive.' R.C.'s dead on impersonation of British snobbery drew smiles from everyone. "I tell you," R.C. continued, "Adam's gaze grew suddenly cold sober and remained focused on the pendant. There was no inflection in his quiet retort, 'That depends on what I consider expensive, doesn't it?'

"The realization that Adam wasn't going to back down easily, caused a wrinkle in the clerk's seamless blanket of smug-aceous cool. Sir Clerk's narrow eyes registered a flicker of surprise, but in a halfbeat's hesitation, he quickly recovered and countered, hauling out his surefire heavyweight shot guaranteed to wipe out all opponents and end the game. With a pompous flourish he announced, 'Yes, of course, Sah. But firstly, the full price is one hundred thousand pounds!' He paused, double chins lifted and thin lips pursed, wearing the confident posture of a champion accustomed to winning many a round in the Un-Professional Clerk's Grinding of the Unknown Axes International Intimidation Tournaments.

"Adam mumbled to himself while reaching inside his jacket. On that note, I was certain he was ready to leave rather than suffer another moment of the clerk's frozen, slightly amused, 'gotcha' expression, but Adam leaned casually against the counter, met the clerk's eyes, and drawled, 'I see, sir, but I feel like I can afford it.'

"At the same time his how-do-you like-me-now-grin came with a profusion of bills, pulled from his pockets, all of which he casually tossed onto the glass. He calculated as he went along, 'OK, that's

$6,500 there, and—nine, oh, yeah, R.C., lend me your cash—thanks man, uh, that's fifteen—I have only about $26,000 American, and 5,000 pounds, but this should cover the difference.' And, raising his pinky finger in the gambler's slow motion 'watch this' flag, he sat his spanking brand new gold card on top of the stack, saying 'You do accept American Express?' I tell you, the clerk swallowed audibly, and I almost fainted. It was plain that Adam's masterful stroke had smooth driven the ball over the fairway and into the eighteenth hole for an impressive hole-in one, but to a commission-only, ex-record hustler like me, the cost of his victory amounted to a king's ransom.

"The clerk eyed the articulate pile and licked the thin line of perspiration that had formed over a quick grimace of his upper lip, which I guessed was supposed to pass for a smiling concession. Still the transaction wasn't complete, for Sir Clerk hadn't finished with us yet. 'Er—that will be quite satisfactory, Sah; however, I am obligated to relate the, how shall I say?—the unusual history of the opal, a history that explains why it has remained in our window for more than eighty years.' That statement commanded our attention, and he knew it. He stopped talking to busy himself blowing invisible dust off the stone while lifting it from its resting place.

"Adam repeated in a near-whisper, 'Eighty years?' The clerk said 'Yes, Sah,' as he ceremoniously and somewhat reluctantly handed the necklace to Adam who held it up and watched it swing and glimmer in the light.

'Actually, Sah, I am obligated to relate the history of the necklace, to every interested customer.' I couldn't have imagined what he was going to say.

'Sah,' he said, 'the story goes that grave robbers sold the pendant to my great uncle when this store first opened in 1893 and, for decades, it was kept in the window as an attention getter, simply to attract customers. My uncle had no intention of selling it and the family held to that tradition after his death. This building had been mercifully spared during the second war's blitz; however, the two wars took an immeasurable toll on the whole country in every way. The last thing on anyone's mind was the acquisition of expensive antique jewelry.

'We managed to buy and sell a few pieces on the black market, but dire hardship forced us to close shop until Hitler was finally defeated. Around the time my father was born, Christmas, 1945, it was, the family had no choice but to go against our late uncle's wishes and offer the necklace up for sale. Straightaway, it was purchased by an American army officer as a wedding gift for his English bride. A fortnight later, the bride's Mum brought it back, tearfully demanding a refund after the officer was blown to Kingdom Come's tiniest fragments when he stepped near a bloody unexploded German bomb. Strange as it seems, no one close by him was injured. The only part of the officer found intact was his right hand, still clutching the pendant, it was. Needless to say, the wife wouldn't go near it.' The clerk added a heavy theatrical sigh as a postscript to the tragic tale.

"When Adam and I, his audience, failed to comment, he shrugged and chattered on while he imprinted the AmEx card, and extracted a black satin box from the cabinet behind him. 'Sah, I would imagine it remains to be seen whether the recipient of this magnificent jewelry will consider herself so fortunate if she learns the truth about it—but, of course, it will be your decision to tell her. I must say that those who inquired after it didn't care how rare and lovely it was; one thing or another about it rather turned them off, so to speak—my family won't believe that someone actually bought it. I remember on one occasion, a customer expressed interest, in spite of the price and its history, but the sale was aborted once the customer detected a trace of a scent about it.'

"Then, Adam lifted the necklace to his nose, breathed in, and closed his eyes briefly, which was hardly necessary; with no identifiable source, a soft, pleasant fragrance had already permeated the air.

'I think the essence is lavender, Sah, as fresh as it was when I was a lad, it tis.'

"For a moment, Adam appeared confused, saying, 'I—I don't believe in curses,' but he quickly recovered. His sudden scowl of displeasure inspired the clerk to conclude his end of the business at a much faster pace, 'You do still wish to purchase it, do you Sah?' Adam's frown deepened. 'Oh, very well,' sighed the clerk, 'at any rate, please keep in mind that it is fully refundable should it prove to be—er—less than satisfactory. Shall I gift wrap it for the lady, Sah?'

"Adam glared at the clerk while it crossed my mind that the day might dawn when Adam would be very glad the opal was refundable, hopefully before he encountered any unexploded bombs—and I didn't envy the giftee, either.

"Nobody could've anticipated what happened next. Adam ignored the box the clerk was holding and slipped the twisted silver chain over his own head. The clerk and I stared at him in confounded surprise. Was he wearing it rather than hand-carry the expensive item through the dark London streets? Or, God forbid, was he buying it for himself? Remember I had just met Adam and I didn't know him very well. It occurred to me the jewelry could've appealed to a hidden poofy streak, you know? Many times after it happened I thought about the weird way Adam found the opal. When I re-played the antique shop incident over in my mind, especially how much at peace he seemed as he let the opal fall under his black turtleneck, his peculiar serenity only added to the mystery. The explanation he stammered made little sense to me then. He said, 'R.C., you can believe this isn't the sort of thing I'd wear ordinarily. See, I just need to keep it close to my heart.'

"Well, I never mentioned it to him again, and since that night the only time the pendant is seen by the public is when he's on stage. I must admit it lends a touch of flash to his performing wardrobe."

As tears rolled freely down Ceeoni's cheeks, R.C. leaned toward Ceeoni and covered her hand with his own. Feeling the tangible power binding all their lives together, she smiled into his understanding eyes, and knew that not even death could diminish the loving life force they shared, one to the other. The thought of grave robbers had given her a chill for a moment, but her newfound awareness and the sharp memories of Clarisse and Elijah's exciting, passionate love warmed the cold away.

x x x

It was 5:30am when Weber brought a fresh pot of steaming Lemon Zinger tea into the living room. Di, carrying her shoes, squeezed past Web on her way out of the doorway, calling, "Smooches, everybody! My lids are droopin'."

"Me, too," Homer echoed.

Stretching and yawning, R.C. said, "Good idea. I'm right behind you. The grand plan is to join Juno and the Ponder Wreckers in the Land of Dreams. It will be daylight in a little while, Ceeoni. You really ought to try to rest if you can. We've all been through a helluva lot in the past few days."

Sleep was next to impossible for her, but she improvised.

"See, I've got plenty of company, Nasrene, Web and Samson are wide awake too, and I'm relaxing, honestly."

She closed her eyes and listened to the closing door and the fading echo of R.C.'s whistled, "Daydream", the haunting Ellington melody vanished into peaceful room sounds: an occasional fireplace crackle, Weber's tinkling spoons and cups for the scented tea, and the faint whooshes Nasrene made sorting through the pages of her journal, all accompanied by the gently splashing waterfall outside. Instead of being soothed by the early morning calm, Ceeoni's emotions took off, speeding into the past, into 1875, into Elijah's arms. Her spirit wandered in circles for what seemed like hours, until Weber's energized voice snatched her back down to earth. Time had lost its way again. A glance at her watch proved that less than five minutes had passed.

"Hey, there's honey and sugar, if anybody's interested," he said. "What's doin' Samson?" Weber took a chair next to Samson and watched him picking through the tapes in Nasrene's bag as if searching for something.

"Oh, I told Nasrene about a kid thing Adam and I used to do, and she agreed we have nothing to lose by checking it out, although it could be another shot in the dark."

"Cool. Do you mind if I hang around?"

"Oh, c'mon Web," Nasrene laughed, "we're all in this same leaky canoe together. Samson, try the one there, that one in your hand, yeah."

Samson installed the cassette into the player and the recorded dissonant notes Adam's fingers had been repeating rang out in the air. Ceeoni was reassured that those notes, or Adam's Song, as she thought of it, was a precursor to his awakening; random neurological spasms of returning memory. Her constant prayer was that no matter what she would have to deal with, when, and if the time came, please God, make Adam wake up sound and in his right mind. Curious, she was about to ask what they were hoping to discover when Nasrene, carrying her journal, rushed to the baby grand and played a few single tones. She struck the same notes Adam played, one at a time, then wrote something down. She signaled for Samson to run the tape backward and forward again.

The sun came up all the way, splashing stark daylight into their tired eyes. Guessing that nobody needed to greet that much of the morning, Ceeoni got up to close the wall of zebra-striped sheers against the brightest sunrise she'd ever seen in her life when Nasrene's whooping, startling scream caught her and everyone else off guard. Weber sat up abruptly, his narrowed eyes alert, the tension in his posture revealing a fleeting glimpse of the wary, cold-blooded fighting machine coiled underneath his mild disposition. But when he saw Nasrene's grin, Weber's features softened into his usual open geniality.

"I've got it! Samson! Baby, you were right!" she yelled. "You were right!"

Strutting to meet her in the center of the room with an elaborate high-five, Samson swept Nasrene off her feet and swung her around. Ceeoni raised her voice to be heard above their laughter. "OK, what? What did you find? Should we call everybody?"

"Right on, yeah, everybody," Weber repeated, reaching for the intercom. "But what am I gonna say?" Samson and Nasrene danced a sliding two-step to the rhythm of Samson's bebop chant, "Splee-deedle-dee-mo—we found the code—we found the code!"

"Code?" Ceeoni and Web asked in unison.

Samson leaned a giggling Nasrene back in an exaggerated formal dip, dropped her onto the soft couch, then pivoted to pull Ceeoni into his waltz without missing a step. "Aha!" he laughed, "A fresh one, waiting in the wings—"

Gesturing with the phone, Weber asked, "Uh, somebody, shall I—?"

"Aw, never mind, Web," Nasrene responded with a dismissing wave. "Might as well let 'em sleep. We can't move on this until we're halfway rested, anyway."

Realizing that Ceeoni wasn't keeping up with his gyrations, Samson stopped dancing, kissed the hand he still held and lisped a not bad Bela Lugosi, "You vant to know vat ve haf concocted in ze la—bora—tory, my beauty? To answer your question, it's about the game I recalled, the game Adam and I devised to exchange fantastic schemes that would rid the universe of bad guys, monsters, and blaaahd-saaahking teachers and vampires!"

She tried to return his teasing smile, but the fact that his face was so like Adam's at that moment increased her anxiety, leaving her motionless. The tink-tink of Nasrene's banging a protesting spoon like a gavel against her cup drew everyone's attention and staunched Ceeoni's ready-to-flow frustrated tears.

"Hear, hear, as in, here we are up to our ears in quite enough suspense, Samson," she chastised, "If you don't hurry up and tell them, I will!"

Reading that the three dead-serious stares focused on his face was probably due to their failure to appreciate the humor in his banter, he quickly apologized.

"Hey, sorry—I guess it was a reaction of relief; you know, the heady thrill of finding a beacon of light penetrating total darkness!" He hesitated a moment and delivered the news in a straight-faced clinical manner contrary to the elation shining in his eyes.

"Anyway, we matched the movement of Adam's fingers to notes in the key of 'C,' and we finally realized that he's playing a message, a message in our old elementary school code."

CHAPTER THIRTY-FIVE

Wednesday's late morning activity centered around mundane conversation and brunch on Homer's patio, but the hushed voices hummed in the distance underneath Ceeoni's noisy, scrambled state of mind. She had gone to her suite for a restless nap around 7am after Samson refused to give in to her plea to divulge the content of what he and Nasrene had discovered. Now, four hours and a steaming shower later, she picked at the honeydew slices on her plate and speculated over the meaning in Adam's Song. Was he identifying a vital clue or the person who had tried to kill him? Or was it something from the past, a message from Elijah? The past and present crashed into each other, overlapping and vying for her attention. She wanted to open the subject as soon as everyone gathered around the table, but Homer perceptively observed, "Well, I take it we won't be cracking the mysterious code until after we've eaten?"

Samson, busy feeding Nasrene a bite of a huge chocolate tipped crimson strawberry, popped the rest into his own mouth and replied with a nodding grin, ignoring the rousing chorus of 'Awwwwws.'

The children finished their meal, chattering with excitement in anticipation of their day in midtown; attending the Center for Puppetry Arts followed by a visit to the King Center. Within seconds, their relatively calm discussion escalated into a shrill squabble over which desserts would be best after dinner at the Atlanta Underground. Immediately, Nanny Ada's eloquent flashing eyes and her singing, musical accent mobilized a moppet kitchen detail, assigning tasks to even the smallest, who refused to comply and only slightly lowered the decibels of her chanted, "Ba-nillwa-Ife-Cweam!" Juno's half of a very effective double-team took over, ending the rebellious tirade that was on its way back up to the top of the child's tiny lungs, "Cweam! Ba-nill-wa-Ife-Cw—"

"Vonna, shussh! You can have any desert you choose, but first, you guys have to soak up some peaceful American educational fun. Hurry along. Now!!"

The way the stair-step Kid Brigade's colorful backpacks bounced in rhythm with their accelerated movements, made Ceeoni smile. The mention of the word 'playhouse' tugged wistfully at her psyche, reminding her how far her concentration had strayed away from her career. Since nearly everything she thought she knew had changed, the Sane Ceeoni's treasured logic was as distant as the moon from the tangle of bizarre unknowns gripping her. That Adam was close to regaining consciousness loomed larger by the hour, and she knew a corner of everyone's mind held the unspoken fear that he could have sustained some form of permanent brain damage.

Another question hovered, towering over her inner landscape like a garish Times Square billboard: If Adam wakes up as he was, what will he think when he hears the tapes of his past life regressions? Of course he'll be awed, as stunned as everyone—but could he be the kind of person who would be shocked into polite, but firm denial? Would any of what had happened there really matter to him, or would it be relegated to party anecdotal material; eerie tidbits saved merely to create titillating chills at social gatherings? What will he do? What will he think? And, when she meets him, the real Adam, not the sensual, romantic Elijah of the past life regressions, or the impossibly Magical Monarch of her dreams, will she care what he thinks?

In the midst of a hail of 'Have-a-good-time' goodbyes, one of the children apparently decided that a hug would be a very good thing. Ceeoni had no idea why she had been chosen, but Carmie, the oldest, spontaneously broke away from the giggling Osh-Kosh-clad crowd Ada and Juno were herding toward the door. She ran back to place chubby arms around Ceeoni's neck, accompanied by a shy cookie-scented kiss on the cheek. Charmed, and more surprised at the full-grown empathy in the solemn baby face, Ceeoni also recognized that a special bond had been sealed, unexpected, yet older than time.

The patio seemed empty after the echoes of the children's laughter faded away. Di and Weber finished refreshing mimosas and the rich custom blend coffee at the same time Juno returned, carrying a fat, once fuzzy Pooh bear sporting a jaunty red bow and a re-sewn ear that she carefully propped up on a black rattan bench.

"Vonna suspected that Teddy wouldn't be properly cared for at home until I promised to feed him and love him and guard him with my life," she said.

All eyes were upon Samson as he handed Weber Nasrene's foldedback journal. "I'm passing our notes around so you can see what the code looks like. An elementary school game Adam and I played appears to be what he, or Elijah, is using to try to get a message through. We found this code in a comic book when Adam was eight and I was about eleven. Damn, if I'd been thinking I'd have instantly realized he was sending a signal, and a simple one, at that. Guess the frantic pace of the last few days obscured my memory. Anyway, each letter of the alphabet corresponds to the C scale, repeated over again until every letter is assigned a musical note, like this," he said, turning the notebook so they could all see:

ALPHABET, top line—CORRESPONDING MUSICAL NOTES, underneath:

ABCDEFG HIJKLMN OPQRSTU VWXYZ
ABCDEFG ABCDEFG ABCDEFG ABCDE

"So, if he played the note A it could mean letters A, H, 0 or V.
"B could mean B, I, P or W.
"C could mean C, J, Q or X.
"D could mean D, K, R or Y.
"E could mean E, L, S or Z.
"F could mean F, M or T.
"G could mean G, N or U.

"We had fun using it a few times to get Adam out of practice early." Samson said. "He would catch my eye and play the notes, E—B—C—D for 'sick.' I'd look over his shoulder to figure out the word and we'd be shown the door as soon as I could muster up a doubled-over case of severe semi-gagging hiccups. See, the first time we tried it Adam had added the statement, 'Oh, he usually throws up!' for good measure. Miss Cora said that for a while she thought I was the sickest child in town. Ha! Why I clearly remember the day we stretched it a bit because my stomach malaise ruse was getting old. He played A C—A—A—A, 'achoo'—at which time my sneezing fit, complete with spraying spittle, caused Miss Cora to throw our little conniving butts out of there, but we had taken note of the funny look in her eye. Crooks, yes, fools, no—due to our healthy respect for Miss Cora Lee's keen nose for rats, we knew it was time to end our short-lived deception."

Looking over Weber's shoulder, R.C. remarked, "Aha, I get it. Now, let's see, the notes Adam's playing are F—B—D—E—B—E—A—C—E. That spells fireplace!"

"Hmm," Samson said, "There's something concerning a fireplace he wants us to see."

"Are you suggesting that Elijah or Adam knows what we're trying to find, and where we can find it?" R.C.'s excitement didn't wait for a reply to his question before he fired off another. "Nasrene, who do you think sent the message?"

"Goodness, this is way out in left field for me. It's true that Adam and Elijah are one, but when Adam is regressed, his fingers stop tapping, so I think Elijah has no awareness of us, or our time. It's more likely that Adam is unconsciously relaying information gleaned from Elijah's memories, using the only method buried in his deeper mind."

Thrilled that Adam was attempting communication, even unconsciously, Ceeoni started to say something about this new development when Homer interrupted her thoughts by banging his fist down hard on the table. An edgy impatience sharpened his louder than usual tones.

"Look, I repeat, I've been over those buildings inch by inch, most of my adult life, and if there's anything meaningful that can be found in a fireplace, I would have found it, wouldn't I? And, if that is what he's saying, we ought to go ask him what it is we're searching for and in which fireplace—"

"Oh Love," Di said, patting Homer's hand, "I don't think there's anyone to ask. After all, Nasrene hasn't gotten a response from Adam after many attempts."

"She's right," Juno agreed, "I think we ought to have a look for ourselves. We'll probably be guided to whatever it is. After all, we've been guided so far!"

Ceeoni spoke immediately, stepping on Juno's trailing remark without thinking, surprised at the firm, sure tone of her own conviction, "We're looking for Miss Letty's hiding place."

"Whoa!" Di said, "You sound so confident, I mean," she lightened the moment by lapsing into half-serious formality, "With all due respect, please allow me to re-phrase R.C.'s most pertinent question. You're saying the hiding place still exists, and Adam is pointing us toward the location?"

Forcing herself to speak slowly, Ceeoni couldn't suppress her enthusiasm as she elaborated, "Look at it this way. It occurred to me how perfectly it fits. The gilded knife tells us the killer has access to a rare antique Spanish artifact, which had to have come from Sybil's dowry, her dowry that was left forgotten in 1849 and hidden with other valuables during the Civil War—ah, but nobody in regression would tell where the 19th century Starcross folk stashed things. We've already established that since the killer found it, the place has got to be where it can be reached, easily. We have quite an advantage because our stalker is certain no one else could possibly be aware of its existence, so he probably didn't see the need to be the least bit careful there. I bet it holds important clues, maybe fingerprints or something else! Now Adam tries to get through to us, and I believe conveying the word 'fireplace' is his answer to Nasrene's request to tell where the secret place lies. Maybe old Elijah put him up to it—."

"Just like in the movies!" Di said, "You know before people had banks they were always hiding valuables, which gave rise to mysterious oddities found in old houses, and fireplaces are a good place to start looking."

"Well, we'll be looking for a while," Homer grumbled, "There are four fireplaces in the theatre and eleven in the house. Plus, they've been thoroughly refurbished. Unless," His bushy eyebrows, knitted into a concentrating frown, failed to cover the dawning uncertainty in his gaze as it shifted to a place above Di's head. Sliding back into her chair, Di crossed her legs, balanced her sleek tan pump on the end of her toe, and stared at him.

"Unless what?" She asked slowly.

When Homer spoke, his shoulders sagged as if the plug had been pulled from the steam engine blowing up his blustery pride. "Well, uh, I do recall the crew bringing an insignificant matter to my attention, er, years ago—" He hesitated again.

Diana's wide eyes blinked slowly and grew wider. "And?"

"It was right at the beginning of the restoration. Somebody made mention that a couple of chimney enclosures seemed a little larger than the others. When I reviewed our measurements, sure enough they were larger, but I'll tell you why I hadn't thought about it until now. For starters, my wildest imaging couldn't have conjured up the murders, the regressions that introduced Miss Letty and the first hand accounts of what happened here in the 19th century, and the possibility of a place hidden inside these walls. I do know that if there's a hollow space behind a chimney wall, and a way to get to it, it would be damned tight. I'm talking a difference in size of maybe only six to eight square feet larger than the rest. Of course, that's large by modern building standards, but in structures old as these that could've been the original builder's deliberate concept, the result of rebuilding or repairs, and you can believe we found evidence of modifications everywhere. Another thing is that it could be because of the planner's mistake; simply leftover space, which isn't uncommon even today. The enclosures seemed rock-solid and sound. We cleaned layers of filth out of those chimneys and forgot about them. It didn't cross my mind to connect that small area with the crimes, even if I knew the extra footage to be hollow, nor would there seem to be a logical tie to the place mentioned in the past life testimonies. A space that small certainly wouldn't provide room for an art collection, Sybil's dowry, a huge supply of canned goods, Talbert's wines and escaping slaves, ya know?"

"Unless," Ceeoni said, "that tiny space, which would be ample for one man, or any number single-file, could conceivably lead to somewhere else. Is that possible?"

"That's a broad 'unless,'" Homer sighed, "and I've already mulled it over, until I asked myself, 'leading to somewhere else where?' Hell, I know for a fact that these chimneys are built on the structures' foundations, extending, of course, all the way to the rooftops."

"Homer," R.C. asked carefully, "What about the attics? Is there space in the attics?"

"Well, yes, but it's only crawlspace, no standing room."

"Is there a way to reach the attics?"

"Uh huh," Homer mumbled, "Drop ladders, one in each building."

R.C. pursued the subject, "I see—by the way, do you recall which chimney enclosures have extra space?"

"Sure I do. There's that big fireplace we uncovered in the Manor dining room, and," in a low tone stripped of all Dinsmore bombast, he added with a sigh, "I think everybody here knows that the other is the double-sided fireplace in Ceeoni's second floor theatre office."

Silence smothered the room as Homer lowered his eyes from all those fixed on him. His downcast head shook from side to side in a slow introspective gesture of coming to grips with bitter truth. Having finally accepted the sobering fact that the killer freely used an area of which he was unaware on the premises of his precious inch-by-inch restoration, he came to terms with the idea that something of such size and significance had the audacity to escape his legendary, eagle-eyed intuition and proud professionalism. Homer's humbled, wounded ego made a rapid recovery. He lifted his hand and kissed one of Di's fingers that had intertwined with his before he lumbered awkwardly to his feet. "OK," he sighed, "although I can't imagine where, the evidence is undeniable. There's a link here somewhere. Let's start at the Manor and see if we can discover the slasher's ways and means."

x x x

R.C., Juno and Samson were the first to head for the front door. Weber caught the keys Homer tossed in his direction. "Pull the Grey Ghost around, Web. We're right behind you."

Waiting for Di to locate her other Jimmy Choo that had somehow made its way under the far end of the table, Nasrene and Ceeoni steadied Di as she hurriedly wriggled her foot into the prized shoe, from a hot new designer she'd discovered.

"So up to the yucky old attic we go, creeping closer to unlocking sinister secrets known only to—" Di's voice dropped to a melodramatic tremble, "the Phantom of the Starcross Theatre," followed by her oddly accurate James Brown growl, "Hit Me!"

Ceeoni retorted, "Look out now, did I hear you say phantom? So why not Phantom-ette, or Phantom-ella? I mean, really, who can forget the perp was probably a girl the last time?" They followed Homer, who phoned while on the move, checking briefly with the Starcross Lakes' contractor, the security company, and Kevin at the restaurant. His next call to Jake raised his end of the conversation to levels high enough for the neighbors to hear,

"Oh man?! Don't tell me the insurance people won't be out 'til Friday! Damn! Every day is putting us further behind. Oh, hell yeah! I know how they are. Just make sure their list of damages matches ours, and not the other way around. Please don't overlook a single item. We can't half-step and let those slicksters get over too much on us. If anything comes up, contact Ceeoni or me."

He answered the jangle that began the instant he stuffed the phone back into his pocket. "Dinsmore! Hey, Nurse Evelyn! He did? We're on our way!" Walking faster, Homer shouted over his shoulder as he swept past the group that had reached the foyer while he was on the phone.

"Whoops! Change of plan. Our attic expedition has to wait. We need to get to the hospital instead. Seems that Nurse Evelyn saw Adam's eyelashes flutter a few times and she thinks some up-close-and personal encouragement might bring him around."

En route to the hospital, a surprise drizzling rain fell from a slate gray sky, confirming Atlanta's reputation for erratic weather. Still, the snarled traffic didn't slow Homer, who weaved around gridlock to pull under Crawford Long's valet parking awning in record time. After informing the nurses' station of their intent to spend a private hour of meditation, they signed in and rearranged containers of flowers and plants to make room for all the chairs.

Watching Adam for any slight movement, Ceeoni noticed that only the fingers of his left hand tapped their persistent coded tattoo on the coverlet. To her eyes, he appeared unchanged.

At R.C.'s signal, Samson dimmed the lights, transforming the room into a charcoal shadowed oasis, layered with the stark hues of a 40's black and white film. R.C. clicked on the latest Delayno recording of Clifton Davis' song that was made famous by Michael Jackson, "Never Can Say Goodbye." Ceeoni's vivid imagination created an outrageously old fashioned romantic fantasy; a blurred image of an anonymous rider in black, galloping in slow motion on a shining black horse across the moonlit movie-scape of her mind. Through a clouded mist, the rider spun the horse around, dismounted and walked slowly toward her just as R.C.'s flat, matter-of-fact statement abruptly shattered Ceeoni's crystal vision.

"Yo, chief," he said. "I really need your input concerning these matters," and he proceeded to tick off several logistical business concerns, as fragments of Ceeoni's imaginary desert rendezvous evaporated with each dry detail. He concluded with a nod to Juno who took over, reading a rave review of the CD, written by disc jockey Jay Edwards of Clark Atlanta University's WCLK jazz radio station. Samson's reading of the CD's rave reviews from "Jazz Times" and "Downbeat" magazines followed, but Adam didn't stir.

"Looks like none of this is getting through to him," Weber said.

"Yeah," Juno agreed, "Nasrene, why don't you have a go before someone comes in?" Without hesitation, Nasrene scooted her chair closer to Adam, set up her tape recorder and spoke the awakening suggestions. As always, Adam didn't respond. She tried again before switching to the regression mode, at which time Adam's fingers ceased their motion, tacitly announcing that another presence was poised to relive a pertinent part of a past reality.

CHAPTER THIRTY-SIX

"What is your name?" Nasrene asked softly. The sadness in the deep voice reply fell like a teardrop in Ceeoni's heart.

'Elijah. Elijah Starcross.'

"Where are you?"

He was having difficulty articulating what he wanted to say. His lips moved, but no sound came forth.

Nasrene reinforced the relaxation suggestions, then repeated, "Elijah? Where are you?"

'I'm—in Geneva. Yes. Switzerland.'

"What is the date?"

'February, 1877.'

Elijah frowned slightly as if trying to understand his own words. 'I wrote to Clarisse every day. For the first few months I made up reasons why I'd received no replies to my letters. Soon, the pain set in, and the constant throbbing ache grew sharper until it became unbearable. My only surcease of sorrow was the music in which I sought refuge. My concert performances were sold out. Concentration on my work gave me a bit of respite, but every night as the last musical strain dissipated, the anguish in my spirit swelled anew. I wondered if I had assumed too much. Had she experienced second thoughts? Had she envisioned the prospect of a lifetime with me as a daunting task? Phineas' words drummed in my head, measuring the seconds of my waking hours and restless nights, repeating, 'Lijah, she may not wanna be down heah in da slave cabin wif us.' I tried to prepare myself for the worst, but the images clamoring for my attention were all too horrible to contemplate.

'I spent days composing what I hoped was an informal, lighthearted note to Wayne Starcross regarding mundane business affairs, and, reluctant to divulge the nature and depth of my heart's anxiety, I mentioned that I hadn't received correspondence from Starcross and I hoped that everyone there was well.

'Spring of 1876 turned into summer and then fall, but still there was no reply from Wayne, Avajay, Phineas or my dear love, Clarisse. I was worried, frantic, tortured by my sense of foreboding and helpless frustration. Sound sleep eluded me, and food was unappetizing. I was told that audiences were enchanted by my passionate performances, but if there was a true scintillating quality in my work, it was born of the pain that was my constant companion. My expensive new wardrobe became loose, as if cut a size too large, but my thinner frame and the haunted eyes staring from my mirror did nothing to dissuade attractive admirers from dispatching various and sundry invitations, to which I declined with one prepared plausible excuse or another.

'Close to Christmas, a packet from Wayne Starcross arrived, containing a thorough Starcross annual financial report and his abject apology for his inability to answer my letter sooner. He explained that his family had been stricken with a relentless fever that by God's grace, all survived. He stated that before receiving my message, his son had attended a Thanksgiving celebration at Starcross and found his cousins, Clarisse and Talbert, along with the entire household, in fine health and spirits. He politely offered the rationale that letters from Starcross hadn't reached me possibly due to the unreliable mail delivery. I kept Wayne's letter with me and read it again and again. It alleviated my most morbid speculations over my loved ones' safety, but his news was proof, the dreaded affirmation of my deepest fear—Clarisse's rejection. I knew I had to face the obvious. She deliberately hadn't answered my ardent declarations of affection. Grief for lost love, for love that never was, overtook my life. For the first time, I hadn't the will to practice. I spent days and nights bound to my darkened rooms, staring into the fire, feeling my one-sided obsession consuming me with the sickening realization that I had been a dimwitted, love struck fool for believing that she returned my devotion.

'Our last hours together, so exquisite to me, probably meant no more to her than a single night of passion she had later come to regret. The quixotic nature of my memories taunted me. At times I could almost feel her sweet presence and taste our blended tears that still filled my eyes and mouth. Then again, I cursed my heart's incessant search for a reason, knowing that reasons didn't matter. She simply did not love me and, God help me, no force on earth was greater than my love for her. I prayed to be released from the shackles of my torment.

'Despondent, I agreed to remain abroad in order to honor contractual options for return engagements. Adding to my agony was the fact that I hadn't heard from Avajay and Phineas, which in itself was most unusual. Hoping against hope and partially out of habit, I dispatched a note addressed to Clarisse saying that I wouldn't be able to return to America for at least eight months. I asked if she would join me in France, if only for a last goodbye.

'Early in January 1877, I was overjoyed to receive a letter from Starcross. Was it from Clarisse? I didn't recognize the handwriting. My trembling fingers tore at the parchment while imagined streams of possibilities crowded all on top of each other, slowing my feverish struggles to extract the contents of the envelope. When I read the message, my excitement turned into a cold vapor that raised the hair on the back of my neck and vibrated a deafening warning knell in my ears:

Deer elaga. J dou not luv you dou not ivir cume bak tou stercros. Verie trulie yrs. "sined" clares

'I was struck by the fact that every word was misspelled. Was I to believe that a graduate of the University of Paris would misspell her own name? Clarisse couldn't have written that note! I was familiar with Phineas' carefully drawn letters, Avajay's precise script and Talbert's stiff, cramped backhand. This childishly overblown writing was adorned with swirling elaborate curlicues, and odd punctuation, as if the illiterate writer possessed a grand sense of supreme self-importance surpassed only by her ignorance. I naturally thought 'her' because there was only one person at Starcross who fit that description—Roxanne Baldwin.

'Clarisse wouldn't have had Roxanne write a note for her, would she? Oh Hell! Of course not! Anger swept over me, wiping away my confusion of the past months. God's eyes, I'd had enough! I'd never discover what had transpired as long as I remained a world away from Starcross and Clarisse. Until such time as they devise a method to take it away from me, Starcross is mine and, damned if I'm welcome or not, I'm going home!

'My decision to cancel the final half of my extended tour infuriated the theatrical agent, but I ignored the man's ranting in my haste to organize my affairs.

'Tonight, I perform my final European concert before I board the ship bound for Savannah. In my fondest dreams, the silent mail will prove to be some sort of mistake, and Clarisse, as beautiful as a summer morning, will be waiting for me.'

x x x

Elijah had apparently said all he intended to say. He stopped talking and Nasrene eventually applied the usual suggestions. There was no further response except the repetitive movement of Adam's left hand. Ceeoni's nerves were strung so tightly, she didn't feel the tears flowing down her cheeks until Di stuffed a tissue into her hand, whispering,

"You OK?" Ceeoni almost managed a smile as she dabbed her eyes.

Nurse Evelyn's bustling entrance normalized the atmosphere. She turned up the lights and adjusted Adam's IV while maneuvering her large form around chairs and plants. "Well," she said, "Y'all know Doctor says that Mr. Delayno's movements are just neurological spasms, but I don't believe it for a moment. I can feel him tryin' to come back, and that's the truth! It won't be long now!"

Homer stopped at an AutoZone on the way back to the Manor and stashed a box in the trunk accompanied by the explanation, "Equipment."

Ceeoni called up her acquired skill of focusing on the moment, but it had never been quite so difficult to do.

In the Manor foyer, R.C. remarked, "Wow! It feels warm and natural in here again. The last time, something about it made me really anxious to run right back out."

The flashlights they pulled from the Auto-Zone box Weber left on the living room floor were the 'hands-free' variety that strapped on like a harness, with a light at the end of a flexible metal coil. Samson passed around one-size-fits-all overalls that generated gales of snickers and finger pointing. R.C. removed his robe, revealing a surprisingly lean, muscular form. There was room for another person inside Di's pants, and after she rolled the legs way up, the result was hilarious. She glared at Homer, who couldn't suppress it, "Well, whad-da-ya-know, you sure look like—"

"Homer," Di said, "If you say another word, I'm taking these things off this instant!" Homer's wide-eyed response raised his eyebrows and caused more laughter. He swooped her up over his shoulder, while her wadded paper missile missed its mark.

"Shoot," he grumbled. "All I was gonna' say is that it looks like a fat sack of potatoes to me, but damn if it don't throw things while it kicks and screams."

It had been a long time since they'd enjoyed a good, hard laugh, the kind that cleanses the cobwebs and strengthens the spirit for the terrifying unknowns ahead.

All eleven fireplaces were checked: six bedrooms, living room, library, parlor and Rose Room. Extra care was taken when examining the dining room fireplace. Ceeoni remarked that the mantle carving of the family crest, a four-pointed star within a cross, surrounded by intricate designs, made assessment impossible.

"Yeah," Di agreed, "I attempted to twist and turn protruding things like they do in the movies, you know, like when the bookcase opens and all. But nothing moved."

"I think we're going to have to know what we're looking for, "Juno said, "It's like ye olde 'needle in a pile of straw.'"

"Give the little lady a Bingo," R.C. cheered, "and somebody please throw in a haystack!"

Weber was the first to climb the ladder pulled down from the hall ceiling between the kitchen and Rose Room. R.C., Samson and Homer followed. Di had almost reached the top of the ladder when

Homer called back, "Ladies, there's no reason for you to come up. I can tell by the thick dust that nobody's been here. Just like I said, there's no standing room, and the chimney stalls are solid. We're on our way down."

By 3:30pm it was obvious that the attic theory was another dead end, and what Adam's code alluded to wasn't sitting out in plain sight, at least not at the Manor. One by one, everybody took off their overalls and ended up on the living room floor. Ceeoni clasped her hands around her knees and tried to recall the illusive memory picking at the edges of her awareness like the remnant of a vivid dream that had faded, leaving only an all-day trace of itself. Nasrene, ever observant, barged into her concentration. "Cee, is that a heavy weight on your mind?" she asked.

"I keep thinking about Clarisse and Elijah's miscommunication, and there's something floating around my recollection. But when I grab for it, it's gone."

Pulling her tape recorder from her bag Nasrene said, "You know what I believe and you know what I'm about to suggest. The solution always lies in the subconscious; some real answers are usually hidden there. So tell me, are you up for it?"

"Sure," Ceeoni, stifling a yawn, replied, "But can I stay here? The floor is so comfortable."

Everybody settled themselves, as Ceeoni stretched out with her head on a sea foam sofa pillow. The light and dark green decor, against the emerald drapes, created a restful cove away from the blind alleys of her private revolving maze. She closed her eyes to the sound of Nasrene's quiet relaxation suggestions.

CHAPTER THIRTY-SEVEN

Once Ceeoni was regressed, a strained, French-accented half whisper, everyone recognized as Clarisse's, said, 'It is November, 1876, nearly a year since Elijah's departure, and I've received no correspondence from him. I've worried about him incessantly, and cried myself to sleep each night. At first, I thought possibly my words of love overwhelmed him. I began to write friendly chats in the vain hope that he would reply, if he could.

'Early in the year, I timidly took Elijah's Symphony out to exercise, under Phineas' careful supervision. The spirited animal seemed know me and to sense that I was troubled, and was therefore quite gentle with me. Beginning by slowly leading her around the pen, I was encouraged by her tender, friendly nuzzles. Within a few days, I was most gratified when she generously allowed me to be the only other person who could ride her. Wandering the meadows and forests of bright Starcross mornings with Symphony, I could almost feel Elijah beside me; a comfort that began to fade as the weeks wore on.

'I was never free from thoughts of my mother's death. I believed Avajay, Phineas and Elijah had told me everything they knew about that fateful night, but their accounts hadn't answered the questions that had haunted me ever since I could remember. I already knew what Roxanne thought. There was no one else to talk to except my father. I decided to defy the clammy silence between us by boldly seating myself across from him at the dinner table while pretending to ignore his obvious discomfort. A guttural mumble was his response to my cheery, 'Good evening!' My father kept his head down to avoid looking at me.

'Although Roxanne served platters of appealing delights, the combination of her sullen presence coupled with my father's disdain crushed my appetite. Even in the dim candlelight, the purplish cast in what I'd seen of Talbert's haggard, blotchy face alarmed me. I realized that a serious illness could take him from this world before I learned what he knew about my mother's death.

'He and I suffered through the same tense, wordless supper ritual for several evenings before I seized upon what I hoped was an appropriate moment to ask the questions I'd rehearsed. After his last mouthful of dripping gravy-sopped biscuit, and before he reached for the brandied peaches, I blurted, 'Father, I'd like to know about the night my mother—'

'My sentence was interrupted by his contemptuous snort. Keeping his watery eyes averted, he gulped the last of his red wine, wriggled his considerable bulk from the armchair and waddled unsteadily out of the room.

'The nervous frustration I felt turned to anger. Damn it all! What had I done to him? Was it his guilt that made him this way? Had my father killed my mother?

'That night, in a vivid dream, Elijah and my father reached out to me from across a wide, stormy abyss. The distance was great and the darkness so deep I could barely discern their features. The sound of my own weeping thundering in my ears in unison with the furious wind awakened me. Tears streaming, I sat up, wondering what, if anything, could I do? I couldn't reach Elijah or my father. Never before had I felt such a lonely helplessness, not even during the dangerous years of my youth in Paris.

'The next day, fate configured a new path for Talbert Bramwell in an unexpected, and most surprising, fashion. It was my Father's habit to stay out all night, or to sleep late, which is why nobody missed him when he failed to ring for his lunch. Phineas said his horses and carriage had remained in the stable all day. When he wasn't present to greet his regular card party guests, we knew something was wrong.

'Hurrying upstairs, calling his name, we were met by my father's faint reply from the other side of his door,'

'I think I've broken my leg.'

After the men forced the lock, we found Talbert Bramwell, all 500 pounds of him, crumpled on the floor. My father was nattily attired in light brown riding clothes with one bootless foot twisted underneath the other. I couldn't help thinking that his equestrian outfit was pure vanity, for no horse on earth could hold him. He rocked back and forth in pain, 'I've been yelling for help since I tripped,' he croaked, 'but I guess nobody heard me.'

'It took four people to lift him onto the bed. While Phineas went for the doctor, Avajay cut away the torn fabric constricting his right calf, exposing the grotesque sight of bright red flesh, swollen to the circumference of a medium-sized tree trunk. Assuming the party had only moved upstairs to Talbert's rooms, his three friends kept up their jovial conversation while settling into comfortable chairs, waiting for Roxanne to set out food and drink.

'Up until that afternoon, I'd felt that nothing could be done about what Phineas called my Father's 'drankin' sickness.' But a rare opportunity presented itself when the short, wiry doctor completed his efficient ministrations and remarked, 'Talbert, no use my fixing this splint on your leg if some of your, shall we say, excesses aren't curtailed. This break won't heal well enough to support you. As it is, you're going to be laid up for months.'

'Right then and there I announced to everyone, the doctor, Roxanne, Talbert and his associates, that I would be supervising my father's meals. I then signaled for Avajay and Phineas to remove the overloaded trays and bottles of spirits Roxanne was arranging. I ended my speech with the concession, 'Gentlemen, your repast awaits you in the dining room.'

'Now see here!' Talbert roared as he tried to sit up, but it sounded more like a cry of pain. He didn't have the strength to put up much of a fight. As I left the room, taking the last tray with me, I felt cold stares piercing my spine from Talbert, his friends and Roxanne. But that was all they could do, seethe to their hearts' content.

'Phineas attended to Talbert's personal necessities and privately joked that a man has a lot of gall to refuse to look at or speak to someone who's holding his chamber pot and giving him his bath.

'My father's loud protests against his new Spartan regime rumbled down the halls at all hours, but he was my prisoner and I had no intention of backing down. Weeks passed before his frequent tantrums, which had upset the household and sent the maids scurrying, ceased. I stayed away from his rooms, preferring that my presence be felt rather than seen.'

x x x

Clarisse hesitated a moment before continuing her testimony. When she began to speak again, her voice sounded weaker. 'Avajay kept the Starcross Theatre presentations colorful for a consistently appreciative audience, but for me, they were brief distractions, indeed. In truth, I spent the year 1876 immersed in the most excruciating inner pain of my life. In my reflections, the ease in which I had loved Elijah came back to haunt me. The night he left, he'd made me believe he returned my love. But after I received a collection of his current published reviews from Cousin Mary LeBlanc in late summer, I knew I had to become resigned to the fact that he was well and my letters had been ignored. Mary LeBlanc had warned me of cads, men without honour. She'd said they were always irresistibly charming, and as disarming as Elijah had been.

'I took the only desperate, albeit futile, measures I could to try to escape my memories of him. I left Symphony's exercise to the grooms and I locked Elijah's quarters, vowing to never again enter what had once been my favorite place. I couldn't bring myself to tear up Elijah's note that had fallen out of my sleeve the night he departed for his tour, for it was all I had.

'Atlanta had been made state capitol of Georgia in 1868. The process of healing was evident in the new buildings and neighborhoods cropping up. Still, there was grinding poverty, especially among the freed slaves. Their plight brought a lump up in my throat. I felt the need to do something. The first time I added clothing and household goods to Avajay's charity donations, Phineas graced me with a bit of wisdom, 'Ya Grandaddy, Ol' Mistuh Ballwin usta say, if ya ain't givin, ya ain't livin, Miz Risse.'

'One rainy afternoon I sat with Avajay at the library table watching her make a list of supplies for the kitchen. She glanced at me from time to time with an unreadable expression in her dark eyes. After a few minutes she asked, 'My dear, you seem so listless and you've lost weight. Are you well?'

'Yes,' I lied. 'I'm fine.'

'Good,' she said. 'I'll get your cape and you can go with us to the Coach Stop! The fresh air will put some roses in those cheeks.' My refusal fell on deaf ears, rather, ears no longer present, for Avajay had already left the room.

'Riding in the breezy carriage on a damp, nippy day proved to be invigorating. At the Coach Stop I browsed the cluttered general store while Avajay and Phineas supervised the loading of bags and boxes onto a wagon driven by a freed slave. Phineas went to visit with his friends at the stable, giving us time to enjoy a bowl of the Inn's special sweet carrot soup before he returned to collect us. I noticed that there was a loaded wagon following closely behind our carriage as Phineas turned in the opposite direction from Starcross. 'Avajay,' I said, 'This isn't the road home.'

'Radiant in her powder blue bonnet, she waved away my remark, 'Oh, I have another errand. I hope you don't mind.'

'I knew that whether I minded or not wouldn't have made a bit of difference. We bounced along a rough road dotted with burned out structures in a part of town that wasn't sharing in Atlanta's sparkling new growth. Phineas pulled up where a group of children of former slaves were playing in front of a dilapidated building that was barely more than a shack. Avajay answered my unspoken question by explaining proudly, 'This is the Fairchild School!'

'Judging from the enthusiastic hugs that greeted Avajay and Phineas, it was obvious this wasn't their first visit. I counted eighteen youngsters in all, ranging in age from toddlers to young adults, joyfully climbing all over the wagon to help unload flour, sugar, beans, potatoes, oranges and other staples. Their contagious exuberance inspired me to pitch in to lift the other end of a flour sack two giggling little ones were tugging, and I heard myself laugh for the first time in months. The teacher, whose light gray eyes contrasted with her brown skin, attempted in vain to quell their joviality. It crossed my mind that the teacher's eyes, bespeaking her mixed blood, would have classified her as a 'Fancy', a woman with such a feature could fetch a high price in the slave markets of not only the recent past, but in the trade that still flourished in the South's secret brothels. As would I.

'All the way home, and throughout the night, the school and the children's faces disturbed my rest. However, I awakened at daybreak, fully alert, feeling a new, unexpected urgency. Phineas chuckled at my request that he drive me back to Miss Fairchild's. 'Ennytime ya reddy,' he replied.'Vacha say ya would, sholey did!'

'During the trip, Phineas told me that Miss Fairchild's was one of the few private schools for former slaves, all of which struggled to stay open with meager resources. He and Avajay had helped Miss Fairchild establish her school by locating the building, and gathering donated supplies all along. The Federal Freedman's Bureau had only started the arduous process of establishing a system of free public education and major institutions of higher learning for former slaves. Complicating matters in 1876 Georgia, the unwanted reconstruction that specified black representation in congress had been defeated by a deluge of opposition, mayhem, beatings and murder, and sometimes by simply excluding Negro office-seekers from the primaries. Federal troops that had occupied the South, had withdrawn from the Southern states, leaving white supremacy, America's albatross, to reign supreme. The practice of lynching began to spread unchecked, placing former slaves in greater danger.

'Although the Freedman's Bureau supplied some poverty relief, only whites were allowed to open schools and other services. Miss Fairchild, ignoring the ostracism for those whites who assisted blacks, was thoroughly dedicated to her school's survival, against all the odds.

'That day, the tall, blonde Miss Fairchild gripped my hand in a warm greeting, her tearful response to my offer to help began a great quest for me. 'Miss Starcross, she said, 'Any assistance we receive will be greatly appreciated.'

'My energetic days working at the school accomplished much and made my lonely life bearable. By Thanksgiving, Miss Fairchild held the deed to a building that had new paint, three new rooms including a kitchen, reinforced walls and roof, three new iron stoves, up-to-date sanitary facilities, desks, cots, books, and adequate funds to accommodate twenty new students. I acknowledged their gratitude but, in fact, everyone, especially the beautiful children at the Fairchild School, gave me far more than I could ever have given them.

'Roxanne faded into the background of my daily life. Avajay kept a close eye on her, making certain that she, the maids and my father's now infrequent guests, hadn't been bribed into smuggling brandy and sweets to Talbert's rooms.

'Talbert's recovery was slow and painful. At first it appeared that my father's leg would never heal, but after a while, I was told he began to hobble about with a cane. I hadn't seen him in the months since the night of his accident until this evening, when Phineas and I found my father sitting on the front porch upon our return from Miss Fairchild's. Phineas took the carriage to the stable, while I approached the steps with my head down and my eyes averted.

'In the fading sunset, a glance at his face showed me that his features had emerged from their casing of fat, revealing a silver-haired version of the handsome counterfeit colonel in the stairway painting. I recalled that Phineas, who had assisted the tailor's fittings for Talbert's new wardrobe, said that over 200 pounds had melted from his tall frame.

'I made up my mind to be politely civil rather than allow his silent intimidation to ensnare me into a state of confused limbo. I nodded in his direction as I stepped up on the porch. My plan was to pass him quickly, but my father quietly called my name. I hesitated, still without looking at him. 'May I have a word with you?' he asked, 'Please?' It was the nicest thing I'd ever heard him say. I took a deep breath and sat in the chair opposite his. The flicker of a single candle from the parlor window reflected in the eyes that held mine. Silence followed. But this wasn't our usual silence. This silence was different. He was different. Facing him, I sat perfectly still, fearing that any movement might break our new, fragile connection.'

'Clarisse,' he began, 'it's time you knew. After I broke my leg, I had to look at some things that I've spent years trying not to see. I don't expect you to understand because I don't understand it myself. It's true, I married your Mother for her money, for selfish reasons. Our wedding allowed me to go against everything my family stood for by turning Starcross into a slave plantation. While I was looking for the joy in getting what I thought I wanted, I fell in love with

Sybil—' He looked away and added, 'madly in love. Lord help me, the day hasn't dawned that I haven't missed her.' I knew from the surprising confession and the tears filling his eyes, that I was meeting my father for the first time.

'Your mother was a good woman who loved me and wanted you with all her heart. I was hard-headed, stupidly cruel and demanding most of the time, and no bigger God-damned fool ever lived.

'Well, that night in the stable, everything happened so fast! Roxanne was down there half-naked. I always thought her brains were in the wrong place, but for once, her ranting rang true, tearing the scab off the festering hatred that had eaten at me all my life. I'm not trying to hide behind piss poor excuses, but until ten months ago, I hadn't known a sober minute since I was fifteen. That night, I was drunk as a hoot owl and mad at the world, as usual. I didn't realize I'd never have another chance to tell my wife how much I loved her.' Talbert shook his shoulders as if trying to shake off his past.

'Suddenly, the fire in the stable was all around us. I think at that point something fell on me. When I came to myself, I found Sybil on the floor. I remember before she lost consciousness she kept screaming something. Because of all the noise and the ringing in my ears, I didn't understand her. I'll always be grateful to Avajay for saving your life. Still, I had to let you go. I guess losing Sybil was too much for me. I spent years wanting to die, unable to be anything to anybody. I wasn't considerate of another living soul, but by the grace of God, and it was only by the grace of God, I never killed anyone. The only time I gave a thought for someone other than my asinine self was that night in the stable when I would've given my life to save you and Sybil.

'Clarisse, to answer your question, that's all I know of your Mother's death. My prayer is that one day you'll forgive me my shortcomings.' Without turning away, he wiped across his eyes with the back of his hand. I sat there stunned, so much so that I could only stare at him. With a bit of difficulty, my father got to his feet. Straightening from a quick formal bow, he said stiffly, 'Your kind indulgence honors me, Miss Bramwell, and although I don't deserve it, I'm proud that you bear my name.' Clarisse sniffed and said no more.

Nasrene waited several minutes before giving Ceeoni the suggestions that she would awaken, free from pain, fully refreshed, remembering everything. Ceeoni sat up, smiling. "No need to ask how you feel," Nasrene said, "that just made my day!"

"Way to go, Ceeoni!" Homer yelled, "Although that didn't lead us any closer to Roxanne's present identity."

"Rightly so," Ceeoni mused, "but in spite of that fact and Clarisse's distress, forgiveness is such a beautiful thing."

The usual quiet prevailed in the Manor's green living room, while outside, straining to comprehend what could be seen through a sliver in the drapery closing, a dark figure blended into the porch shadows. The ominous presence remained still and undetected until an on-foot security patrol, including a pair of attack German shepherds, noisily approached from around the bend in the lane. Swiftly, without making a sound, the prowler abandoned the window before the patrol was close enough to discern movement on the porch.

CHAPTER THIRTY-EIGHT

Ceeoni, lulled by the living room's dimly lit, subdued atmosphere, didn't miss recognizing a glance between Homer and Nasrene as a page straight out of Miss Letty's and Avajay's private lexicon. A plan was brewing.

Paying closer attention, Ceeoni realized that Homer was putting some wheels in motion when he said, "Say, Weber, have you ever had a deja vu experience, or any psychic visions?"

"I've had a mild sense of having been somewhere I knew I'd never been, but that's about all, why?"

"Hmm—what I mean is, well, you haven't said much about past life regression one way or the other. Web, would you, you know—"

"Oh, I see where this is going," Weber laughed, "Homer you know me well enough to know that I'm intrigued. This is all new to me, but I think I'd like to see what a regression would reveal."

"No time like the present," Nasrene said.

"Yep," Homer agreed, "As long as we get to the theatre to approve Jake's fabric samples before he leaves."

Weber's next statement was tinged with an edge of apprehension, "I've been wondering if I had a less than positive role in this pattern."

"If the shoe fits, Dog!" Homer teased.

"C'mon Homer," Di said, "You remember how nervous you felt when you were first regressed."

Weber smiled his gentle smile, "That's OK—I guess he's forgotten how he got his butt brought to him back in grade school." He stretched his mauve silken-clad form out on the sofa, "Go ahead, Nasrene, I can handle this."

All attention became focused on Weber and Nasrene as Nasrene installed a fresh tape into the recorder. Eyes closed, he responded very quickly to the relaxation suggestions. In answer to her first question,

'What is your name?' an enthusiastic rich contralto replied proudly, 'Mrs. Sybil Baldwin Bramwell!'

"Where are you?"

'In my bed. Oh! Oh heavens! It's nearly 3am and that Talbert's gone again! He keeps such late hours,' she sighed. 'He was sound asleep right here just a little while ago! Now, where could he be?'

"What year is it?"

'1849. October. We're newly married and I'm expecting our first baby any day! I've had terrible cramps lately. Doctor will be here first thing in the morning to see after me.' Sybil rattled on as if chatting with an old friend, 'My Talbert can be such a grump sometimes, but I understand him, I really do. I've seen a part of him that very few have witnessed, and I know he'll be better after our baby is born. Men are that way, you know. My father said something might be wrong with my baby, but I believe this little one will be perfect. Oh fudge! There goes another cramp! I can't wait to get my teeny weeny waist back. I'll bet Mister Talbert will spend more nights at home then! Right now, I have something very important to tell him. Guess I'll have to brave that devilish staircase again to try to find him. My husband needs to know about this!'

"You have something to tell him?"

'Oh, yes! Yes! You won't believe what I saw tonight!'

"What's that?"

'Well, it was about two hours ago! I didn't want to ring for the maid and disturb Talbert's rest, so I went down to fill my water pitcher myself. I tell you, while I was standing at the kitchen cistern, I heard somebody making an effort to be quiet, coming in the back door. I doused my candle and hid in the broom closet. Peeking out in the darkness, I could see Miss Letty and Avajay escorting slaves into the kitchen! Slaves! Into my kitchen! There was a woman, a buck and two small children. I recognize that buck! He's the one that helps Phineas out in the stable sometime. He's from the Birdlaw Plantation! They had no candles! And then, I saw Roxanne sneaking along right behind them! I had to see where they were going! I followed them to see, but they all seemed to disappear in the direction of the Dining Room! Hmmph! And all the time Talbert thought his Mother was afraid of the slaves! Oh ho! Now I know! I know! She didn't want to own slaves because she's really an abolitionist! And they hid somewhere, too! Miss Letty helped them hide somewhere around here! Why, that's against all the laws of our land!' Sybil rubbed her stomach, saying, 'Getting back upstairs was so tiring, I slipped back into bed quietly so as not to disturb Talbert. He can be such a bear sometimes! Well, I guess I dozed off until just now, and wouldn't you know that Talbert must have gone out while I was taking that little nap. Now where are my slippers?

'I don't hear him in the water closet. Now where could he be? I want to tell him what I saw! Imagine, Miss Letty and her maid setting our slaves free! I'll see to it that my husband puts a stop to those shenanigans! Ouch! Another cramp! That one was a little closer than the last. Doctor says that's a good sign. I'm going to find Talbert this instant!

'Uh, now that I'm outside, uh, I hear voices! Voices? Oh! It's Talbert! He's out here yelling at—Roxanne?! Feels like these gravel rocks are digging clean through my itsy bitsy shoes! Talbert! What are you two doing down here, in the stable! Together! Roxanne! Why are you screeching like that? Whose baby? Talbert! Spain! My Mother was from Spain! I, OhGod, ohGod, ohGod!—Oh! Fire! Roxanne, stop! Roxanne, why are you hitting me?! Talbert! Roxanne she, she hit me! Oh, Talbert, our baby! Save our baby! Don't cry! Oh, don't cry, darling, please don't cry—'

Nasrene didn't hesitate to start the pain reduction and awakening suggestions as quickly as she could, although Weber kicked and gripped his stomach as he struggled to get up. Nasrene finally calmed him.

"Weber, it's OK, it's OK!"

Clearly upset, but clearly moved, Weber looked from one face to another.

"You alright, Web?" Homer asked.

"Yeah, I'm fine," he answered slowly, wiping his eyes. "You know, I can't fully describe it. What bothered Sybil most was her husband's indifference and the fact that Miss Letty was freeing slaves. Now that I've been there, I understand what you meant. I feel like I've discovered eternity, but it was all completely familiar, it was all a part of me that had always been apart of me, there was nothing foreign."

Homer patted him on the back, "We know, Web. The past life experience is a big leap into the unknown, but once you get over the jolt, it's like finding an old photo album, filled with pictures of yourself and your life, from a hundred years ago."

"Now we know that Talbert didn't kill Sybil," R.C. said, "and it appears that Roxanne is still killing for revenge."

"It's true our unreasonable compulsions and hatreds come with us from past lives," Nasrene interjected, "I've heard of vendettas like Roxanne's continuing on through many lifetimes. Her hatred is so blind, she probably doesn't understand why she's doing what she's doing."

"Well," Samson offered as he opened a bottle of Clos du Bois Merlot, "Your premise helps me understand the weird justifications people have for the atrocious deeds they commit, but actually, most legal cases involve desires far more complicated than what I'm guessing is Roxanne's motivation. I said that to say that I believe Roxanne has another cause underlying her rampage. It was her reason in the 19th century, and it's her reason now."

"So Samson," Homer asked, "What do you think she wants?"

"Homer, my friend, she wants Starcross! That's why Basil Cassidy was murdered. He negotiated the sale of it to Adam, and Adam was almost killed twice because he bought it. And the detectives had to go because they were getting close to the truth. I think Ceeoni's brakes were sabotaged and Minette was clobbered simply to throw the investigation off."

"Aw," Homer protested, "that doesn't make sense. How could anybody get Starcross if Adam dies?" His voice spat out the word, 'get.'

"That's the golden question that hopefully we'll answer when we find out who she is," Samson replied.

Weber's slow drawl cut to the heart of a point to be considered, "Seems to me Homer, since she trashed the theatre and torched one of your estates, you can't afford to be complacent. You sold it to Adam, which means, my brother, you're on her list too."

x x x

I'm not scheduled to meet Jake until 8pm," Homer said, "why don't we all walk to the theatre? There's a worn path through the woods and we could all use the exercise."

"I hate exercise," Di groaned.

"C'mon girl!" he coaxed, "All we've done is sleepwalk and be scared!"

"Yeah, Di," Ceeoni said, "It won't hurt us to walk two and a half blocks."

"Actually, the way through the woods is shorter," Homer added, "After we've checked the fabric samples and the attics and fireplaces, we can come back here for the car, grab a bite, then head for the hospital."

"Sounds like a plan," R.C. said, but Di had reservations, "What about the slasher?"

"Di-Di," Homer answered, "There are six two-man security teams, each with two attack dogs on the premises at all times, and remember, there's eight of us."

"Well, alright Sweetheart, but s'pose she stops slashin' and goes to shootin'?"

"I think most murderers rarely change their M.O.," Samson offered, seriously, "They choose the method of killing based upon complicated personal reasons, that is, of course, unless they reach the point of desperation."

Ceeoni suspected, as did everyone else, that the 'Starcross Slasher' had already passed the point of desperation.

Outside the Manor's kitchen door, a full moon infused the thickening fog with moving shadows. Ceeoni was conscious of the fact that this was the doorway that Sybil spoke of the night she watched the escaping Birdlaw slaves sneaking through the kitchen, on the night of the stable fire. But where did they go from there? Did they go to somewhere in the Manor? But where?

Homer led the way into the dark stand of pines covering sinister patches of misty underbrush, reminiscent of classic horror movies.

Keeping their flashlights down on the smooth path, they were abruptly halted halfway to the theatre by R.C.'s yelp of joyous discovery.

"Wow!" He picked something shiny off the ground. "Oh, cool! Oh màn! I've wondered where this was! Adam was found near here! Guess it fell off when he was attacked. This is an omen! I know it!"

Samson turned his flashlight on the glittering object R.C. held up by its double-twisted chain. Everyone gathered to look closely at R.C.'s find, as the opal and diamonds spun in a lazy, sparkling circle.

"Bean-gao!" Juno whispered.

R.C. ceremoniously slipped the chain over Ceeoni's head, "Here, Cee, keep this for him. Recognize it?"

Unable to speak, she nodded, inhaling a trace of lavender that took her all the way back to the night in the rosewood bed where Clarisse knelt before Elijah, placing the pendant around his neck. She held the opal as the scene replayed in her mind like a slide show.

"Adam hasn't been without this since he bought it," R.C. said, "Call me superstitious, but I believe if anything will help him, this is it. Homer?"

"I'm on it, R.C. The theatre will wait until tomorrow!" Already turning back toward the car, Homer dialed his phone.

"Let's upgrade to a faster mode of transpo. I've gotta notify Jake."

"It's so good to finally sit," Di gasped, as she climbed into the car. "Walkin' shoes these are not. I can't wait to get that pendant to Adam. Cee, do you think he'll react?"

Outwardly, she answered with a shrug, while her fingers gripped the pendant around her neck, and the sane self inside chased hyperactive butterflies that refused to be still.

Starting the engine, Homer asked R.C. to call and check on Adam, but R.C.'s call to the hospital only served to postpone the urgency of the moment. Nurse Evelyn's side of the conversation bounced around the car at full volume.

"Mr. D.'s doing great, but he underwent a battery of tests earlier and Doctor has prohibited any visitors until morning." R.C. pulled the phone away from his ear and looked at it as if it had bitten him.

"Mr. Ponder, are you there? Mr. Ponder?!" Her voice lowered to a stage whisper, still loud enough for everyone to hear, "Oh, OK, OK! You're wearin' me down! Twice today I noticed some changes. I'm not sure when, but the fingers on that left hand have stopped moving. Then, late afternoon, I saw his closed eyes twitch as if he were in the REM stage, you know, like he was dreaming or something. It's against Doctor's orders, but I'll be the only nurse on the late shift after eleven tonight. You guys won't be stopped if you come through the emergency entrance. Anytime after eleven!"

"Look out, Juno!" R.C. laughed as he broke the connection, "That girl is after my own heart."

"Well now," Weber suggested, "since we've got to wait until after eleven, and since we have time on our hands, why don't we venture south of the border to savor Senor Weber's fabulous Mexican fantasy, which is almost ready and is in need of just a pinch of love, if you ladies will join me in Homer's kitchen. It was for tomorrow, but what better time than now?"

Di, Nasrene, Ceeoni and Juno sipped Sangria while admiring Weber's artistic culinary flair, evident in his tastefully coordinated blending of ingredients. Soon, spicy scents of cumin, cilantro, onions and peppers wafted through the house, inspiring the kitchen crew to enthusiastically sample the platters they arranged and carried to the living room. Steaming homemade corn tortillas, salsa, seasoned rice, refried beans, shrimp fajitas, chicken quesadillas, enchiladas and perfect guacamole were topped off with the coldest, creamiest flan Ceeoni had ever tasted. Weber had outdone himself again.

R.C. and Juno excused themselves to read bedtime stories upstairs. Leaving the others to the after-dinner brandy veg-out before the fire, Ceeoni cleared the dishes with Nasrene. After searching her mind for a fresh approach to the regressions, she mentioned her idea.

"Nasrene, do you think Miss Letty would talk to you about the secret place if she thought she was talking to Avajay?"

"Hey! That's a thought, and frankly, I don't have a clue. But we have to remember that a deliberate, purposeful energy is at work here, causing it all, and guiding our way. It's only 9:30, we can certainly try!"

CHAPTER THIRTY-NINE

Samson called Juno on the intercom, asking if they would like to witness Homer's experimental past life regression. R.C. and Juno returned from saying 'Goodnight' to their children, while Homer situated himself on the sofa. Tension electrified the air. Everyone, hoping for a breakthrough, settled down to observe.

At the completion of the relaxation and regression sequence, Nasrene said,

"This is Avajay. What is your name?"

'Leticia Starcross Bramwell,' Homer answered in Miss Letty's voice.

"What year is it?"

'Why Avajay, you know the year is 1849!'

"Uh, yes, Letty, the secret place was a wonderful idea, wasn't it?

Miss Letty chuckled softly, 'Ah Yes, Avajay, your design worked out just the way you said it would.'

Again, Miss Letty's unexpected reply caused Nasrene a moment's hesitation. 'Uh, yes—yes—'

'But Avajay, we shouldn't discuss this now, there are others present,' Miss Letty cautioned in a lowered tone.

"Letty, these people are our friends, sympathetic to our cause. They are here to help us. It is necessary that you relate everything in detail about our secret place, so that your memory of our tasks will be well understood. You must tell everything. It is safe." After a long pause, Miss Letty asked, 'Of this you are certain?'

"Quite so"

'Because I have implicit trust in your judgment, I will comply.'

With lofty pride, Miss Letty explained, 'By 1822, Starcross had one of the new indoor kitchens, built to satisfy those who might be curious about our construction. At the same time, remember, you and Thurman supervised the building of one large chamber with a connecting tunnel system, all of it located fifteen feet underground, underneath the Manor's foundation.

"Chambers—tunnels—underneath the foundation," Nasrene repeated, "I'm trying to recall the way it was built. You know my memory is not as good as it was."

'Well,' Avajay said, 'I could never forget! Hidden narrow stair-steps lead to the entrances to the secret place. One entrance is through the Manor fireplace. The other is through the back room fireplace, upstairs in the church. Of course, one can enter freely through the hidden outdoor outlets, if the locations are known, which made it easy to hide slaves. Both underground tunnels connect at a point halfway between the Manor and church in the Starcross Forest, where there is a concealed outlet. The longer tunnel continues from the church for half-mile to other outlets deep in the woods. The system allows us secret access to the Manor, the church and the outside, at will. No one ever suspected!

'Avajay, sent by God, is what Thurman said of your design and the unusual method of execution that your instructions provided. Our friends in the Abolitionists' Movement were notified that we had a concealed station when it was completed, and the slaves who built it, used it to go north.

'Oh, I am so afraid! In all the years since the secret place was built, nobody except our group knew of its existence until tonight. Now, everything we've worked for all these years could be ruined! Avajay, you said you would figure out what to do before morning. You always know what to do!'

Nasrene improvised her response. "Yes, yes, I will have the solution—before morning. Now Letty, it is important that you continue with your version of the shocking incident, so our friends will understand."

'Yes.' Letty began to talk faster, 'As you know, our schedule earlier this evening could no longer be postponed. Too much and too many lives always depends on our keeping a reliable timetable!

To save time, Phineas stood watch in the front, while we brought the family from the Birdlaw Plantation through the kitchen, rather than our usual route through the more secluded solarium door. The family had already crisscrossed the creek several times to confuse the slave hunters' hounds.

'Although they were all blindfolded and it was pitch black dark, the two children never whimpered. They had a long way to go before reaching the next station near the Tennessee border. Remember Avajay? After we sent them on their way through the tunnels with torches, instructions, maps and provisions, we came back upstairs for our usual cup of sassafras tea. That's when we made the sickening discovery that Roxanne had been following our every move—down to the hidden chamber—she knows! Oh, Avajay! She knows! Remember how she was half-dressed in one of Sybil's sheer dressing gowns, and all puffed up with her forbidden revelation—remember how she confronted us? 'I saw you!' she screamed. 'You're setting Talbert's slaves free! I saw your hiding place, and I know how you've been getting down there, and I'm telling Talbert right now, and you'll be sorry!' She slammed the kitchen door as she headed out into the night. 'You'll be really sorry, sorry, sor—ry—you slave-loving bitches will be sooo Goddamn sorry!!' Her hollow laughter echoed in the air long after she was gone.' Oh, Avajay, every word she screamed is burned in my memory!'

Tears formed in the corners of Homer's eyes as Miss Letty said, 'I'm terribly afraid for all of those who stand to be killed because of this hate-filled 12-year-old. Avajay, she knows our secret!' Homer's hands wrung in a familiar gesture of frustration.

Nasrene reduced Miss Letty's pain, and asked, "Letty, can you tell us what happened next?"

'Well, I went up to bed and took a sleeping draught like you said, but the noise woke me up.'

"What noise?"

Letty's voice wavered, as she sobbed, 'The fire! Oh! It was horrible! Horses screaming, people shouting—I heard the popping and snapping of a great crackling inferno! Sparks, glowing like burning snow, blew from the direction of the stable and floated against my windowpane. Before I finished dressing, the frantic noises outside began to subside and the fiery reflections on my walls were fading. I was pulling on my shawl when you knocked on my door a few minutes ago. 'Heaven forbid, Avajay! Your bloody, sooty appearance alarmed me! There you stood, holding a squirming blue bundle—I'll never forget what you said—' Smiling happily, Miss Letty didn't finish her thought until Nasrene prompted her.

"But what did I say, Dear?" Nasrene asked.

'Why, you know what you said, you said, 'Letty, this is Clarisse Starcross Bramwell, who must leave us for a while, but we will all meet again. You told me not to fret about Roxanne Baldwin knowing the truth about our hiding place. She will not be believed when she tells our secret. As always, God has provided the perfect solutions. Tomorrow, everything will be understood, and everything is fine. Avajay, you always know what to do.'

Homer then held out his arms, 'I'll take her now,' Miss Letty whispered. Homer's arms swayed gently as if rocking a baby, as Miss Letty sang a lullaby in a soft tuneful voice:

> Oh can ye sew cushions? And can ye sew sheets?
> And can ye sing baa la loo, when the wind breaks?
>   Oh hee and baa birdie
>   Oh hee and baa lamb,
>   Oh hee and baa birdie,
>   My bonnie wee lamb—

Nasrene gently awakened Homer after Miss Letty refused to say anything else. Samson helped him sit up, "That singing was alright, Homes," he laughed.

Homer appeared totally perplexed, "How about that? Me singing! And I can't carry a tune in a bucket with a lid on it."

"Well now", Di kissed Homer's forehead, "Miss Letty's lovely song is captured on tape for posterity." A round of applause was met with Homer's theatrical bow.

"Nasrene," Samson asked, "what about the critical missing piece? With all of Miss Letty's wealth of info, we still don't know how to gain entrance into the tunnels. But Roxanne found out, and so did our killer."

"Oh!" Nasrene's hand flew to her mouth, "I got all wrapped up in the excitement and neglected to ask Miss Letty."

"In that case," Homer asked, "can we try to contact Miss Letty again?" He was already stretching out on the sofa. Nasrene turned on her tape recorder and repeated the relaxation and regression suggestions several times, but despite Nasrene's best efforts, Homer didn't respond.

"Well," Nasrene sighed, "Seems that Miss Letty isn't coming back, at least, not right now."

After a few moments of contemplative silence Ceeoni asked,

"Nasrene, would a regression similar to the last one be effective?"

"What do you mean?"

"Would Avajay return and divulge more if she thought she was talking to Clarisse? I was thinking that I could say that I'm Clarisse. Avajay may tell Clarisse the way to enter the secret place."

"Miss Cee, you missed your calling, you've got a natural ability!" Nasrene gave Ceeoni the hastily scribbled instructions, and composed herself in the spot on the sofa Homer had vacated. Ceeoni, trying not to rattle her paper, began to apply the suggestions.

Once Nasrene was relaxed, Ceeoni said, "This is Clarisse, what is your name?"

Right away, they recognized Avajay's familiar tones,

'Hello Clarisse!'

'Hello Avajay,' Ceeoni answered cordially.

"What is the year?"

'Clarisse, have you forgotten? The year is 1877!'

Surprised, Ceeoni didn't read the next statement until Di tapped her arm.

"Avajay, we need to help Elijah. It is necessary that I learn how to reach the secret place underneath the Manor."

'Did you lose your earrings and the pendant Miss Letty gave you?'

"I still have them."

'Then use them!'

"Use them?"

'Yes. Miss Letty told you that your opals are magic, remember?'

"Yes, she did, but how—?"

'The magic in your opals is that they are keys. The earrings belonged to Miss Letty, the pendant hung on Mr. Bramwell's watch fob, and the matching ring was mine. My ring was lost around the time of Miss Letty's death, but that didn't present a problem, because nobody goes down there to the hiding place anymore. We never told you, but those tunnels saved our lives and countless others, and helped souls go free, before, during and after the war.'

"How are the keys used?" Ceeoni asked.

'Any one of the opals fits into the center of the crossed star family crest on the fireplace mantle—but only in the dining room and in the room that is now Elijah's quarters over the theatre. With one turn to the right, the fireplace back wall opens, exposing the stairs.

'But Clarisse, there is a pressing matter that I must discuss with you. I could see that you tried to keep your love for Elijah secret, still I guessed the truth and shared your pain and grief when I knew you'd received no letters from him. Phineas and I hadn't received any correspondence from Elijah either, and we were worried sick. But Wayne Starcross brought wonderful news when he arrived for Talbert's Christmas Ball. Wayne's news made Christmas, 1876 one of the best Holidays of my life! Wayne said that he'd received a letter from Elijah! Clarisse, he also said that Elijah's note stated that he hadn't heard from anyone at Starcross! My Dear Child, now it is the end of March, 1877, and Elijah has been away since December, 1875, and all during that time, we haven't received Elijah's letters, and he never received ours!

'Wayne said that Elijah wondered if we were all well. Right away I knew Roxanne Baldwin had managed to sabotage the mail. I decided to search for the letters that I guessed Roxanne's demented mind would save, considering them souvenirs of her twisted triumph. Weeks passed before I felt strong enough to put my plan in action.

'I waited until Roxanne went to the Coach Stop for her daily shopping trip, before I searched her rooms. I looked under the rugs, the mattress, and even in the water closet, and found nothing. But she left two important clues—my lost opal ring was in her jewelry box. I remembered that she had followed us to the tunnels on the night of the stable fire—the night you were born, and she saw how we used the ring. Obviously, she stole it later on. And there was another thing—hidden in a dresser drawer—was one of Sybil's artifacts from Spain, a jewel-handled stiletto! Sybil had a set of two identical stilettos. I knew Sybil's things had been stored with other valuables in the secret place before the war. Right away, I knew Roxanne had been going down to our secret place, and I knew that is where she probably hid the stolen letters. I left the opal ring and the stiletto where I'd found them to keep Roxanne from becoming suspicious.

'Clarisse, I hurried to your suite and grabbed up the silver box containing your earrings, in order to gain entrance to the hidden chamber. One day, when I was certain that Roxanne was gone, I put my plan in action. Because of my advanced years, and the lit candle I carried, the trip down the narrow steps was difficult. I had to stop half way down to rest. It was dark, but the chamber was dry and cool. There were new torches and flints in the box at the bottom of the stairs, attesting to recent visits, but I didn't dare use one.

'The dim candlelight played on Miss Letty's and Sybil's things, dresses, artifacts and jewelry, laid out as if in use. I noticed a box of unopened letters. I chose one addressed to you, from Elijah, and another that had been addressed to the Milledgevillle Asylum from Miss Letty, both of which I stuffed into my pocket. Miss Letty's inquiry to the Asylum never got there! Dear Jesus, how did Roxanne do this? Miss Letty wrote that letter the day after Roxanne returned to Starcross.

'The light from my torch fell on a stack of placards bearing a passable rendering of Roxanne's face. Cold stark fear crawled up the back of my neck as I read:

-WANTED January 25, 1873-
Roxanne Baldwin Age: 36
Hair: Blonde Eyes: Light Brown
Escaped, Milledgeville Lunatic Asylum
Wanted for murder of her husband Dr. Kenneth Pendleton by strangulation, and for the stabbing murders of Gwenyth and Sara Pendleton, two hospital attendants and three patients.

This fugitive is criminally insane and is considered extremely dangerous. If whereabouts are known, please contact:
The Georgia State Lunatic Asylum,
Milledgeville, Georgia'

Avajay said that standing there in the dark, she realized the great danger that had threatened them all at Starcross, every day. Roxanne was a killer and Roxanne hated Clarisse. It was especially dangerous for Clarisse. Avajay had always suspected that the night Roxanne knew Clarisse was born alive, her survival was so galling to Roxanne, she was unable to maintain even her usual partial mask of sanity. Terrified, Avajay said that she struggled to get back upstairs before Roxanne came home.

When Avajay finally reached the library where she could slow her hammering heart and collect her thoughts, she decided not to tell anyone of Roxanne's crimes until she could notify the proper authorities. She wanted to give Elijah's letter to Clarisse before going to the Coach Stop to arrange for Roxanne's capture. Roxanne had gotten away with murder for a long time, but now she would have to answer for what she had done.

An hour later, Clarisse arrived home from the Fairchild School and Avajay called to her, saying she had a surprise. Avajay said it was one of the greatest joys of her life to know that Clarisse's and Elijah's love had defied the onslaught of interference and deception, and that nothing could ever change that.

Clarisse's face lit up as she read the address on the letter Avajay handed her. 'Avajay!' she cried, 'It's really from him!' Tears of sheer happiness spilled down her cheeks. 'Where did you get this??' Clarisse's trembling fingers carefully extracted the onionskin paper from its envelope.

'Suffice to say that Elijah has written you dozens of letters, in spite of the fact that he never received any from you.'

'What? Oh! Oh God! Oh no! What must he think? Why didn't he receive my letters? Oh, Avajay, he doesn't know how I feel about him! Oh, listen to this! I'm sure he won't mind if I read it to you.

My Dearest Love,

It is raining here again, and I always get lonely when it rains.

As I said in yesterday's missive, every concert on this tour is sold out.

I hope and pray that all is well there, although I still haven't received a letter from you.

There is much political unrest in Europe these days, but I believe that if you do decide to visit, you will be safe. We can talk about everything as we did during those precious, unforgettable days at Starcross. Please meet me in Paris, in the spring.

Loving you with all my heart, forever,

E.

'Avajay! He's got to hear from me, right away. I'll go to France! But first, I'll post the letter I've started to him—I'll post it myself! Oh, Avajay, my goodness! I've got to get ready! I'll ask Phineas to start the preparations, and I need to borrow the big sea trunk in Elijah's quarters? I can probably get everything in it.'

'Certainly, Clarisse, I'm so happy you decided to go.'

'I want to see if that trunk is as large as I remember. Walk with me? I'll go get our wraps!' She almost ran out of the room.

Exhausted, Avajay said she sank into the wing chair to wait for Clarisse with her head resting in her hands. Her glance down at her little dusty shoes revealed a horrifying sight. The vanilla Aubusson rug underfoot was smudged with gray marks, footprints she'd tracked from the tunnel, making a trail straight from the dining room fireplace to her library chair; a tell-tale map written on Miss Letty's lovely pastel carpets. Avajay summoned a maid to immediately remove the stains, before Roxanne saw the evidence of Avajay's visit to the secret place.

'Here's your shawl,' Clarisse said, as she placed the garment over Avajay's shoulders. 'March in Georgia brings pneumonia weather.'

Clarisse's joviality was contagious. Avajay found herself smiling as they walked quickly along the dogwood-lined lane. The early blooming branches overlapped overhead, creating a white sanctuary of sumptuous fragile blossoms. At this time of year, she always had the sensation she'd invaded a place that was not on this earth; an untouched world made of flowers.

Up in Elijah's quarters, they pulled the trunk away from the wall, and opened it. It was almost empty except for a few sheets of music and some blue sari material that Avajay had intended to use, but never did.

'Elijah stored his scores in this trunk until he needed them.' Avajay remarked, as she pushed the fabric aside. 'Look at this feature, Clarisse. We used to hide valuables in here when Letty and Thurman and I were running around Europe, see? You pull this brad, here.'

Clarisse was delighted to see the trunk's false bottom pop up.

'Ha!' she laughed, 'You can put your things in that space and no one will ever know!''

Avajay took the silver box from her pocket and gave it to Clarisse,

'Here's something to start with,' she said.

'My earrings! Of course! That's exactly where I'll keep them!' She placed the silver box down in the false bottom and closed the cover, 'It fits perfectly! And that's a fat little box!'

Their laughter masked the sound of footsteps moving up behind them. They didn't hear the swish of the fireplace poker. Neither did they anticipate the swift, fatal blows impacting the backs of their heads—first Clarisse, then Avajay, both skulls smashed within a fraction of a second. Avajay said she lived a while longer, long enough to watch Roxanne raise the glittering jeweled knife high in the air. Through excruciating pain, fading vision and spraying blood, she saw Roxanne's slack mouth twisted into a wet smile of total ecstasy. From a great distance, Avajay could faintly hear the savage guttural grunts and heaving breaths Roxanne uttered with every quick thrust, as she stabbed and slashed at Clarisse's already dead body, over and over again.

Nasrene bolted upright, screaming, "Clarisse! Clarisse—I'm sorry! I'm so—I'm—"

Immediately, Ceeoni applied the pain reduction and awakening suggestions.

Shaken, everyone tried to overcome the stunned emotions they felt as Samson rushed to take Nasrene, still dazed and trembling, tenderly into his arms.

CHAPTER FORTY

Avajay's testimony left a dense aura of sadness, but Nasrene wouldn't let it linger. Ready to forge ahead, she unwound herself from Samson's embrace, asking, "Ceeoni, are you feeling OK enough to proceed to the hidden chamber?"

"I'm very ready," she replied, "no matter where I am, it's going to take time for the vision of Clarisse and Avajay's murder to wear off. And, I know we're all eager to see what's down in the secret place."

Just then, Homer picked up his ringing phone.

Nurse Evelyn's excited voice exploded,

"I thought y'all were coming to the hospital?"

"Yeah, well, we are, but something else came up."

"Mr. Homer, wait'll you hear this! I supervised Mr. D.'s bath today and I could tell there's something going on. Make no mistake, his shoulders and facial muscles moved slightly, you could say deliberately, and it was more than a little old twitch. I've got a feeling you guys oughtta get to the hospital right away!"

"Bingo!" R.C. shouted, "I'm anxious to get that pendant back around his neck."

"But we just made some real progress here!" Homer grumbled.

"We can't be in two places at once," Di said as she tossed Homer's jacket over his arm, "To quote that great philosopher, Homer Dinsmore, 'We gotta go where the Spirit moves us!'" Weber opted to stay home from the hospital trip rather than squeeze into the already crowded car.

They reached Adam's room close to midnight. Arranging chairs and plants with R.C., Ceeoni felt a subtle stirring underneath the antiseptic, floral calm surrounding the still figure in the bed.

Empathetic Di felt it too. She nudged Ceeoni's elbow with the old 'check this out' signal from their long-past partying days. Ceeoni nodded in silent agreement.

"I know he's glad to see you," Nurse Evelyn whispered as she left the room, "Stay as long as you like."

As soon as everyone was settled, R.C. beckoned to Ceeoni,

"Cee, you ought to be the one to place the pendant on him," he said softly. Ceeoni stood at bedside, and took the pendant off. She kept it warm in her palm until Samson, on the other side of the bed, tenderly lifted Adam's head, allowing her to slip the twisted chain around his neck. Enjoying the touch of his skin, she moved slowly, as if in a dream from a forgotten memory. She dropped the opal down inside the neck of his light blue hospital garment against his skin. Everyone paid close attention, watching for a slight reaction, but Adam didn't move.

"You know, I can feel him coming closer," Nasrene said, "Why don't I try? I'm thinking maybe he didn't respond to his lucky pendant because Elijah has more to say. The last time we heard from him, he'd cancelled all his concerts and was on his way to Georgia, driven by the peculiar note he'd received; the warning message that he knew could not have been written by Clarisse."

Nasrene didn't wait for agreement, she simply scooted her chair closer, switched on the recorder and began the hypnosis process, finishing with, "You are now going back to a time affecting your life now."

To Nasrene's question, "What is your name?" His answer sounded hoarse with fatigue,

'Elijah Starcross.'

The year was 1877. Disembarking in Savannah, and anxious to get to Starcross, Elijah said that he hired a horse and sent his cases by the slower coach. The chestnut stallion he rode for the last horse exchange slowed after turning into the Starcross Lane, as if knowing that the final throes of blooming dogwoods was still a sight to behold. The winding, tree-lined lane wore a carpet of fading clumps of yellowing and brownish blossoms. He shook off the feeling of dread that came over him when he passed the theatre billboard where a 'Closed' sign was posted in place of the usual list of coming attractions.

Rounding the bend in the lane, he realized that the tall slender stranger chatting easily with Phineas while they both brushed down a fine gray mare was Talbert Bramwell. Talbert nodded curtly in Elijah's direction and led the mare away while Phineas, nearly as vigorous as ever, quickly strode the few yards to greet him with a bear-hug,

'Lijah, oh, Son, iss, iss so good ta see ya—'

'Phineas! How are you?' Elijah could feel that something was wrong.

Phineas' face fell and his voice cracked, 'Ah—Lijah, iss Miss Risse and Vacha—dey missin! Dey jis up 'n vaniss two day ago, in da middel o' da nigh, wifou uh trace! Ah ben worryn, worryn mysef sick!' He wiped away freely flowing tears.

Elijah couldn't reply right away. 'What?'

'Rokann say dey gon ta Urripp, but Lijah, ya knows dem! It ain lak dem ta go off lak dat! Ah teeng iss serriss. Rokann ackin mo funny! 'N all Mis Risse n Vacha close 'n all da trunks 'n bags, cases, wagons, carrage 'n hosses is still heah! If 'n dey lef, dey lef walkin wif nuttin but da close on dey backs!' Elijah said he tried to blink back his own hot tears. His mouth felt stiff, and the earth was no longer beneath his feet. He felt himself floating in a blinding red nightmare, far from what he thought of as reality. Hot and cold and numb, he listened to Phineas saying that he and Talbert had searched every acre of the Starcross property over and over again, and they'd inquired at the Coach Stop, the Coach Stop Inn, the drivers, and the neighbors, and no one had seen anything.

Elijah followed Phineas into the stable where, with an equine wheeze and several rearing kicks to her stall, Symphony heralded her happiness to see him.

Elijah was bone tired, but he saddled her and spoke to her in their special language. She nuzzled his cheek, telling him with her articulate eyes that she'd missed him and how healing a hard ride with an old friend could be. He let her have her way in a fast gallop, across the lane, through the forest and out into the open meadow. Everything he saw around him held ghosts; memories of a lifetime of love and pain clung to the lush scenery that flew past his tear-filled eyes.

Phineas waited at the stable to take the reins when man and horse, dripping with sweat, returned.

'I sweah, Lijah, dat hoss smartuh den mos peeples. Ah lets da skule chirren ride huh 'n she be gennel a uh lam, but don let noboduh else teeng dey gon git up on huh back—sepn Miss Risse!'

Elijah followed Phineas into the kitchen, where he poured out two glasses of his sweet, scuppernong wine, made in the shed every year for anybody who didn't mind staggering around for a few hours. But the wine had no effect on his anxiety.

As they sat at the table, drinking Phineas' potent, pink concoction, Phineas told Elijah about Talbert's accident, and how 'Miss Risse 'n Jeezis fix im up.' Elijah enjoyed the story of the Fairchild School, and Clarisse's role in rebuilding it. Then Phineas asked a question that tore at Elijah's heart. He said,

'Ah knows Vacha, 'n me, we ben real hurt wondern—n' Miss Risse, she ben lookin righ poley—wall, we wuz wondern, Lijah, Son, why din cha write?'

His torn expression showed the pain of asking a question he'd hoped Elijah would explain on his own.

'But Phineas! I did write! I wrote to her five, six letters a week, and I wrote to you and Avajay at least once a week. Phineas, I never received a single letter from you, Avajay or Clarisse!'

The two men stared at each other with dawning certainty. No amount of words could describe the sinking sensation that turned each man's world to total darkness at that moment.

'Roxanne took our letters!' Elijah said evenly, his eyes never leaving his old friend's.

Elijah had always suspected that Phineas was in love with Avajay, and Phineas' next words confirmed the fact,

'Ya lucky ya gots suthin' she lef fo ya. Ah jis has memrees.' He reached into his shirt pocket and handed Elijah a letter Clarisse hadn't had the opportunity to complete.

'Ah foun dis 'n huh room.'

The pale linen paper contained only a few sentences, but Clarisse's words of love would sustain Elijah and give him solace in his grief, until he ran toward the Light a year later in London. He had never seen her writing before. He read her beautiful measured script:

My Dear Love,

There! My nightly prayers are finished—as ever, I ask that God keep his protection around you until we are together again. I sorrow because I have no word from you, and that there is no child

Propelled by the agony of anger and regret, Elijah bounded from his chair, 'Phineas! Where are the torches? We've got to look again!' He recalled Roxanne's great physical strength at the age of twelve. He always knew she had been capable of murder, but he'd assumed the rage in her unbalanced mind had settled over the years. Now, his fears for Clarisse and Avajay were wrapped up in his memories of Roxanne's mindless cruelty.

'Look,' he said. 'I know we don't have solid proof yet, but I'm seeing to it that Roxanne will be leaving Starcross tomorrow, and the authorities will be properly notified of our plan to keep track of her movements. If something has happened to Clarisse and Avajay, I'll arrange for a Pinkerton agent to follow Roxanne wherever she goes, until her crimes are brought to justice.' He berated himself for not sending her away before he went to Europe.

In spite of Phineas' sad pronouncement, 'Dey ain heah—we don ben ovah dis tree time!' Elijah insisted on searching the grounds and buildings again. Although he didn't expect to get sensible answers from Roxanne, he nevertheless banged on her door in pure frustration, but she didn't respond. He would have continued banging on Roxanne's door, but Phineas drew him gently aside, restraining his futile pounding,

'She ain gwine nowheah. She don teeng we knows.' 'You're right,' Elijah replied, 'but you can rest assured she's leaving Starcross at first light, if I have to carry her out of here myself!'

Rita Graham

x x x

Elijah's pocket watch had a little chime that rang twice before he finally gave up and slowly walked the shadowed lane to his quarters. The moon shone in the window of his rooms that were undisturbed, just as he'd left them, except for Miss Letty's old sea trunk, sitting away from its place against the wall, atop the Persian rug. The rug belonged on the other side of his bed, but he barely noticed. Distracted by the atmosphere that was saturated with Clarisse's presence, he even detected a faint scent of lavender drifting up from the sheets on the neatly made bed. Thoughts of what was, and what might have been, danced before his eyes as he undressed down to his black breeches. The more he thought of his loved ones' disappearance, the stolen mail and Roxanne, the more bitterly furious he became. He buried his face in the pillow and vowed again to put everything he could to rights before he returned to England. Exhausted, he fell into a hazy, fitful half-sleep wherein all of his bad dreams came true.

His night visions turned into an erotic fantasy, as the voluptuous, real woman in bed beside him began to grind her sweating body tightly against him. 'Clarisse—' he mumbled. He rolled over, still not fully awake, ready to seek more of her. He'd had such delusions night after night, but tonight, the familiar high-pitched titter caused him to awaken, every nerve alert, feeling the shock of ice replacing the warm blood running through his veins. 'What the hell??' he shouted. 'How did you get in here?' He was certain he'd turned the lock. When they were children, she'd had the advantage of being older, stronger and almost a mistress, who had to be dutifully obeyed. But times had changed. Now, he was six-foot, three inches tall and well over two hundred pounds, and this woman had taken his life away. Roxanne was unprepared for the speed and strength of purpose with which he threw one foot over the side of the bed to brace himself while easily locking both of her arms in a vise grip.

'I heard you outside my door!' she screamed, 'You're going to send me away! You—'

'Where are they?!!—' He shook her, hard, demanding 'Dammit, Roxanne, where are they?'

'What do you want with Clarisse? I'm a white woman! I can make you happy! I can really, really please you!' The force of his fury tempted him to break every bone in her body, and he knew he could. There was superior strength in his hands and arms from years of working in the fields and playing the piano, and the torment in his heart made him stronger. He wanted to kill her. Right then and there.

'Where are they?!' he yelled again, while jerking her nearly nude form out of his bed. Her kicking, spitting, and attempts to bite him didn't phase him. None of her frantic struggles made any difference. He heard something metallic drop to the floor.

'My ring!' she screeched. 'Let me get my ring! I've dropped my ring! You're nothing but a slave, a god-damn black slave! I'll have you whipped! My ring—!' He ignored her ranting and continued to drag her out of his room and down the wooden staircase to the theatre's back door. His plan was to take her to the Manor and have her restrained as a part of the official investigation of Clarisse and Avajay's disappearance.

He opened the door to the cold outside as Talbert Bramwell dismounted the gray mare. Elijah knew how they must have appeared; both of them breathing hard from exertion; him stripped down to his breeches, and Roxanne, wearing only a pale yellow dressing gown tied loosely at the waist. He was about to explain when Roxanne stopped kicking, shook her head and smoothed the stringy hair out of her eyes, to find Talbert standing a few feet away. Her long hatred for him spewed out in trills of hysterical laughter.

'Oho, Talbert, you stupid son of a bitch! I won! Damn you! I killed them all!'

Talbert stared at her with contempt before asking quietly, 'Roxanne, what in God's name have you done?'

Her mood switched instantly to condescending sarcasm. 'Why, I just told you, you stupid fool! I killed them all!'

'Let her go,' Talbert said quietly.

Knowing he could always catch her if she tried to run, Elijah released his hold on her. With a pious lift of her chin, she bragged, 'I put them where they can never come back! I got rid of stupid Sybil, and her black baby, Clar-isse, and that stupid lackey, Avajay, and I put a pillow over that bitch, Miss Letty's face, too! Now they're gone, and they can't bother me anymore!'

Pulling a pistol from his waistband, Talbert said, as if talking to himself in a flat monotone, 'You murdered my mother, my wife, and my daughter.' Elijah heard the stark suffering in the barely audible statement, but Roxanne's elation took wings.

'Oh, yes I did!' she screeched, 'And you should've been there!' She laughed so hard, tears squeezed out of her colorless eyes. 'You should've seen how they died! The blood sprayed all over, and—'

Quickly, Talbert raised the weapon and growled, 'Stand clear, Elijah!' Without aiming, he almost casually shot her between the eyes, as if he were eliminating a wild animal. Watching her body spiral and slump to the ground, Elijah was reminded of the final eradication of a deadly plague.

'I came to leave this for you.' Talbert said as he handed Elijah a newspaper. 'Go back to bed, I'll finish up—' he said, in a low, flat tone. Elijah turned away, but Talbert's voice lowered to a rumbling whisper, fell on the air between them, 'I don't know how, but you know she won.'

Elijah said he went upstairs, built a fire, and poured himself a brandy with shaking hands before he read what Talbert had given him. It was the latest edition of the local paper, dated that day, stating that one Roxanne Baldwin Pendleton, wanted on several counts of murder, had been traced to the Atlanta area. The front page article listed various victims: her husband, Dr. Kenneth Pendleton, Dr. Pendleton's two sisters, staff and patients from the Milledgeville Asylum, as well as an innkeeper and a mail coach driver. The news was accompanied by a drawing of her face. With that, Elijah ended his testimony. He sighed deeply and would not say anything more.

Nasrene gave Adam the familiar suggestions.

x x x

Ceeoni leaned forward with her eyes closed, breathing deeply, hoping her torn emotions would dissipate quickly. Several moments passed before anyone spoke.

"Nasrene," Juno asked, "Why is it that Ceeoni and Adam are now more like they were in that life? I mean the rest of us are totally different from the way we were then."

"You know how the Bible speaks of choice? It's the Soul's choice. The body and life situations are the Soul's expression. They are the way we've chosen, or the lessons we've chosen, on the path to loving God, ourselves, each other and the earth, which is the only path to a life filled with Light."

After sitting with Adam for nearly two hours and he didn't rally, Homer said, "Well, maybe tonight's not the night, but, my friends, the secret place awaits! We might as well explore!" In the usual noisy shuffling of chairs, Samson patted his brother's shoulder, "See ya in the AM, Bro—" he murmured.

Juno leaned over and kissed Adam's cheek, and last of all, Ceeoni lightly kissed his warm lips. Suddenly, Adam's strong fingers reached out and quickly trapped her wrist in a steely vise-like grip. His eyes, open, dark, mysterious, and unreadable searched her face. She started, trying instinctively to step back, but his silent intensity held her fast.

"Say something," he demanded.

"W—what?" Ceeoni's breath caught in her throat.

"Please—say anything—"

"I—uh, we, well—" she began, but Adam, smiling, quickly sat up, reaching for her, pulling her body into the circle of his arms. He enfolded her, nestling his face against her heart.

Slightly dizzy, and thoroughly lost in what seemed unreal, her spirit came to rest, as if she and Adam had never been apart. She heard everybody gathering around them, heard Juno's quiet sobs, heard Adam breathing in spasms of pent up emotion, and felt her own pulse pound with endless joy. She closed her eyes, let the tears fall and wondered if she'd ever grow accustomed to the way he made her feel.

"I had to hear your voice, to be sure," Adam said, as they finally broke apart. Samson, Juno and R.C. hovered, all talking and hugging him at once. Adam correctly identified Di, and Nasrene, who hung back behind the others. Adam turned to Homer,

"I always looked forward to hearing you coming down the hall, because I knew we were getting closer to understanding the reasons we're here together. And Diana, you're as beautiful as your voice. Nasrene, thank you for teaching that truth lies underneath what appears to be chaos. After the regressions, I'd have known you anywhere. You have Avajay's eyes." He was quiet for a moment, and then he added, "Let me begin by saying that I did as I was told. I remember everything. I remember every single thing."

Stunned silence followed Adam's statement, as each person stared at him, absorbing what he'd just said.

CHAPTER FORTY-ONE

Di drove the Rolls, while Homer, R.C., Samson and Adam followed in a taxi. Nurse Evelyn had grudgingly assisted them with disconnecting Adam from his IV, while fussing over Adam's self-styled hospital discharge against doctor's orders. "Y'all should just wait till the doctor okays this in the morning!" she protested for about the twentieth time in as many minutes, as the elevator doors closed on a load of smiling people.

Weber met them and saw to it that the flashlights, overalls, his snacks, herb tea and cocktails were available. The lively discourse in the Homer's living room revolved around the past five days, and all they'd learned collectively about Roxanne, and 19th century Starcross. They concluded that Elijah never learned of Miss Letty's covert activities, unless he discovered it on his own, and Talbert would never have believed that his mother and Avajay were able to free his slaves without leaving a trace, unless he saw it with his own eyes.

Leaning back in his chair, Adam, in black sweater and sleek black pants, stretched his long legs, "First of all, I'm anxious to hear those tapes. There in the hospital, I realized that because of the regressions, and all of you, I am not the same man who went in." He gazed at Ceeoni, who sat across from him, trying to appear calm.

"Getting back to our dilemma," Adam said, "I wish I could identify my attacker, but I didn't see what blindsided me. I'd sat down with a sandwich before Saturday's concert, and when I went to investigate a noise in the kitchen, I was attacked from behind. I woke up in what appeared to be a dark tunnel. My stab wounds were bleeding and painful. I kept waking up and passing out, as I crawled along. It seemed like it took me hours to climb to the top of a long narrow stone stairway. With all the limited strength I could muster, I pushed at the wooden slab that was weighted on the topside. After many tries, it opened and I fell out in a spot under a thicket. I crawled a few more yards in a wooded area before I passed out again. The next thing I knew, I was in the hospital bed, unable to move, but I felt completely at ease. For the first time in my life, my usual vague anxiety was gone. I didn't recognize myself, and I didn't care. Eventually I realized that the Force keeping me in that state wanted me to be aware of everything going on in the regressions and all around me."

"Apparently," Samson said, "since the Slasher hasn't left a single clue, without the info we've gathered, the crimes here would remain unsolved forever. Adam, we think we're getting closer to the whole truth."

"And," R.C. added, "since Roxanne's motives were from a past life, and there're no clues—piecing together a motive couldn't happen."

"So Roxanne's present identity is still a secret, huh?" Adam asked.
"Well, for a time," Ceeoni said, "I thought I might be Roxanne, until I dug up the courage to consent to a regression."

"Ceeoni, I knew who you were the moment you touched me. I don't know how I knew, but when your fingers met mine, I felt as if a solid block of ice inside me had melted away. Warmth exploded like thousands of fireworks lighting the lonely corners of my heart. The prayers of my childhood came to my remembrance, and I said them all. I needed a piano, and I needed to see what was in your eyes."

Ceeoni had stopped trying to think. Her new little voice whispered, 'You lost faith in his love in 1875. This is no time to have a faint heart.'

"Another thing that shocked us," Homer said, "was your poisoned IV bottle."

"Yeah, that was the one time I felt frustrated at not being able to move, I knew there was something weird about the way that unusual person approached my bed. I knew she wasn't one of my nurses, and I could feel her anxiety in her heavy breathing, along with her nervous fiddling with the bottle. She ran out of the room when footsteps came close. Today, I heard the doctor say that the substance wasn't detectable in blood tests, but there was enough thallium nitrate in that bottle to kill a lot of people."

"So, it was a woman?" Homer asked.

"Come to think of it, I'm not sure. I said it was a woman because she pulled the covers down to my knees, and was actually raising the robe I was wearing. I mean, would a man have—"

"Damn!" Homer commented.

"That," Samson concluded, "is an understatement!"

"Oh Homer," Weber said, "Minette called and wants me to pick her up at Hartsfield at 2:45am."

"Minette?"

"Yeah, Adam," Homer replied, "She manages the Starcross Restaurant."

Adam sat up in his chair, "She came to the hospital, right?"

Homer nodded. A slight frown passed over Adam's features.

"There was something odd about her voice—an unusual undertone, but I can't quite put my finger on it."

"Do you think she's Roxanne?" Di asked.

"Minette couldn't be Roxanne," Weber said, "Minette's been in New York."

"Or—maybe she just wants everyone to think she was in New York. His voice emphasized the word, 'think'. I'm familiar with those tricks, from way back in my bachelor days," R.C. laughed, as Juno punched his shoulder.

"Why don't we try to entice her into allowing Nasrene to regress her, and see what happens?" Di suggested.

"Web, if you'll bring her back to Homer's under the pretense of having a homecoming party for Adam, we'll make a run for it."

"Good idea, Di," R.C. agreed, "Meanwhile, I feel like the secret place has got to contain real clues. I'm taking Adam's pendant and going down there if have to go by myself."

"I've got a little over an hour before I have to get Minette," Weber said. "I'm right behind you."

They all slipped the overalls back on, the legs of which proved to be a bit short for Adam, who joked, "Steve Urkel, eat your heart out!"

445

In the dining room, Adam's pendant fit perfectly into the center of the family crest star, and with one turn, the back wall of the fireplace slid out of sight, exposing dark, narrow, steep steps. Their flashlights lit up the walls. They waited in a huddle at the bottom of the steps until Homer, leading the way, pushed open the door to the right. At the same time they heard a 'whoosh' and the loud slam of a door closing from somewhere behind the rows of shelves across the large chamber. R.C., Samson and Weber took off through that door in hot pursuit, their flashlights rebounding madly as they maneuvered around the rare artifacts and nineteenth century paintings scattered about. Homer moved to follow, but Di held onto his shirt sleeve,

"Oh, no you don't! We need somebody to stay with us in this spooky place!"

Nasrene played her light slowly, methodically covering the area, bit by bit. They gasped in unison at the illuminated figure of Detective David Saxon, unconscious on the floor. Di immediately dialed 911. From what they could see, David's clothes were covered with blood and he appeared to have a nasty wound on his temple, but he was breathing.

The men returned empty-handed. They hadn't caught anybody.

"It's true we don't know our way around down here," Samson fumed, "but we were either too slow, or she has somewhere else to hide."

"Yeah," R.C. shook his head in disbelief, "She just freakin disappeared!"

Then he saw the body on the floor, "Oh, wow! David!" He went over and examined the detective closely. "Well, he's still alive, we shouldn't touch him. Somebody will be here in a few minutes. Moving him is out of the question."

Weber went upstairs to greet the paramedics while the others explored the large chamber below. Ceeoni was very glad that Adam was behind her when her light fell on two skeletons with flowing hair, propped up against each other in a corner. She shivered as she recognized Avajay's silvery braid, falling over her clavicle bone, and patches of Claisse's thick ringlets clinging to parts of her skull. Dusty, blood-stained fabric that had once been elegant gowns were draped over their bones. Ceeoni felt her knees start to quiver, but Adam kept his arms around her.

"Steady, Baby," he whispered, "It's alright now." Her trembling nausea passed quickly, and soon she felt well enough to examine all the wonderful things that had been left in the room. Candlesticks, mirrors, silverware and jewelry of Spanish design, had probably belonged to Sybil. Discarded iron manacles, reminded her that this place had known slaves, running for their lives, sometimes with children, blindfolded until they were ushered into what must have appeared, in their eyes, to be a frightening dungeon.

In the prevailing climate of that era, a slave had to be extremely brave to even try to escape. Harriet Tubman had gone back to the South nineteen times to lead several hundred slaves to freedom. Seeing those chains made Ceeoni acutely aware of the enormity of that feat.

She recalled a history professor saying that over one-hundred million slaves were displaced and killed from the time slavery began in the 16th century until its ending in the mid-19th century. When a student expressed doubt that the number could be so high, the professor had replied, 'Imagine how many victims Hitler and thousands of his henchmen would have eliminated if they'd had three-hundred years to do what they pleased without any interference or opposition.'

Within a half hour, the police and paramedics had carefully transported Detective Saxon up the stairs and on to the hospital. Everyone went back to Homer's to get out of their overalls, and to wait for Weber to return from the airport with Minette.

x x x

"We should find out who the perp is as soon as David comes back to himself," Samson said, "hopefully in the morning. They said his vital signs are stable."

Di followed R.C. and Juno into Homer's kitchen in a raid for more grapes and cheese, saying, "If we're gonna stay up all night again, we might as well eat."

Taking Ceeoni's hand, Adam suggested an escape to the patio, but Weber and Minette's entrance interrupted their privacy plans.

"That was quick!" Adam whispered to Ceeoni, "You know the old adage that one day, we'll look back on all this and laugh? Well, I won't laugh about this part. I'm ready to throw you over my shoulder and run off to a deserted island." Ceeoni thought that was a fabulous idea.

Minette, fresh as a daisy, appeared very pleased to meet Adam Delayno. They munched the late night repast while Minette demonstrated how charming she could be. Adam's new CD played softly.

Homer broke the ice. "Minette, do you believe in reincarnation?"

"No, but I've read about it."

"I'm a licensed therapist," Nasrene said, "I specialize in helping people remember things in their deeper minds; things they believe, that may be affecting their lives today. We don't actually know how it works, but this very simple process is called past life regression, and it can help eliminate unresolved issues like nothing else. I was wondering if you'd like to try it."

"Oh, no!" Minette glared at her, "Past lives? I would never submit to anything like that!" With that said, she got up, went to the bar and perched on the edge of the stool next to Adam. Di's eyes lifted up toward the ceiling, as she puffed up her cheeks in exasperation.

"Adam," Minette asked, "Have you ever submitted to this, this past life thing?"

He nodded, "It's an indescribable experience. Having just met me, you have no reason to trust me," he lit her cigarette from the gold elephant lighter at his elbow, "however, knowing or simply believing that I've lived before has imparted a feeling of freedom that one has to feel to understand."

She smiled her phony cordial smile and murmured, "How nice for you—er, please excuse me."

With tossed hair and swinging hips she sauntered off in the direction of the powder room, her shoulder bag banging in rhythm against her body, leaving a trail of blue smoke.

"She's jivin'," Di said in a loud whisper, "and I didn't see a bruise on Ms. SistahGirl's forehead, either!"

"O.K." Adam asked, "So what alternatives are there? If she's unconsciously hiding something important from her past life and consciously hiding her crimes in this life, how can we crack it, I mean, what do we do then?"

"We can't do anything," Nasrene answered quietly, "except be patient until David Saxon can talk and identify his attacker."

CHAPTER FORTY-TWO

While everyone in Homer's living room turned inwardly to their own thoughts, Adam's eyes followed Ceeoni as she curled up next to him. His sensual smile inspired her to snuggle closer, whispering,

"I'm ready to keep Clarisse and Elijah's date in Paris anytime you are."

"My love, I'll settle for our house tonight, it's closer, and I can't wait. Hey, but we are scheduled to go to France in a few weeks. C'mon let's tour the patio, and I'll tell you all about it." Outside, Adam eagerly wrapped her up in his arms, and buried his face in the soft skin of her neck, "I said I can't wait—Oh, Ceeoni, there's so much I know I don't need to say, but I feel like I want to tell you everything I've ever thought—" She understood what he felt, because she felt the same way.

Suddenly, his entire body froze, stiffening as if in shock.

"What do you want?" Adam asked, slowly. Detective David Saxon, still in his filthy, bloody clothes, wearing a cold, impersonal expression, stood behind Adam. Where did he come from?

"David!?" she blurted, but Adam's eyes warned her. Wondering how David had managed to get up over the second story balcony, she quickly put it all together and angrily admonished herself, 'Why the hell didn't I see through him sooner?'

David jammed his service revolver into Adam's back, and pushed him hard.

"Move it, Delayno," he hissed, "and you too, Goodie Two Shoes!"

David's eyes shifted rapidly from side to side in his flushed face. As they entered the room, Homer, Samson, R.C. and Weber read the situation right away. Nasrene, Di and Juno took a little longer to realize that David was actually herding them all into the dining area with a service revolver. "I want everybody sitting at that table—with all hands up on the table where I can see them!"

"Aw, man!" Homer said. "I've known you most of your life! I gave you your first job!—You and me, we've been—"

"Oh, shut up, Mister Rich Bitch Ass!" he hissed as his eyes bucked into a crazed glare, "You took away the only thing I had!"

Everybody stared in shock at the detective who no longer resembled the handsome, self-possessed young lion they knew. It dawned on Ceeoni that David looked like—Roxanne! David had taken on another persona, one with an exaggerated femininity, a higher hollow-sounding voice, a slight lisp and a dangerous edge. Recognizing the surreal transformation, Homer softened his approach. "David, please—what do you mean?"

David's arms swept in a wide inclusive gesture, "All of this! Starcross! It's mine, dammit, and you fucking took it!"

"How do you figure that?"

Smug in his conviction, he replied proudly, "My great, great-grandfather was a slave named Phineas Baldwin!"

There was a vacuum of silence before Homer slowly said, "Well, I can't argue with that, but why was Starcross up for sale?"

"I was just a kid when you bought it! Years later, I discovered who I was. When I first came here, I knew in my heart that it was mine—I knew it! But I couldn't find proof! That stupid Basil Cassidy promised me he'd find proof!" he whined petulantly, "But he never found proof! He let it get sold to that asshole!" He pointed to Homer with the revolver.

"Now Old Pal, you're going to sign your confession to the murders, and you're going to sign Starcross over to me!"

David pulled a crumpled piece of paper from his pocket, and threw it on the marble table in front of Homer. Homer's hesitation pushed his anger up a notch, "I said, Now!" he screamed.

Ceeoni, realizing that something had to be done quickly to diffuse his fever pitch, ventured in her lowest, softest voice, "David?"

Surprised at the unexpected gentle sound, he dropped his guard a little. "Wha—what do you want?"

"Poor, poor Baby, I can tell you're wounded," she purred slowly.

"Oh that! Ha! I collected my blood and saved it for that purpose," he gloated, "And—and the bruise on my head happened when my stupid partner tried to stop me from taking his nosey ass out, and then I cut myself in the side with a razor, just enough to make a bleeding wound. I got away from those idiots at the hospital before they had a chance to examine me. See, I'm smarter than all of those dumbass keystone kops!"

"Do you think you're going to get away with this?" Adam asked.

"Delayno, Delayno, De-layno!" he sang. "Don't be so naive! Has playing that piano addled your Goddamn brains? My badge is a license to kill, you know, Double-O-Seven? Hell-O! A good cop has the law on his side! The proof ain't on me, dog! If I'd had my way, your ass woulda' been dead!"

"Ah," Samson said, "downstairs, the person we chased got away—who helped you, David?"

Laughing hysterically, he wiped his runny nose with the back of his hand,

"Was that a stroke of luck or what?? I had just come in that door, and when you opened the door on the opposite side, a gust of wind caused it to close on its own! There was never-never-never anyone there!" His laughter cut off abruptly, pushing the pen closer to Homer, he screamed, "Sign, Bitch!"

Ceeoni recognized her pen; her lucky gift from Di. The fact that this monster had taken her precious pen took her blood to the boiling point. She noticed that Adam hadn't pushed his chair as close to the table as the others, and he inched the chair away from the table a little more when David wasn't looking. Weber, who sat next to Homer, hadn't moved a muscle.

"Alright, David," Homer sighed, "Tell me just one more thing? How did you get down to the underground chamber in the first place? You do realize there's a fortune in valuables down there, don't you?"

"Oh, Basil always said that, but I don't care about that stuff! What's important is my Destiny! See, even when I was little I dreamed that I had a ring, a beautiful black ring with pretty colors that would take me through a fireplace and down some stone steps to my own sanctuary—and there I would fulfill my heart's desire! My dream came true on the day Homer's crew broke through to that back room in my theatre. It was My Destiny that brought me there that day! Homer, you remember that day! While you were on your knees, rifling through that old trunk, I saw it! It was right there—my beautiful ring, sparkling, beckoning to me from under the bed. At last! My ring! I knew My Destiny had come true!

"As soon as I found it, I knew from my dreams what it was for. I've been going down to my special place ever since, after hours, after you and your dumb-ass crews went home!" He sniffed, "I used to take Basil down there, and—we—" David's focus shifted, and to everyone's disgust, he began to sob, while reaching down to squeeze his swelling crotch.

"I didn't want to kill Basil! I loved him—I—really did!"

"Basil always took care of you, didn't he?" Homer asked.

"Shut up! Just shut up!" His sniveling lasted only a few seconds, then, in another rapid mood swing, David's head jerked and he laughed as if he'd suddenly heard something funny in his head. Homer shifted uncomfortably in his seat, a move that infuriated David. "Homer," he yelled, "I swear, I'm counting to three, and I count backward!" He shoved the weapon violently against Homer's temple and cocked it.

"Stop! Wait!" Ceeoni cried. Forcing herself to speak in soft tones, she cooed, "It's only playing fair if you tell us what's going to happen once Homer's dead. If he's dead, he won't be able to sign."

"Oh, that's easy," he snickered, "I'll sign it myself after I shoot all you fuckers, and this will be in Homer's hand!" He waved the gun for emphasis. "I'm the Star of the God-Damn Department! No one would ever doubt my word!"

'He's going to kill all of us anyway,' whispered the little voice in the back of Ceeoni's mind. 'Take a chance, remember Daddy's advice'—Ceeoni recalled Eddie Jones saying, 'Whenever you're cornered, play crazy.' She never understood what that meant until this moment. With slow, high—pitched childish inflections, she pouted, "Da-vid, you didn't never, ever, ever, ever, ever let me see you pwetty wing."

His sick mind slid easily into her psychodrama. "Noooo! You might try to take it! I saw your 'ol cheap ass earrings!"

"Aw, c'mon, OK?" she coaxed, "You can see one of my earrings up close. Just let me see you pwetty, pwetty wing for a teeny-weeny minute—it's sooo pwetty—pweasee?"

"Nooooo! No—no—no!" he screamed.

Very slowly, she took off her earring and held it out to him. He watched her, fascinated. "Wanna twade?" she asked, "You can hold mine, while I see yours."

Thinking about it, he blinked, "Well, OK, but only for a little while!"

He snatched her earring with his free hand, while turning the hand that held the gun sideways, in order to proudly waggle the opal and diamond ring on his pinky finger in her direction. Weber, moving with unexpected lightning speed, karate chopped it, but the weapon remained in David's hand. Homer ducked—R.C. dove across the table after David, but he backed away, firing, wounding Weber in the lower arm. Samson knocked over his chair in time to push Nasrene from harm's way, as a second bullet grazed his forehead. Screaming, Juno scrambled under the table. Adam was almost able to reach David, when David, seeing the movement out of the corner of his eye, fired in that direction. The shot missed Adam, but it got everybody's attention. David had gained control of the situation again as he leisurely waved the revolver, bringing the foray to a halt, ushering them back to their seats, screaming,

"I said sit, sit sit! Goddammit! Sit-the-fuck-down!!"

Everyone was still except Homer, who, in an act of pure defiance, walked over to stand in front of Di, protectively. David roared, grabbed Ceeoni by her hair, pulled her up against his body and locked his free arm around her neck in a tight chokehold. She could see that he'd stepped only inches away from the edge of the Lucite walkway.

"I trusted you, you whore!" David yelled into her ear. Ceeoni cringed at feeling his muscles tighten in the process of raising the weapon, "Homer! You and all these assholes think you don't have to do what I say! Y'all are goin' outta' here in fuckin' body bags, one by one!"

Fighting for consciousness, nearly out of air, Ceeoni knew another few seconds would expend the last bit of breath in her lungs. She wanted Adam's face to be the last face she saw. She searched for him with her eyes, finding him to her right, at the outer perimeter of her line of vision. Adam's eyes flashed briefly to a spot at her left. Catching his signal, she shifted her eyes in that direction where a startled, wide-eyed Minette stood in the entryway, frozen, except for her right hand that slowly reached into her shoulder-bag.

Time had run out. There was no more air in her lungs. Feeling lightheaded, she prayed that somebody would have an eleventh hour plan. She did the only thing she could. She jerked her elbow backward, serving only to tighten David's hold on her neck. With his quick, furious reaction he turned his face toward the doorway just in time to catch the clean shot from Minette's Derringer that left a tiny hole, oozing a trickle of blood, dead center between his shocked eyes.

Adam, moving fast, deflected David's aim while catching Ceeoni's waist and pulling her, gasping and choking, out of his line of fire, as a stray bullet whizzed past her ear. David's last two wild shots penetrated the wall behind where she'd stood, as he crumpled and collapsed—gurgling, head bobbing, arms flailing, David sank into the sapphire water, while Minette dropped her pistol and fell to her knees, sobbing.

x x x

The sound of approaching sirens proved to be the result of the unauthorized disappearance of Detective Saxon and a police car from the hospital emergency area. Weber and Samson were treated for their injuries, while Minette, still trembling from the trauma of her rescue ordeal, hugged her knees in a zebra chair. Everyone expressed eternal gratitude to Minette, but she kept saying, "I had to do it—I don't know why—he was going to kill us all. All I knew was that I had to kill him—"

"Minette, God sent you to save us," Homer said, "but why are you packing the heat?"

"It was for my ex-husband. He stalked me for years, so I bought the Derringer in case he turned up."

Weber, arm bandage and all, handed her a cup of his herb tea, "Hey, it's good to know we have you around for protection," he joked. For the first time, Minette smiled genuinely. Without her makeup, her purplish forehead bruise and her nose, red from crying, made her a lot more likeable.

"Nasrene?" she asked, "I—I know it's after 4am, but if you don't mind, can you—? Well, I think I'd like to be—you know—I'd like to be—"

"Regressed? Yes! Oh Minette, if you'll make yourself comfortable, we can try. And I think you'll find it to be a pleasant, if not life changing, experience. Most of the time, something wonderful happens in the human conscience after scenes of a past life are brought to our remembrance."

Curiosity overcame fatigue as everyone got comfortable to observe.

After Weber helped Minette arrange herself on the sofa, Nasrene applied the relaxation and regression suggestions. Minette proved to be an easy subject. To the question, 'What is your name?' she answered in a heavy rumbling baritone,

'Talbert Starcross Bramwell'.

"I knew it!" Adam whispered, "It was Talbert's low timbre in her voice that I recognized in the hospital."

Nasrene asked, "Where are you?"

'Starcross—it's so lonely here. Jesus, I couldn't stop it! I was too late. I was too God-damn late!' Minette's head tossed from side to side as tears flowed freely from her closed eyes.

"What's too late?"

'By the time I found out what that crazy Roxanne was up to, it was too late!'

Nasrene quickly applied the pain reduction suggestions to settle Talbert down. After a few minutes he began to speak quietly.

He said that when Clarisse and Avajay had been missing for two days, he went to the Coach Stop Inn to ask around again, just in case anyone had seen anything. Having his bourbon and branchwater at the bar, he saw a heavily veiled, dark haired woman walk by.

'Who's the brunette?' he asked Max, the bartender.

'Talbert, you lost your eyesight along with that tub of blubber? That's your cousin, Mary Starcross.'

'Oh yeah,' Talbert lied. 'New outfit.'

'Yeah, well, shame about that scar that messed up her face.'

'Yeah, shame.'

'Everybody around here feels sorry for her, having to cover up like that,' Max said, 'even in summer. She used to come in here every other day to spend a few minutes upstairs with Zeke, the mail coach driver, 'til they found him stabbed to death last week.'

Max leaned over the bar and whispered, 'They think some crazy beer-serk blonde escaped from Milledgeville and killed Ol' Zeke along with a whole slew of people, ya know! It's all there in the paper. They even have a picture of her in there! Whodda thought Ol' Zeke had woman trouble!'

Stunned, Talbert said he didn't know what to think. Needing to know more, he picked up the daily paper on his way out. Talbert began to speak very slowly.

'Elijah had returned from Europe earlier that day and, later on I heard Phineas tell one of the maids that Clarisse and Elijah had both failed to receive their mail. After I read my newspaper, I pieced it all together. Roxanne had put on a wig as soon as she left the Manor, and she hadn't let the folk at the Coach Stop see her face or let her real identity be known, because she knew the authorities were hot on her tail. She would probably steal the mail that Phineas had left on the day he left it, right out of Zeke's room—well, right then and there, I made up my mind that Roxanne had done all the damage she was going to do! Later on, in the middle of the night, I followed her to the theatre and saw to that!'

Talbert said that Phineas took the horses and moved to his family's place up north, leaving him to wander the grounds of Starcross alone with his painful memories and a lifetime of bitter regrets. During one of his midnight walks, divine lightning struck him down in front of his mother's theatre, ending his suffering.

"Do you know everyone in the room?" Nasrene asked him.

'Yes,' Talbert whispered.

It was the last thing he would say. Nasrene applied the awakening suggestions. Minette opened her eyes and looked at each face around her, as if seeing them for the first time.

"I need time to think about all of this," she said slowly.

"Get ready, girl," Homer laughed, "We have a bunch of tapes for you to listen to."

Minette blinked her eyelashes at Weber and asked,

"Hey, have you guys got a spare bunk around here where a lady can sack out?"

"Sure, Minnie, right this way. We can compare recipes."

Juno, Nasrene, Samson, Homer, and Di, carrying shoes under her arm, bid goodnights' all around, leaving Ceeoni, Adam and R.C. in the living room. It was a beautiful time of morning, just before daybreak when deep blue darkness begins to turn gold.

"So, Adam," R.C. said, "I am so totally ready for business to go on as usual. Now that my mind is free to think about it, we're only a few days behind schedule."

"Right. It's time to roll up out of here. You know what to do—alert the band, and hook up ground transpo. We can boogie with the airlines in the morning."

"Cool. Uh, by the way, did I hear the lovely lady on your arm say that she can count? You know we need somebody—"

"She did, she did, and since we don't do that so well, and Juno doesn't have time for us, I plan to put her to work—" R.C. turned around at the door, signaling a two-thumbs-up salute accompanied by a parting, whispered, "Bing-Bing-Go!"

Ceeoni blew out the last burning candle, "Adam, you know if we ever have a mind to, we can always read Clarisse's and Elijah's letters—they're all down there, unopened."

"Well, I think we should clear it and seal that area off completely. We don't want our children discovering hidden tunnels." His warm lips tasted hers. She closed her eyes and let her spirit slowly drift away into the sunshine of a new day dawning. He drew her closer into the shelter of his love,

"Ceeoni, Baby, all my life I knew something was missing, but I didn't know what. I had given up. I thought I'd never find you."

"And now," she asked, smiling into his eyes, "how does it feel to know we have forever?"

Made in the USA
Lexington, KY
19 January 2012